The Orphans of Halfpenny Street

Cathy Sharp

W F HOWES LTD

This large print edition published in 2016 by
W F Howes Ltd
Unit 5, St George's House, Rearsby Business Park,
Gaddesby Lane, Rearsby, Leicester LE7 4YH

1 3 5 7 9 10 8 6 4 2

First published in the United Kingdom in 2015
by HarperCollins*Publishers*

A CIP catalogue record for this book is available
from the British Library

ISBN 978 1 51001 799 3

Typeset by Palimpsest Book Production Limited,
Falkirk, Stirlingshire

Printed and bound in Great Britain
by TJ International Ltd, Padstow, Cornwall

MIX
Paper from
responsible sources
FSC
www.fsc.org   FSC® C013056

For my wonderful agent, Judith Murdoch,
who gave me the chance to write these books,
and for my equally wonderful editor,
Kate Bradley, for inspiring me.

CHAPTER 1

'Mary Ellen, I need you,' her mother's voice called from the front door of their terraced house as she approached. 'Hurry up, love . . .'

Mary Ellen sighed and walked faster. She'd been all the way to the busy market in the heart of Spitalfields and her basket was heavy with the items her mother had asked her to bring. There was a ham bone, which would be made into soup with some turnips, potatoes, pearl barley and carrots, all of which she'd bought from the market, because they were cheaper, and her arm ached from carrying them.

She hoped Ma wasn't going to send her anywhere else until she'd had a drink of water, because it was hot and sticky and she was feeling tired after her long walk. She'd been up at six that morning to wash the kitchen floor and the sink, before going to school for a few hours. After returning home for lunch, Ma had sent her shopping because it was only sports and games in the afternoon, and Ma said she didn't need to bother with them, though Mary Ellen knew her teacher would give her a black mark next time she attended school; but that might not be for a few days, because Ma had been coughing all night. Mary Ellen had seen spots of blood on her nightgown when she'd taken her a cup of tea before she left for school that morning.

'I'm sorry, love,' her ma said as she reached the door. 'You'll have to go back out for my medicine. I've got none for tonight and I can't seem to stop this . . .' She couldn't finish her sentence because the coughing fit seized her and she sounded terrible. Her body bent double with the pain and her face went an awful pasty white. Mary Ellen could see bright red spots on the handkerchief that Ma held to her lips, and her heart caught with fear. 'Mary Ellen . . .'

Ma gave a strange little cry and then sort of crumpled up in a heap at Mary Ellen's feet. She bent over her, trying to make her open her eyes, but her mother wasn't responding.

'Don't be ill, Ma,' she said, tears welling up. She didn't know what to do and she'd been living alone with her mother since her big sister Rose went off to train as a nurse. 'Please . . . wake up, Ma . . .'

Mary Ellen was conscious of the slightly grubby lace curtains twitching at the neighbouring house, then the door opened and Mrs Prentice came out and looked at her for a moment before asking, 'What's up wiv yer ma, Mary Ellen?'

'She's not well,' Mary Ellen said. 'She told me to go for her medicine but then she just fell down.'

'I expect she fainted,' the neighbour said. 'I reckon your ma has been proper poorly. Your Rose should be ashamed of herself. You not even nine yet and 'er goin' orf and leavin' her to cope on her own . . . and you with no pa.'

'Pa died before we moved here,' Mary Ellen said defensively, because she knew some of her neighbours thought she'd never had a father. Her tears began to spring in her eyes once more. 'Ma's never been well since . . .'

'We'd best get someone to go fer the doctor, and I'll tell my husband to go round and fetch your Rose when he comes home . . .' Mrs Prentice went into her house and shouted and a lad of about thirteen came out and stared at them. His trousers were too big and falling off him and his boots had holes in the toes, but he smiled at Mary Ellen.

'What's wrong, Ma?'

Mary Ellen's mother was stirring. Mrs Prentice signalled to her son and between them they helped Ma to her feet. She stood swaying for a moment, seeming bewildered, and then straightened up.

'I'll be all right now,' she said. 'Thank you, Lil. It's just the heat.'

'Not from what I've seen,' Mrs Prentice said. 'Get orf and fetch the doctor to her, Rip, and then yer can cut orf down the Docks and tell yer father to fetch Rose O'Hanran back tonight.'

'No, you mustn't,' Ma protested faintly. 'Rose is busy; she hasn't got time . . . and I can't afford the doctor . . .'

3

'Likely he won't charge yer, as long as it's all goin' ter be free soon, that's what the papers say anyway, though I'll believe it when I bleedin' see it,' Mrs Prentice said. 'Go on in, Mary Ellen, and make yer ma a cup of tea. I'll bring her in and settle her down and then you can go and fetch that medicine.'

Mary Ellen nodded. The last thing she wanted was another walk to the High Street, but she had to go, because Ma needed it.

'Ma, you're ill.' Rose's voice was sharp and the sound of it sent a tingle down Mary Ellen's spine as she sat on the bottom stair behind the half-opened door into the kitchen, listening to her mother and sister. She was supposed to be in bed. 'You've got to see the doctor. You can't go on like this – and you know I can't come home and look after you. I'm taking my final exams next week and if I miss them I'll have to do at least another term and perhaps an extra year.'

'I don't expect you to come home,' Ma said, sounding weary and defeated to Mary Ellen's ears. 'I saw the doctor weeks ago, Rose. He did some tests and it seems I have consumption. According to Dr Marlow I'll have to go to an isolation hospital in Norfolk, by the sea – and what is going to happen to Mary Ellen then?'

Mary Ellen stiffened. No one knew better than her how tired Ma was; she'd been neglecting all the things she'd once taken pride in and that

4

included looking after her younger daughter. It wasn't that her mother didn't care; Mary Ellen knew she was loved, but Ma couldn't raise the energy to fetch in the bath and see that her daughter was clean. Instead, she told her to wash in the sink and got cross if Mary Ellen's clothes were dirty too soon. Instead of baking pies and cakes and making delicious stews, she gave Mary Ellen three pennies to fetch chips and mushy peas from the pie shop most days.

Mary Ellen was hungry all the time and Ma said there was no money to buy good food, because Pa's employers had stopped paying the pension they'd given her. Mary Ellen didn't understand why it had happened; she just knew that her mother could barely manage. Pa's firm had said because of the accident Ma was entitled to a generous amount, but now it seemed they'd changed their minds and they'd cut it to just a pound a month. They'd offered her a job cleaning offices but Ma was too ill to work.

Mary Ellen thought Ma's illness had got much worse in the past few weeks. At first it had been just a little cough, but now she coughed all the time and there were sometimes spots of blood on her mouth. Rose didn't come home often so she didn't see how tired Ma looked; she wasn't the one who had to scrub the kitchen floor and wash their clothes in the copper in the scullery. Ma tried to help her with the mangle but she was so tired afterwards that she had to go to bed. It was Mary

Ellen who had to peel vegetables when they did have a proper meal, and her mother just watched her as she put the pans on the stove and told her when the soup was ready.

She didn't mind helping out, but because of her mother's illness Mary Ellen had missed school three times this week and two the week before. If they weren't careful the inspector would be knocking at their door and Ma would be in trouble.

'Mary Ellen will have to go into a home,' Rose said and the determination in her words sent chills through her sister. 'I've got a couple of days off after I've taken my exams next week. I'll come and arrange to take her in myself, to that place in Halfpenny Street – and you must agree to go away for that treatment.'

In the semi-darkness, Mary Ellen hugged herself, tears trickling down her cheeks. She didn't want to be sent away; she wanted to be with her mother and look after her. Forgetting that she was supposed to be in bed, she jumped up and rushed into the kitchen, temper flaring.

'I won't go away and nor will Ma,' she cried. 'You're mean, Rose O'Hanran. I hate you.'

'Oh, Mary Ellen, love,' her mother said. 'You should be in bed. You don't understand. Rose is only trying to help us. I can't look after you properly . . . you would be better in St Saviour's, if they'll take you.'

'I'll go round and ask Father Joe if he thinks

6

they'll take her,' Rose said. She looked at Mary Ellen in the yellowish light of the gas lamps and sighed. 'Your hair could do with a wash, child. Come here, and I'll do it before I go and see Father Joe.'

Grabbing Mary Ellen's arm and ignoring her protests that she'd washed her own hair only two days previously her sister filled a jug with water from the kettle and added cold, then bent Mary Ellen's head over the sink and poured the water, rubbing at her hair and scalp with the carbolic soap they used for everything.

'Your neck is as black as ink . . .'

'Liar! I washed it this week . . .' Mary Ellen retorted.

'Well, you didn't make much of a job of it.'

'I hate you, Rose.'

'Stop quarrelling, the pair of you,' Ma said wearily.

'I shan't come back when I've been to see Father Joe,' Rose said as she rubbed at Mary Ellen's head, her nails scratching as she bent to her task. She poured out the rest of the jug, washing away the soap and making Mary Ellen gasp because it was too cold and the soap stung her eyes. 'I need to get some sleep and I've got to work on my revision every day. I don't want to fail my exams after all the work I've put in . . .'

Mary Ellen's eyes watered. She didn't want Rose to come back home, because in that moment she hated her. Rose was selfish and mean and they didn't need her, because Mary Ellen could look after her mother.

Rose was giving her hair a rough rub with the towel. Next, she took a comb and began to pull the teeth through the long hair, making Mary Ellen yell because it tangled and hurt her.

'Don't make such a fuss,' Rose said crossly. 'You're not a baby.'

'I can do it myself,' Mary Ellen said. 'You're a brute and a bully, Rose. Just go back to nursing and leave us alone. I'll look after Ma.'

Rose looked at her and her face softened a little. 'You're not old enough, love,' she said in a kinder tone. 'You've done your best, Mary Ellen, but you're not nine yet and you need to go to school. Ma told me how you make her a cup of tea before you go and do as much of the work as you can when you get back – but you're missing school and Ma will be in trouble if it continues. I'm sorry, but you will have to go into a home – just until Ma is better. You do want her to get better?'

'Yes.' Mary Ellen looked at her mother in alarm. 'Ma . . . I don't want to go to that place . . .'

'I know you don't, love. Come here.' Her mother held out her arms. 'I don't want to go away either, but Rose is right. I am ill and if I stay I could make you ill too – so they will make me go soon even if I try to stay. You do as Rose says. Rose, give me that comb.' She took it and began to smooth it through Mary Ellen's hair

8

without pulling anywhere near as much. 'You get off, Rose. I'll see the doctor tomorrow and make arrangements to go to that hospital . . . and you can ask at St Saviour's if they'll take our Mary Ellen . . .'

Mary Ellen's throat was tight and painful, but she knew it was useless to resist. Ma's illness was getting worse all the time and neither of them had enough food to eat. It was summer now but in the winter this damp old house would make Ma's chest even worse.

Holding back her tears, she bowed her head, accepting defeat. 'I'll do what you want, Ma,' she said.

'There's my good girl,' her mother said and kissed the top of her head. 'I'll put some milk on and we'll have a cup of the cocoa Rose brought us. It was good of her, wasn't it?'

Mary Ellen nodded. 'Yes, I like cocoa.'

'You like ham too,' Rose said and smiled at her. 'When I come on my day off I'll bring some ham and tomatoes. You'll like that, won't you?'

Ham was a rare treat these days, because even if you had the money it was hard to find in the shops, but the manager of Home and Colonial, the grocers where Rose had worked until she left to train as a nurse, had a soft spot for his former employee and he would find her a couple of slices.

'Yes, I'll like that,' Mary Ellen agreed, but a slice of ham and tomatoes wouldn't make up for the way she was being cast out of her home . . . it wouldn't take away the grief of losing her mother and not knowing if she would ever see her again.

'Wotcha! Lovely day, ain't it?'

Mary Ellen O'Hanran ignored the cheery greeting as the delivery boy whizzed by her on his shop bicycle. Ma would say he was common and tell her to ignore the likes of Bertie Carter. Even though they were forced to live in the dirty little houses crammed close to the Docks, they did not have to lower their standards.

'You know better, Mary Ellen, and don't you forget it. We may live here, but we came from better things and one day we'll be back where we belong,' her mother had used to say when they first came to Dock Lane, but that was nearly four years ago, just after her father had died and her mother had still been fit and healthy.

Even the last rays of a late summer sun could not cheer the grime of the dingy street, its narrow gutters choked with rubbish. Peeling paint on the doors of terraced houses and windows that were almost uniformly filthy from the dirt of the slums were at odds with the spotless white lace curtains at number ten Dock Lane. A scrawny tabby arched its back and hissed at a scavenging rat amongst the debris, and the cheeky delivery boy whistled loudly as he swerved to avoid two snarling dogs fighting over a scrap of food further down. He waved as he turned the corner of the narrow lane, before disappearing out of sight. Mary Ellen stared after him, a small, lonely figure with her fair hair curling about a thin, pale face in wayward wisps that had escaped from her plait.

A single tear trickled from the corner of her eye but she dashed it away with her hand, refusing to give in to the feeling of misery that kept threatening to overcome her, because Ma had shouted and told her to keep out of the way. Ma never shouted, but she was so tired, at the end of her tether. She was lying down on her bed after another bout of terrible coughing, her face so pale and drawn that Mary Ellen was afraid she might collapse again. In the distance, the towering cranes on the East India Docks and the smoking chimneystacks of merchant vessels out on the river were outlined against a clear sky. The sound of a ship's horn blasted suddenly through the mean streets and the foul stench from the oily water had worsened with the heat of the day. The noise of the trams clanging their way through the main thoroughfare echoed in the stillness of the unusually quiet lane. For once there were no gossiping women standing at their front doors, the heat having driven them all inside, thick lace curtains closed to shut out what had been a relentless sun.

Mary Ellen's home stood out from the crowd, because until these last few weeks, when she'd got so ill, Ma had kept her doorstep scrubbed and her curtains washed despite the constant struggle against the filth of the East End of London. Mary Ellen had scrubbed the step herself this morning, and Ma told her it looked lovely, but the soap had stung her hands and her knees hurt where she'd grazed them on the stone. Yet Mary Ellen would do it again tomorrow, because Ma had been used to better and her pride made her battle against the poverty and wretchedness of her surroundings.

Hunting for the right kind of stone, Mary Ellen was set on playing a game of hopscotch to while away the hours until Rose came home as she'd promised, and it was time to go in for her tea. Maybe one of the other children in the lane would come and play with her, though because Ma kept herself to herself, her neighbours thought they were stuck up and the other kids often refused to notice the O'Hanran girl.

'Who does she think she is, with her airs and graces?' their mothers whispered to each other when Ma put her spotless washing out to dry in the back yard. Hair in wire curlers peeping out beneath their headscarves, they made faces at the woman whose hair shone like silk and wore no apron over her dress when she came into the street. 'Just because her father owns a shop over the river she needn't think she's better than the rest of us.'

Mary Ellen bet some of them were gloating to see her mother's pride tumbled in the dust and tears of anger stung her eyes when she thought of what was going to happen when Rose came home. She knew where she was going, because she'd passed St Saviour's on her way to visit the park

12

with her school, St Mary's. There she'd seen the St Saviour's girls, all dressed in grey skirts, white blouses and dark red coats.

The other kids at St Mary's laughed and pointed at the orphans, calling them the 'Alfpenny kids, because that was the name of the street the home was in, and now Mary Ellen was going to be one of them. The idea filled her with dread.

Why couldn't she stay at home? Rebellious thoughts filled her head, though sometimes, her mother looked so pale and fragile that Mary Ellen grew frightened. When she saw the blood on the handkerchief that Ma tried to hide, she prayed to that God in the sky her father had impressed on her was there to save them, especially little children.

'Ah, whist, me darlin',' Tom O'Hanran would say, as he sat her on his knee and stroked her head, his breath always smelling faintly of good Irish whiskey. 'Sure, Jesus in His heaven and Mary Mother of God will smile on you, my Mary. You've the charm of the Irish and the smile of an angel, and no one could help but love you.'

'Now then, Tom O'Hanran.' Ma would smile fondly on them. 'Don't you be spoiling her with your daft stories. Mary Ellen has to learn that life does not always flow smoothly for the likes of us.'

Mary Ellen still missed her father. Sometimes it hurt so much that it was like a big hole in her chest, but Ma didn't talk about him so she had to keep her grief inside.

Ma was English, not Irish, and in the opinion of her shopkeeper father she had disgraced herself by marrying a wild Irish Catholic, who would, he prophesied, ruin her. Ma had been in love with her handsome husband in those days, and she'd even converted to his faith at the start, though after his death she had lapsed and no longer sent her children to the Catholic Church. Ma seldom went to church at all, but when she did, she chose the Methodist one because the minister did not scold her for changing her mind over the matter of religion. In a huge city teeming with people of all faiths, the minister had long grown used to accepting those in need, whatever their denomination, and did what he could to help the poor of the area, regardless of whether they attended his church.

Ma's father had disowned her when she married, and he had not relented when she became a widow, even though he could have helped her to stay in the nice little cottage she'd gone to when she wed. Mary Ellen's elder sister Rose said that Grandpa would've given Ma money if she'd grovelled and begged him, but Ma was too proud to beg. Instead, she'd been forced to come here to this slum and fight her battles against an encroaching illness and the tide of dirt that threatened to engulf them.

Rose still attended the Catholic Church, not out of devotion but because, she said, they had allowed her to take a scholarship under their aegis that had enabled her to enter nursing college. Rose was determined to better herself, to make a good life, and her only way of getting the chance she needed had been to take advantage of being a good Catholic. Father Joe had been a friend to all of them and he took an interest in Rose's future, telling Ma that she should be proud of her daughter's hard work.

'You've a good daughter there, Mrs O'Hanran,' he'd said when he came to visit. 'Respectable and devout, she'll make a wonderful nurse.'

Ever since she was Mary Ellen's age, Rose had dreamed of becoming a nurse one day, and the recent terrible war which had ended only two years earlier had made her even more eager to take up the profession.

'When I see men fresh home from the war, with legs missing and awful scars, some of them so weak that they will never recover, I want to help them,' Rose had told her young sister. 'I only wish I had been old enough to go out to the Front – somewhere the fighting was at its worst – to help nurse the men. I could never work in an office or a dress shop when there is something more worthwhile to be done. Hitler is beaten, and London will recover from the Blitz in time, but the injuries some of those men received will never be healed.'

Rose wanted to help sick people, but she hated the slum area they'd been forced to live in after Pa died, and Mary Ellen knew she wanted to become a nurse so that she need never come back here. She was ashamed of their home and wanted something better. Mary Ellen didn't care about such things, she just wanted to be at home with her mother . . . but after today she would be sent away and she wouldn't be able to see or touch Ma . . .

Mary Ellen had often sat unseen on the stairs in the evenings and listened to her mother and sister talking in the kitchen. At nights, Ma lit the gas lamps and made a pot of tea, which they drank together, discussing subjects that they considered her too young to comprehend, but life hadn't been easy since Pa died, and Mary Ellen understood grief all too well. She heard things that worried her, though she often made sense of only a fraction.

Yet she knew that Britain was still struggling to pay back its war debts and there were not enough decent jobs for able-bodied men, let alone those who could not do a full day's work.

Everyone had hoped rationing would end with the war, but instead it seemed that every month they were told there would be less of something else. 'Only one ounce of bacon per person per week now, and three pounds of potatoes,' Ma complained when Rose came home with whatever she could find. 'We shall all starve before they've done – and what was it all about, that's what I'd like to know.'

'Governments falling out like spoiled children,' Rose said in a harsh tone. Ma sometimes complained

16

that Rose was becoming a radical and too critical of politics and things that were best left to men, but that just made Rose toss her head and retort, 'You'll see, Ma. Women are going to have more to say in the future. It's time ordinary people had enough to eat and decent homes to live in – it's time women were equal to men, in wages and everything else.'

Ma would laugh and warn her that pride came before a fall, but Mary Ellen thought that her sister was right. Why shouldn't women have more say in their lives? And it wasn't right that people went hungry. Yet when she said so both Ma and Rose told her she was too young.

'It's not really the Government's fault,' Ma said. 'There isn't enough of everything to go round and things haven't got going yet after the war.'

'And who is to blame for all the shortages, the way the shops are empty even though the war has been over for months and months; more than two years? Who says we have to go on being rationed? No one has enough to eat, Ma. I can't even buy a decent pair of shoes for work. What did all those men fight for if it wasn't to make life better for us all? If those fat idiots in Westminster stopped rabbiting on and sorted things out perhaps we shouldn't have to put up with all this austerity. With a country to rebuild there should be plenty of work for everyone and money to live decently – but it's still hard to find work for most of the men, even though it may not be as bad as it was after the first big war.'

Mary Ellen sort of understood, because she was good at listening to people talking and because she was small and quiet they didn't always realise she was there. She heard Mr Jones the butcher talking about the fact that he couldn't get supplies of lamb from his usual suppliers.

The big freeze in January and February had made it seem that life in Austerity Britain could not get worse. And the floods in April with the resulting catastrophic loss of livestock, with millions of sheep drowned and arable crops flooded, had only aggravated the situation.

Yet here in the East End, which had taken much of the damage during those terrible nights of war when waves of bombers flew like great birds of prey over the city, disease and poverty still haunted the streets. Life had always been hard for these people and somehow they endured, though they never stopped moaning about the bloody Government. Moved by the pity and despair she saw in the faces of wounded men, returned to a life without work and precious little to eat, Rose was fired with a zeal to do what she could to put things right, to make life better for others as well as herself. A nursing career was the only way she knew to leave the poverty of the East End behind her and find the kind of life she wanted: a way of forgetting the drabness of life in Austerity Britain.

Mary Ellen admired her sister. Rose was dark-haired and beautiful, with her pert nose, full red lips and firm chin. She was also one of the most determined people that Mary Ellen had ever come across.

Mary Ellen finished chalking the squares for her game of hopscotch and then selected a flat stone from amongst the filth in the gutters. Her chores finished for the day, she'd come out to play while Ma had a rest on the bed, and they waited for Rose to return home from work with food for their tea.

Mary Ellen threw her stone into the first square and hopped into the one after it. She was preparing to perform a hop, skip and jump before turning to go back and pick up her stone when a voice spoke from behind her and made her start and lose her balance.

Turning, she saw a boy of similar age to her own. He was a little taller, dressed in long trousers that had been cut down from an old pair of his brother's, a washed-out shirt and scuffed black boots. His dark auburn hair was tousled and un-washed, his nose red and dripping and there were streaks of dirt on his face where he'd rubbed it with his filthy hands. As she watched he wiped his nose on the back of his hand and then, to her disgust, slid his hand down his trousers. Ma might be ill and they might be poor, but Mary Ellen was clothed in an almost clean cotton pinafore skirt and blouse her mother had made before she became ill, and she had better manners than to wipe snot on her dress.

'That's rude, that is, Billy Baggins,' she said.

'What did you make me jump for? I shall have to start again now.'

'I didn't mean to, Mary Ellen,' he answered meekly. 'Can I play?'

'You'll have to find a stone,' she said, looking at him curiously but without malice. Billy Baggins had no mother and his father had recently been killed in an incident on the Docks. Mr Baggins had been a bully with a loud voice, who hit both his sons whenever he was drunk, but at least he'd kept the family together and they hadn't starved. Since his death, Billy's elder brother had cleared off to no one knew where, and Billy had been collared by the *authorities* who had said he was going to be put into care.

Mary Ellen had felt sorry for him, because he might look unkempt and his manners were rough, but she knew he was kind and generous. When her own father had died, Billy had been the only one who understood how she felt, sharing his sherbet dip with her as they sat on the doorstep and she battled with her tears. He was her one real friend in these lanes and she'd missed him when he'd gone off to stay with his nanna. She knew how bad he must feel now that his own father was dead and all he had was an old lady and his rogue of a brother. 'I thought you'd gone away?' she said now.

'Not yet,' he said. 'I've been stayin' with me nanna in Whitechapel, but she was taken into hospital sudden and I came home ter see if Arfur had come back.'

'Has he?' Mary Ellen asked sympathetically, but with little expectation of a good outcome. Everyone knew that Arthur Baggins was a bad 'un.

'Nah, didn't fink he would've,' Billy said. 'Came ter make sure 'cos the bloody council bloke will 'ave me in a home afore you can sneeze if I don't watch it.'

'That's bad, that is,' Mary Ellen said, feeling her eyes sting with tears she would never dream of letting Billy see. They weren't just for him, because it was going to happen to her too – and she hadn't got anyone else she could go to, because her grandfather hadn't even opened the door to them when Ma had tried to tell him she was ill. She hated the thought of leaving her home and being with people she didn't know, and her voice wobbled as she asked, 'What are you going to do?'

'Don't know,' he said and pounced on a stone with glee. 'This is a good 'un, this is.' He showed it to Mary Ellen, who nodded her agreement. Because she was feeling sorry for him, she told him he could have first go. He grinned, showing a gap in his bottom set of teeth. 'You're the best friend I've got. I wish I could stay wiv you and your ma.'

'Ma's not well.' Her heart felt as if it were being squeezed, because she was afraid of what was going to happen to her. 'She's got to go away . . . and that means I can't stay here.'

'Why ain't your Rose 'ere then, if yer ma is bad?'

'She's going to be a nurse. She'll work in a hospital and live in the home for nurses. She's too busy to look after me, she said so.'

'That's bad fer yer then, Mary Ellen.'

'Yes,' Mary Ellen agreed unhappily, moving from one foot to the other. 'Rose said they're going to put me in St Saviour's. I heard them talking about it the other night. I think Ma might go away to the hospital . . . somewhere a long way off . . .'

'That's rotten luck,' Billy said. Then he threw his stone, did the feet-apart jump and the hopping motions, as he went up the squares and down again to retrieve his stone without a fault. 'I reckon that's where they might send me, St Saviour's. I wouldn't mind being sent there if I thought you would be there an' all . . .'

'No,' she replied doubtfully, watching as he threw for the next square and set off again. He performed the actions perfectly. She wasn't going to get a turn for ages at this rate. 'What do you think they do to you at that place? Is it a house of correction? I don't know what that is but I heard someone say they ought to send your Arthur there when they thought he broke into the corner shop . . .'

Billy looked anxious, because his brother had been in trouble with the police over that years ago, but no one could prove he'd done it and so he'd got away with the crime.

'Nah,' he said and threw his stone, which missed. He swore, a word that would have earned him a cuff round the ear from Mary Ellen's mother. 'It's your turn. Proper put me off, that did – but St Saviour's ain't a punishment house. Those places are for bad boys, not orphans. Not that you're an orphan, yer ma is still alive. Still, sometimes they put yer in a home even if both of 'em are still around. I heard as they're all right at St Saviour's – not like some places where they treat yer rotten. Nanna told me I should go there. She warned me she was too old to have the care of a young lad, and I reckon it's the worry of it wot's made her bad.'

'I put you off; you can throw again,' Mary Ellen offered, because he looked worried about his nanna, but he insisted it was her turn. She threw, hopped up the squares and executed a perfect turn, coming back to balance on one leg as she picked up her stone. 'I reckon we'd be all right there together – it wouldn't be as bad as if we were on our own and didn't know anyone.'

'All right,' he said and gave her a wide grin. 'If they say that's where I'm goin' I'll let them put me there. I can always run orf if I don't like it.'

'Where would you go?'

'Don't know; I'd probably just hang about the streets until I could find Arfur. There's plenty of bombsites wiv 'ouses half standin' where you can hide. Me bruvver won't have left the East End and he might let me stay wiv him if I asked,' he said hopefully.

'It would be better than living on the streets alone,

23

I suppose.' Mary Ellen didn't much like Billy's brother. He was mean and vicious and made her feel nervous when he looked at her. 'Besides, you're nine, aren't you? How long can they keep you at places like that?'

'If Dad was alive I should've gone to work down the Docks as soon as I was twelve, that's wot he told me. I ain't sure if it was legal but he said he'd be damned if he kept me any longer than me twelfth birthday. He was an old devil but I wish he was still around.'

'You've only got three years until you can work then,' Mary Ellen said with a sigh. 'I've got ages more before I can train to be a nurse like Rose.'

'Work's a waste of time if yer ask me,' he said, watching as she completed a second turn. 'Arfur says he can earn more in one night than me farvver made in a month.'

'What does Arthur do?'

'I dunno,' Billy said, but Mary Ellen thought he was lying. She could always tell, because his ears went red and so did his neck. Rose said Arthur was a thief for certain, but she couldn't say that to her friend. She threw for a top square and missed, and Billy chortled, stepping in to throw his own stone. This time he landed it exactly where he wanted and set off up the squares. He was on his way back when Mary Ellen saw her sister coming down the lane and knew it was time to call a halt. Before she could speak the delivery boy screeched to a stop beside her.

'Wotcha, Billy,' Bertie Carter called. 'I ain't seen yer for a while. Where yer been?'

'To stay wiv me nanna,' Billy said, his attention turned. 'What yer doin', then?'

'Got a job delivering sausages,' Bertie said. 'Me bloody pa's drunk all his pay again so ma told me to get out and find a job.'

Mary Ellen saw Rose glaring at her and knew she would be annoyed to see her talking to two boys she would describe as being rogues.

'I've got to go, Billy,' she said. 'It's time for my tea now.'

'All right,' he agreed but looked disappointed. 'It was nice seein' yer, Mary Ellen. Don't forget, if they put me in that home I shall be there waitin' fer yer . . .'

'I'm orf,' Bertie said. 'Yer can come wiv me, Billy. I'll get a bag of chips on me way home and you can share 'em.'

'All right,' Billy agreed.

Whistling, he ran off after Bertie, the pair of them reaching the end of the lane just as Rose came up to Mary Ellen. She stared after him with a look of annoyance on her pretty face. 'Was that that Baggins boy?'

'Yes. His nanna's gone into hospital and he came to see if his brother is back, but he isn't – and they're going to put him in a home.'

'In my opinion they should have done it long ago,' Rose said. 'If he's left to run the streets he will turn out just like that good-for-nothing brother of his . . .'

'Billy isn't like his brother.'

'Ma told you not to have anything to do with him, Mary Ellen, and now I'm telling you. He comes from bad blood and we do not want you getting into trouble because of him. Go in now and wash your hands. Then you can help me set the table and get the tea on . . .'

'I thought we were going to have ham and tomatoes tonight?'

It was Friday night and before Ma got ill they'd always had ham for tea, because it was pay day, but now there wasn't enough money for treats like that unless Rose brought them.

'There was no ham left by four this afternoon, and Mr Brown wouldn't cut a new one until tomorrow. I bought a bit of fish and I'll mash some potatoes to go with it.'

Mary Ellen pulled a face behind her sister's back. She didn't like fish and she'd been looking forward to a slice of ham all day, because all she'd had at midday was a slice of bread and dripping. Rose could be mean sometimes, finding fault with Billy for no reason, and then bringing fish for tea when she knew Mary Ellen hated it.

She would rather have a piece of bread and jam and if Rose hadn't brought a fresh loaf, she would make toast of the old bread and put the last of the strawberry jam on it.

CHAPTER 2

'Angela, this is a welcome surprise.' Mark Adderbury rose to his feet, offering his hand as his guest entered the study of his old, rambling, but rather lovely house, which adjoined the surgery attended by his private patients. Situated at the edge of the small but charming Sussex village where they both lived, its appearance was testament to his status as a respected and expensive psychiatrist. He'd come down for a long weekend and did not return until the following day. 'What may I do for you?'

'I haven't come as a patient,' Angela said with the sweet smile that won hearts but these days did not quite reach her eyes. Mark understood the sadness that lay behind those expressive eyes, because when her husband John had been killed in the war, he too had felt the sharp pang of loss for his best friend. It had been then that Angela had drawn closer to him, glad of his sympathy and understanding. 'I wanted to ask your advice.'

His eyes moved over her, noting the style of her dress, the New Look which Christian Dior had introduced that April, with its longer full skirt and shaped waist that gave women's figures that hour-glass shape. The rag trade in London had copied it within hours, getting cheaper versions into their shop windows to tempt women who were sick to death of the Utility dresses that were all that had been available during the war. However, by the look of Angela's dress, she had probably bought it in Paris when she stopped there on her way back from Switzerland, where she'd been on behalf of some patients; military personnel with private means, whose families had sent them for a rest cure after their traumatic experiences.

In her capacity as an administrator for the military hospital in Portsmouth, she'd sought Mark's advice when it was deemed necessary to find a clinic which might just be able to mend the minds of some badly damaged war heroes. Yet Angela had known only too well that it wasn't just their minds that had been damaged; in many cases they had lost a leg or arm, sometimes both, but there was help for amputees these days. It was the men with faces so severely burned that they looked like something from a horror film that Angela had felt for the most, skin blistered, eyes damaged, sometimes sightless – and some poor devils didn't even have a nose. Yes, there were wonderful surgeons ready to reconstruct a face, but it would mean endless pain and operations. She'd told Mark afterwards that she believed a lot of men would rather be dead than endure the look in the eyes of friends and family . . .

and he knew she'd broken her heart over the hopeless cases.

He'd told her about the clinic, of which he was a co-owner, and she'd managed the rest herself, though she'd complained bitterly because she wasn't able to offer the same service to deserving soldiers who didn't have private means. He suspected that she'd paid for one or two of her lame ducks to have the special treatment out of her own pocket; he'd often done the same himself and thought that having money to spare came in handy sometimes.

It was a pity that the job of hospital administrator had been her last, because she had excellent managerial skills. The hospital had been loath to lose her but Angela's mother had wanted her to come home, and since she was recovering from a severe bout of flu and seemed very low, Angela had obliged her – perhaps because she too needed to rest and recover her spirits.

Mark saw the signs of strain in her face and the dullness of those eyes that had once seemed to glow with life and vitality. Only five years ago she had been considered beautiful, with her dark blonde hair, azure eyes and sensual mouth, the only daughter of middle-class parents, her father a much respected family lawyer. Angela had been expected by her parents – some would say required – to make a brilliant marriage, and indeed she had, though rather later than had been hoped. For years she had led a butterfly existence, playing at being her father's secretary and enjoying the social whirl, despite her mother's frequent hints that it was time she settled down. Even though she was presented to several eligible men, Angela just hadn't found anyone she could bear to think of as a husband and stubbornly refused to give way to her mother's urging, even though they argued often. However, after meeting Captain John Morton, a handsome and charming Army officer, at a Young Farmer's ball at the age of twenty-nine, she had fallen madly in love, been swept off her feet and married him within a month. Much to her mother's displeasure, she had chosen a quiet wedding without any fuss and drama. Angela told her closest friends that her mother had never forgiven her for cheating her out of a big society wedding, but as she had also been fond of saying, 'With a war going on we just didn't have time to waste, besides, it would have seemed wrong when everyone was suffering.'

'You know you can count on me as your friend,' Mark said now, giving her his comforting smile, which, he was well aware, his wealthy patients declared was worth every penny of the exorbitant fees he charged for consultations. 'You are feeling less tired now, I think?'

'Yes, absolutely,' Angela replied. 'In fact I have so much energy that I am bored to tears. I just cannot live at home and help my mother with her charity work or I shall go mad . . .' She laughed softly, and his heart caught because it was a while since he'd heard her do so – not since John was killed. 'Not literally. I'm not going to have a break-down or anything. I just want something to do with my life – something worthwhile. I've had enough of endless society engagements and dinners with my mother's friends. Besides, Mother wants to find me another husband and I can't . . . I won't let her bully me into another marriage.'

'I agree that three years is too soon for you to think of anyone else, because you were so much in love with John,' he said, although he wished it were otherwise, because he would have liked the chance to offer her love and a reason to be happy again. 'Do you want me to speak to her for you?'

'No, thank you. I need work, proper work that takes me away from here – away from my comfortable life. I want to live in the real world rather than Mother's. I find most of her friends shallow and selfish and I want to help those in need. I'm not hysterical, even though Mother looks at me as if she thinks I am when I say something like that. She thinks she helps people because she sits on the board of a charity and raises funds for her pet projects but she has no true idea of what goes on.'

'A little unkind, wouldn't you say?' Mark raised his brows. 'Your mother does help others less fortunate in her own way; she just doesn't wish to get her hands dirty. That's what you're after, isn't it?'

'Yes.' Angela's smile was rueful. 'It sounds awful

31

put like that – as if I'm a middle-class do-gooder trying to earn my Brownie points.'

'Have you considered that that is how you may appear to people who truly have to get their hands dirty to survive? If I were to find you a job – or at least point you in the right direction – you would almost certainly come up against prejudice because of your background.'

'Do you know of something that might suit me? All I want is a chance . . . something to make it worthwhile getting up in the morning. Something to take away this emptiness . . .'

Her eagerness touched him, the sudden glow in her eyes making him realise that she was truly in earnest. Although the perfect beauty she'd once enjoyed had gone, she retained the clean symmetry of good bones, her face a little angular these days, but perhaps more arresting because it told of her suffering – and she had the best ankles Mark had ever seen on a woman. It couldn't hurt to help her on her way. She might change her mind once the reality of hard work came home to roost, but there was no harm in letting her try. He realised now that it had been in his mind to ask her for a while, because she would be perfect for the role of the new Administrator of St Saviour's – and of course it would give Mark the perfect excuse to see her more often. He smiled inwardly, because he knew his own feelings had played their part in his decision.

'As it happens, I do know of something. I was

actually thinking of mentioning it to you, Angela. You may not be aware, but I am on the board of a charity that runs a children's home in the East End of London . . .'

'Daddy told me a little about it. It's why I came to you, because I thought you might know of someone needing help? I don't have to be paid.'

Mark nodded, because he knew that John had left her well provided for; Angela didn't need to work, but he could see that she needed the discipline of it. Outwardly, she appeared to have coped well with her bereavement, but one had only to watch her to see the grief that lived inside her. She'd come home for her mother's sake, but he'd never approved of her giving up work for such a reason; of course if John had lived he would have expected it, but then she would have had a busy life caring for a home and a husband she adored.

Mark had been attracted to Angela from the first time he saw her, at a charity dance her mother had arranged when she was about twenty-two and he just twenty-six. He'd still been married then, of course, and working in a London hospital, down for the weekend to look at a house he hoped to purchase with a small inheritance from an uncle. He'd simply admired the bright and beautiful girl that she was from a distance, arranged to put a deposit on his house and gone back to London the next day, visiting occasionally to oversee the renovations at the property. He'd acquired the house mostly for Edine's sake, thinking it might suit her health to live in the country, but he'd often wondered since if it had been a mistake. Over the years Edine and he had met Angela and her parents at various social affairs, but by the time Mark had suddenly found himself free, Angela had been in the throes of falling in love with his best friend. It was really only after John's death, when he'd held her in his arms and let her cry against his broad shoulder, that he'd realised how deep his feelings ran.

Mark felt the ache like a yearning hunger deep in his guts. It was hard behaving like a perfect gentleman and a good friend, when what he really wanted was to take her in his arms and kiss her until she melted into him, submitting herself to his loving . . . but that was the daydream of a man in love and Mark had to face reality.

He got up and went over to the sideboard to pour a small glass of sherry for each of them, and brought the tray back to the desk, giving himself time to think over how to answer her.

'St Saviour's has recently been given a Government grant, which is wonderful, but it means big changes, and that's where you could help, Angela. Sister Beatrice is an excellent nurse. She has been in charge of the home for the past two years and we are delighted with the improvements she's made on the nursing side; but good as she is, she dislikes paperwork – and she does tend to drag her feet a bit when it comes to change. Her desk is always piled high with papers in no order

34

whatsoever, and her reports are always late and usually leave much to be desired. She is a nurse first and foremost: a dedicated, hard-working and intelligent woman, but the office work is beginning to slip. Some of the governors are growing concerned and I think she may find the new order hard to accept.'

'She sounds a wonderful person, Mark.'

'She is, but we do need to bring St Saviour's into the modern world, Angela. Right-thinking people are questioning the way some homes have been run in the past – especially after that fiasco when all those children were sent overseas. Three thousand of them went down on that ship the Germans torpedoed and it caused an outcry against the high-handed men who sent them off without a thought for what the children wanted. In my opinion it's time we started to think about the wishes of the child involved. Look at the way they were just shipped off to the country at the start of the war – and some of them went missing; others had a terrible time. Instead of being kept safe and cared for they were treated little better than servants.'

'That was awful,' Angela said. 'If they were going to send them off like that, they could at least have made sure the homes they went to were properly vetted.'

'From what I heard, people just turned up and selected who they wanted and took them off. Some mothers didn't even know where their kids were

. . . but that's not what concerns us now. I want to make sure that our home is run for the benefit of the children in order to give them a better future – education comes into that and it helps if their minds are stimulated, not just at school, but in their home too. I want us to show them there is another way of life . . .'

'You mean take them to places of interest, outings that they will enjoy but will open their minds too?'

'Yes, but perhaps there are other ways you could encourage them to think for themselves, Angela? I should like you to consider what we could do to change both the way St Saviour's is run and any improvements to both the old and the new building. You have a clear mind and I'm sure your views and your sense of order would help Sister Beatrice. I am not asking you to take over from her, Angela, but she is struggling to cope with all the responsibility, and once the Board approves any changes, it will be your task to implement them. You are not supplanting Sister but you could help her find her way.'

'I did quite a bit of reorganising at the hospital.'

'Yes, so I've been told, and they were grateful for the changes you suggested. The difference is that change will not be welcome to everyone at St Saviour's, Angela.'

'I'm prepared for that,' she said and sipped her sherry thoughtfully. 'I need a challenge, Mark. At the moment life feels a bit empty . . .'

'You will have more than enough to do if you take this on. Make no bones about it, Angela; the children you will meet are often the casualties of violent and broken homes. Some are so damaged mentally that I'm not sure we shall ever get them right, others are physically ill. St Saviour's takes in any children in need of help, no matter what their background or religion.'

'That's perfect,' Angela said and leaned forward, her face alight with interest. Mark caught a breath of her perfume; it was light and sensual and made his guts ache with the need to take her in his arms.

Mark continued, 'It is a poor area; many of the old houses are not far off being slums. Hitler got rid of some of the worst, but there are still too many narrow lanes and rundown streets. St Saviour's itself is in Halfpenny Street, but there are lots of alleys and lanes leading off it, though locals refer to the whole area as the 'Alfpenny or if they really want to bamboozle you, as the Two Farthin's.'

'That's clever.'

Angela laughed and Mark nodded his appreciation of her humour. 'Yes, they're unique, these people. It doesn't seem to matter what hardships they have to endure, they will come up with something to laugh at.'

'I can't wait to find out for myself. Please go on, Mark; it's fascinating.'

'The house was once a Georgian mansion, quite beautiful inside, I believe, but all that grandeur was lost when it became a hospital for contagious

37

illnesses. The people of the area have never had enough to eat and rationing hasn't made that much difference to some of them, because they couldn't afford to buy more even if food was plentiful. Indeed, at St Saviour's our children eat better than they ever have in their lives; they wear decent clothes and have shoes without holes. Of course, you'll find decent families living in the vicinity, businesses and shops too, but it's the kind of area where in the old days diphtheria would have swept through like wildfire. Thank goodness we have a vaccine for that now, but there are plenty of other diseases to cope with. Polio is a terrible illness and there's too much of it about these days.'

'Terrible,' she agreed. 'I do understand that it is a poor area, but that is why I think I might be able to do some good.' Angela gave him a hot, urgent look, her eyes full of passion. Mark wished she felt as passionate about him. 'What would I be asked to do?'

'Your job would be mainly in the office, but they cannot afford as many carers as they would like, and you would undoubtedly be asked to help out – perhaps with trips outside, pleasure outings, if you like. If Sister Beatrice likes and trust you, she may allow you to help with the children. Mrs Burrows – or Nan, as everyone calls her – is a surrogate mother to the children. She is the one who looks after those most damaged by trauma, and she often puts the young ones to bed, and cares for them if they are ill – at least, with small things that do not require they be placed in the nursing ward. Make a friend of her and she will put you right.'

'Oh, if only they will take me. It sounds just exactly what I should like. If I had trained as a nurse I could have been of more help, but Mother hated the idea and when the military hospital discovered I was good at keeping order they made me one of the administrators; it was a bit of a shambles when I arrived. They were always inundated with casualties and often out of their depth. We had to provide temporary wards wherever we could find space and that took a lot of co-ordinating, so I think I can manage to bring in some changes at St Saviour's. However, I also did an extensive first aid course and I know a little about helping out in a crisis.'

'A lot of your time will be spent dealing with the setup of a new wing and the paperwork, also some fundraising. With the grant from the Government's department to help with repairing war-damaged infrastructure, we've been able to purchase an old building just next door. We've had the architects in and the plans have been approved. The builders expect to move in shortly, perhaps next month if things go well. It has to be completely gutted and refurbished, which is a big job and will cost a great deal of money. We have also been given a small grant to help with running costs for the first year; it's a part of the grand new welfare scheme that is coming in next year. Even with the grant we are going to need to raise a lot of money in the future . . . I'm hoping you will take that on, Angela? We need to get some wealthy people interested – and you know quite a few through John's family.'

Mark saw the colour leave her face and wished he hadn't spoken, because it was obvious that her grief lay hidden just beneath the surface, but he also knew from experience that grief had to be brought out and dealt with.

'Do you think it sounds like something you want to tackle?'

'Do you think they will give me an interview?' she countered, and her stricken look had gone. 'It's just what I need, Mark.'

'You're sure you feel able to cope with an area like Halfpenny Street? Local legend has it that the street earned its name from the ragged orphans that would do any job, not matter how demeaning, just to earn a halfpence or two. It is part of the Spitalfields, Stepney and Bethnal Green area, at the heart of the East End, once a prosperous area when the rich silk merchants lived there. However, when the richer people moved out, the area went into a slow decline and was taken over by less well-off immigrants, Used as a fever hospital, the building was damaged inside but the shell survived and is the only one that has managed to do so in this particular area. We took it over in a neglected state and made it habitable again. However, it is a dingy area, teeming with all kinds of people, all nationalities these days. The Huguenots were there from the start, of course, but then it became very much a Jewish centre; you will see evidence of that in the old synagogues and shops. Many of the synagogues are now used as factories or storehouses. There are lots of little manufacturers and craftsmen working in the lanes and streets around the home, and most look grimy and neglected.'

'What does any of that matter if I can be of use?'

'You are prepared to do whatever they ask at St Saviour's?'

'Yes, of course.'

'You are quite sure it's what you want?'

'I'm absolutely certain. I need to feel useful, Mark – to do something other than sit around and try not to be bored stiff by Mother's friends.'

Mark wanted to please her, to see that quick smile he found so attractive. 'I shall speak to the Board tomorrow; it's our monthly meeting and if I recommend you . . . I can't promise you, because Sister Beatrice is going to resist, but I think I know how to bring her round.'

'Thank you so very much,' Angela said, her face lighting up. 'You are wonderful, Mark. So much to do but you always make time for me. I almost didn't ask because you are so busy . . .'

'As I've told you before, I am your friend and always here for you.' He wanted to tell her that he cared about John's cruel death too but she wouldn't want to hear that just yet. Mark had

41

served overseas with the Army Medical Corps for a while; he and John had both been at the horror of the nightmare that had been Dunkirk and survived it, but then Mark had been transferred to the Military Hospital in Aldershot. John had served out in Egypt for some months. He'd been home for a short visit, which was when he'd met and married Angela, returning to his unit for another tour of duty overseas, before his last leave. John's unit had been one of those that stormed Normandy in the D-Day assault and it was there that he'd been so horrifically wounded that his CO had hardly recognised him.

Sent out to France in the vanguard of the advancing troops, Mark had worked with the other medics as part of a team, because this time round there was an understanding that it wasn't just physical injuries the men suffered from, but deep psychological harm too. When John's body was brought into the makeshift hospital, Mark was working with one of the surgeons on the burns cases, trying to prepare men for the ordeal they faced when they returned home, and he was there when John was carried into the ward, his injuries so severe that he was not expected to survive the night. Indeed, it had been a mercy that he'd never regained consciousness, but the memory was one that Mark could never share with his friend's wife, because it was too shocking and painful.

'Well, I must not take any more of your time.' Angela rose to her feet. His gaze took in the grace

42

of her movement as she uncrossed her legs, the smooth whisper-thin nylon stockings and sensible Cuban-heeled black shoes. Mark stood too and they shook hands.

'Good luck. I imagine you will get a letter quite soon asking you to go up for an interview.'

'I can't wait,' she said and went out.

Mark turned to stare out of the window at his very beautiful and extensive gardens. He was comfortably off, able to live much as he pleased these days. Indeed, he had no need to work all the time, and certainly the unpaid work he did at St Saviour's was unnecessary to his career, but he too had known the urge to do something useful, to give back a little of what hard graft and Fortune had brought him. Perhaps it was merely a salve to his conscience, because he knew that many of the middle-class and rich women who patronised his clinics were not truly ill – at least their symptoms were real enough, but the mischief lay in the idleness of their comfortable lives. If more of them had Angela's strength he would soon be out of a job, he thought with a wry smile.

Mark was thirty-eight, and had an unhappy marriage behind him. It had ended because his wife died in a diabetic coma, brought on by her total lack of discipline. She had disregarded her diet, eaten foods that were too sugary, and forgotten her insulin, often leading to an emergency dash to the hospital. He suspected that these frequent crises were cries for help, which had sometimes been

43

ignored because he was working too hard to think about her unhappiness. In fact he suspected that she had deliberately taken her own life, because she'd known what her reckless behaviour would lead to, and it was her way of paying him back for neglecting her. He blamed himself for not recognising the signs of depression that ought to have been plain; his only excuse was that the pressure of work with men who were suffering terrible trauma had led him to imagine that Edine was happy enough in her comfortable home.

Mark knew that he had neglected her. It hadn't been his fault that their son was born deformed, but he knew that in some peculiar way his wife felt it was. Unable to accept what had happened, she accused him of paying more attention to his patients, as if that had somehow caused the child's death. He blamed himself on both counts, though he knew it was ridiculous. Had Edine's misery and depression contributed to his son's tragic condition? Or was it partly her illness that had starved the boy of the oxygen he'd needed at birth?

The child had died only a few days later in the hospital. Mark had been told the hole in little Michael's heart had never closed and by the time the doctors realised what was wrong, it was too late. Considering his other deformities, it was perhaps a merciful release. The pity of it was that Edine could never have another child, because the boy's birth had damaged her inside.

It had all gone wrong after that.

Nursing his own disappointment and grief, Mark had buried himself in his work and neglected his wife without realising what he was doing. She'd turned away from him and he'd believed she blamed him for what had gone wrong, but he should have tried harder to reach her. Edine's miserable death would lie forever on his conscience. He did not deserve another chance. Why should he be alive and able to love again when both his wife and their child were buried in their graves? It must have been his fault somehow. Because he'd been too selfish or too busy to realise how unhappy Edine was, to take more care of her, something had gone wrong inside her. He did not deserve to be happy again or to be loved by Angela. Besides, he was not even sure she saw him as a man, but rather as a friend of the man she still adored.

Angela's perfume still lingered, haunting him, making him wish for something he knew was beyond his reach, for the moment anyway.

Sighing, Mark went back to his desk and pulled out the folder he'd been dealing with earlier. In this case the woman was suffering from a mental condition that might result in her having to be shut away for the sake of her family and her own safety. He was reminded of Edine and the way she'd brooded towards the end and the guilt was hard to bear. Sometimes he could see her resentful, sullen face, blaming him for her unhappiness. Why hadn't he realised that her frequent illnesses were a cry for help? Yet this was a different case, and he must not allow personal feelings to come into it. It was rather a sad matter, and he didn't want to make the decision himself. Mark would ask a trusted colleague to examine his patient and give him his thoughts.

Walking back to her parents' house, a modern red-brick building set some distance from the village, Angela was feeling more cheerful than she had for weeks. Of course Mark Adderbury couldn't promise that St Saviour's would take her on, but he obviously had some influence with the Board, having been a member since it was opened just four years earlier to deal with an influx of orphans created by the war. So many lives had been lost in the terrible bombings, both during the Blitz and from the terrifying V2 rockets in the last year of the war. Sometimes whole families had been killed, but at others children lost mothers, aunts, and grandmothers. In the worst cases their fathers were also killed while away fighting for King and Country and they had no one to take them in. Angela knew from something that her father had once told her in confidence, that the first matron employed to run the children's home had been sacked after two years for various misdemeanours, including embezzling the funds. Mark had been very angry at the time and they had been more careful in their choice of the nursing sister who replaced her.

Her father had told her that Mark had been the

one who pushed for Sister Beatrice and therefore if he recommended Angela for the post of Administrator, surely his word would carry some weight? Her mother would be horrified at the idea of her daughter working at a place like St Saviour's, but her father would understand.

Angela had never doubted that her parents loved her. Daddy was wonderful, always trying to understand yet doing everything wrong, petting her as though she was still his little girl. What no one understood was that she'd lost her soul mate, the only man she'd ever loved.

For a moment the pain of her grief caught her off guard and she had to fight to get her breath. She must not let her grief overpower her. She must face what had happened to her, face the fact that the man she'd adored was never coming back to her . . . face the knowledge that his body had been so badly mutilated that it was only his identity tags that convinced his CO it actually was John. Of course Angela should never have known the truth of his death. Her official letter had been brief, merely telling her that he had died in action and was a brave soldier.

Angela should have accepted that but in her despair she'd cajoled her father into discovering more. He hadn't wanted to tell her the truth, believing it would make her grief worse, but she'd wanted to know even though it had caused her unbearable pain. For some time she'd felt numb, and that had helped her to carry on at work as if

47

nothing had happened. Perhaps she would have gone on like that if she hadn't come home after the war ended, but her father had telephoned her, telling her that her mother had flu and was very depressed. She'd come home on a short visit and stayed on because her mother cried and begged her not to go back, and since the war was over there had seemed no reason to return. Angela had promised to stay for a while, and at first it hadn't been too bad, but now that her mother had recovered she wouldn't stop plotting and planning to get her married again.

Mrs Hendry was determined that her daughter was going to enter the circles she had only ever watched from the edge. John's family was landed gentry, and Mrs Hendry thought that Angela should use his parents to launch herself into society and make a second marriage. She would have had a brilliant social life if John had returned from the war, of course, because he was set to enter politics. They would have lived in London most of the time, enjoying a full life of children, a loving relationship, and entertaining their friends, but his death had left her with nothing and she felt so empty – and the one thing she didn't want was the kind of marriage her mother craved for her.

Angela might have stayed with John's family had she wished, but they were busy people and though they tried to make her welcome she knew she didn't fit into their world of hunting and shooting, high society. Had there not been a war on, Angela doubted that she and John would ever have met. He was home on leave from the Army some three years or so after the war had started, and would not normally have been in the district. Like Angela, he'd been invited to a dance by a friend and because he was at a loose end tagged along for something to do. The truth was, their worlds were far apart and only love had brought them together. She was just a well-educated, middle-class girl with faintly socialist ideas, pink rather than red, her father teased, and without John she was a fish out of water in his world.

Mark had been the person who got through to her after she came home, becoming a frequent visitor. He'd taken her out to dinner a few times, telling her about some of the work he did with damaged and vulnerable children in a London clinic; he'd woken something in her with his stories of suffering. She'd never had cause to think of poverty, of people living on the edge, dying of terrible illnesses that were the result of dirty living conditions and poor diet. His words had made her aware of a desire to do something in return for all that she'd been given, all that she'd taken for granted until a cruel fate swept away the only thing that truly mattered. The feeling of numbness had left her, but that made her more conscious of what she'd lost – of the emptiness of her life. The kind of position Mark had outlined was perfect for her, almost as if it had been engineered for her sake.

He wouldn't do that, would he? She decided it was unlikely.

Feeling a flicker of excitement at the prospect of a new job and a new life, Angela knew she had to keep it to herself. Mother wasn't going to like it when she discovered that she was going to live in London and work in a slum area. Daddy would support her, of course; he was such a darling, but he didn't like arguments in the house. Once Angela was sure of her ground she would fight her own battles. She wasn't a child any longer.

Walking into the highly polished hall of her parents' house, Angela saw that her mother was just setting a bowl of the most beautiful roses on the half-moon table. An antique handed down through her father's family, it was just one of the beautiful things in a house that was furnished in the best of taste, because Phyllis Hendry did everything well. Having set down the roses, she turned and saw her daughter enter, her brow furrowing in slight annoyance.

'Where have you been all morning? Mrs Finch called to invite us to a dinner she is giving next week. Did you not promise that you would give her a cutting from our garden?'

'Yes, I had forgotten. She wanted a piece of the white lilac, because she has the blue but particularly admired our white blossoms in the spring. I'll take a few cuttings to her this afternoon. There are some other bits and pieces she might like . . .'

'We have tea at the Robinsons' this afternoon,'

her mother reminded her. 'Really, Angela, can you not even remember our social engagements from one day to the next?'

'I'm sorry, it had slipped my mind. Do I have to go? I have nothing in common with Mrs Robinson.'

'You accepted her invitation. It would be rude to cry off now. Besides, you may take those cuttings to Mrs Finch in the morning, unless you have engagements of your own?'

Angela shook her head, heading towards the stairs. Her mother took it for granted that she would resume the life she'd led before she married John, but she couldn't. Angela found the whole idea tiresome. Endless tea parties, mindless chatter about unimportant matters, and women who thought that social position and money were everything, bored her. What her mother found shocking she often thought vaguely amusing, and when the last vicar's wife had run away with her lover Angela had silently cheered her on, while all her mother's friends tore her character to shreds. In fact she no longer fitted into the snug and comfortable world her mother had made for her family. She wasn't the same person that had frittered her time away before her marriage, and she could only pray that soon she would have a chance to do something worthwhile with her life . . .

CHAPTER 3

Sister Beatrice pushed the clutter of paper, pins, elastic bands and pens on her desk to one side with a sigh. She had never expected there to be quite so much accounting to do when she'd accepted the post as Warden of St Saviour's. She felt it to be such a waste of time when the children and staff needed her. The home was understaffed as it was and she could not spare the time to write endless reports and keep the accounts, which, as a devout nun, she found distasteful. Having made her point clear at the last meeting of the Board, which she was forced to attend each month – another waste of time – she hoped that they would accept the admittedly skimpy report she'd written up in the early hours of that morning.

She'd set aside the evening to do it, but three new inmates had been admitted; suddenly orphaned by the loss of their mother to some kind of violent poisoning, probably from food contaminated by flies or worse, the children had nowhere else to go. Had Nan been on duty she might have stuck to her plan, but the woman she trusted most in the world had gone down with a bout of influenza the previous day and was at home in bed. Sister Beatrice did not consider any of her nursing staff competent to admit three terrified children late at night. Sally, a dedicated young carer but with no nursing training, had washed them and put them to bed, but they had first to be examined to make certain they did not have any symptoms. If the illness that had taken their mother was not food poisoning, as she'd been informed by Constable Barker, but an infectious disease, it could have wreaked havoc amongst the other inmates. However, since the woman was a known prostitute and drank too much, it seemed likely that a nasty bout of food poisoning would be enough to kill her.

Sister Beatrice had examined them all herself, and apart from some bruises to their arms and legs, a couple of untreated sores on the eldest boy's leg, which needed bathing with antiseptic and the application of a soothing salve, and the fact that they all looked emaciated, she passed them as fit. No sign of disease, thank goodness; no lice either, which was quite often the case with children from the slums around Halfpenny Street. She'd asked if they were hungry, or if they'd eaten anything that made them feel sick, and the elder boy had piped up.

'We ain't had nuffin' but a crust fer two days, miss. Ma said she had no money to buy food, but then she and her fancy man went out drinking and they ate jellied eels from the stall near the pub. Ma said it was that as made her bad . . . and she ate two dishes of it, greedy pig. Didn't bring so much as a chip home fer us.'

Assuming that the jellied eels were quite possibly the cause of the food poisoning – she'd always thought them nasty things – Sister Beatrice mentally thanked Providence that the selfish mother had not brought any of her treats back for the children. The evidence of the children's near starvation and the bruises told her that they were victims of neglect and brutality, which was rife in the lanes about St Saviour's. It was more than likely that the mother had had a succession of men and probable that the children had suffered at their hands; she didn't think from looking at them that they all had the same father, since their colouring was quite different. However, she thought a decent meal and some loving care would put right the most obvious symptoms of their distress, though in cases of abuse the mental trauma often didn't come out immediately.

After two years of running the home, and years of experience in the Abbey of All Saints' Infirmary, she ought to be used to cases like these, but the sight of obvious abuse never failed to rouse her to fury. Hers was a nursing order, and though Beatrice had given up all thought of having a family of her own when she entered the convent, she had a deep need to help those unfortunates she thought of as the forgotten ones: the lost children, abused by those who should love them and abandoned by society.

54

She must be careful not to be side-tracked by her indignation. Her order forbade her from speaking out in a public way, but inwardly she burned with resentment at the way unfortunate children had been treated in the past. It was not so long ago that they had been sent down the mines at a tender age and used shamefully. Even as recently as the beginning of the terrible war they had all endured, when children had been sent off to the country, to people they did not know and sometimes against their parents' wishes.

Beatrice had been reading an article about the distress this had caused to some unfortunate children, who had been put to work rather than being cared for, and it was that which had aroused her anger, because it seemed that there were either no proper records or they had been lost in the war. And then there were the misplaced children in Europe, homeless and orphaned, what chance had they of finding a safe haven?

'May God protect and keep you,' Sister Beatrice murmured to herself, crossing her breast. Only the Good Lord knew what would happen to them. At least here at St Saviour's the children would be safe from the horrors left behind from a cruel war.

She fingered the silver cross she always wore as a sign of her faith and pondered the injustices of what at times seemed an uncaring world. It was not for her to make judgements. Her duty was to serve and she did her duty to the best of her ability.

55

'Help me not to fail, I beg you, Lord. Prevent me from the sin of pride and give me the grace to serve with humility.'

Sometimes, Sister Beatrice was weighed down by her fear of failure. When faced with ignorance, poverty and cruelty, she wondered if she could ever do enough to make a difference, or was she like the little Dutch boy who had stood with his finger in a hole trying to keep out the flood of the sea? Perhaps God had His purpose for her and to do His will she must be humbled.

This would do no good at all!

Smothering a sigh of annoyance, she reached for the dark grey coat that would cover her habit. Having reached the age of forty-nine, she no longer glanced at her reflection, other than to make sure her cap was straight and her uniform worn as precisely as she demanded from her staff. Once, she'd been considered attractive, more than that if the truth be told, but beauty was skin deep, and in Beatrice's opinion only brought unhappiness.

'Sister Beatrice, may I have a word with you please?'

She turned, frowning in annoyance as the pretty young woman came into her office. 'Staff Nurse Michelle, what may I do for you? I am in a hurry . . .'

'Oh, are you going out?'

'It is the monthly meeting and I'm already running late so make it quick.'

'One of the new inmates is running a fever. I thought you ought to know.'

'You had better put them all in the isolation ward just in case.' Sister Beatrice picked up her battered but once-good leather bag and her gloves. 'I shall visit them there when I return. Surely you can cope, Nurse?'

'Yes, of course.' Staff Nurse Michelle looked as if she wanted to sink, but raised her chin. 'I thought you should know. I shall keep an eye on them myself just in case they have contracted something infectious.'

'Well, you did the right thing, but I am in a hurry. Get on with it!'

The girl scuttled, making Beatrice smile grimly. Staff Nurse Michelle was usually reliable, as she ought to be, having trained as a nurse at the outbreak of war and done service in both civilian and military hospitals. She shouldn't be so nervous of being reprimanded, but she was still fairly new to St Saviour's and would get used to their ways in time. Perhaps she was in awe of her superior, because she wore the clothes of a nun?

Did her nurses think she was too strict because she tried to follow her conscience and do the work of the Lord? Was she too set in her ways, too accustomed to the years of suffering to accept that things were changing? At times her uncertainty pricked at her, but she took refuge in her faith. God would provide.

Sister Beatrice had suffered enough reprimands

during her years of training at the convent infirmary. Her sin had been one of pride and she feared that she had been a disappointment to Mother Abbess many times, before she learned to control her anger and her pride. She'd worked many years with the sick and dying in the infirmary before she'd been permitted to care for the children. And it was only by special dispensation that she had been allowed to take up her position here, and because the Church wished to have a representative in a position of authority. It was the Bishop's intention that she should maintain the strict moral discipline he believed desirable. Too many children's homes had been called into question in recent years and she'd been told in confidence that it was her strong sense of discipline that was needed here.

'With you at the helm I am sure our standards will not slip, as they have at other institutions, Sister Beatrice. I am relying on you to remember the old values. Children need to learn what is right and proper, but they must also be protected and cared for.'

'Spare the rod and spoil the child?'

'Exactly.' The Bishop smiled at her. 'I know I can rely on you to see that St Saviour's does not fail in its duty to these poor ignorant children, Sister.'

'If God grants me strength I will do what I believe to be right, my lord.'

'I know we can trust you, Sister Beatrice,' Mark

Adderbury had told her later. 'I've watched you working with sick children and I know you to be stern but compassionate – exactly the qualities needed. You will be their guardian and also their champion.'

Sometimes, she wondered if she'd been a fool to be flattered by Mark Adderbury into taking on the position of Warden. He was such an eminent man, so well respected, and charming. His smile could make most women melt and even she – who ought to know better – had experienced a few heart flutters when he smiled at her.

They'd met at the children's hospital, which was part of the Church-run infirmary, where she had been the Sister in charge of the traumatic cases: children who had been the victims of violent abuse, children who often had lost the power of speech and would only stare at the wall by their bed. Mark Adderbury had been the visiting specialist and she'd admired his professionalism, his manner with the young patients, and the success rate he'd had amongst what had been thought to be hopeless cases. Of course he had as many failures as successes, but even one child brought back from the hell of despair was cause for celebration in Beatrice's eyes.

Walking along the busy London street, her eyes moved over dingy paint and dirty windows. The narrow lanes about Halfpenny Street were, she supposed, marginally better than those many of the children came from in that the gutters were not choked with filth. When the charity – formed by several well-meaning persons of influence and wealth, including a Catholic Bishop and an Earl, though the latter did no more than contribute to the funds and allow his name to be printed on their headings – had bought St Saviour's for a song, it had cost a small fortune to make it habitable again. However, its situation made it ideal for taking in the orphaned or mistreated children from the surrounding slums and giving them a safe home where they would be fed, cared for and given a new start in life. Although various council-run homes existed, and of course Dr Barnardos had places all over London and the rest of the country, there were none quite like St Saviour's, in her opinion. Everyone seemed intent on getting the children out of the city, sending them to scattered locations in the country, where they would lose touch with any friends they might have and would eventually lose their London identity. Here they gave their children individual attention, with each child loved and cared for, which wasn't always the case in other homes. Beatrice liked to think that it was a place of hope for those poor forgotten children who might otherwise have lived on the streets.

St Saviour's was the first place a harassed council and busy police force thought of when needing somewhere to place these children. Some would move back when their families were able to cope; some would go to new homes with kind people who took them in and cared for them. The worst cases sometimes went into specialist homes because their minds or bodies were beyond repair but St Saviour's took as many children as they could squeeze into their premises. Because she knew only too well how desperately the home had been needed, Sister Beatrice could not truly regret having given up her life at the Catholic convent, which was situated in a quiet suburb on the outskirts of London, though she sometimes missed the peace of the evenings spent in prayer or quiet contemplation. She'd been convinced of her vocation and content to do the work God had given her; it was only since coming to St Saviour's that she had sometimes wondered if she was strong enough for the task. However, Mark Adderbury was right when he said that not all children in need were ill. Many were simply undernourished and ill-treated, and it was these that St Saviour's had mainly been set up to help because the established homes were overflowing and some had closed during the Blitz and taken their children out of London. This particular area had been chosen because it was at the heart of one of the poorest in the city, and would provide an instant refuge and in some cases a home for life.

The disastrous war the country had just come through had left many additional orphans in London, which was why the scheme had found favour amongst so many of Mark Adderbury's friends and acquaintances. Sister Beatrice had no doubt at all that his was the driving force that had got everything up and running in the first place. She'd found herself responding to his charm and promising to think about it, and after inspecting the home, which she instantly saw was in need of better management, had allowed herself to be persuaded. On the whole, she found her work satisfying and often rewarding, but she had not reckoned with that wretched paperwork.

Entering the rather dark and austere church rooms, where the meetings were held each month, she saw that the committee were already assembled and waiting for her. The Bishop looked annoyed, glancing at the gold watch he carried in the pocket of his dark waistcoat, and one or two of the others seemed frustrated because she'd kept them waiting. Mark Adderbury rose to his feet instantly and drew out a chair for her, his easy smile making her forget that she found these meetings a waste of time.

'I'm afraid my report is sketchy,' she announced. 'We had an emergency last night and I had to write it earlier this morning . . .' Taking a deep breath, she went on, 'I am aware that the committee has been petitioning the Government for extra funds. If the new building is to be converted to more dormitories, I may not have time to complete a monthly report or keep the accounts accurately. I should need a secretary . . .'

'This really cannot continue,' the Bishop said fussily. 'I do understand that the position carries many responsibilities but we must have our reports and the accounts were late last quarter. There are limited funds and I really do not see how we can find the money for a secretary . . .'

'I disagree,' one of the committee members said. 'With the new grant we ought to afford more staff.'

'The grant is to provide and maintain additional accommodation for the children,' the Bishop said. 'Really, if it is too much for you to administer the . . .'

'Perhaps I may have the answer,' Mark Adderbury said smoothly. His air of authority held them silent, every eye trained on his distinguished figure as he rose to his feet. 'We should not expect such a caring and dedicated nurse to be bothered with reports and accounts and I propose that we should appoint a new administrator for St Saviour's. She would be there to assist in any way necessary, typing reports and keeping the accounts would be a part of her duties, but she would also oversee the building work and the setting up of the new wards, and be in charge of raising funds, leaving Sister Beatrice free to do what she does so well – caring for the children and her staff with all the dedication we have seen.'

'But the cost . . .' began the Bishop, who was cut short by Mark Adderbury once more.

'There are to be two grants, sir. The first and largest is a single one-off grant from the Government for the setting up of the new building; the other is a provisional yearly grant. Our good work has been recognised and we shall be given a generous grant for the coming year, which would pay for the new administrator. After that, we must apply for future grants – but I have every hope that Mrs Morton will raise additional funds to carry us through so that we do not have to wait in line for council funds, which are always stretched to the limit.'

'Sounds good to me, Adderbury. Who is this lady – and what experience has she had?'

'I've known her some time and a few days ago I asked her if she would be interested in perhaps taking on the post. Mrs Morton is a war widow, like so many others – but she has worked as an administrator for a military hospital; she was in the Wrens during the war and took an extensive course in first aid. Although she has no actual nursing experience on the wards, she does have good office skills and I know she was very well thought of in Portsmouth. Indeed, during one air raid, in which the hospital was damaged, she worked side by side with the nurses and was of great assistance in saving the life of one of the doctors. In fact they wanted her to stay on after the duration, but for personal reasons she left . . .'

Administrator! Over her dead body. Beatrice looked at him in annoyance. Was he implying that she couldn't do her job?

'I might be glad of help in the office but I do not need help in running the home itself.'

Her flat announcement brought all eyes to her.

Some of the committee looked impatient, for Mark Adderbury's suggestion had met with favour, but he was smiling at her, his manner as calm and reassuring as ever.

'Mrs Morton would not dream of usurping your position. We all know that we have a treasure in you, Sister Beatrice. For my part, I have been afraid that we might lose you because too much pressure was being put on your shoulders . . . No, no, Mrs Morton will naturally co-ordinate her ideas with yours but I believe you will find her helpful. We do need to move with the times, because now that the war is over things are going to change. In fact some of the changes are mandatory. Mrs Morton will help you guide St Saviour's into the new and better future we all long for, and oversee the setup of the new wing. She is a friendly person and has independent means, and if she were to become attached to the project she might be inclined to contribute.'

He paused to draw breath. 'As we all know, we need every penny we can get – and Mrs Morton has experience in fundraising. Her family is well connected, and I am sure she would be happy to write to people she knows to ask for funds. Her late husband's family are wealthy people, and she would have a wide-reaching net . . .'

Sister Beatrice glared at him. Begging for money was the one thing she had flatly refused to do, for she did not know anyone who might contribute to their charity and she could not have begged to save her own life. Pleading for money was against her religious beliefs and her principles and she didn't think she would be much good at it.

'Well, I think that settles it,' Bishop Trevor said. 'Will you write to Mrs Morton and ask if she would take the position of Administrator, Adderbury? Since you know her personally, I believe we may dispense with the formality of an interview. I think we all have complete confidence in your judgement. After all, someone like that does not come along very often.'

There was a murmur of approval and the motion was passed, leaving Beatrice with nothing to say. Of course she could have threatened to resign. That would have thrown them, but she was at heart a sensible woman and there was no point in cutting off her nose to spite her face. The Board – particularly Mark Adderbury – was pushing for big changes to come into line with new thinking, and she had to let it happen . . . even though it touched a raw nerve inside. She knew that her methods and perhaps her standards might be considered old-fashioned by this young woman, who sounded very efficient and clever. Once she became established at St Saviour's, Beatrice might find her own position threatened.

Well, it was in God's hands, she thought. She'd been called to this position of trust and if she was found wanting then it must be because God had another purpose for her – and yet she did not feel resigned to giving up even a part of her authority.

She truly loved her work at St Saviour's and the thought of all the changes ahead made her nervous. Would she be able to cope in this brave new world?

CHAPTER 4

'She was in a right old mood this morning,' Michelle said as she flopped down in one of the comfortable but shabby armchairs provided for the carers and nurses in their staff room. Accepting a cup of hot milky coffee from Sally's hand, she smiled at her. 'I only told her because if she discovered I'd put the children in the isolation ward without her permission she would have cut up rough.'

Sally was as attractive as she was pleasant, with reddish brown hair cut short so that it framed her face and brushed her smooth forehead with a pretty fringe. Her eyes were a greenish blue and honest, instantly making her everyone's friend. In contrast, Michelle had hair that was almost inky midnight blue-black, cut in a shoulder-length pageboy which she wore clipped back under her cap for work; her eyes were a deep blue that could cloud over when she was distressed. Dressed in their different uniforms neither of them appeared at their best, but anyone seeing the girls for the first time would be bound to take a second glance, for they were both outstanding in their separate ways.

The different uniforms were necessary, because the nurses were in charge of the sick bay and the isolation ward, and the carers were expected to check with the nurse on duty before attending to sick children. They each had their own table in the dining room, although Michelle often sat with Sally or another carer rather than by herself if she was the only one on duty. Some of the nurses were inclined to look down their noses at the carers, especially when they came from a different class. Michelle, however, was an East End girl, and in the few months she'd been there, she'd made friends with everyone.

'Don't worry about Sister. It's the monthly meeting; she's always a bit touchy on those days,' Sally said, eyes bright with amusement as she sank down with her own tea and a vaguely gingery ginger biscuit made by the kitchen staff. 'She's not a bad old stick, you know. She can be harsh, and she's strict to work for, but she really cares for these kids deep down.'

'Yes, I do know,' Michelle said, the last of her ill temper vanishing as she looked at her colleague. 'Are you going out tonight? A few of us are visiting the Odeon in Bethnal Green. We can get a bus that takes you right outside the door, and it's *Gone With the Wind* this week – it's come back again.'

'Oh, I've seen that,' Sally sighed dreamily. 'It was lovely and I'd love to see it again – but I'm going dancing at the Pally with my brother Jim, Madge and Brenda tonight . . .'

'Who is Madge?'

'Jim and Madge have been courting for two years,' Sally said. 'She would've got married ages ago, but he's saving up so that they can start off right with a decent house and proper furniture. He says he's never going to settle for a dump like we had before we got re-housed. We've got a lovely modern council house now, much better than the old back-to-back houses they've replaced. In some ways Hitler did us a favour, bombing the area. It meant the council had to get us moved so that they could pull the lot down – so we were first on the list.'

'We're still stuck in a two-up and two-down back-to-back with no bathroom. Hitler missed us, though the houses in the next street got a direct hit.'

Sally Rush's family were lucky. One of the council's first projects after the war had been to clear the area where they had lived: a small cluster of six old houses close to the Docks. It was just the start of a huge clearance scheme, which was going to take years and hundreds of thousands of pounds to complete. The problem was that the furnaces couldn't produce enough bricks, and timber was scarce, and so in a lot of areas they were putting up temporary prefabs.

'What do you think of all the fuss about Princess Elizabeth's wedding?' Sally said, glancing at the newspaper lying on the table next to her. 'Fancy her going to marry Philip Mountbatten. He's the son of a Greek prince, isn't he? – and very handsome . . .'

'Yes, he looks nice,' Michelle agreed. 'I wish I'd been there outside the palace when it was announced in July. They say the crowds went mad with delight at the news.'

'I wonder what she'll do about a wedding dress. You have to save coupons for ages to buy a proper gown. I know there's a little more material about now, but she will need yards and yards.'

'Oh, I expect they'll find some extra coupons for her – she deserves it. I reckon the whole royal family have been bricks. They could have gone off to the wilds of Scotland and been safe in one of their big houses, but they chose to stay here with the rest of us.'

'Yes, I love the King – he's so like everyone's favourite family doctor . . .'

'Sally! You can't say that about the King!'

'Why not? He's kind and comforting and I don't think he would mind.'

'Probably not,' Michelle agreed, smiling, then, 'What about going dancing together another week?'

Whatever Sally was about to answer was lost as they heard a child's scream of rage and then the door of the staff room was flung open and a rather scruffy-looking boy with red hair rushed in followed by Alice Cobb, another of the carers. A little plumper than the other two, she was very pretty. She was wearing a big rubber apron over her uniform and it was obvious that her intention had been to bathe the lad. Her pretty face was blotched with red, her soft fair hair sticking to her forehead, and she was obviously feeling hot and bothered.

The lad looked angry rather than frightened, and seeing a cake knife lying on the table, picked it up and held it in front of him like a weapon as Alice advanced on him purposefully.

'Put that down, Billy,' Alice said in a severe tone. 'You've been told you have to have a bath when you're admitted for the first time. Nurse needs to examine you to make sure . . .' She gave a little scream and flinched back as he made a threatening gesture at her. 'I shall tell Sister on you and she'll send you to a home for bad boys. We don't want the likes of you here.'

'What do you think you're doing, Billy Baggins?' Sally asked and got calmly to her feet. 'You should be ashamed. Your father would skin you if he saw you threaten Nurse like that . . .'

'He ain't around to skin me no more,' Billy said but grinned and lowered his arm. 'Wot you doin' 'ere, Sally Rush?'

'I work here, that's what,' she said. 'Give me the knife, Billy. You know you're not going to use it. You're not a bad boy so don't be a dafty.'

'She wanted me ter take orf me clothes in front of 'er!' he retorted indignantly. 'Then she yelled at me when I kicked her shins so I hopped it . . .' He looked at the cakes on the table. 'Blimey, they look good. I ain't had nuthin' decent since me nanna went in the hospital.'

'Well, you can have a corned beef sandwich with

pickle and a rock cake when you've had your bath,' Sally said. 'Come on, I shan't look at your willie so you can stop making a dafty of yourself. You don't want to go where they give you nothing but bread and water, do you?'

'Nah.' He gave in and passed her the cake knife by its handle. 'I reckon I don't mind you givin' me a bath – if yer promise not ter look.'

'I promise,' Sally said but didn't give way to the smile that Michelle knew was hovering. 'Nurse might have to examine you if you've got sores but she'll let you keep your underpants on.'

'Ain't got none. Ain't got no sores neither. Me nanna made sure of that when she looked after me. I 'ad a bath only last month, afore she went in the 'ospital.'

'You will have clean pants now. Your clothes need a good boil, so you'll be issued with new things. Clothes that fit. You'd like that, wouldn't you?'

'Suppose so . . .' He stared at her, clearly still reluctant, but when Alice took off her apron and handed it to Sally, he submitted, asking as they headed to the bathrooms, 'You promise you'll give me that sandwich and a cake?'

Michelle smiled at Alice as she flopped down in an empty chair and kicked off her shoes, sympathising with her friend. 'Sally has a way with the stubborn ones, doesn't she?'

'He took offence when I asked him if he had lice . . .'

'A lot of the kids think you're looking down on

73

them if you ask questions like that, you know. He looked scruffy but that was mainly those old clothes. I should think his grandmother kept him clean until she was taken into hospital. Is she still alive?'

'I've no idea,' Alice said. 'I only know Constable Sallis brought him in. He said he'd been found wandering the streets and the magistrate said he should come here if we could take him, while they decide what to do with him. I suppose they are waiting to see if his family can be found – Constable Sallis said he has a brother but he's gone missing.'

'Probably in trouble with the law,' Michelle said and stood up. 'I think I'll go and see how Sally is getting on – but first I need to look in at last night's new arrivals. Are you coming to the cinema this evening?'

'No. I've got the afternoon off and then I'm on again for the evening shift tonight. I wish I was coming. I wanted to see that film. I missed it last time and I shall probably miss it this time as well.'

'If you want, I'll swap duties with you,' Michelle offered. 'I don't mind, Alice, honest.'

'I daren't. Sister Beatrice would have my guts for garters if she caught you doing my job. Thanks for offering though, you're a mate. Why don't you come round ours on Sunday? We could go for a walk in the park and have tea out. Anything to get away from our house when the kids are home.'

'All right, I'd like that,' Michelle said. 'Cheer up, love, you did your best and some of the kids we get are that stubborn.'

'That one is – he'll end up getting the cane off of Sister if he doesn't watch it.'

Michelle nodded and left her. She doubted whether Sister Beatrice would have minded if they changed duties, if she'd even noticed, but Alice was too often in trouble to risk it. Shrugging, she turned her steps towards the isolation ward. She thought the elder boy, whose name was Dick, probably just had a bit of a chill, but she was glad she'd acted quickly. The last thing they needed was for an infectious disease to spread through the home. She was sure that Sally was all right; she was better at managing the children than Alice.

Going into the ward, she checked as she saw that Sister Beatrice was sitting by the eldest boy's bed. She was wearing a white apron to cover her habit and checking her patient's pulse. Looking up as Michelle approached, she nodded her approval.

'Well spotted, Staff Nurse Michelle. Dick has the early stages of chicken pox. I hope we may avoid an outbreak because of your prompt action, though I think his brother and sister have probably taken it from him. I'm putting you in charge of them and taking you off other duties. You can choose one of the carers to help you and you two will be the only ones other than myself to enter the ward. Remember your hand washing routine, and you must change your apron in the side room before leaving, and send your clothes to the dirty laundry, so that you do not carry the infection to the other nurses.'

'Yes, Sister,' Michelle said. 'I don't mind giving up my evening off if it will help.'

'You may decide the shifts as you please, but no one else is to enter until the infectious stage is over. Chicken pox is not normally dangerous, but I do not want half the children in the home going down with it or the staff. We just couldn't cope with such an outbreak. I take it that you've had it yourself?'

'Yes, Sister. I know Sally has had it but I think she has plans for this evening.'

'One of you must be around all night,' Sister Beatrice said. 'Take it in turns, but I expect both of you to remain here. You can get some rest in the room next door, but I don't want this boy neglected. In his state it could be dangerous – he is seriously undernourished. He will not fight off the infection as well as a healthy child would.'

'Yes, I know,' Michelle said. 'I am quite happy to stay this evening, and for as long as you think it necessary . . .' She wasn't sure that Sally would feel the same, but she would much rather work with her than any of the other carers.

'Good, that is what I like to hear. I shall send Miss Rush to you.'

Michelle watched as Sister left the room. Sister had been bathing Dick's forehead, and Michelle took over, wringing the cloth out in the cool water as the boy moaned and writhed, obviously feverish and in pain. He hardly seemed aware of her, calling out and begging someone not to hit him.

Michelle's heart felt as if it were being squeezed. How could these people be so cruel to their children? She'd learned from the younger boy that their own father had died three years ago, and the man who had lived with them was an unofficial stepfather. No doubt their mother was under this man's domination, powerless to stop him beating the children – but he wouldn't do so again, because now they were here and safe. By the way the little girl wept for her mother, *she* at least couldn't have been entirely bad, just weak and unable to protect her children from the unsuitable men she had living in her home. Unfortunately, it was something they saw over and over again and it never failed to make Michelle angry.

Little Susie was whimpering again. Michelle went to comfort her and saw the telltale signs of red spots on her face. She had taken the sickness too, though it looked as if Jake was all right so far. He got out of his own bed and came to stand by the side of his sister's.

'She's got it too, ain't she?'

'I'm afraid she has, but she isn't quite as bad as Dick.' Michelle looked at him anxiously, because he was the most undernourished of them all, his spirit much stronger than his poor little body. 'How are you – any headache or feeling hot?'

'Nah, I never get nuffin' like the others,' Jake said proudly. 'Shall I sit wiv me sister?'

'You get back in bed, there's a good lad,' Michelle said. 'Would you like some comics to look at? I'm sure we've got some Rupert Bear copies in the cupboard somewhere, or there might be a *Beano* . . . one about an ancient caveman?'

'I'd rather 'ave an adventure story,' Jake said, 'but if there ain't none the comics will do.'

'I'll have a look in a minute, after I get Susie to swallow this draught . . .'

'Wot is it?' he asked, looking interested. 'Susie don't like medicine, but Ma always takes an Aspro for 'er 'eadaches.'

'It's just a special medicine we use in hospital but you can't buy in the shops – that will stop her feeling so bad, helps to cool the fever. You can't use Aspirin for children with chicken pox, you see.' She held the glass to the little girl's lips, but Susie had clamped them shut and refused to swallow.

'You 'ave ter be firm wiv her,' Jake said, leaning over and pinching his sister's nose so that she was forced to open her mouth and gulp the mixture down. 'That's wot me dad used ter do wiv me when I were a nipper. He were a good 'un, me dad. We were all right afore he died . . .'

Michelle smiled as he retired to his bed, lying on top of it in the striped cotton pyjamas the home had supplied. She would find something for him to read if she had to send one of the carers out to buy him an adventure story.

Sally entered the ward just as Michelle was looking in the cupboard for the promised comics. The nurse turned her head, giving her colleague a wry smile.

'Are you furious with me for picking you to help?'

'No, of course not,' Sally said. 'I've rung my sister Brenda at her office and told her I shan't be going dancing with them tonight. We can share the nursing.' She looked at Dick as he flung out his arms and muttered something unintelligible. 'Are they all ill?'

'Jake says he is feeling all right,' Michelle said, pouncing on a pile of comics and two much-read Biggles books in triumph. 'I knew we had this somewhere. Give them to Jake; it will save him from being bored for a while.'

Sally took the pile of comics and sat on the edge of Jake's bed, smiling as he grabbed them eagerly. Clearly he'd been taught to read at school, even though he probably wouldn't have had much help from his mother. 'My brother likes these Biggles books. He still reads them even though he's grown up and I bring them in for the children when he's finished with them, though Sister would have my guts for garters if she knew . . .' Sister Beatrice didn't like books and comics brought into the sick ward, because of the germs they might hold. She thought the violence portrayed in some of the comics unacceptable.

'I shan't tell her,' Jake said solemnly and drew a finger across his throat. 'I'm awful thirsty, miss.'

'Do we have any lemon barley in the rest room?' Sally asked Michelle.

'There's bound to be something – and you can put the kettle on and make us a cup of tea . . .'

Michelle pulled back the covers and smoothed her cool cloth over Susie's heated body, dried her gently and applied calamine lotion to the spots to help stop the itching.

Sally went into the next room and filled a kettle for their tea, but when she looked in the cupboard there was nothing to make a drink for the thirsty little boy. Michelle looked impatient when she told her.

'Oh, for goodness' sake, can't the kitchen staff ever do their job properly? You'll have to take off your apron and wash your hands, then go down there . . .'

Just as Sally was about to obey, there was a knock at the door. Discovering one of the kitchen girls with a loaded trolley, including a jug of iced lemon barley, some milk in a jug and a bottle of concentrated orange squash, she laughed.

'You must be psychic,' she said. 'I was just coming to fetch some of this.'

'Sister Beatrice told me to bring this to you – and I'm to bring another jug up before I go off for the evening.'

Carrying the loaded tray to a table, Sally set it down and filled a glass for the thirsty child. Then she went through to the little room next door just as the kettle boiled. She made a pot of tea and took back two steaming mugs.

'Fancy Sister Beatrice thinking of all this,' she said as she put Michelle's tea on a table and sipped her own.

'She's very efficient,' Michelle said. 'Just don't get on the wrong side of her, that's all . . .'

'Well, I think she's a brick,' Sally said, sipping her tea, 'but I wouldn't dare tell her so.'

Michelle smiled, finished her tea and went back to Dick, who was tossing from side to side again. Poor little boy, he was really feeling very ill and it was no wonder that Sister was worried about him. In cases where the patient was already weakened, chicken pox might lead to pneumonia, and Dick just wasn't strong enough to go through that; none of them were.

CHAPTER 5

Alice left St Saviour's at just after eleven that evening, shivering a little because it had turned colder and her coat was thin, almost threadbare in places. She was saving for a new one from the market, but there was always a crisis at home and her mother needed most of Alice's wages. Although she didn't really grudge the money, it made her as mad as fire when her father got drunk on pay night, having spent more than half of what he earned all week. The rows in their house on a Friday night were awful, and she was glad that she could get out of it because she was working the late shift.

She walked quickly, wishing that she could have afforded to catch the tram that would take her to the end of their road, which was not far from Commercial Street. She had to cross over the wide thoroughfare, which, during the day, was always choked with traffic, horses and carts, buses and lorries, delivering goods to the shops. Her way took her down Brushfield Street towards Gun Street and Artillery Lane, where her family were housed in part of an old town house that had been turned into multiple dwellings by the landlord. To reach home she would have to pass the ugly building that served as a night refuge for women; these destitutes were always poorly dressed and often drunk, their faces grey with the exhaustion that came from poverty. Nearby was what Alice knew to be one of the finest Georgian shop-fronts left over from a grander past, because this area had once been most respectable. London was such a hotchpotch of the ugly and the beautiful, sometimes standing side by side.

As she turned the corner, Alice thought about the home she shared with her parents and brothers and sister, which was within walking distance of Halfpenny Street. The house had once been a large property but was now partitioned off with entrances to the front and rear; the latter reached through a narrow passage at the side. All six of her family were crowded into three rooms, with a tiny scullery; the only toilet was in the back yard and shared by two other families. The stench from the old-fashioned closet on a warm night was almost unbearable and Alice never used it, preferring a pot behind the screen, which she emptied in the morning before leaving for work, averting her head and trying not to breathe as she did so. She and her sister Mavis, who was just a year younger and working in the cardboard factory, shared one half of the front bedroom. Behind a curtain hung from a thin brass rail her two younger brothers, Saul and Joseph, slept in one small bed, head to tail. If Alice woke in the night it was usually to the sound of her brothers quarrelling.

Her parents had the smaller bedroom at the back, and since the walls were painfully thin it was possible to hear what went on when they retired for the night. If they weren't shouting at each other the bed springs would be pounding, Alice's mother protesting unfairly at what she termed her lout of a husband's brutality, because he wasn't a violent man. To Alice's knowledge, he'd never hit her mother and it was more likely that she would use her rolling pin on him.

Sometimes, Alice wished that her father would leave home again, for his sake, because she couldn't bear to see him looking so miserable. He wasn't all bad; she knew it was her mother's tongue that drove him to the drink and wondered why he stayed, yet she knew his leaving would not improve her mother's temper. Mrs Cobb was a scold with a nasty tongue and she used it on her family and neighbours, quarrelling regularly with everyone that shared the crumbling building.

Houses like theirs ought to have been pulled down long since. The council had talked about it long before the war but nothing was ever done. Even Hitler hadn't obliged them by dropping a bomb on the place, though his Luftwaffe had left gaping holes everywhere you looked.

Why couldn't her family be moved to one of those smashing new council houses like Sally

Rush's lived in? Alice envied them their warm home – and it wasn't just the lovely new stove that made Sally's home seem warm. Her parents didn't row all the time.

If only she could find somewhere else to live, Alice thought. She'd asked Sister Beatrice if she could have a room in the Nurse's Home, but had been told that she lived too close to need it. It wasn't the walking she minded, though on cold nights it was far enough, but she longed for some peace and privacy.

'Where are you off to at this hour, then?' Accosted by a voice she knew, Alice refused to turn round, though she fluffed up her hair, wanting to look her best even though she ought to ignore him. She didn't want anything to do with Jack Shaw, because he was no good. He might have film star looks with his black hair, slicked down with Brylcreem, and bold blue eyes, and he always had money in his pocket to spend, but that was only because he ran with the local bad boys. Alice's father had warned her when he'd seen her talking to Jack once, and since then she'd tried to avoid speaking to him.

'Aw, don't be like that, Alice luv,' Jack said, coming up to her and swinging her round to face him. 'Why are yer avoiding me these days?'

'I don't want anything to do with the likes of you, Jack Shaw. I keep meself out of trouble – and you're bad news.'

'Now where did you get that idea?' Jack said,

grinning at her. They were standing in the light of a street lamp, giving him a yellowish and slightly malevolent look as he gazed down into her face. 'I could be good news for a girl like you. I'm going places, Alice, and I might take you with me if you're nice to me.'

'Go away and leave me alone,' she said sharply. 'I've asked you politely, but if you persist I'll scream.'

Jack laughed, seeming delighted with her resistance. 'A fat lot of good that will do you round 'ere,' he teased. 'There's girls screamin' all the time, most of 'em because they like it – they make out they don't want it, but they do . . . just like you do, Alice Cobb.'

'You just shut your filthy mouth,' Alice said fiercely. 'I know how to protect myself and I'll kick you where it hurts if you touch me.'

'She's a feisty one,' Jack said and his grin broadened. 'Maybe that's why I like you, Alice. You ain't easy. I know you ain't been with anyone and that's why I'm interested. If you went out with me, you'd soon see I'm a proper gent. Jack Shaw knows how to treat a girl right. I'll give you a good time, and I'm not talking about a quick one up against the wall either. I'll take you to a dance or a nightclub and dinner – and then we'll go back to my place. I've got somewhere really cosy but I only take special girls there.'

'I don't want to be one of your special girls,' Alice said. She glared at him as he edged closer and then made a grab for her. Even though she tried to escape, he had her in his arms, pressed hard against him as his mouth closed over hers. His kiss surprised her, because she'd expected the kind of slobbery mess that some of the lads at school had tried on with her; instead his mouth was firm but soft, exploring hers sweetly in a way that made her heart jerk with fright because it aroused new feelings. His tongue explored the shape of her lips, trying to force entry but she kept it firmly shut and suddenly brought her knee up sharply. He yelled as she made contact with him and jerked back, clearly hurt and shocked. 'I warned you. Just stay away from me, Jack. That was just a friendly reminder, next time I'll really hurt you.'

Alice walked away swiftly, knowing that he was watching her. She half-expected him to run after her and give her a good hiding but he didn't, though after a moment he called out, 'I'll have you begging me yet, Alice Cobb, and you just see if I don't. I've got something you want even if you don't know it yet.'

Alice didn't dare to answer in case he changed his mind and decided to punish her for daring to protect herself. She knew that some of the gang he ran with would have slapped her about if she'd done the same to one of them, and a little shiver went through her as she wondered whether he would take his revenge another time.

He was mixed up in bad things, Alice knew he was, and she wasn't going to let the sweetness of that kiss blind her to his character. Alice had no intention of ending up like her mother, tied to a smelly house with four children, no money, a drunken husband and no prospects of a better life. When she got married, if she did, she wanted to live in a decent place – perhaps out of London, in the suburbs. She wanted no more than two children and the money to raise them properly . . . but in her heart she knew that life wasn't so simple. Girls like her too often gave their hearts to the wrong men and ended up having to get married to a man who would make them miserable – or even worse, ending up having a backstreet abortion in one of those filthy houses everyone knew existed but pretended they didn't. Alice didn't want that. No sweet-talking charmer was going to do that to her. She had too much of her mother in her.

Alice smiled as she recalled an incident from her childhood when her mother had chased her father up the lane with a rolling pin, and she'd battered him when she caught him. Sid Cobb went off for a while after that but in the end he'd returned to his wife and family. If she'd been him she would have stayed away, but it seemed her mother had something he liked even if he did drink half his pay every Friday night. Alice wasn't sure whether it was her cooking or what they got up to in bed; they made enough noise to waken the dead sometimes.

She was still thoughtful, torn between anger and the memory of that sweet kiss, as she paused outside the house where she lived. The smell of stale cooking, the stink from the back yard and the odour of mildew greeted her as she opened the front door and went in. Immediately, she heard her mother screaming abuse at someone, but this time it didn't seem to be her father. As she hesitated in the parlour that led in off the street, the kitchen door opened and a woman with long, straggling dark hair and a filthy apron came storming out.

'I'll swing for your ma one of these days, Alice,' she said. 'I swear I'll take the meat cleaver to her if she clouts my Bertie one more time.'

'I'm sorry, Matty,' Alice apologised, because she liked the woman, despite her frowsy appearance. Matty Carter cared about her children and did her best to keep them clean, though she was losing the battle in this awful place, which three families shared, because her husband drank more than Alice's father. In Mr Cobb's case, he'd been driven to it by his nagging wife, but Matty never nagged her husband; he was just a bully and a brute. 'What happened?'

'He was fighting with your Saul as usual, and she waded in and gave Bertie a black eye.'

'Oh dear, she shouldn't have done that – I'm sure it was half a dozen of one and six of the other.'

'Alice, you're a treasure and that vixen doesn't deserve you,' Matty said and smiled at her before going out of the door and banging it behind her.

'Alice, is that you?' her mother's voice screeched at her from the scullery. 'About bloody time too. Where the hell have you been to until this time, girl?'

'I worked late at the home, Ma. I told you this morning,' Alice said. 'You shouldn't wait up for me, just leave the key on the string and I'll let myself in.'

'I'm waitin' up fer yer father and he'll catch it when he gets back, I'm tellin' yer.'

'It's not Friday night . . .' Alice said.

'I bloody know it's not and I want ter know where he is.'

'Perhaps he had to work late?' Alice suggested, though it wasn't likely.

'He's took money from my pot to go drinking, that's what he's done. Saul give me half a crown from his wages from the delivery round and that bugger's took it. I'll teach him when he gets back, you see if I don't . . .'

Alice sighed, because she could smell the beer on her mother's breath and knew she drank whenever she got the chance; it was a case of the pot calling the kettle black, but she wouldn't dare to suggest it.

'Why don't you try understanding him for once? Perhaps you wouldn't quarrel so much then.' Alice wished her father didn't drink so much and would stand up to her shrew of a mother sometimes, but a part of her still remembered the man he'd been before his wife's nagging drove him to despair.

'You'll feel the back of me 'and if you cheek me, girl. Get through to yer room or I'll give you a hiding an' all!'

Alice sighed as she went through to the shared bedroom. She tried not to disturb anyone but she knew almost at once that they were all awake, the boys lying in their beds and giggling, waiting for Pa to come home with bated breath. Alice sometimes wondered what sort of men they would turn into; their parents' example certainly wasn't a good one.

'Listen to her,' Mavis whispered as Alice undressed and crawled into bed beside her. 'Rantin' and carryin' on. I shall be glad when I can get out of here. I've had enough.'

'You don't earn enough to get your own place.'

'Who says I'll need to? I've got a lad and he wants me to get married – and I'm goin' to as soon as we can.'

'Mavis! You're only seventeen. Surely you want a bit of fun before you get married – besides, who is he? You haven't brought him home.'

'Bring Ted Baker here? You must be mad,' her sister said. 'I don't want him to run a mile before he even gets the ring on my finger. His father owns a small newspaper and tobacconist shop and there's a flat over the top. It's in Bethnal Green – and Mr Baker says we can have the flat and I can work in the shop until we have kids. He's all for it, says he likes me.'

'Keep him away from Ma then,' Alice advised

and yawned. 'I'm so tired. Go to sleep, Mavis. We'll talk about it another time . . .'

Closing her eyes, Alice remembered the way Jack's mouth had tasted, not beery and foul like so many of the lads she'd met at the local dance, but pleasant. He'd had a faint taste of peppermint about him, and he smelled nice too – but he was a bad one. Her father had warned her, and she knew she mustn't let the memory of a kiss break down her reserve, even if it had been sweet . . .

CHAPTER 6

'Yes, how can I help you?' Sister Beatrice looked up as the woman entered her office. She was elegant in a pale grey fine wool dress and darker grey suede court shoes with a matching belt around her waist. Her short blue jacket had a fashionable pleated swing back, and she carried a small clutch bag in her hand. 'I don't recall – did we have an appointment?'

'Well, I was told to report to you as soon as I arrived.' The young woman offered her hand, from which she had just removed her leather glove. 'I'm Angela Morton.'

'Good grief, are you here already? I didn't expect you for at least another week.'

'Mark's letter said he was anxious for me to start as soon as possible, but I couldn't come until last night.'

'Well, your office isn't ready yet. I've asked the caretaker to install a desk, chair and filing cabinet in the room next door. It's small but I think adequate for your needs.'

'I am sure it will be fine,' the young woman said breezily. 'I'm so happy to meet you – and grateful for this chance to do something useful. My mother thinks I'm mad, but my father sort of approves . . .'

Beatrice answered sharply, irritated by her confident manner. 'Well, I dare say they both think their daughter should spend her days doing something more suited to a girl of your class.'

The smile left Angela's face. 'I'm just turned thirty-four, a widow, and I'm tired of sitting at home doing nothing much. I think it's time I started to do something worthwhile with my life.'

'Indeed?' Beatrice was aware that she'd been sharp and stood up, extending her hand to the younger woman. 'I'm afraid you've caught me at a bad time. We have three very sick children in the isolation ward with chicken pox at the moment. I've done what I could to stop the infection spreading, but one of my kitchen staff seems to have gone down with it. The stupid girl told me that she'd had it, but it turns out she'd had the measles. She ought not to have taken it even so, but she ignored my instructions and went into the ward when my nurses were busy. I know she thought she was saving them time, but some people have no sense . . .'

'Oh, what a shame,' Angela said. 'Has she taken it badly?'

'I've no idea. She was sent home when she started to show signs of fever. It is a nuisance because none of the other girls in the kitchens have had it, and I'm afraid of sending any of them

94

up in her place, so it looks as if I shall have to run after Michelle and Sally myself.'

Beatrice wondered why she felt a need to explain. There was something about this woman that pricked at her, made her feel inadequate despite all her years of experience.

'Would you allow me to help? I did have the chicken pox when was I was ten, and the measles. It would give me something to do until I can start work on the accounts.'

Beatrice was silent for a moment; she was reluctant to hand over even this small task to the woman she still thought of as an intruder, but she had too much to do as it was and it would keep Angela out of her hair for a while.

'Well, if you're certain, you may take up their trays, but stay outside the ward. I do not want another casualty going down to it – and God forbid that it should spread to the other children. Although it is usually not serious, it can affect the weaker ones badly – and we have enough to do without an epidemic.'

'Yes, of course. I can understand your concerns, Sister. I have had some experience of hospital routines, even though I'm not a nurse. And I took an extensive first aid course in the war because I thought it might help in a crisis – and it did.'

Beatrice sighed and heaved herself to her feet. She was feeling a little under the weather herself, just a bit of a sore throat, which she was dosing herself for, but this was an unwanted distraction.

'I shall take you down to the kitchens myself. Have you thought where you will live? If you would like a room in the Nurses' Home for the time being it could be arranged. It is situated at the back of the home and once housed the Warden of the fever hospital. These days, it is divided into rooms with a shared kitchen and a communal sitting room. I use it myself, because there are too many nights when it would not be convenient for me to be away from the children, though I do have my own room at the convent, which is my home. Some of my nurses stay in the Nurses' Home during the week and go home when they have a two-day leave – but you have no parents in London and might not wish to live there permanently.'

Beatrice gave her a challenging look, because Angela was obviously used to better things.

'I should like to take a room if there is one available. It would be better than the hotel and I could look round for an apartment at my leisure.'

Beatrice was surprised; she'd expected a flat refusal.

'I'll arrange it for you. Now follow me and I'll point out the various rooms as we go . . .'

Hearing the knock at the door, Michelle went to open it, and looked blankly at the elegant woman standing there with her trolley. Michelle was feeling hot and irritated, because Sally had gone for her break an hour ago and all three children were now suffering the debilitating effects of an illness that might not be serious as childhood diseases went, but was certainly causing her patients a great deal of distress.

'Who are you?' she asked sharply. 'Who gave you permission to come here?'

'Sister Beatrice,' the woman replied. 'I'm Angela Morton and I'm here to help out with the office work – and anything else that is needed.'

'The new Administrator? Oh, right, I didn't realise. Sorry, I'll take that now. For goodness' sake do not come in here, even if we don't answer the door promptly. Just leave the trolley here and one of us will fetch the tray.'

'Of course, if that's what you wish. I should tell you that I have definitely had the chicken pox years ago, and the measles. I do know the difference – and I helped nurse my young cousin when he took it a few years back.'

Michelle sighed impatiently. 'You just don't understand, do you? We have probably more than sixty children here at any one time. If you carry the infection to another person in this home, we could have half of them down with it in days – and we do not have enough nursing staff to cope with an epidemic. I just hope the kitchen staff hasn't taken it from Maisie, because it could spread through the place like wildfire . . .'

'Yes, I perfectly understand. Please do not worry. I shall not risk carrying it back to others. I'm sorry that I distressed you. You must have more than enough to cope with as it is.'

'To be honest, I could do with more help, but I dare not risk it.' Michelle picked up the tray and took it inside, kicking the door to with the heel of her shoe. She felt a bit mean for tearing Angela Morton off a strip like that, but Jake had taken the chicken pox despite his proud boast that he never did get ill, and, as luck would have it, he was worse than either his sister or his elder brother.

Sister Beatrice had done her best to contain the sickness to the three children in the isolation ward, and so far her precautions were working. The trouble was that there just weren't enough trained nurses to cope if a really nasty infection were to spread to the dormitories. Even Sister took extreme precautions when visiting the children, covering up her uniform in the rest room and donning a clean apron before going about her business afterwards.

Neither Michelle nor Sally had had an evening off since Dick first went down with the sickness, several days earlier. They were taking it in turns to rest, but for a lot of the time it needed both of them to keep the children cool and comfortable. If Sister Beatrice had not taken her turn, Michelle thought she couldn't have coped.

Holding back another sigh, she poured herself a mug of tea, but before she could take more than a sip, Jake was calling out. She put the cup down and went to sit by his bed, soothing his heated brow and watching him with sympathy. He felt so ill and on top of all that he'd suffered in the short years of his life, the sickness was taking its toll on him. He'd certainly got much worse in the last few hours. Seeing how pale and vulnerable he looked, a shiver of fear went through her because she was already fond of him. He was such a likeable little boy and his serious looks had tugged at her heart.

'Please get better,' Michelle murmured fervently, hardly knowing whether she was entreating him or praying to God. 'Don't die . . . please don't die . . .' Michelle was afraid that he was slipping away from them, despite all the love and care he'd been given, his once-vital spirit all but extinguished. Yet what more could she do to save him? Although a bright, intelligent boy, his physical strength had been affected by the years of neglect. Her throat caught with tears and she felt a surge of rebellion and despair.

She left him as Susie started to whimper and gave the child a drink to ease her headache. Susie was actually on the mend; she'd only taken it lightly and apart from a tendency to scratch her face because the scabs itched, she was causing less anxiety than either of her brothers.

The door from the rest room opened and Sally entered. 'I thought I heard the tea tray. How is Jake now?'

'Still restless. I'm worried about him, Sally, but there's nothing more Sister Beatrice can do if she comes – and she was up half the night with him, because she insisted we get some rest. Unless, do you think we should have the doctor?'

'Why don't you go and speak to Sister about it? The poor little thing seems to be getting worse all the time and perhaps we should have the doctor out.'

'Normally, we try to manage ourselves. Sister doesn't like to waste the doctor's time,' Michelle said but she was uneasy, fearful that the child might slip away from them.

'I know,' Sally agreed. 'Shall I sponge him down while you drink your tea?'

'Yes, please,' Michelle said. 'He has so many spots now, far more than either of the other two . . . if Sister Beatrice hadn't looked at him herself last night I should wonder if what he has is something worse . . .' She hesitated. 'Perhaps I'll go and talk to her and suggest the doctor just in case of . . .'

'What?' Sally stared at her in horror. 'You don't mean smallpox? No, it can't be . . . that's a killer. My father's mother died of it years ago.'

'Well, it has crossed my mind – but I'm sure I'm wrong. It's just a severe case of the chicken pox, but I'll ask Sister to take a look and tell her that I'm worried about him. If he needs a doctor we shouldn't leave it too long. Can you hold the fort while I speak to Sister?'

'Of course I shall,' Sally said. 'You look almost all in, Michelle. After you've spoken to Sister, why don't you take your tea into the rest room and have a little sleep?'

'If you're sure you can manage . . .' Michelle

arched back, feeling the ache in the small of her spine. 'I'm so tired, but you must call me if Jake takes a turn for the worse . . . and I'll ask Sister now if we should call the doctor out . . .'

Angela looked round the room that had been offered to her. It was clean but basic with none of the comforts she was used to, but it would do for a while and would be useful on those nights when she stayed over at the home to help out, even if she found an apartment she liked. There was no point in staying at a hotel that entailed a long bus ride when she had the use of a bed here. As soon as she got used to St Saviour's and its occupants, she would look for a nice little flat she could make into a home.

A rueful smile touched her mouth, because so far she hadn't been made to feel welcome here. Sister Beatrice had greeted her politely but she'd sensed an underlying hostility that she couldn't explain. Why would the woman want to put a barrier between them from the start? Angela had been sent to help her, and was very willing to do whatever was asked of her, even though Mark had made it clear that her main task was to bring St Saviour's in line with more modern thinking . . . but the stern Sister wasn't the only one to show dislike. Cook had told her that she must ask for what she wanted and not go making tea or sandwiches herself.

'That's our job,' she'd said, scowling as Angela

began to lay out the tray. 'Just ask for what you want, and we'll give you the proper menu for the nurses and carers. The children have different, of course. Sister Beatrice decides what special diets they need, if any – so don't go getting food for them without my say-so. You might end up doing more harm than good; besides, I don't want my precious rations being wasted. We can't afford to waste a scrap.'

'Of course not, Mrs Jones. I wouldn't even know where to start . . .'

She'd let her gaze wander around the large kitchen with its array of copper-bottomed pans hanging above a huge range, the painted wooden dresser and shelves crowded with an assortment of crockery. A large scrubbed pine table occupied the middle of the long room and was littered with dishes and wire trays, which held freshly cooked pies and jam tarts. The food, she'd discovered, was kept in a huge cold pantry and there was a refrigerator for the perishables. It made a loud chirring noise and sounded as if it were overloaded and might give out at any moment. She guessed that it was some years old. They could really do with a new one, more modern and efficient. Perhaps she could make that one of her first priorities, raise some money towards it – that was if a new one could be found. The shops were still struggling to buy in goods like refrigerators, which had been considered a luxury and expendable when metal was in such short supply during the war.

Yes, already she'd begun to make a mental list of changes, but once she got inside the building next door destined for the new wing, her job would really begin.

'Well, just remember what I've said and we'll get on all right.' Cook glared at her. 'We're short-staffed at the moment so you'll have to wait until I've done this semolina pudding for the children . . .'

Angela had waited patiently, wishing that she could just prepare the tray herself, but she didn't want to tread on anyone's toes, and would rather not make an enemy of the cook right from the word go.

She'd thought the nurses in the isolation ward would at least be glad to get a plate of both chicken paste and tomato sandwiches, a pot of tea, and the jugs of cold lemon barley for their patients. However, that very pretty nurse had snapped her head off and made her begin to wonder why on earth she'd ever accepted this post. Mark Adderbury had spoken of her being needed and wanted, but it certainly didn't look that way at the moment.

Perhaps she should have taken the offer to return to her old posting in Portsmouth, and yet there were too many memories there – of happier days when she'd met and married John . . . but that hurt too much and she was determined to put her grief behind her and throw herself into her new life.

Angela's mother had been upset that she was

leaving home again and had done her best to dissuade her; they had argued so many times over foolish little things that in the end Angela had just packed her cases and left. Her father had been staunch in his support but the arguments had left a little shadow hanging over her.

Putting aside all thought of her mother's reproachful looks as she left, Angela opened her bag and took out the key to the building next door. Its last purpose had been commercial, some sort of offices she understood, and Mark had warned her that it was in a bit of a state.

'Take a look straight away and refer to the drawings I've sent you,' he'd said when he telephoned to make sure she'd received his letter. 'I'd like your opinion, Angela. The architect has opened it up and made a lot of the small rooms into much larger ones. It's more economical that way, I suppose, to have larger groups of children together, but I'm not sure it's right. If you have any suggestions then we should like to hear them – before the builders move in, please.'

'Yes, of course. I can't tell you how much I appreciate this, Mark. You've been such a good friend to me since . . . John died.'

'You know I was fond of him, and he would expect me to help you.'

Mark's reply had been non-committal, and she'd sensed something . . . as if he were holding back whatever he wanted to say. Perhaps he understood how sensitive she still was on the subject of her late husband; it still hurt so much and she'd grown a protective barrier to keep everyone away from the source of her pain.

She sighed as she went out of the main building and into the rather dilapidated one next door. The door stuck and she had to put some force into getting it open. A brief inspection told her that the frame had moved out of true, possibly caused by an explosion a few doors down where builders were presently taking down a fire-damaged bakery. The front of their new wing looked as if it might need a bit of rebuilding, but inside was worse.

Angela's heart sank as she looked about her at the debris. Whoever had left this place had done so in a hurry. Broken furniture lay about and there were old newspapers scattered on the floor, cabinets hanging off the walls and plaster from the cracked ceilings was scattered everywhere. Its condition was daunting to say the least and would cost a great deal to put right.

No doubt the architects and builders had taken all this into account. Her job was to make certain that the plans drawn up were to the best advantage of the children who would live here. She frowned as she saw the clean, clinical layout of the upstairs floors. Down here, there were recreation rooms, and that was a definite improvement. Angela gave that a big tick, because safe space for the children to play was at a premium; they did have a small garden, she'd already observed, but on cool or wet days they needed more to do and this large room at the back with space for them to play various games was excellent. At the front a modern reception area and an office had been planned, which seemed a good use of the available space. She wasn't so sure about the layout upstairs. With only one shower room for the girls and one for the boys, it did not provide for any kind of privacy and modesty, and in her opinion that ought to be a consideration; there ought at least to be separate cubicles. It would add to the cost, she imagined, which might not go down well with the Board, but perhaps it might not be necessary to knock down so many walls . . .

As she went upstairs to investigate, Angela was still wondering whether she would be able to break down the resistance of the staff here. Perhaps Cook had taken the lead from Sister Beatrice, who was clearly hostile. It was obvious she felt challenged by Angela's appointment, far more so than Mark had imagined. A wry smile touched her mouth as she recalled what he'd said about the Warden.

'You'll manage her, Angela,' Mark had told her. 'She is a little stubborn and set in her ways – but once she sees that you have the good of the children and the staff in mind she will accept you.'

Angela could only hope that was true. She'd been filled with hope when she arrived, keyed up by his encouragement, but after just a few hours she was beginning to wonder if she had done the right thing. No one seemed to want her here; they thought her one of those middle-class do-gooders.

Mark had warned her that might be the case at the start. She'd dismissed his warning, but now she knew that it wouldn't be easy working with people who resented her.

Well, she'd taken the first step to her new life. Whether she'd chosen well or not, her path was set. She would find a niche for herself here, however long it took . . . and the main thing was to go over this place with a fine-tooth comb and then write her report so that any changes she decided on, and there were a few already, could be sorted out before the builders moved in.

CHAPTER 7

Rose stood outside St Saviour's, looking up at the forbidding stone walls and three storeys of tiny windows with what seemed to be attic rooms above. She had always thought it was like a prison from the outside, and, indeed, when the old house underwent major alterations in the late eighteenth century, the fever hospital had been intended as a place to keep some people in and others out. Back in the bad old days, men, women and children had been brought here to die. They had been shut away because they were known to have infectious diseases and the authorities of the time saw them as a danger to others. When diseases like smallpox, typhoid or cholera raged through a city they decimated the population, leaving swathes of dead in their wake. In most cases nothing could be done to save those who had contracted these virulent infections, and so they were often locked away from the population and left to die. The warders who were supposed to treat them gave them food and water and precious little else according to the tales that still circulated in the lanes surrounding the old place. It had been a house of fear and death then, but now it had become a place of hope – at least Rose trusted it would be.

Above the door was a stone heart split in two by an arrow, as if warning of the perils of life and death, and underneath in some ancient script the words: *St Saviour's Hospital – Make peace with God and render unto Him all that is due for He is the Light and the Way.*

A cold shiver went down Rose's spine as she thought of her mother's probable fate. She wouldn't be treated as harshly as the people who'd been incarcerated here in those far-off days, but she *was* being sent to an isolation unit near the sea, because she had tuberculosis. Her illness had progressed to the stage where she coughed up great lumps of blood and she found it difficult to get her breath. Dr Marlow had told them that she ought to have come to see him long ago, and to Rose, when she'd spoken to him later alone, he'd confessed his doubts about her mother's chances of getting over the disease.

'If she'd come to me earlier there might have been a good chance that they could save her, but now . . . well, I'll be honest with you, Rose, it is one chance in ten that she will recover. The best we can do for her is to put her somewhere pleasant and quiet, where she will receive treatment and kindness . . .'

'Is it really as bad as that?' Rose had asked, a sob rising to her throat, because she couldn't bear to think of Ma being so ill. 'She kept saying it was nothing, just a little cough, but then I saw the blood on her mouth – and she's so exhausted all the time.'

'Your mother was a very strong woman. Had she not been she would have collapsed long before this, Rose. I wish I could offer you more hope but . . .' He shook his head. 'There *is* treatment for her illness these days, but I think it may be too late for her.'

'I think she knows it,' Rose said in a choked voice. 'She is worried about Mary Ellen, and so am I. I've been offered a place on the staff at the London Hospital if my exam results are satisfactory, but I'm required to live in the Nurses' Home for the first year or so. If I go home and look after my sister, I might never get another chance – and all that training would have been wasted.'

'You must not do that,' he protested, concerned. 'Being a nurse and rising in your profession is your one chance of getting on, of making a good life for yourself and your sister. It is what your mother wants for you. Have you considered my suggestion?'

'Putting Mary Ellen in St Saviour's? We spoke of it. I let my mother think it was my suggestion. She wouldn't like it if she thought I'd been talking to you behind her back. Do you think they will take Mary Ellen? I heard they were bursting at the seams . . .'

'Have a word with Father Joseph,' the doctor

advised. 'He stands on good terms with the Warden. I'm sure Sister Beatrice will squeeze one more in, she always does. Remember, it's going to take me two to three weeks to find the right place for your mother and the child may as well stay at home until then.'

Apparently, the Catholic priest had had a word in Mary Ellen's favour, because a week after she spoke to him, Father Joe had visited Rose at work and told her she should go to see the Warden of St Saviour's after she'd finished her shift on the wards the next day.

'I'm not promising anything, Rose, but I think Sister Beatrice will find a place for her, though I know they are pressed for space, not to say funds.'

'Everyone is,' Rose agreed. 'There was so much devastation, so many factories, houses and commercial buildings bombed and burned to the ground. The manager at the Home and Colonial, where I used to work, reckons that it will take years before they clear the bombsites, let alone rebuild all the houses. We just don't have the raw materials we need.'

'I dare say it will take years,' Father Joe agreed. 'And the trouble never seems to end. There was a fire at a bombed-out factory a couple of weeks ago, caused by an unexploded bomb going off and rupturing a gas main. The people in the streets nearby thought the war had started again.'

'God help us, I hope that won't happen; we've had enough.'

'Now then, my child. Don't you be taking the Lord's name in vain. Remember what I've told you, and don't be late for your appointment with Sister Beatrice.'

That had been the previous day. Now, standing before the daunting building, Rose took a deep breath and stepped up to the door to ring the bell. Nothing happened, so after a couple of minutes she rang again. A young woman who looked as if she had been scrubbing the floor, her hands red from being in hot water and soda, opened it. She looked Rose up and down, sniffing as she asked what she wanted.

'I'm here to see Sister Beatrice. Can you take me to her?'

'I daresn't do that, miss,' the girl said. 'I've got to finish me work afore I goes home, see – and me ma will go on somethin' awful if I'm late, 'cos she wants ter get orf ter 'er job at the pub.'

'Well, can you point me in the right direction please?' Rose asked, stepping into the rather dim hallway without being invited. The floors were some sort of dark slate tiles and there was a grand staircase with mahogany banisters at the end of the hall, its wooden steps covered in a dull red carpet.

'I reckon it's up them there stairs and down the corridor to the right. You'll see the notice on 'er door. I ain't never bin in there 'cos I'm the downstairs skivvy, see.'

'Then you've no business to be opening the door.'

''Ad ter or you'd 'ave stood there all night, I reckon. Nan's been orf sick fer a week or more and they're all run orf their feet . . .'

Deciding that it was useless to reason with her, Rose started for the stairs. She was annoyed because she'd had to take extra time off to come here and so far had not formed a very good opinion of the place. Had there been an alternative, she would not have gone any further. However, people generally spoke well of St Saviour's and she could only think something must have gone wrong if a young and ignorant kitchen girl was answering the door.

She walked up the stairs without looking back and turned right. Sister Beatrice's room was at the end, the door firmly closed but with a little plaque on it inviting visitors to knock. Rose clenched her hands at her sides, because if they wouldn't accept Mary Ellen it meant that she would have to give up her plans to take up the position she'd been offered. Rose couldn't work as a nurse and be at home with her sister, and if she had to look after Mary Ellen and work in a shop, she would never manage to pay the bills. Besides, she'd set her heart on becoming a nurse. When she had a little more experience in nursing she would earn more than she did as a shop girl, and she could take care of her sister. In her heart she knew that her mother hadn't much longer to live and Mary Ellen couldn't be left to fend for herself. A girl as pretty as she was couldn't be left to wander the streets on her own after school, because anything might happen. Yet you heard of shocking things happening at some children's homes . . . Despite her doubts, Rose really had no choice because, if she sacrificed her dreams, both she and Mary Ellen would soon be trapped in the kind of grinding poverty that was impossible to escape. Her sister would just have to make the best of things until Rose could afford to make other arrangements.

Standing outside the Warden's door, Rose knocked and after a moment was invited to enter. The room was large and furnished with a big oak desk, its green leather-covered top crowded with bits and pieces. Two armchairs with worn arms and sagging seats were beside the fireplace, though no fire was burning, and a small table stood next to one of them, a book lying on top. Apart from some bookshelves and a small cupboard the room looked sparsely furnished, though someone had brought in some plants in bright pots, to stand along the windowsill.

'Yes, what do you want?'

The question was barked at her, bringing her startled gaze back to the woman behind the desk. She was dressed in the habit of a religious order, her head covered by a hood and wimple, no trace of hair showing beneath it. On her nose was perched a pair of gold-rimmed spectacles, over which she peered at Rose in a distinctly hostile manner.

'Are you deaf and dumb?'

'No, Sister Beatrice.' Rose was stung into a reply. 'I'm Rose O'Hanran. I've come to ask about a place for my sister Mary Ellen. Father Joe sent me . . .'

'Oh.' Sister Beatrice blinked and sighed audibly, removing her spectacles. She pinched the bridge of her nose between thumb and forefinger, looking tired. 'Why didn't you say so at once? I can't remember everything. We are very busy at the moment.'

Rose swallowed hard, nails turned into the palms of her hands as she battled with the urge to tell this woman just what she thought of her. She hated being made to feel she was begging, but what was her alternative? Giving up her dreams wasn't an option and she wouldn't do it.

'Please, would you consider taking her? She has nowhere else to go and I have to take up my place as a nurse in the hospital next week. I could bring her here on Monday morning. My mother has to go away. She has advanced TB.' Rose spoke as calmly as she could manage, holding back the caustic comments that rose all too easily to her mind.

'I hope neither you nor your sister is infected? I suppose you've been checked?' Rose nodded. 'We've got enough problems as it is . . .' Sister Beatrice made a noise of frustration as someone knocked, barking out that whoever it was might enter. 'Oh, it's you, Angela. I've been waiting for those updated lists all afternoon . . .'

115

'Sorry, Sister,' the elegant woman in a silver-grey dress said apologetically. 'I wanted to get it right and it was rather a muddle . . .' She broke off as she saw the indignant look in Sister's eyes. 'We've had a lot of coming and going recently.'

'I am well aware of that – tell me, what beds are available on the girls' ward, aged about . . .' She glanced down at a paper on her desk. 'Eight, this says . . . is that right, Miss O'Hanran?'

'Mary Ellen will be nine in two weeks' time.'

'Near enough then. Well, what is the situation?'

Rose thought how rude she was and felt sorry for the woman who might be her secretary, though she was very well-dressed for such a position; she looked a bit uncertain as she shuffled her papers while the Sister drummed her fingers on the arm of her chair.

'We have two emergency beds in the sick ward . . .'

'No use, we have to keep those in case we need them. What else?'

'There is a bed free but in the ward with the nine- to twelve-year-olds . . .'

'Well, I suppose that would do at a pinch.' Sister Beatrice glared at Rose. 'You are certain she doesn't have an aunt who would look after her – or a kind neighbour? Children are better in their own surroundings if at all possible.'

'There is no one I would trust to look after her. If there were I should not be here. God knows, it seems a terrible place . . . I was admitted by a girl who was scrubbing the hall floor . . .'

'I resent that comment, Miss O'Hanran. We pride ourselves on giving our children the best care we can manage and on being a warm and welcoming place for those who need us. If as you say you were admitted by one of the kitchen staff, it is because things are difficult just now. We have three members of staff down with influenza, and we have some very sick children in isolation,' Sister Beatrice said coldly. 'Normally, Nan sees to the new arrivals at first and then the nurses and carers take over . . . well, do you want the place or not? I doubt you'll find anyone else to take her.'

Rose swallowed hard. She wanted to march out right now and tell her mother that she would stay home to look after Mary Ellen, but if she did that they would never get out of the slums that her father's untimely death had brought them to. Her chest caught with pain, because even now she couldn't bear to think of Pa's death and her mother's terrible illness. Yet she knew she had spoken out of turn and must apologise.

'I'm sorry. I didn't realise. Naturally, your staff problems must make things difficult.'

'We have limited funds, Miss O'Hanran, but St Saviour's never turns away a child that really needs us however stretched we are – so do you want her to come to us?'

'Yes, please,' Rose said. 'I shall bring her next Monday morning, which is my only free time before I start my new job, if that is all right?'

'Yes, bring her on Monday. Mrs Morton can

take you down and arrange the time with you. She will be admitting your sister unless Nan is back by then. I simply do not have the time.'

Rose clamped her mouth shut, walking out before she lost her temper and told that awful old woman what she could do with her bed. If only Pa hadn't died she could have left Mary Ellen in his care; he might have liked a drop of good Irish whiskey but he'd been fond of his daughters, especially the youngest one. Her heart ached, because it was hard to lose the people you loved, and Rose was carrying a burden that was almost too much to bear. Seeing her mother grow weaker, knowing she was probably going to die, had been made worse because she couldn't share her grief with anyone. She had to keep the truth from Mary Ellen as long as she could.

Hearing hurried footsteps behind her, she turned to see Angela trying to keep up with her. She slowed down, because she needed to find out a few things that she hadn't felt like asking Sister Beatrice.

'I'm sorry,' Angela apologised. 'I know Sister can be a bit harsh but she has good reason for it today – we lost a child early this morning. He only came in a week ago and went down with chicken pox. Unfortunately, he was very weak and he contracted pneumonia. The nurses did everything they could but we lost him, though his elder brother and sister are recovering, I'm thankful to say.'

'Oh, I'm sorry.' Rose bit her lip, because that

put her firmly in the wrong and she knew she'd bordered on rudeness. 'I didn't realise . . .' she said, but she hadn't changed her mind about the nun. She'd made Rose feel like something dragged in off the streets and she wouldn't take that from anyone.

'She was up all night with him. I saw her when she left after performing the last offices; Father Joe was with her, because the boy's family was Catholic. Sister was truly devastated, though she hides it behind a brusque manner.'

'Well, that explains it,' Rose said. 'We don't want Mary Ellen to go out for adoption. Either Ma will come home after she's cured . . . or I'll look after her once I'm in a position to do so.'

'Yes, I think we've understood that,' Angela said, checking her list. 'She is a temporary . . . but she'll need to live here until you can provide a home for her. I must take some more details and there are some forms for you to sign and then we'll discuss what she needs to bring with her . . . and her feelings about coming here. Perhaps we could go back to my office and talk before you leave?'

'Yes, all right.' Rose realised that Mrs Morton had more authority than she had first thought and sighed; a shadow descended as she imagined her sister's reaction to the news. 'She can be a bit stubborn, and she isn't going to take kindly to the idea . . .'

'Don't worry, we'll look after her. She will soon settle in.'

119

The trouble was Mrs Morton didn't know how stubborn Mary Ellen could be when she didn't like something and Rose wasn't looking forward to telling her the news.

Mary Ellen stared at the faces looking down at her, mutiny flaring. Rose kept on saying that she had to go into St Saviour's until Ma returned from hospital, but something in the way her mother looked at her told Mary Ellen that Ma didn't think she would be coming back. She could feel a sick lump in her chest and she wanted to scream and stamp her feet, but Ma looked so sad and so tired.

'I don't want to go,' she mumbled in a voice barely above a whisper. 'I want to stay here with Rose and you . . .' Her eyes entreated her mother, but Ma looked as if she too wanted to cry and that was worse than all the rest. Mary Ellen longed to make her better, to bring back her loving smile, but there was nothing she could do and that hurt – it hurt so much that Mary Ellen thought she would die of it. How could they just send her away to that horrible place, as if she were an unwanted stray? She wanted to be with her mother, to feel Ma's loving arms holding her close and see her smile. Her chest felt as if it would burst for the pain of it.

'I can't look after you, love,' Ma said, and tears spilled from her eyes, dripping slowly down her pale cheeks. 'I don't want to leave you, Mary Ellen – but I have to go to the hospital. If I stay with you, you may get my illness and I don't want you to suffer like me. Anything is better than that . . .'

Mary Ellen didn't want that either, but she longed for Ma to laugh and take her in her arms as she had in the old days when her father was alive and Ma was always happy and singing.

'Why can't Rose stay and look after me?' Mary Ellen didn't particularly want to be in her sister's care, because Rose was so sharp, but it was better than going away to a place she didn't know – a home for orphans. Surely that was for kids who had no family? Mary Ellen had a mother and a sister and she wanted her own home.

'Because Rose has worked hard to get that place in the hospital and she needs to work her way up until she's a senior staff nurse or a sister and then she will earn enough to have a house that we can all live in. I'll be able to move from here too, Mary Ellen. Let Rose go and do what she has to – and then we can all be together again.'

'I would rather she stayed here until you come home from the hospital.'

'Well, I can't,' Rose snapped. 'I have to go now or not at all. Stop complaining, Mary Ellen. Ma is ill and she has to go to the hospital. She doesn't want to go either but you don't hear her whining and moaning. I've made the arrangements and I shall take you on Monday morning and that's that.'

'Well, I think you're mean and rotten and . . .' Mary Ellen broke off with a gasp as Rose gave her a smack round the face. Tears welled in her eyes but she didn't sob or carry on because the slap had shocked her more than hurt her. Rose had never hit her before and something in her sister's manner told her that she had reached the end of her tether. In that moment Mary Ellen understood that her sister was suffering too, even though she was trying not to show it. 'I'm sorry . . .'

Rose was looking pale, as if she were shocked by what she'd done, and Mary Ellen felt her resistance ebbing. She'd known ever since Ma told them she had to go away that this was coming, but she'd been hoping something would happen and everything would be all right again.

'Rose, love, don't quarrel with your sister. It's hard enough for all of us – and Mary Ellen . . .' Ma looked at her sadly, her eyes wet with tears. 'Please try to understand, my love. I'm really ill. I wouldn't leave you if I didn't have to but it's my only chance. . . .'

'If Ma doesn't go she'll only get worse,' Rose said but her mother shook her head. 'She's got to understand, Ma. There is no other way for us. I can't work and look after her properly – and I need to complete my training. The exams I took are only the first hurdle; there will be so much to learn that I couldn't possibly look after a child. If I don't do this, we'll be stuck in this rotten slum for the rest of our lives. It's living here that has made you ill. Do you want her to die young too?'

Mary Ellen ran at her mother, clinging to her legs and hiding her face in her skirt. She felt gentle hands on her head but knew Ma wouldn't kiss her: she didn't kiss either of them these days and tried not to breathe on them in case she infected them with her illness. She was always holding a handkerchief to her mouth and that was usually speckled with bloodstains.

'Please, love,' her mother begged, a break in her voice. 'You're tearing me apart. I can't bear it . . .'

Mary Ellen heard the pain in Ma's voice and was immediately contrite. She buried herself in the skirts of Ma's dress and mumbled that she was sorry.

'I'll go,' she said, voice thick with misery. 'I'll go – but Rose had better come and get me sometimes or I shall run away.'

'Of course I'll visit when I can and bring you sweets or something,' Rose told her, relieved and trying to be kind now that she'd won. 'The time will pass quickly. You'll see, Mary Ellen, before you know it I'll be visiting and then I'll be a nurse and we'll have a much better house to live in than this old thing . . .'

'You promise you won't leave me there and forget me?'

'Cross my heart and hope to die,' Rose said and smiled. 'You're my sister and I care about you. Please try to understand. I've got a lovely fresh loaf, some real butter, ham and tomatoes for tea. Come on and help me set the table like a good girl. We don't want to upset Ma, do we, love?'

Mary Ellen stared at her with reproachful eyes.

It was all right for Rose, she was going to do something she'd always wanted to do, but Mary Ellen would be stuck in that home – and she knew how forbidding it looked from the outside. She felt abandoned, unwanted, and it was breaking her heart. Mary Ellen just knew it would be horrible there. It would be like being locked away in prison, except that she hadn't done anything wrong and it wasn't fair. Ma was going to a hospital where she would have people to look after her, and Rose was going to be a nurse but she would be sent away, because no one loved or wanted her . . .

CHAPTER 8

Michelle luxuriated in the warm scented bath water, thoroughly enjoying the sensation of being pampered and lazy. She'd bagged the bathroom at the Nurses' Home first that evening, and the water was still hot, which it wouldn't be by the time three or four of the inmates had run a bath, because Michelle had used more than she was supposed to and the old geyser that heated it wasn't really up to all the demands made on it. She was using the remainder of the lilac-scented bath salts she'd had for her last birthday, because it was a special occasion that evening. She had the next two whole days off and tonight she was going dancing at the Co-op hall in Bethnal Green with a group of her friends.

Sally's friend Keith, an apprentice plumber who often did small jobs for people in the Halfpenny Street area, had asked her if she had some friends who would like to support the dance, which was in aid of the local darts team of which he was a member. So Sally had roped in Alice, her cousin and a friend of his from the Army.

Michelle had hesitated when she was asked along

too but something in the way Sally had looked at her had made her give in, because they both needed cheering up after what had happened to Jake. A night out in the company of friends would stop them both brooding over his death. Besides, if Michelle had guessed right, Sally didn't want to spend all night with just Keith for company. She too had the luxury of a weekend off, because Sister Beatrice said they both deserved it. The Warden hadn't blamed either of them for what had happened to their patient, though they bitterly blamed themselves. Losing such a lovely little boy had been unbearable and felt so wrong. Surely, if they'd tried harder, they could have done something – though they both knew they had neglected nothing in their care of the boy. He'd just been too weak to fight the pneumonia.

Nurses were not supposed to get involved with the children in their care: it was one of the first things they learned, to toughen up, because otherwise they were going to break their hearts over every child that was lost. Michelle had believed that she'd managed to grow a thick skin; she could mostly cope with whatever the wards threw at her, but somehow Jake had got beneath her shield. Perhaps it was because he was so bright and intelligent, so interested in everything going on around him. He'd watched her nursing the others and one night he'd confided that he was going to be a nurse when he grew up so that he could look after sick people. And then, suddenly, he'd become silent, a pathetic, tortured child, as the fever gripped him and turned into an illness that was so often a killer. A doctor had been summoned, but he'd endorsed all they were doing, praised them for their devotion, yet it still hadn't been enough. Jake had slipped away from them just before the dawn, his last gasping breath taken. The sight of him lying pale and silent had torn her heart in two.

Michelle felt the sting of tears. Her throat was tight and for a moment she felt overwhelmed by a deep sadness that threatened to undo her, but she fought it back. Jake's struggle was ended and his pathetic little life was over. The awful thing was that he'd had such a rotten one. With parents who starved and beat him, he'd never had a chance, and yet he hadn't been bitter. Instead, he'd loved his little sister and wanted to protect her – had wanted to grow up to be a nurse so that he could help sick people.

'Why?' Michelle asked of no one in particular. There were plenty of bad people in the world; why, if a soul had been needed, couldn't it have been one of them instead of that innocent boy?

She shook her head and jumped out of the rapidly cooling water. It was time she got ready for the dance that evening. Sally and Alice were coming back here to start with and they would catch the bus to meet up with the men outside the dance hall. Keith had wanted to pay for all the girls to go in, but Sally said that wasn't fair on him, because apprentices didn't have much money to spare so they'd agreed that everyone would buy their own tickets at the door.

Michelle looked through her wardrobe, settling on a pale blue dress with white spots that had a halter strap and a sweetheart neckline, adding a little white bolero with capped sleeves. The skirt was gored and because of the restrictions during the war it didn't have the fashionable fullness she would have liked, but it finished below her knees and suited her well. Her white leather shoes were almost new and hadn't yet needed to be cleaned with whitening, though after this evening they probably would. You never knew who you would end up with as a partner in the progressive barn dance; sometimes you got lucky and they danced well, but half of the young men who filled the popular dance hall seemed to have two left feet.

Michelle didn't mind who she danced with much. She'd been let down once by a man she'd thought she was in love with, but he'd turned out to be as selfish as most men were in her opinion. From then on, she'd devoted her life to her nursing. Her life revolved around her family – her two younger brothers, mother and father – and her work and, of course, the children that came into her care. Perhaps she would meet someone one day, but for the moment she wasn't much bothered about a relationship and preferred going out with her friends.

★　★　★

'Oh, there they are,' Sally said, hugging Alice's arm and giving a nervous giggle. 'I was afraid they might not be here. It's awkward if there aren't enough men to go round.'

'Oh, I knew I could trust Eric to turn up on time,' Alice said, looking at her cousin with pride. 'And he promised to bring Bob Manning, a mate of his from the Army. Eric only came because you were coming, Michelle. I think he's sweet on you.' The teasing look in her eyes made Michelle shake her head impatiently. She wasn't interested in Alice's cousin that way, though he was a decent partner on the dance floor and she didn't mind spending an evening with him.

Because so many young men had died or been injured in the recent war, it was not unusual to find that there were not enough men of the right age to go round and some girls danced together rather than sit out most of the evening. It wasn't going to happen tonight, though, because there were two very good-looking men ready and willing to be their escorts. Dressed in Army uniform Alice's cousin looked very handsome, his short hair black and his eyes a brilliant blue. His friend had light brown hair and greenish eyes, and seemed a bit quiet.

'Eric is the best looking of all three,' Michelle said to Alice. 'But don't tell him I said so, will you?'

''Course I shan't,' Alice laughed and ran up to her cousin. 'You found Keith all right then?'

'He found us,' Eric Wright said. 'I'm glad you roped us in tonight, Allie, love. We would probably have spent the night in the pub. This will be much more fun . . .' His gaze roved over Michelle and Sally, seeming to favour Michelle, and he swooped on her as she fiddled with her purse. 'Put that away, I'm paying for you. Beautiful ladies should not have to pay for their own ticket.'

Michelle demurred, but seeing he was determined put her purse away. Eric paid for himself, his friend and all the girls.

Sally protested and tried to give him the five shillings entrance fee but he pushed her hand away with a frown so she shoved it back in her coat pocket. Seeing that Keith had to pay for himself, she felt annoyed with Eric Wright for throwing his money around, and with the others for simply accepting it. Keith had offered to pay, even though they all knew he didn't get much money, and Eric had made him look like a fool, almost shutting him out when it had been his idea to come as a group in the first place.

Feeling protective of Keith, she slipped her arm through his and smiled up at him.

'This was a lovely idea,' she said. 'I'm going to take my coat off but will you dance with me first when I come back? I would much rather dance with you than the others . . .'

Keith's lovely soft eyes smiled down at her. With his sandy hair and rather long nose, he wasn't as good-looking as either of the other two men, but she thought much nicer. He was a good friend and she liked him, but lately he'd started hinting that he wanted to go steady and Sally wasn't sure she wanted to settle for Keith, at least not yet. 'I'll buy you a drink first. What would you like? I think they do a pleasant white wine or you could have gin and orange, something like that if you prefer?' Michelle had hardly ever drunk wine, but realised Keith was trying to impress her with the offer.

'I wouldn't mind a port and lemon, as long as it's more lemonade than port please.'

'All right,' he said. 'I'll buy a small port in a big glass and a small bottle of lemonade so you can put in what you want yourself.'

Sally thanked him and followed the other girls to the cloakroom. Michelle and Alice were whispering together and giggling. It seemed that Alice rather liked her cousin's friend, but though she wouldn't be rude enough to say it, Sally didn't really care for either of the Army boys. She much preferred the young apprentice plumber, though she didn't get those funny feelings in her tummy when he smiled or kissed her.

Sally had never had a proper boyfriend, although she'd been out to the flicks with Keith a few times during the war when he was home on leave, and she'd let him have a goodnight kiss; all the girls let the blokes in the forces have a kiss, a memory to take back with them, but she'd been careful never to let it go further. She usually went out with her sister Brenda and brother Jim or with a group of friends from work, but although some of the young men she met made suggestions about meeting up alone, she'd never felt the desire to oblige them. Sometimes, when she saw other girls meeting their sweethearts after work, she wished she could fall in love, but none of the men that showed an interest touched her heart.

Not that it really mattered. Sally hadn't time for a serious relationship, because she wanted to be a nurse. She admired girls like Michelle and Anna, one of the other nurses at St Saviour's, who had taken their training and passed their exams, and wanted to follow in their footsteps. It wasn't that she didn't enjoy working at St Saviour's, she did – most of the time. She hadn't enjoyed it when Jake died. Caring for him and his brother and sister as a special assignment, she'd come too close to the child for comfort. The charm in his smile had won her over and she'd felt she would break apart when she saw the colour fade from his lips and realised they had lost him, despite all they'd done.

Sister Beatrice had seen her distress and told her that death was something she had to learn to accept. In the mean streets of London's East End there were too many children suffering from malnutrition and all the debilitating diseases that filth and depravation fostered.

Determined not to let the shadow of a child's untimely death spoil her evening, Sally tidied her hair, slid her lip-gloss over her full lips and left the mirror to the next girl. Her nails were short and neat, polished with a pale varnish that was a natural pink. Alice was wearing bright red polish on her nails to match the lipstick she'd borrowed from Michelle but Sally would not have felt confident with that colour. She headed back to the ballroom, wending her way through the crowds of laughing girls and men to the seats near the bar.

The band was playing one of the hit tunes of the previous year – 'They Say It's Wonderful' – and people were smooching to it as they danced. Looking at the smiling faces, Sally thought that no one would have known that the country was enduring yet another year of austerity. Most people felt safe because the war was over and they were not going to receive a telegram to tell them that a loved one had been killed.

Keith sat down beside her, depositing his tray on the little table. 'I asked Michelle and Alice if they wanted a drink, but they decided to dance. It looks as if they've paired off for the evening. I hope you don't mind being stuck with me?'

'I wouldn't call it being stuck,' Sally smiled and poured lemonade into her small glass of port. 'I wouldn't have come if I felt like that, Keith. You know I like you, I always have.'

'You're a nice girl,' Keith said. 'I would've asked just you, but I thought you might not come out on your own? We've mostly gone out in a crowd, haven't we?'

Sally nodded, because she was glad he'd asked

her friends. While Keith was in the Army, he'd seemed content with the arrangement they'd had of going out in a crowd. She enjoyed his company, but just lately he'd seemed to be more interested in getting her alone and he'd spoken about what he intended to do once he'd finished his training as a plumber.

'Most of the chaps moan about being called up for the Army,' Keith had told her once as he'd walked her home, 'but I learned a lot out there and I got into plumbing when they put me on latrine duty for a while. I had to help fix the toilets and the showers, which were forever blocking, but then they sent me up the line when there was a big push on. After I caught a Blighty in my leg, they said I couldn't go back up to the front to fight so they stuck me on duty back home as one of the repair squad and I did a bit of all sorts. At least I had some sort of idea what I wanted to do when they demobbed me, but it took me a while to get taken on by a firm. It's a well-paid job when you're qualified, Sally. I'll be able to support a wife and family.'

Because she didn't want to promise she would go out with him alone in future, she said, 'How are you getting on at work? Do you have to work terribly long hours?'

'Yes, sometimes. I did a job for someone you might know this morning. He had a leaking tap and I fixed it for him. I reckon he visits St Saviour's quite often – Mr Markham?'

'I think Mr Markham comes to teach some of the children?' Sally had only seen the man in question as she passed him in the corridor and didn't know much about him.

'I don't know,' Keith said. 'He just happened to say he was going to St Saviour's and that made me think of you . . .'

'I think it's a kind of play therapy that he has developed. Michelle says he thinks that damaged and backward children need remedial teaching – and he is working on the theory that it could be applied to all infants' schools to help the children to learn. His real job is as a surgeon and he's brilliant, so Michelle says.'

Keith shrugged. 'I only went there because he wanted a plumber in a hurry. He's got a nice house. I should think he's well-off – bound to be if he's a surgeon.' He took a sip of his drink. 'That is enough work for now.' He put down his glass and stood up. 'Shall we dance now? It's a waltz. I enjoy waltzing.'

'So do I, even though I'm not much good at it . . .'

'Oh, listen, they're playing a Vera Lynn song from the war. I love her records.'

Sally stood up and gave him her hand. He was really nice and she was glad she'd come, just as long as he knew that they were only friends. She didn't have time for anything else at the moment.

CHAPTER 9

Mary Ellen dragged her feet as they approached the large, rather forbidding building. She looked all the way up to the tiny attic windows that were shuttered and dark and wondered if that was where they would put her. Would they shut her away somewhere and forget her? She remembered a scandal in the lane years ago, when the body of a young boy had been discovered hidden in the attics of one of the old houses after the occupants of the house had run away and left him there. People said that he must have starved to death and whispered about it in hushed tones. What was going to happen to her after Rose left her here in this horrid place?

'Come on, love,' Rose said crossly. 'I've got to get to work and if I don't arrive by ten I might not be allowed to start today.'

'Good, you can come home with me,' Mary Ellen said, struggling to keep from showing her fear, her voice rising as she begged, 'Don't leave me here, please. Rose, I'm frightened . . .'

'Now you're just being silly,' Rose said and

tugged on her sister's arm, half-lifting her from the ground as she forced her up the steps to the front door.

Mary Ellen could hear a bell clanging inside. It seemed to echo and a chill slithered down her spine. She felt sick and miserable and wished she could run away, run back home to Ma . . . but her mother wasn't there any longer . . .

'Hello,' a woman said, opening the door to them, a wide smile on her face. She had short light brown hair that looked as if it had a natural curl, friendly chocolate brown eyes and a soft mouth. Mary Ellen thought she looked about Ma's age or a little younger, but plumper than Ma had ever been. 'You must be Rose and Mary Ellen. Come in, my dears. Sister Beatrice told me to expect you. I'm Mrs Burrows or Nan to my friends. And I'm going to look after you, Mary Ellen, so we shall be friends, shan't we?'

'Oh . . .' Some of the fear drained out of Mary Ellen. Nan looked nice, exactly like a mother ought to look, and not at all like the wicked monster she'd been expecting. She gave her a wide-eyed straight look. 'You won't lock me in the attics and leave me to starve, will you?'

'Mary Ellen!' Rose cried indignantly and shook her shoulder. 'Say you're sorry at once. As if I would leave you here if they mistreated children. I don't know what gets inside your head.'

'I promise you we shan't put you in the attics and forget you, and I'm sure we can find you something nice to eat just as soon as we've got you settled . . .' A look passed from Nan to Rose, warning her not to prolong the parting.

'Go on,' she said and dropped down to look into Mary Ellen's face. 'I have to leave, but I shan't forget you, love, and I'll visit when I can, send you things. I'm sorry but there's nothing else I can do.'

Rose handed over Mary Ellen's parcel tied up in brown paper and string. Making a grab at her big sister's sleeve, Mary Ellen tried to hold on to her, but she shrugged away, her face set. 'Please . . .' Her mind formed the word but no sound came out as Rose strode away. Mary Ellen felt abandoned, her eyes stinging with tears, but Nan was reaching for her hand, talking to her in a cheerful voice. Mary Ellen choked back her sob. She wasn't a cry-baby!

'I don't know if you've been told what happens, Mary Ellen?'

'No . . .' She looked up at the motherly woman, her tummy clenching with nerves as she battled against the need to cry. 'Only that I have to stay here . . .'

'Well, I am going to admit you as one of our children,' Nan said. 'First of all we give you a little wash and some different clothes to wear . . .'

'Rose washed me this morning and I'm wearing my best skirt.'

'Yes, and a very nice skirt it is,' Nan said, 'and much too good for playing with the other children.

All our girls and boys wear a uniform, you see, because when we go out it makes it easier to know that you all belong to us . . . and some children are not as fortunate as you, Mary Ellen. They do not have nice things of their own to wear so they might feel upset if they saw you in such a smart skirt.'

'Oh . . .' Mary Ellen digested this for a moment, then, 'Are we often allowed to play?'

'When you're not at lessons or mealtimes, yes, there is time to play games or read books and do puzzles.'

Mary Ellen felt a flicker of interest. 'I can read words and I like puzzles, but I only had one and some pieces got lost.'

'We have lots of puzzles and books with pictures in as well as words. You are allowed to look at them, Mary Ellen – but I'm sure you are going to make lots of new friends and . . .' Nan stopped as a very pretty lady with blonde hair came towards them. 'Oh, you must be Mrs Morton.' Nan turned back to her. 'This is Mary Ellen. I believe you spoke to her sister Rose the other day?'

The pretty lady smiled and looked down at Mary Ellen, then held out her hand to her. 'How nice to see you, Mary Ellen. I'm Mrs Morton and I'm very pleased to meet you.'

Mary Ellen felt shy and gravitated towards Nan's side, eyeing the newcomer speculatively. She'd never seen anyone so posh. Her dress was much smarter than even Rose's Sunday costume, and she spoke in a funny, posh way, but seemed nice;

her hair was soft and the colour of the dark honey Ma had used to give her for tea when her pa was alive, and her eyes were a kind of blue that Mary Ellen couldn't describe, except sometimes the sky looked that way. She was like a princess rather than the wicked witch she'd expected. Maybe it wouldn't be too bad living here for a while.

'Mrs Burrows,' Angela said and winked at Mary Ellen, a twinkle of laughter in her eyes as she looked at Nan. 'Sister Beatrice told me you were back. I do hope you are feeling better?'

'Oh, much,' Nan replied. 'It was just a bit of flu but nasty for a couple of days and the doctor told me to stay in bed until I was properly over it. We must have a talk and get to know each other later, and do call me Nan. I have to look after Mary Ellen for a while, but we might have a cup of tea in my room – in an hour, say? Mary Ellen might like a drink and some cake at that time too?'

'Oh, I should enjoy that,' Angela said and Mary Ellen thought she looked really pleased. 'Will that be all right with you, Mary Ellen?'

Grownups didn't ask children if things were all right for them. Some of the shadows lifted and she felt better than she had since Ma told her she was ill, and she gave the woman a fleeting smile. 'Yes, please,' she said. 'I think it would be nice . . .' She looked up at Nan. 'I'm ready to be washed now if you like.' Angela gave her another wink and went on up the stairs ahead of them. Mary Ellen held tightly to Nan's hand and climbed after her.

She wasn't frightened now, but she still wished she could be at home with Ma, helping her with the baking or hanging washing on the line in the back yard – but Nan had said there was time for play and Mary Ellen wanted to make friends. She wanted that more than anything, except to see Ma looking happy and well again.

'If Sister Beatrice finds out you've been playing truant, Billy Baggins, you'll be in for it,' Alice warned him. She'd grabbed him as he came sneaking into the home by the back door hoping to snatch his tea from the dining room and disappear again before anyone saw him. 'You're trusted to go to school in the mornings and come back at lunchtime but that's the second day you've skipped lunch, and you're late back – so where have you been?'

Billy stared up at her truculently, wondering if he could get away with lying but he knew Alice had two young brothers at home and she didn't let much get past her. Deciding to tough it out, he squared his shoulders and put on a defiant air.

'I couldn't do the daft sums and it was a test so I give it a miss – went down the river and got talkin' ter a man on a barge. He were unloading wood in the dry dock and I give 'im a 'and. Paid me sixpence, 'e did . . .'

'Indeed?' Alice glared at him wrathfully. 'I suppose you think that's clever, Billy Baggins, but let me tell you it will get you nowhere. Unless you want to work for pennies when you grow up? Without schooling you'll never get a decent job – and maths is important.'

'Wot do you know? Arfur says learnin' never done him no good . . .'

'You have to learn or you'll be as ignorant as that brother of yours. Hand over that sixpence. I'll put it in the swear box for foreign aid and you can buckle down to trying harder at school.'

'Shan't,' Billy said. ''Sides, I can't. I spent it.'

'I don't believe you. Hand it over this minute or I'll tell Sister Beatrice.'

'I don't care what you tell that old battleaxe! I'll run away if she canes me . . .'

'You are a wicked boy,' Alice said and grabbed him by the shoulders. 'I'm going to take you to Sister now.'

'No, you can't make me . . .' Billy yelled and tried to pull away from her. Alice lost her temper and cuffed him round the ear, not hard but enough to make him sing out again.

'I hate yer!' he yelled and kicked at her ankle but missed it.

Alice shook him but an icy voice stopped her hitting him again.

'What is the meaning of this disgraceful scene?' Sister Beatrice sailed down on them in awful majesty, causing Alice to shiver in her shoes and look apprehensive and Billy to glare at her as if she were the devil himself.

'You do not hit the children, Alice Cobb, nor do

you shake them. You were given the guidelines when you were first employed. I expect you to read them and abide by them. If a child needs discipline you send them to me and I will deal with the culprit as I see fit.'

'Yes, Sister. I'm sorry, Sister – but I was trying to bring him to you and he wouldn't come.'

'Then you should simply report the incident to me, and leave me to deal with it. Aren't you on the tea roster this afternoon?' Alice nodded, twin spots of bright colour in her cheeks. 'Go along then and leave the boy with me if you please . . . and you may come to see me in my office before you leave this evening.'

Alice looked scared, as well she might. Being called to Sister's office could be an unpleasant experience and she'd been warned once already for not sticking to the guidelines. She shot Billy a look of venom and walked off with her head down.

Billy stared up at Sister Beatrice, his cocky manner a little deflated as her sharp eyes surveyed him. He'd also been warned that the next time he caused trouble he wouldn't get off lightly. Last time he'd merely been sent to bed without supper, but that hadn't bothered him, because he got three meals a day here, which was more than he'd ever had in his life.

'What have you to say for yourself? What did you do to make Alice so cross with you?'

'Nuffin' . . .' he said and sniffed, wiping his nose on his sleeve.

'Have you no handkerchief? You must learn a few manners, Billy. What are we going to do with you?'

'Dunno,' he muttered and hung his head. 'Send me orf somewhere?'

'I really do not wish to do that, Billy.' Sister shook her head. 'I suppose I could cane you – and next time I shall, but I think Alice was as much at fault here. I think detention when the children go to the church fete next Saturday should be sufficient punishment. Yes, you will remain here and miss the treats in store for you all.'

Billy sniffed hard and set his lip. He'd been looking forward to the fete, because it was always good fun if you had a few pennies to spend on the stalls – and the donkey rides were free to St Saviour's children.

'As for Alice, well, I shall have to see.' Sister made this remark to herself rather than to him, but Billy was alarmed by the severity of her expression, because he knew he'd provoked the young woman.

''Ere, you ain't gonna give 'er the push? It weren't 'er fault. She got on to me for playing truant, that's all . . .'

'You're speaking up for her?' Sister's eyes narrowed in suspicion.

'She nags all the time but she ain't that bad.'

Sister looked at him intently for a moment. 'Go to tea then, child. I dare say you are hungry.'

'Thanks, Sister,' Billy said and ran off before she

could change her mind. His stomach was growling with hunger now and he was looking forward to warm scones and butter with lashings of strawberry jam, and a slice of ginger sponge with custard or perhaps a piece of plum cake.

Entering the long dining room, which was noisy and filled with children from little toddlers to boys and girls of nearly fifteen, he was met by the sound of their voices as they filed in an orderly line and selected what they wanted from the loaded tables. There was always plenty of good thick bread and marge and usually a cake or some sort of tart with treacle or jam, also tomatoes and cucumber when they were in season, sliced to make into sandwiches, and three days a week there would be hard-boiled eggs cut in halves, or sardines, which were good for you, but not many of the children chose them. On Sundays as a special treat they had Spam and pickle sandwiches or very occasionally some Canadian pink salmon out of tins. Salmon was something Billy had never even seen until he came here; his nanna was more likely to give him bread and dripping or a bit of stew and dumplings if he were lucky. He wasn't sure what he felt about the salmon and sniffed at it doubtfully the first time it was offered, until he took his first bite of a sandwich and then he grinned and wolfed it down, though he still reckoned his nanna made the best stews.

Billy made his selection. He'd missed all the scones, which were popular – and that was that rotten Alice's fault – but he took two thick slices of bread and marge and two big spoonfuls of jam, a slice of seed cake and half a banana. It was so long since Billy had had a banana that he almost didn't recognise it, but there was one piece left so he grabbed it and then looked round for a space to sit, letting his eyes roam the tables to see who was already there. He couldn't believe his eyes when he saw the girl sitting by herself at a table in the corner. Mary Ellen here, and looking as if she wanted to burst into tears! Armed with his loaded plate and a glass of orange squash, he made a beeline towards her. She looked up as he approached and her expression lightened.

'When did you get here?' he asked and sat down on a spare chair without asking. He looked at her plate and saw she'd only got a buttered scone and some jam. 'Is that all you wanted?'

'Rose brought me this morning,' Mary Ellen said and gulped, her bottom lip trembling. 'I didn't feel hungry, because . . . I don't like it here . . .'

'Nor me fer a start,' Billy said, beginning to spread jam thickly on his bread and marge. 'I ain't got no mates 'ere and I wanted ter run orf, but I promised me nanna I'd give it a try.'

'I promised Ma I would try, but it's horrid,' Mary Ellen sniffed, tears suspiciously close. 'I'm in a room with two girls older than me and they don't like me – they look down their noses at me and don't answer if I speak to them.'

'They don't know yer,' Billy said. 'If they did

they would like yer – you've got ter give it time, Mary Ellen.'

'I know.' She gave him a wobbly smile. 'I feel better now I know you're here, Billy. You've got a banana; I didn't see them. It's ages since Rose brought one home from the shop.'

''Ere, you 'ave it,' Billy said generously and transferred it onto her plate. 'You need ter eat somethin', Mary Ellen.'

'Ta, Billy,' she said and offered her plate. 'You have half of this instead.'

'Fair exchange,' he said and spread jam on the scone and scoffed it down, speaking with his mouth full. 'I wus in trouble wiv Sister just now. Alice give me a clip round the ear for playing truant. I hope she don't get the push fer it – she's a nagger but she's all right really.'

'I've met Alice,' Mary Ellen said, munching her half of the scone. 'Nan told her to help me wash and bring me some fresh clothes. Nan's nice. I told her my clothes were clean, but she said everyone has to wear the clothes they're given unless they go out for a day with family. Trouble is, our Rose won't have much time to visit me. She'll be busy all the time.'

'We all get taken out on trips sometimes,' Billy said gloomily. 'There's an outing to the church fete this next Saturday, but I can't go . . .'

'Why not?' Mary Ellen was indignant on his behalf.

'Because I played truant and then I cheeked

Alice so Sister did it to punish me. Alice said Sister would cane me, but she didn't – she says next time I shall catch it. I'd rather she caned me and let me go to the treat. They do all sorts of stuff there: you'll love it, Mary Ellen. There's games and cartoon shows from a projector and a special tea with ham and jelly and ice cream sometimes.'

'I shan't because I shan't go,' she said. 'If you've got to stay here then I'll stay too. You're my only friend in the whole world now, Billy, and we'll stick together. Whatever they do to us, we'll be there for each other.'

Billy looked at her in surprise, then solemnly put his hand over hers. 'It's a pact,' he said in hushed tones. 'A promise to keep until we die.'

'A promise to keep until we die,' Mary Ellen repeated. 'Ooh, that sounds important, doesn't it? But we will be friends always, Billy. They shan't part us whatever they do . . .'

CHAPTER 10

Angela saw the girl sitting outside in the garden as she came across from the Nurses' Home. For the first few days she'd worked flat out on various lists and reports for Sister Beatrice, but today she'd had the afternoon off and had taken the chance to do some shopping, buying a few pretty things for her room at the home; the glass vases and china ornaments had already brightened the place up a bit. As soon as she was sure that she would be staying on at St Saviour's she could look for her own small apartment, but she was still concerned about fitting in here, because she couldn't just force the changes she considered necessary and needed to win the staff's confidence first. However, Nan had welcomed her without reserve and Angela had enjoyed having her morning break with her and Mary Ellen. She didn't know why, but something about the little girl's woebegone face had reached out and grabbed at her heart. She'd winked at her, because she'd wanted to see her smile, and had seen the child's solemn look ease a little.

Already, Angela had become immersed in the

lives of the children who lived here at St Saviour's. There were so many of them, and they seemed to arrive with alarming regularity. Some were here only for a few hours while relatives were contacted, some a few days or weeks until a mother or father was able to come and collect them, but most would be here for a long time unless they were lucky enough to be adopted, and that was a difficult and complicated affair. Most suitable couples who wanted to adopt were looking for babies or very young children; the older the children were, the less likely it was that they would find a new family, and that was heartbreaking.

Angela was aware of a burning desire to help all those she could; a new-found zeal for righting the wrongs of a cruel world had begun to fill the empty spaces inside her. She no longer lay awake late into the night aching for the sound of a voice she would never hear again, though at times something would remind her and catch her out. Her love for John was still there deep in her heart, but she knew she had to make a new life, find a purpose for her existence.

She believed she could be happy here, but Sister Beatrice was still treating her as if she were a leper and how she would react when she knew Angela was here to recommend changes she might not like, Angela dare not think. There would certainly be personality clashes before too long! It would be much better if she could win the starchy Sister over to her point of view by gentle persuasion.

Hearing a loud sniff followed by a wail of grief, Angela pushed her own problems to the back of her mind. She knew that girl. Alice was one of the carers, dressed in the pink-striped shirtwaist and white apron they all wore, to distinguish them from the nurses who had a pale grey uniform. She'd noticed Alice, because she always seemed to be working hard, though she had a sharp voice and sometimes raised it to the children. Of course, some of them could be very naughty; they weren't all little angels and could drive anyone to distraction. Alice wasn't the sort to give way to tears easily and so Angela stopped and sat down beside her on the wooden bench.

'It is a bit chilly out here,' she said conversationally. 'Is something the matter, Alice? Have you had bad news from home?'

'No, thanks for asking.' Alice took out a large handkerchief and blew her nose. She seemed to consider for a moment, then, 'I'm in trouble with Sister Beatrice. I have to see her before I go home and I'm afraid she's going to sack me. Ma will go mad if she does. My father's on short time at the Docks and we need my wages coming in . . .'

'I'm sure you can't have done anything very terrible,' Angela said in a reassuring tone. 'You always seem to me to be conscientious in your work, Alice.'

'I try my best, miss – but it was that Billy Baggins. He was playing up and Sister saw me shake him . . . I know I shouldn't lose my temper with the children, but he's enough to try the patience of a saint!'

Angela laughed softly and shook her head. 'Yes, I know he is a bit of a terror. Sally was telling me he'd tried to play her up the other evening. She made a joke of it, though. I think she likes him despite his bad manners and his wilfulness.'

'He takes more notice of Sally than of me. I suppose I should ignore him, but I can't help getting cross. He's a bright lad, but he just wastes his time . . . thinks it's clever to be like that good-for-nothing brother of his.'

'He will grow out of it sooner or later,' Angela said. 'Next time count to ten before you lose your temper. If he sees he can rile you he will do it all the more.'

'I know.' Alice sighed. 'He reminds me of my brother Saul, always in trouble at school and thinks it's funny. Oh well, I may not be here much longer to worry about Billy . . .'

'I'm sure Sister will just want to remind you of your duty to the children. Why should she sack you? You are a good worker.' Angela glanced at her neat gold wristwatch. 'When do you go to see her?'

'In another hour. I've got to help get the trays ready for supper before I leave.'

'Look, I'm going back to my office now. Shall I have a word with Sister? Tell her that you were just doing your job?'

'It's good of you to offer.' Alice gave her a grateful

glance but then shook her head. 'Best you don't say anything, though. It might make her angry.'

'Very well, but cheer up, I'm sure she's a fair woman underneath and she won't be too harsh with you.'

Angela left the girl to return to the kitchens while she continued into the home and upstairs. She hesitated outside Sister's office but then went into her own. She had decided to build a register of the illnesses that each child presently living at the home was known to have suffered in the past. She'd enlisted Sally and Michelle to help her collect the information. It was always useful to know how many children might be susceptible to infectious diseases. She intended to make a similar list for the staff, because Maisie hadn't contracted chicken pox after all; she'd gone down with the influenza, which had affected six of the staff in turn – four of them from the kitchen and two carers.

It was Cook finding herself with almost no helpers that had induced her to allow Angela to help prepare tea trays for the staff room and for the sick children's ward. She'd had strict instructions to consult Cook's list, but at least she could now be useful in the kitchen. The present inmates of the sick ward were not suffering from infectious diseases; thankfully, the outbreak of chicken pox had been confined to the three children who had brought it in, thanks to Nurse Michelle's quick thinking and Sister's strict hygiene measures.

Angela had begun to make friends with the staff here. Most of the carers were talkative, lively girls, though she knew that they were still a little suspicious of her, because she came from a different background, and even though she chose her plainest clothes, and wore no other jewellery but her wedding ring for work, she was conscious that they might seem expensive to girls who lived in the East End of London.

Busy typing up her lists for the files, Angela became aware that her door had opened and Sister was standing there looking at her.

'What are you doing? I thought the accounts were ready for tomorrow's meeting?'

'Yes, they are. I've been creating lists so that we know what illnesses our children have had – in case we should have a visitation from something nasty. I think we ought to have the medical records of all our children on file. In fact I'm sure it will soon be a statuary obligation.'

'Humph . . .' Sister's lips twisted as if she thought it a waste of time. 'I want you to prepare Alice Cobb's wage sheet. I'm going to dismiss her and I shall give her a month's wages . . .'

'Oh, but you can't,' Angela exclaimed. 'I mean, isn't that a bit drastic – surely she didn't do anything so very terrible?'

'I think that is for me to judge, don't you? Please do not interfere in what does not concern you. I am the Warden here and it is my decision that Alice should leave. She hit a child and shook him.

If I hadn't arrived she was going to hit him again. I will not tolerate girls who lose their temper and take it out on the children. Physical chastisement is to be restricted to the minimum. I am perfectly prepared to deal with troublesome boys myself, and all she had to do was report the incident to me.'

'Yes, but she didn't hit him hard, and her family need her wages . . .' Angela saw the flash of anger in Sister Beatrice's eyes and knew she'd made things worse. Of course Sister was right; Angela had no authority as far as the staff were concerned. Even though she'd been asked to bring the home into line with modern thinking that didn't mean she could interfere with the Warden's day-to-day running of St Saviour's. 'Forgive me. It's not my place . . . I know she ought not to have slapped him, but – please, can't you give the girl another chance? Make it clear that she is never to hit a child? She was crying in the garden . . . and we have difficulty in recruiting hard-working girls as it is.'

'If there is one thing I will not tolerate it is bullying,' Sister Beatrice said sharply. 'You have no idea what you are asking, Angela. Allow a bully to get away with it and they do it again, and if you threaten and do nothing they get worse and worse.' She frowned and shook her head as if a memory had intruded. 'Please bring me that wage sheet.'

'Yes, Sister. I'll find the file for you,' Angela said

and sat staring at the door as it closed with a snap behind the woman. She had spoken out of turn and Sister had every right to be angry – and poor Alice would bear the brunt of it.

She got up and went over to the metal file, looking through the drawers for Alice's details. The girl was one of a large family, and by the looks of things they didn't have much money. Alice's wage would be a big loss to them, but there was nothing more that Angela could do; in fact if she said anything more she would only make things worse.

She placed the wage sheet on top of the other pages in the file and took it to Sister's office. Sister didn't look at her, merely indicating that she should leave it on the desk. Angela hesitated, but the stony expression on the Warden's face made her leave without another word. Really, the woman had no need to be so intolerant! Alice was in the wrong, but everyone deserved a second chance – didn't they? Alice didn't strike her as being a bully. Yet she couldn't do more than she had already; it was up to the Warden to decide Alice's fate.

Beatrice sat at her desk, the file open before her. She frowned, because it did not make for easy reading. Alice came from a difficult background. No one knew better than she did that the girl would have difficulty in finding work if she were sacked from St Saviour's – but what else could she do?

A deep sigh escaped Beatrice. What was best for everyone? Alice had worked hard to secure her place here, and she was well aware how diligent she was – but she had a temper. Now and then she lost it and that frightened Beatrice. Supposing she really lost her head and hurt a child, badly? How could Beatrice live with herself then?

Squaring her shoulders, she wrote down the sum of money that she must pay Alice to sever her service here, and then took the key from her belt and unlocked her drawer, taking out a large cash box. Beatrice counted out the notes and then added another pound. It distressed her to know that she would be condemning a girl who had shown promise to a life of drudgery, because that was all Alice would find after this, but she really had no choice. Or was she being too harsh because of memories that were best forgotten?

Should she give the girl one more chance? Hearing a knock at the door, she invited Alice to enter. The scared look on the girl's face made her cover the money she'd placed on her desk. 'Come in, Alice,' she said, trying not to sound too harsh. 'I think you know what I have to say to you . . .'

'I'm sorry, Sister,' Alice mumbled, her eyes red with crying. 'I wouldn't have hurt him. It's just that boys like that need a bit of discipline or they run rings round you.' She drew a deep sobbing breath, then, 'Please, Sister. Will you give me another chance? I shan't get another job like this and I really love what I do . . . and me ma will kill me . . . I didn't mean to hurt him. I wouldn't never do that.'

Beatrice sat for a moment, her thoughts sombre. Perhaps it was too harsh to dismiss her. Beatrice's calling taught her to be merciful and just this once she would allow herself to relent; but there would not be a second chance.

'Very well, I shall not be hard this time. I am aware that Billy Baggins is a cheeky and undisciplined lad, but I prefer that you refer him to me for punishment in future. Do you understand me? This is your last chance, Alice. If it happens again, I shall dismiss you without a reference. Just remember that I gave you a chance to better yourself when I took you on here. Such chances do not come often – and there are hundreds of girls in Spitalfields and Bethnal Green alone who would jump at the opportunity you've been given. Do not let me down or you may end up in trouble, like many other girls in your situation.'

'You're not sacking me?' Alice stared at her, seeming unable to believe in her reprieve. 'Oh, thank you, Sister. I'm truly sorry for what I did and I won't do it again, I promise.'

'Very well, I shall take your word that you have learned your lesson. Self-discipline is important, Alice, particularly when working with children. Remember that, please. You may go now. I think you've finished your duty for today?'

'Yes, Sister, but I don't mind staying on if there's something you need me to do.'

'Nothing, thank you. Just get off home to your family.'

'Thank you so much,' Alice said and went out quickly as if she were afraid that the Warden would change her mind.

Beatrice smiled wryly. She wasn't sure what had changed her mind . . . except that both Angela and Billy himself had stood up for the girl. Oh, well, perhaps everyone deserved a second chance in life – but next time she would not be so lenient.

CHAPTER 11

Alice splashed her face in cold water in the cloakroom before leaving St Saviour's. She didn't want Ma to know she'd nearly been sacked, because her mother would take on something awful; she would probably give Alice a good slapping for getting into trouble.

Satisfied that she didn't look too bad, Alice walked swiftly away from her place of work. Now that she'd got over her fear of losing her job, she let her thoughts drift to the dance she'd gone to with Michelle and Sally. She'd been partnered by her cousin Eric a couple of times, but most of the time she'd sat talking to his friend. Bob was a quiet bloke and she'd found it difficult to find a topic he was interested in at first. He wasn't much of a mover on the floor, though he tried the easy ones like the barn dance, but he was clumsy in the waltz and he simply couldn't do the foxtrot or the quickstep, one of Alice's favourites.

'I'm not much company, am I?' he'd said when he brought her a second lemonade shandy. 'If you want to go off and dance with another fella I shan't mind.'

'No, there's no one else here I want to dance with,' Alice said, wishing she could think of something to interest him. 'What do you do when you're not in the Army, then?'

'I was a gas fitter; it was a protected job during the war,' Bob told her. 'I got the push when the blokes senior to me came back from fighting. They was promised their jobs, see, so I got downgraded. I decided to sign up for the Army myself – and they've trained me to be a mechanic.'

'Do you like it?'

Bob shrugged. 'It's all right – steady job anyway.'

Almost in despair, Alice had tried again. 'What do you like doing in your spare time?'

'You don't want to hear that . . .'

'Yes, I do,' Alice insisted though she longed to be on the dance floor.

'I like playing football. We've got a good team and we play against the other services, see. It's a real needle match with the flyboys, because they think they're better than anyone else.'

Alice smiled, because this was something she understood. 'My dad supports West Ham,' she said. 'My brothers like Arsenal and Manchester United, because they collect cigarette cards of all the players, and they go down the road on Saturday afternoons, to listen to football on the wireless at old Mr Griggs', the newsagent's. He has it on in his back room and all the kids go to listen and buy a penny sherbet dip. Saul reckons Manchester United is going to win the FA Cup this year, but

Joe says it will be Arsenal. We have a real ding dong in our house on a Saturday afternoon when Dad gets the *Evening Standard* and reads out all the results.'

Bob's eyes had lit up then. It turned out he was on her father's side and had been a regular West Ham supporter until he signed up for the Army life.

Alice's eyes had wandered round the room, noticing a crowd of young women and men, one of whom was Jack Shaw. She bit down on her lip, because some of the people he was with were the wrong sort, and it brought home all her father's warnings. He was talking to Arthur Baggins, and Alice believed he was a thief, because she'd seen the police after him down the market. Arthur was always in trouble, and if Jack hung around with him, her father was right; he was a bad lot. He always had at least two or three young girls hanging after him, and he'd got his arm round one with blonde hair now. Alice bet that colour had come out of a peroxide bottle and she frowned her disgust. Jack had spotted her looking in his direction and grinned. Alice looked away immediately.

'What do you reckon?' Bob was saying to her. She blinked, because she hadn't heard him. 'Would you come to the flicks with me one night? I'm home for five more days yet.'

'Yes, yes, I should like to come,' Alice said and smiled at him. 'You're not enjoying this dance much, are you? Why don't we go for a walk? We could get some chips on the way – if you want to walk me home?'

Bob grinned at her, looking pleased. 'Yeah, I'd like that fine, Alice. I can call for you on Tuesday evening if you like and we'll go to the Regal – or the Odeon if you prefer?'

'The Odeon is the posh one with comfy seats,' Alice said. 'I like that best, if there's anything good on.' She stood up. 'I'll get my coat. Wait for me by the door. I shan't be long.'

'All right, Alice.'

Bob went to have a word with her cousin, probably to tell him he would see her safely home. Alice said goodbye to Sally but Michelle was dancing so she just nodded in her direction on her way to fetch her jacket. As she emerged from the cloakroom, a man moved in front of her and she found herself staring up at Jack Shaw.

'Not goin' already, Alice? You ain't danced with me yet.'

'And I don't intend to,' she'd said. 'I'm with someone.'

'Yeah, I saw – the Army bloke.' Jack frowned. 'You don't want to hang around with that lot, Alice, love. He'll only go off and leave yer – watch out he don't give you one up the spout.'

Alice's hand itched to slap him, but she controlled her temper. 'One of these days I'll wipe the smile off your face, Jack Shaw,' she said and tried to move past him, but he caught her arm. 'Leave me be.'

'Come on, just one little dance . . .'

'No! Just get out of my way or I'll hit you.'

'I wouldn't try that here if I were you. I might have to give you a slap just to show me mates who's the boss.'

'Get off me then . . .'

'Why don't you leave her alone?' Michelle had come up to them. 'Alice doesn't want anything to do with the likes of you, Jack Shaw. We all know what you are.' She rounded on Alice, concern in her eyes. 'Don't be taken in by him, love. I know his sort and he's rotten through and through.'

'Mind your own business, bitch,' Jack said and grabbed her arm.

'I don't allow scum like you to touch me,' Michelle said and wrenched away from him.

Seeing that Jack was about to hit her, Alice pushed in front of them, glaring at her colleague. 'Stay out of this,' she warned. 'It's none of your business . . .'

'Too right,' Jack leered at Michelle. 'Alice is going home with me, aren't you, love?'

'You've been drinking,' Alice accused him. 'Let me alone, Jack. Just go away and leave us both alone . . .'

'Something wrong, Alice?'

She drew a deep breath and looked into the face of the man she'd thought of as being a quiet meek sort. Bob's eyes had gone cold and hard and the way he was looking at Jack spelled trouble.

'What are you gonna do if there is?' Jack challenged.

'Come outside and I'll show you,' Bob said. 'Where I come from we know better than to use violence in front of a lady.'

For a moment fury blazed in Jack's eyes and Alice feared he would go for Bob, but then he grinned in a mocking way and stood back.

'I should keep hold of this one, Alice love,' he said. 'Lady now, is it? Well, well, the Cobbs are goin' up in the world.'

He turned and walked off. Alice thought Bob would go after him, and caught his sleeve. 'He isn't worth it, Bob. His sort would pull a knife without giving it a thought. Please, I don't want you to be hurt.'

'It might not be me that gets hurt. They teach you a few tricks in the Army – like how to deal with bullies. But I don't want to spoil our evening. He will keep for another time.'

'Yes,' Alice said and tugged at his arm. 'Come on, Bob, let's go. I'm looking forward to a bag of chips – and we can walk by the river and talk for a while . . .'

'I'm glad I came tonight now,' Bob said. 'I didn't want to when Eric suggested it, but you're a nice girl, Alice. I'd like to be your friend.' The look in his eyes made her think that perhaps he wanted more than mere friendship.

Alice had murmured something encouraging. She liked Bob and wouldn't have minded going out with him sometimes, but he didn't make her heart thump the way Jack Shaw did. Sometimes, she dreamed about Jack and he was different; he had a steady job and he cared about her, wanted her to be his wife – but that was a load of rubbish. Her father had told her what he did for his wages and Alice didn't want anything to do with a man who went round with one of the big crime bosses extorting money out of restaurant and club owners.

Jack worked for one of the most feared men in the East End of London. Alice wished she didn't know, because she would have liked him if he'd chosen to work on the Docks or gone into the armed forces.

'On your own tonight then?'

Alice jumped; because of her mind wandering back to the dance as she walked through the dim streets, she hadn't seen him coming. Jack had sneaked up behind her, and now he grabbed her arm and swung her round to face him, gripping her so tightly that she almost screamed out.

'What do you think you're doing?'

'Making sure you know whose girl you are,' Jack replied, looking down at her angrily. 'I'm warning you, Alice. Stay away from that Army bloke – unless you want me to teach him a lesson?'

'You wouldn't!' Alice was shocked, because he looked so menacing and it terrified her. 'Why would you do something like that over me? There's lots of girls prettier than me, better figures too. Why pick on me?'

'Because I picked you out long ago,' Jack said, but he was grinning now, eyes bright with laughter.

'I don't mind you not being one of those skinny girls, Alice, love. I like a good armful, me. You're mine and I'm going to have you one of these days so make up your mind to it. I'm warning you to stay away from other men – especially Army boys. I don't like them, see. If I discover you've been seeing him, he'll be the one who pays. I shan't hurt you, Alice, because I like you. Just remember you belong to me and everything will be all right.'

'I don't want to be yours,' Alice said. 'My father says you're bad and I believe him. I've seen the girls running after you, and I'm not one of them – and never will . . .'

Alice never got to finish, because Jack had her tight against him, his breath hot on her face as he gazed down at her. Something in his eyes sent a thrill of excitement through her, and she could feel the hardness of his arousal through her thin coat and dress. For a moment she couldn't breathe and then his mouth covered hers in a kiss that sent her senses swooning. For the life of her she couldn't prevent her arms going up about his neck as she clung on, as if she would fall if he let go. His face lit with triumph as he released her.

'Now you know you're mine . . .' he began, but incensed by his behaviour, Alice hit him round the ear as hard as she could. For a moment he looked as if he might throttle her, but then he laughed.

'I like a bit of spirit in a girl, Alice. I'll let you get away with that one – but if you keep seeing that Army bloke you'll be sorry . . .'

Alice stood stock still, trying to catch her breath as he walked away. Her head was in a whirl and she didn't know what to think. Part of her was furious with him for behaving as if he owned her, but the other part couldn't forget the way her body had responded to that kiss.

When she'd let Bob give her a peck on the cheek on Saturday night she'd felt nothing. She was puzzled why she reacted like this to a man she knew was no good for her and never would be – but she didn't think he was a murderer, despite his threats. He was just trying to frighten her off Bob – and yet there was something in the way he'd spoken about the *Army boys* that bothered her. Did Jack bear a grudge against the Army?

Alice wished she knew more about him. Her father wasn't going to tell her anything she wanted to know; he would just forbid her to speak to Jack – but maybe Eric would know something. She would tell him what Jack had said to her, because he was a local man and would know whether she ought to be worried or not. Bob had said he was able to take care of himself, but to Alice he seemed a modest, quiet person and she doubted he could defend himself against Jack Shaw and his like. Besides, there were a lot of bad men in this area and if Jack put the word out . . . Alice shivered, because she wouldn't want anything to happen to Bob because of her.

CHAPTER 12

'Would you take a tray up to the sick ward, Angela?' Cook asked when Angela carried down the tea tray, which she had enjoyed in her office at eleven that morning. 'I'm still so short-handed.' The older woman gave a little shake of the head. 'This flu bug has taken against my staff, I think.'

'Yes, your girls have had more than their fair share,' Angela agreed. 'You know you have only to ask and I can help. We could always take on a temporary girl if you're really pushed. I'm sure I could find an agency with an honest working girl on their list.'

'You've a good heart, Angela, but I'm not sure Sister Beatrice would agree to that,' Cook said and nodded approvingly. 'I wasn't sure you would fit in here when you first came, but I think you'll do – and you can call me Muriel in future.' She patted her hair, which had been freshly washed and Marcel-waved with heated tongs the previous day.

'Thank you.' Angela smiled, touched by the compliment. 'Your hair looks lovely. I must find a good hairdresser to cut mine soon.' She picked up

169

the loaded tray and put it on the trolley. 'I'll bring what you need later, but for now I'll take this tray up to the ward. At least visitors are allowed now that we don't have any nasty infections.'

'I'll give you the phone number of my hairdresser,' Muriel said. 'If you meant what you said about extra staff . . . Well, I have a niece who is looking for a Saturday job until she takes up nursing. She doesn't care about wages but wants to work with children – because she hopes to be a children's nurse when she has finished all her exams.'

'I'll mention the possibility to Sister Beatrice, but your niece ought to be paid something,' Angela said.

Walking upstairs with the loaded trolley, Angela was thoughtful. She was beginning to find her way about now and the list of changes she wanted to make was growing. Some were just small things, but she had a feeling that Sister Beatrice was going to fight her all the way. For one thing, she'd noticed that the staff always used certain tables in the dining room, and there were places to spare at some of the children's tables, so the carers could quite easily sit with the children sometimes to give it more of a family feeling. They were going to need more tables when the new wing was up and running; it didn't make sense to have another dining room, because the kitchen was here. Perhaps they could expand out into the caretaker's room and move him to the new wing?

As she heard the happy laughter coming from the children's ward, Angela's frown lifted. The children here suffered from a variety of ailments, from little Johnny who had experienced a bad bout of rheumatic fever, which had left him with a weak heart, to little Susie, and young Marion Jason, a pretty child who'd had a nasty fall and broken both her arms and her right leg. Her arms had mended well, but her leg was still sore and festering from an infected wound that had almost drained her life from her before she was brought into the home. Marion's father had beaten the child black and blue and then thrown her down the stairs; the wonder was that she hadn't broken her neck. She'd been in the infirmary's children's ward for seven weeks, and then transferred to St Saviour's once the wound had begun to heal. The infection was no longer a danger to her life but the wound still caused her pain, and she was just beginning to regain some mobility. However, the terrible experience had left her feeling nervous and for a long time she'd hardly spoken a word. The nurses and carers believed that she was beginning to trust them, but she seldom smiled or chattered as most of their children did.

When Angela entered the ward and placed her tray of egg and cress sandwiches, and three dishes of plum tart and custard, on the table together with a jug of milk and another of orange squash, Marion was sitting on the edge of her bed. She was enraptured as Mr Markham read his story about a giant, who had captured a little girl and was going to eat her, but a big hairy spider had come to frighten the giant away and Johnny Goodboy had arrived to rescue Little Susie from the monster.

Hearing the children giggling as the monster was vanquished by the big spider, which then sat down and drank a glass of milk, made Angela's heart lift. She smiled at the brilliant young surgeon who gave so much of his time to children free of charge. She'd been told that he'd been introduced to St Saviour's by Mark and had become a regular visitor of late. He was perhaps thirty years of age, she supposed, with rather too long light brown hair that fell forward over his brow and into his eyes, a pair of horn-rimmed glasses perched on the end of his nose for reading. He became aware of her, closed his book, removed his glasses and smiled, then stood up, nodding to Sally, who had been quietly watching in the background.

'It's time for your lunch already, my dears. We shall have another story next time – or perhaps you would prefer to work on a puzzle?'

There were squeals of protest from the children, who begged him not to go, but he shook his head, telling him that he had patients waiting for him to cut lumps out of their tummies that afternoon. His words caused his audience to give little screams of delight, because to them it was no more than the wicked giant being chopped into little pieces and eaten by the big hairy spider – which, of course, was Mr Markham's object in telling them gory stories. He believed it helped them to come to terms with what had happened to them at the hands of violent parents, preparing them for a future that would in most cases be hard. His stories always had a happy ending, an ending that gave them hope, reassuring them that, no matter what, there were people who could help: like those here at St Saviour's.

'Now then, children,' Sally said. 'Say thank you to Mr Markham. He has lots of sick people to make better and you have to eat your lunch.'

'Can we have sandwiches made out of giant's fingers and toes?' Johnny said and shot a sly look at her.

'Oh dear, what kind of monsters have I created here?' Mr Markham twinkled at the young carer, and Sally's blush made Angela wonder if his reasons for visiting so often might include a desire to see a pretty young woman.

'They love your stories,' Sally replied with a shy smile.

'I'll leave you to get on with it,' Angela said and turned towards the door so as not to intrude if these two wanted a few moments alone. However, he was clearly about to leave himself, ushering her to go ahead and holding the door for her.

'Bloodthirsty little monsters, aren't they?' Mr Markham remarked to Angela as he followed her into the corridor. 'I find that children are very resilient. If you tread round them on tiptoe you do more harm than good. Most of them have known pain and unkindness. I think it far better to make up stories of wicked giants who get their comeuppance and work through their fear than to try to pretend that none of it happened. Facing up to it is always better in the long run.'

'Yes, I believe that is the same for all of us. Mark Adderbury works on similar principles, I know.'

'Yes, sound man. It was he that got me to try my stuff out here, more his field in a way, but I've always been interested in working with children in need of help – whether they are the casualties of life or simply underprivileged, and that isn't necessarily always the same thing.'

'No, I know what you mean; a child doesn't have to be poor to suffer from bullying, and not all deprived children are unhappy. Some of the poorer families are brave and make excellent parents, but unfortunately society doesn't see fit to pay them a living wage and the children suffer. It is the vulnerable ones, the ones that have slipped through the net, forgotten by those who should care, that are most at risk.'

'Exactly.' He smiled at her. 'How are you getting on here? Mark told me you had joined the staff. Fitting in all right?'

'Yes, thank you, I think so,' Angela replied with enthusiasm. 'It was nice to hear the children laughing just now. Yet we can only help a few and there must be so many still out there needing and wanting the love that is denied to them by uncaring parents or . . .' She broke off and blushed as she realised that she must sound like a well-meaning do-gooder.

'It's what we all need, isn't it?' he said and gave her an amused but approving look. 'I must leave you now. I really do have to go and cut some lumps out of people's tummies . . .'

Angela watched as he went down the stairs and out of the front door. She'd told him she was fitting in, and she really believed she was finding her feet at last. Her work was mostly in the office thus far, but from next week she would be supervising the building work as well. Since making a friend of Muriel, she'd helped out with trays and cutting sandwiches, and she'd been on a trip to the park with some of the older children one afternoon. Sally had gone with her, and they'd taken the children on a pleasure boat on the Serpentine, and then given them tea at Lyons' Corner House afterwards: little round ice creams and small fancy cakes washed down by ginger beer.

One day in the future Angela was hoping there would be sufficient funds to take the kids into the Essex countryside or even the seaside, but that would happen only if she managed to bring in enough donations for next year. The money for their trips was raised by outside helpers who held flag days and went round shops and factories, collecting pennies in tins. Angela had chipped in with three pounds of her own money, which had paid for the special tea rather than just a cornet in the park. The children had been so excited by all they'd seen and done. Yet she knew this was only the beginning but her ideas would have to be introduced gradually. For the moment she wanted to see how things worked and what could be done to improve them.

She longed to do more – much more, and not just as an administrator. Angela hadn't realised until she came here that there was a deep well of love inside her, just waiting to pour out. Some of the sights she'd seen here, the stories she'd been told of children brought in off the streets with sores all over their bodies, half-starving – it was enough to make her weep, yet she also had tremendous satisfaction in seeing those same children sitting down to a decent meal and hearing their laughter and chatter. St Saviour's was certainly a place of safety and hope, and she wanted to be a part of it all, to stay here and do what she could for the children.

As yet Angela had seen virtually nothing of Mark Adderbury, though she knew he'd been to the home at least twice since she'd started working there. Once she'd been out shopping, and the second time she'd just caught a glimpse of him with Sister Beatrice. They had been deep in conversation so she hadn't liked to intrude; she was aware that she felt disappointed that he hadn't rung her, because she'd thought they might now see more of each other. Mark was such a good friend to her and she wasn't sure how she would have got through without him, but she mustn't allow herself to think of him as more than a friend. She still loved John and even to think of putting another man in his place was disloyal.

Angela was glad that Sister had changed her mind and allowed Alice Cobb to stay on, but she wasn't sure how much she'd had to do with it. Perhaps Sister had her own reasons for relenting.

Alice had thanked her for helping her, obviously believing that she'd had some influence with Sister Beatrice. The girl had seemed cheerful that morning, but since then Angela had seen her looking anxious and wondered if Alice was in trouble with Sister again. Perhaps it was a personal problem. With her family that was quite possible, but Angela didn't yet know her well enough to ask if something was wrong. Michelle was Alice's special friend and she believed they went out together often. So far, Angela hadn't made friends here, perhaps because of the perceived social divide, though she didn't feel as much of an intruder as she had at first.

CHAPTER 13

'I got told off again fer runnin' in the corridor,' Billy said to Mary Ellen one morning at breakfast. 'She says if she catches me again she'll give me the cane.'

'Sister's a mean old thing.' Mary Ellen looked at him uncertainly. 'I heard she threatened to sack Alice for giving you a clip round the ear – it didn't hurt, did it?'

'Nah, not a bit. I've had worse flea bites. Pa really used to thrash me when he was drunk, but Ma was all right and so was me nanna. I ain't 'eard a word about her. I wish she'd get better and have me home – and you could come wiv me, Mary Ellen. Nanna's all right, she wouldn't turn you away if she could look after us.'

'I wish I could go home to me ma.' Mary Ellen sighed. 'I wrote to her and Rose. Sally got me envelopes and stamps, but I haven't had any letters yet . . . I miss my mother so bad.'

'Yeah, I know how yer feel,' Billy said. 'I missed my ma somethin' awful when she died. It ain't bad 'ere sometimes – but others I feel like I'm in prison. All them rules they make us keep; like

178

wearing yer cap whenever yer go out, washin' every day and havin' clean clothes all the time, and puttin' the lights out at half past eight, and not runnin' anywhere . . . and puttin' things away neat in the dorm, and not talkin' when we're told to be quiet for mornin' prayers.'

Mary Ellen nodded, even though she didn't mind some of Billy's long list. 'I think it's just that Sister Beatrice. Our Rose said she was sharp with her when she asked for me to come here. I wasn't supposed to hear that, but I did, because I stood on the stairs and listened. It's the only way to find out what they're saying in our house, 'cos they think I'm too young and they tell me lies.'

'Bloomin' grownups are all the same like that,' Billy said. 'Think yer a kid and can't be trusted if they tell yer the truth.'

'They keep telling me Ma is going to hospital to get better, but she thinks she's going to die. I heard her making Rose promise to look after me when she's gone.' Mary Ellen sniffed hard, struggling against her tears.

'Rotten luck.' Billy looked sympathetic. 'I'd better finish my breakfast. I've got ter go ter school; it's football practice and I don't want to miss that – are you going to school today?'

'I don't think so, 'cos I've had to change schools, but I think I'll be going with you now the school holidays are over.' Mary Ellen looked anxious. 'Nan says I'll hear about my place this week . . . and she's putting me in a dorm with the girls of eight and nine instead of with the older ones.'

'You'll like that,' Billy said, finished his glass of orange squash and pushed back his chair. 'I'd better go. If they send you to school next week we can walk there together.'

'Are you going to attend school regular then?'

'I might, seein' as you'll be there,' he said, grinned at her and dashed off, only to be reprimanded by one of the staff for running in the dining area.

Billy stuck his head in the air and went off whistling. He had made up his mind to keep a low profile for the moment, because he didn't want to give Sister a chance to cane him: the mean old crow! But he didn't want to be late for football practice so he ran to fetch his boots.

'No running in the corridors!'

Billy saw Sister bearing down on him and made a ferocious face at her. If he'd dared he would have kicked her ankles and told her just what he thought of her rules, but he was here on probation so he'd best keep his mouth shut for a while, or he might find himself in a house of correction. He hadn't cared at the start whether he stayed or not, but now that Mary Ellen was here he would hate to be sent away . . .

Billy was feeling pleased with life when he went home for lunch after football practice. He'd done well and the master in charge had praised him, telling him that he was showing promise and might be selected for the school team. Used to being scolded for being lazy or neglecting his work, Billy had glowed with pride. He couldn't wait to see Mary Ellen and tell her that he'd scored a goal.

'I thought I told you this morning not to run?' Sister Beatrice put out a hand and caught hold of Billy's jacket, forcing him to turn and look at her. 'Do you not understand that the rules are meant for a reason? If you run you could fall and hurt yourself, but also you could knock into one of the staff and cause them to drop whatever they happen to be carrying. It might be a tray of glass or perhaps sterilised bandages and medicines, which are expensive to replace.'

'Sorry, Sister.' Billy looked up at her defiantly. He wasn't doing any harm, but he had to find Mary Ellen and have his lunch before returning to school. He'd been told that his inclusion in the team would depend on his attending regularly. Besides, most of the boys ran when they could get away with it, the Warden just had it in for him. 'We were late back from football practice and if I don't hurry I'll miss lunch and be late this afternoon.'

'You will report to me after school this evening, Billy. I've warned you several times and you ought to know the rules by now. As you continue to flout them I shall have to administer punishment.'

Billy glowered, hanging his head but defiant. If she thought giving him the cane would break him, she was wrong. He didn't look back so he never saw the anxious way the Sister's eyes followed him until he was out of sight, before turning away.

'Well, this is your own fault,' Beatrice said as Billy looked at her with those stubborn eyes of his. 'I have warned you repeatedly about running in corridors. Please hold out your hands.'

Billy hesitated, clearly wondering whether he could get away with defying her, then reluctantly held them out. Taking a deep breath, Beatrice gave him three strokes on his left hand and then prepared to repeat the action on his right. The boy held his gasp of pain inside, gritting his teeth fiercely and refusing to let her see it hurt. His bravery only made Beatrice the more angry and she decided to teach him his lesson once and for all. She had just brought the thin cane down when the door to her office opened and Angela walked in carrying a sheaf of papers.

'What are you doing?' Angela cried. 'No, not the cane . . .'

Beatrice glared at her and gave Billy two more strokes before dismissing him. Billy had not made a sound and stared at her with proud defiance, as if daring her to hit him again, but she hardly noticed as she turned to her assistant in rising anger. She saw the righteous indignation in Angela's eyes and held her tongue until the boy had departed, slamming the door after him. No doubt he was already running, defying her to the last.

'How dare you interfere with my punishment of

a troublesome boy? How dare you come barging in here and speak to me in that manner?'

Angela seemed to hesitate, and then raised her head, looking her in the eyes. 'I dare because I cannot stand by and see a boy beaten . . .'

'You have no right to interfere with my decision. I am the Warden here, Mrs Morton, and I will thank you to knock before you enter in future.'

'I am perfectly prepared to knock and for that I apologise,' Angela replied. 'However, I do have the right to object as a compassionate bystander if nothing more, though of course I should have done so in private. I do not believe in beating a child for small misdemeanours, though of course there are times when it might be necessary – but in my opinion it is time that all corporal punishment for children was banned. You claim to care for the children in your care – how can you inflict it on a child that has in all probability been beaten too often in the past?'

Beatrice was outraged. How dare this newcomer insinuate that she was given to cruel treatment of her children? All she had ever done was to see they were well fed and cared for, but discipline must be maintained. The Bishop had told her himself that he expected her to maintain strict rules at St Saviour's.

'I have repeatedly warned the boy not to run in corridors. He chose to ignore me and so I punished him. It was my decision and my word is law here.'

'Not exactly,' Angela informed her quietly.

'Naturally, it is not my business to interfere in the way you run the home – unless I believe you mistaken in your thinking and in that case I shall speak my mind. The Board has authorised me to suggest changes as and where I see fit. I do not believe in corporal punishment and I think we should try other methods. Withdrawing privileges in extreme cases of bad behaviour is one – but for small things, perhaps an hour in detention or some lines?'

'I think I am the best judge of what is right for my children. I believe that if you spare the rod you spoil the child.'

'Do you not think that a little outdated? Have our children not already suffered enough unkindness and often brutality? To hit them is surely telling them that we are no different to the fathers who beat them. If Billy's spirit has not been broken by a brutal upbringing, why should a few strokes of the cane teach him to obey the rules? Surely it is better to explain and teach, to show him there are rewards for being a better person? We are moving towards a new and I believe brighter future. Laws will be made to protect children, though they will not come all at once. I may be ahead of popular thinking, but I believe that any form of physical punishment will eventually be forbidden in schools and anywhere that children might be at risk.'

'Indeed? Are you telling me that this rule will apply here?'

'I would hope so . . .'

'Not while I am the Warden.'

'I do not want to make an unfavourable report on your handling of the children,' Angela said, still in that quiet tone that Beatrice was beginning to find infuriating, 'but if I have to I shall speak to the Board myself. I could not lend my authority to an institution that condoned such punishment. I should warn you that I feel strongly about this, Sister.'

Beatrice was so angry that she could hardly speak, but then she remembered her calling. Had she not been taught that humility was her duty? If God had not wanted Angela here, He would not have sent her. This was meant to be a test of Beatrice's strength.

She took a deep steadying breath. 'Until such time that I am aware of the Board's wishes in this matter I shall continue to administer the punishment I feel appropriate. Now, was there anything more?'

'You might like to look through this,' Angela said. 'It is a preliminary list of suggestions for improving both the building and the running of St Saviour's. I wanted you to see it before I sent it in. I was asked to suggest anything that needed to be improved, with the buildings themselves and the way St Saviour's is run – though of course I do not have the authority to change anything unless both you and the Board agree.'

'We may be able to agree on some of it. I will

185

look at it when I have time,' Beatrice replied. 'Please leave it on my desk. I am rather busy.'

With that, she walked past Angela into the hall before she lost her temper again.

Angela returned to her office, feeling a little shaken by her first real argument with Sister Beatrice. She was not at all certain she'd done the right thing in letting her feelings overrule her head. It would, she reflected, have been better to wait and then tell Sister Beatrice that Mark considered they needed to change considerably if they were to bring St Saviour's up to the proper standards. She'd been putting it off, waiting for the right moment, but her distress at seeing the Warden caning a young boy had made her act without sufficient thought.

She would have to apologise, of course, because she ought not to have spoken in front of the boy – and yet could it ever be right to subject a child to such treatment? Angela thought not.

The telephone on her desk rang at that moment, recalling her thoughts to the present. She picked it up with a little frown. 'Angela Morton, how may I help you?'

'Angela, it's Mark. How are you?'

'I'm fine,' she lied, managing to sound cheerful. 'We seem to keep missing each other. How are you?'

'Busy.' His warm laugh banished her frowns and she remembered how much he'd helped her since John died. 'Work – and I've been helping a friend clear up his late father's affairs.'

'I'm so sorry,' Angela said and meant it. 'What can I do for you?'

'I just wanted to hear the sound of your voice,' Mark said. 'Work has been pretty bloody recently – and I need someone to cheer me up. How about coming out for a drink and a snack this evening? There's a decent pub I know that does simple meals – how does that sound?'

'Perfect. I could really do with a night out with my best friend.'

For a moment Mark seemed to catch his breath, then, 'Am I your best friend, Angela?'

'Surely you know that?' she murmured huskily because emotion caught at her throat. 'You're the only one who understands me, Mark – the only one I feel I can turn to.'

'That sounds a little desperate? Bad day at the office too?'

'You could say that . . . no, just a little tactical error on my part. I shan't bore you with the details; in general everything is fine.'

'Shall I pick you up at seven then?'

'Yes, please. I'm so glad you rang me, Mark. I want to help when you need me – just as you've helped me.'

'I'll always be your friend,' he promised and something in his voice made her heart jolt as the receiver went down at the other end.

Angela nursed the receiver at her end before hanging up. She'd always thought of Mark as a friend, nothing more. He was much the same age as John, perhaps a year older, and attractive – more sophisticated and serious than her husband had been when she fell in love with him. It had been a whirlwind affair and Angela had been swept off her feet by the handsome Army officer, snatching at happiness even though she knew what might happen. War had changed John, and she'd sensed a new reserve in him, a new resentment that hadn't previously been there when he came home on leave, and it had felt as if he'd somehow shut her out, even though he'd made love to her with an almost frantic passion, as if he could never have enough of her – but later, he'd left their bed and gone down to the sitting room, where she'd found him staring out at the night sky.

'What's wrong, darling?' she'd asked and gone to him, putting her arms around him and nuzzling the back of his neck. He'd gone stiff and still in her arms, almost as if he rejected her touch. 'John?'

'Go back to bed, Angela. I need to be alone – please, just do as I ask.'

Angela had done as he asked and in the morning he brought her flowers, tea and toast and then he made love to her so sweetly that all her fears were banished and she was filled with love for him. But it hadn't been the end of the sudden tiffs that flared between them . . . they'd argued over her desire to do something useful with her life, because she wasn't the kind of woman who could just sit at home and twiddle her fingers.

Angela dismissed the memory. She'd loved John

no matter what the war had done to their perfect relationship and she always would; to even think about loving someone else was a betrayal of the promise she'd made on her wedding day. She could never betray their love; it was unthinkable. Perhaps if they'd had the children they'd both longed for she wouldn't feel this emptiness inside, but they'd had so little time together because of the demands of war, and it just hadn't happened.

Why had she even thought about a new relationship? She was ridiculous to imagine that that soft, deep note in Mark's voice spoke of a feeling he was afraid of revealing. No, he was content to be her friend, of course he was – and that was all she wanted. If a tiny voice inside her head asked questions about the future, demanding to know if she was content to sleep alone forever, she drove it away.

She ought to seek out Sister Beatrice and talk to her, tell her that she had no wish to interfere with her day-to-day running of the home, make her understand that Angela's task was to work beside her and not to flout her authority, and apologise for speaking out in front of the boy . . . yet nothing would ever make her condone the sort of punishment Sister had handed out. Her feelings of outrage at what she saw as injustice would always make her speak out, though she was aware that if she wanted to fit in here she needed to get on with the Warden . . .

CHAPTER 14

'I'm bone weary,' Sally said when she got in one late September evening and found her mother dishing up cottage pie for her sister, brother and father. 'We're short-handed because a couple of the carers have left; they were fed up with all the rules and found jobs in the factory. There's only Nan, Alice, Sarah, and me on days at the moment, besides the nurses, and it isn't enough at bedtimes or when we're getting the younger ones up in the mornings. The girls on nights don't have as much to do as a rule, just walking round the dorms to make sure all the children are in their beds and peaceful. Sometimes there's a wet bed to change, or a sick child, but that doesn't happen too often.'

'What about the nurses, can't they help out in the mornings?' her mother asked, looking at her sympathetically. She was a slightly plump woman in her forties with soft brown hair that waved naturally back from a face free of powder and eyes that sometimes looked hazel and sometimes green. Dressed in a floral cotton dress with short sleeves and a white collar, she wore a pink spotted apron over it and a pair of sensible flat shoes, and looked younger than she was.

'They do, of course, but they have the sick ward to see to, and the new arrivals to check over before they are allocated a bed. Besides, they're trained nurses and they're not employed to do our job – and there's always one of the kids complaining of feeling sick or having a tummy ache. I think a lot of them do it to get out of school. The nurse is our first port of call before asking a doctor to come out. Besides, we only have three nurses apart from Sister Beatrice at the moment and mostly only one is on duty, because they split the shifts.' Sally washed her hands at the sink, groaning as she looked at the clock. 'Keith will be here in half an hour. We're just going for a drink but I don't want to keep him waiting.'

'He will wait while you get ready,' her mother said. 'Sit down and eat your tea, girl. Surely Sister Beatrice knows you need more help with the children?'

'No doubt she'll get someone as soon as she can and until then we shall just have to manage. Nurse Anna doesn't like being on nights, because she has a steady boyfriend, but at the moment she has no choice, and I know both she and Michelle feel they need another senior nurse.'

Brenda looked at her speculatively. 'I've thought about applying for a job at St Saviour's as a carer, but I earn more where I am. Besides, I don't think I'd want to work the hours you do, Sally.'

'Of course you earn more,' her mother said sharply. 'You didn't do that secretarial course to throw it away after a few months for a job that takes half the training. Sally is only there until she saves enough money to see her through nursing college; she's going to proper nursing school because she wants to be a state registered nurse, perhaps become a ward sister one day. Your father worked hard to keep you girls at school and give you a good start in life.' Their mother looked proud of her daughters. 'You've both chosen good professions so just stick at what you're doing.'

'I know . . .' Brenda sighed. 'It's just so boring stuck in the office. I should like to do what that Angela Morton does, Sally – office work and helping out. I'm stuck in front of a typewriter all day long.'

'It's what you wanted to do, and I don't think you would like scrubbing nits out of the children's hair when they first arrive,' Sally said and swallowed a mouthful of the delicious pie of minced meat, vegetables and soft potatoes with a crispy top. Her sister pulled a face of disgust and went on eating her meal. 'I don't think I could stand office work – but then I've always wanted to be a nurse. I'm going to specialise with children, because they are a delight to look after. We've got a little girl in the sick ward now. You wouldn't believe what her father did to her, poor little thing, and yet when she was listening to Mr Markham's stories she was giggling as if she'd never been hurt in her life.'

'That was in the paper, if she's the one whose father threw her down the stairs in a drunken rage. I hope they throw him in prison and lose the key,' Mr Rush said. 'If I had my way men like that would be strung up by their privates and left to rot until the crows took their eyes out . . .'

Sally laughed at her father's righteous anger. 'That's the sort of story Mr Markham tells the children, only his bullies are giants and they get chopped up and eaten by big hairy spiders.'

Brenda squealed. 'Do you two mind? I'm eating my tea. What sort of a teacher is he?'

'He's a surgeon actually, but he's interested in remedial work with damaged children. He and Mr Adderbury work together at the hospital sometimes, and Mr Markham has published some children's books that he wrote and drew. He's so clever! I think Mr Adderbury asked him to try his stories on the kids at St Saviour's and they love them, can't get enough of them. He comes every week now, just two mornings. I didn't know him at first, but I was on duty in the sick room when he came today and he's lovely . . .'

'It sounds as if you can't get enough of Mr Markham yourself,' Brenda remarked dryly. 'You want to watch it, sis, he's probably got a wife and six kids at home.'

Sally flushed bright red and shook her head. Mr Markham had spoken to her a few times, and his smile did funny things to her insides, but she knew he was only being kind. 'Don't be daft, Bren. I know he wouldn't look at me – besides, he's about thirty I think . . .'

'Too old for you,' her mother said sternly. 'You stick to that nice young man who is taking you out tonight. He's got his head on the right way, learning to be a plumber. He could have his own business and a nice house one day. Doctors are way out of our league, Sally.'

'It isn't really a date. I've known Keith for ages, Mum, but he's only a friend,' Sally said, though she knew that was her fault: Keith wanted more but she wasn't ready to give it. 'We were all going together, Michelle and Alice and some other friends, but Michelle is stuck on the evening shift for a week now, and Alice had a proper date. So, Keith said if I liked, he would pick me up and go for a drink . . .' Yet even as she denied it to her mother, Sally knew that Keith was starting to get serious, to talk about getting married one day.

'That's a date in my book,' Brenda said, interrupting her thoughts. 'One thing, Keith can't afford to get married for years, because he's only training to be a plumber. Besides, you'd probably have to live with his parents. I don't think you would care for that?' She gave Sally a straight look. 'I thought you wanted to be a nurse?'

'I haven't changed my mind,' Sally replied and pushed back her empty plate. 'No, I don't want any afters, thanks, Mum. I'm going to have a quick wash and get changed into my blue dress . . .' The navy blue cotton with a tiny white daisy pattern

194

was one she'd made herself with material from the market and because she'd saved her coupons, she'd been able to make a fuller skirt than any of the ugly Utility dresses they could buy during the war. A few nicer things were appearing in the shops now, but Sally still couldn't afford them on her wages. She and Brenda made their own dresses, and Brenda was much better than Sally, helping her to cut out the Butterick pattern.

Ignoring her sister's smirk, Sally left the large warm kitchen and went into her cold bedroom. The linoleum was icy under her feet and she shivered as she kicked off her shoes. Sally wore thick lisle stockings for work, because nylons would never stand up to the treatment they got crawling about on the floor with the little children. Just now she didn't have a pair of nylons without a ladder, but she'd got used to browning her legs with gravy powder in the war and going without stockings, and besides, what did it matter? Keith wouldn't notice.

As she finished dressing her mind was on her work. She wondered if Sister Beatrice knew that the last few days Angela had been stepping in to help the carers with the washing and dressing at bedtime. It wasn't truly her job, but she didn't seem to mind what she did, and Sally really liked her. She looked and sounded posh, but underneath she was just like anyone else . . . nicer than many of the carers, some of whom came and went with alarming regularity. They didn't like the dirty jobs they had to do, like bathing filthy kids who had lice crawling over them when they arrived, and changing sheets soaked in urine or mopping up sick off the floor. A lot of girls would rather work in a department store if they could, but Sally loved her job and had no patience with those who spent most of their day staring at the clock and wishing it was time to go home.

A little frown touched her forehead as she wondered about Alice. She was usually very friendly, but the last few days she'd been a bit distant, as though she was bothered about something. When Sally asked if anything was wrong the young woman had snapped her nose off, though the next moment she'd apologised and said she had a headache. But somehow Sally suspected there was more, though she wasn't close enough to the other carer to press her for details she clearly had no intention of giving. Alice was Michelle's special friend, but Sally liked her and hoped that whatever was troubling her wouldn't interfere with her work at St Saviour's. They were short-staffed enough as it was and if Alice left it would just make the situation worse.

Alice looked at Bob as they sat together on the tram heading back to Whitechapel. She'd really enjoyed the evening, even though the main film had starred Errol Flynn and she wasn't keen on him, but Bob had brought her a small box of Cadbury's Milk Tray and the best tickets. She'd relished being treated like a lady, because mostly in the past she'd gone out with boys from school who'd tried it on all through the picture, their hands always trying to touch her breasts or inch up her skirt. Bob hadn't even put his arm around her shoulders.

In the interval he'd gone to the cloakroom and on the way back he brought them ice-creams from the girl who walked round with a tray.

'I wasn't sure what sort you liked so I brought a choc ice?'

'Lovely,' Alice said and cracked the thin chocolate round the soft centre of vanilla. The ice cream had melted a bit and she liked it that way. 'You're very generous, Bob. Thanks for bringing me and everything.'

'My pleasure,' he said. 'I'd like to take you for a drink on Thursday, if you'll come? It's my last night of freedom for a while before I go back to my base.'

'When will you get another leave?'

'Perhaps in a couple of weeks. Sometimes we only get a twelve-hour pass and then I can't come home, but we get longer leave once a month and I could see you then, Alice – if you were interested?'

Alice wasn't sure what to say, because she couldn't forget Jack Shaw's threats. She'd kept her word to come to the pictures with Bob, but would she be doing him a bad turn if she went out with him regularly?

'I know I'm not much of a catch,' Bob said as

she hesitated. 'But I'm in line for promotion – and the married quarters on the base are really nice, better than most places round here.'

'Better than my home,' Alice said, because he'd seen where she lived and it hadn't put him off; she liked him for that, because a lot of blokes would've run a mile. 'I'll come out with you sometimes – but I'm not sure about settling down. I like going out with my friends . . . and I want to be sure. I'm never goin' to end up like Ma.'

Bob laughed softly. 'I wasn't proposing, Alice, not yet. I was just sayin' so that you don't think I'm a complete loss. I know I don't have a flash car like that bloke who seemed to think you belonged to him . . . but I'm steady and I'll have a nice house of my own one day.'

'I didn't know Jack had a car?'

'I saw him driving round town the other night. Him and that Arthur Baggins. He's a known thief, Alice, and violent too if what I've seen down the boxing club is anything to go by. Jack drew up and tried showing off but me and Eric saw them off all right.'

'How many of them were there?' Alice knew her cousin was good at boxing, but fists were not much good against men who used knives when they fought. 'You want to be careful, Bob. Jack and his friends . . . well, I wouldn't put anything past them.'

'One of them pulled a knife, but I think we showed them we wouldn't be intimidated,' Bob said. 'Eric is good with his fists. I like watching it down the club but I'm more into martial arts. I've got a mate in the Army who's a black belt, and I'm pretty good myself.'

'What's a black belt?' Alice looked at him as the lights went down.

'Hush now, I'll tell you another time. It's the main film starting.'

Alice nodded, and finished her ice cream. They'd eaten all the chocolates during the earlier cartoons and the Pathé news, but she was feeling warm and contented. Perhaps she didn't need to worry about Bob getting into trouble if she saw him again.

'I'll go out with you for that drink,' she whispered in his ear and saw him smile.

It was on the way home that Bob explained the art of judo to her. 'If you went to a club you could learn to do it too,' he told her. 'I think all women should learn to protect themselves. There are too many men about who think they can take liberties. I'd take you and show you if you were interested?'

'I don't think I'd like that, besides, I can manage to take care of myself,' Alice said, though she knew that if Jack had wanted to punish her for kneeing him where it hurt he could easily have done so. 'I'd like to watch you sometime, though.'

'I'll take you to the club one day,' Bob promised and grinned. 'It's not as rough as that crowd down the boxing club.'

They'd caught a tram on leaving the cinema and it stopped just down the road from Alice's home.

Bob insisted on walking to her door. Outside, he hesitated, then bent his head and kissed her softly on the mouth. Alice didn't turn away, even though she didn't feel that thrill of excitement that went through her when Jack kissed her so thoroughly. It was quite nice being kissed by Bob, just not special.

'I like you a lot, Alice,' he said. 'I'll call for you on Thursday at seven.'

'All right,' she smiled up at him. 'Thanks. I'll look forward to it.'

CHAPTER 15

Angela was almost ready to leave for the evening. She could hardly believe that more than a month had passed since she arrived that warm day in late August. She was looking forward to meeting Mark, but before that there was something she needed to do. It wasn't going to be easy, but she had to make her peace with Sister Beatrice.

She went into the hall, hesitating outside the Warden's office, then knocked and was invited to enter.

'Yes?' Sister Beatrice asked, looking at her imperiously. 'I was about to make a tour of the sick wards and the dorms – is this important?'

She was so obviously hostile that Angela was tempted to turn round and walk right out again, but if she did that she might as well keep on walking.

'I think so,' she said carefully. 'I wanted to apologise for speaking out as I did in front of the boy. I should not have embarrassed you like that. I assure you it will not happen again. In future I shall always knock.'

Sister Beatrice glared at her. 'I should imagine so,' she said, unimpressed.

'I am sorry that I called your judgement into question, although I can never and would never condone corporal punishment for small misdemeanours. However, I ought not to have spoken to you as I did. I do regret that and hope that you can forgive me.'

Sister Beatrice was silent for a moment and then she inclined her head. 'Very well, we shall forget it happened. However, I expect you to respect my position in future, at least in public, if you cannot do so in private.'

'I do respect you, Sister, in many ways. I cannot promise always to agree with you. However, perhaps we could try to meet in the middle wherever possible.'

'I imagine some people find you an irresistible force,' Sister Beatrice said dryly, 'but I am not one of them. However, I shall read your proposals carefully, and endorse anything I believe to be for the good of the children and St Saviour's in general. Anything else we will put to the Board and allow them to decide. I cannot say more at this time.'

'Thank you, it is all I could ask,' Angela said. 'Excuse me now, I am about to leave – unless there was anything you needed?'

'I dare say we shall manage without you, Angela.'

Feeling rather like a scolded schoolgirl, Angela left her. It was hard to swallow her pride but she had done what she felt right, although it had a left a bitter taste in her mouth. Even so, she would not give one inch on the principle that corporal punishment of a child was wrong – and she would fight tooth and nail to get Sister Beatrice to see that there were other ways.

'You look beautiful,' Mark said as he leaned in to kiss her cheek. The smell of her perfume was intoxicating and it was all he could do not to put his arms about her and bring her closer. A kiss on the cheek only left him wanting more, much more. A primeval urge to carry her off to his lair and kiss every inch of her delicious body before making love to her surged through him, making him ache with need. 'That's a lovely perfume, Angela.'

'Yes, it's a favourite of mine by Elizabeth Arden,' she said and slid inside the car. Once she was safely tucked into the passenger seat, Mark went round and got behind the wheel.

As he drew away from the kerb he could sense her eyes on him, but he resisted the need to look at her, reminding himself that she valued him as her friend and nothing more. To make her aware of the intense feelings she aroused in him might scare her away and that was the last thing he wanted.

'How are you settling in?' he asked in a casual tone as they drove along the embankment. It was good to have the lights on in London again, despite the ravages of the recent war and the empty spaces where bombed-out buildings had been pulled down and grass was growing through the rubble. The cast-iron Victorian lampposts shed a yellow light over the water, making it look mysterious and beautiful rather than oily and dirty as it did in daylight. 'Finding the work to your liking?'

'Yes, I enjoy it,' she answered easily, but he detected a note of reserve in her voice.

'Something bothering you?'

'No, not really. I had a small disagreement over punishing the children with Sister Beatrice earlier today, but we've settled it, I think. I spoke out of turn but this evening, just before I left, I went to her office and I've made my peace with her.'

'I expect it was inevitable that you would clash,' Mark said. 'She is used to a harsher regime than we need these days. I suppose it comes from the strict discipline she has been accustomed to as a nun.'

'Yes, I imagine so. She mentioned doing her duty as she thought right and I believe she had mulled over what I said to her. Actually, I think she agreed with some of the changes I have in mind, but we decided to put the ones we couldn't agree on to the Board and abide by their ruling.'

'What kind of things?'

'Are you sure you want to hear this?' Angela said. 'I thought you wanted to get away from work?'

'My work can be pretty depressing at times,' Mark replied. The night was dark and he was concentrating on weaving his way through the press of traffic. 'I'm interested in your ideas for St Saviour's, Angela. What have you come up with?'

'Well, I think the showers should have individual cubicles instead of being all in together. I realise that is more expense, but particularly for the girls I think it important.'

Mark frowned but nodded. 'What else?'

'I don't like the idea of such large dormitories in the new wing. What we have at the moment is ideal, three or four children together – it's more like a little family then.'

'Did Sister Beatrice agree with you?'

'When I apologised to her, she mentioned that the important thing is to get more beds and the bigger dorms will provide that – also the smaller rooms make more work for the carers.'

'She's right about that,' Mark said. 'Purely on the point of cost – and that's what the Board went on when the new plans were drawn up.'

'I suppose it could be made to work if you had a couple of older children in with the smaller ones, to take on the role of a big brother or sister . . . however, in my view dorms can be too big and feel as if they have no privacy, which does sometimes intimidate the smaller, more timid children. My suggestion would be to cut them into units of four at most, unless that is impossible because of cost. It must be for the Board to decide, of course.' Angela was thoughtful. 'We're going to need more tables in the dining room, because we want to keep that as it is. I thought if we expanded into what is the caretaker's room at the moment we could make space. Perhaps give the caretaker the small room at the back of the new wing. It's pencilled in as a store room, but might be put to better use, because he has the cellars to store his tools.'

'Sounds good to me.'

'I've also suggested that instead of having a staff table we split up and sit with the children for meals, move round a bit so we get to know and talk to all the children over time. There are spare seats on several tables, and I think it might make it a little bit less them and us . . .'

'Hmm,' Mark said and indicated as he turned off the main road. 'I can't see Sister agreeing to that one?'

'No, she didn't. I imagine she will continue to eat at the table set aside for her or take her meals in her office, and the nurses may feel they are entitled to eat their meals in peace – though I hope the carers will follow my suggestion.'

'Yes, that sounds more likely,' Mark laughed softly. 'So what else?'

'Sister Beatrice has a list of repairs she wants to the main building, and I've agreed with all of them, because I think she's right – but I also think we need a room where Sister can address the children and staff, a place to say prayers and give the children any news we think they should know.'

'Yes. I believe the dining room is used for

imparting any instructions or messages at the moment, and you say grace I believe?'

'Only once a day at tea, because Sister is often too busy to come down for meals. And we have a prayer before supper and bedtime.' Angela paused. 'Most of the other changes are not structural and concern the actual running of the home – and it's there that Sister and I part company altogether.'

'Ah, yes, I think I understand. She's afraid that you want to take over her job and downgrade her.'

'Yes, possibly,' Angela agreed. 'I've just made suggestions about various practices but they aren't meant to be mandatory, simply ideas of what might work better.'

'Go on, tell me about them,' Mark invited as he peered ahead. 'I think the pub I want is just down here on the left . . . ah yes, that's it. Do go on, Angela. I want to hear . . .'

'I'd like to stop all corporal punishment and replace it with less draconian measures. I think we could appoint monitors amongst the older girls and boys and give them some responsibility for maintaining discipline, in the dorms and the corridors.

'Also, I think we might get some teams together, with a team leader appointed by the children themselves so that they do not feel as if they are being forced into the new activities. We want more outings than the staff can manage, and perhaps these older children can take younger ones to the zoo or the waxworks occasionally, but they would also organise a system of points and the points have to be earned . . .'

'Whoa,' Mark laughed. 'I can see this could go on all night.'

'Yes,' Angela admitted ruefully. 'These suggestions are only the tip of the iceberg. I'm not even sure of half of them myself – it's just that I think at the moment there is not enough community spirit. It's more a case of the children doing what they're told and being as quiet as possible.'

'Yes, rather like the old workhouse atmosphere without the work,' Mark agreed and brought the car to a standstill. He turned to look at her and smiled in approval. 'You've vindicated my faith in you, Angela. No matter what Sister Beatrice is saying now, I feel you can find a way to either lead her or bring her struggling into the light.'

'Yes, I'm sure . . . well, I'll do my best,' she said and gave a reluctant laugh. 'I've chewed your ear off, Mark. Now, let's have that drink and then you can tell me your troubles . . .'

It was only when she was getting into bed that night that Angela allowed herself to dwell on how much she'd enjoyed her evening with Mark. They'd eaten delicious mushroom omelettes with jacket potatoes and a mixed salad, followed by apple pie and custard and real coffee. It was amazing how good simple food could be when well-cooked and shared with someone you really liked.

Afterwards, Mark had driven her home, promising

to be in touch again soon. He'd got out to open the door for her, taking her hand and holding it in his for a few seconds longer before he kissed her briefly, on the lips this time rather than the cheek. His kiss was light and not meant to show passion, but just as a token of friendship, Angela thought – although for a moment before he turned away he seemed to hesitate, and the look in his eyes sent a little frisson of anticipation down her spine. For a moment her heart raced and her mouth was dry, a need that she'd almost forgotten gripping her. It was a long time since she'd felt this way and she longed to have Mark's lips on hers, his tongue teasing and arousing her and . . . . What was she thinking! Her thoughts came to an abrupt halt as she realised that she'd wanted him to make love to her.

No, it would be a betrayal of her love for John. Thank goodness she'd come to her senses almost at once.

Mark was handsome, charming and, she'd real-ised that evening, very physical. He liked to touch her when they laughed and his hands had lingered at her shoulders when he'd helped her off with her coat. For a moment she'd wanted to lay her cheek against his hand, because the gesture reminded her of something John had often done, but in another moment she recalled that it was Mark and not John and she'd turned away before he noticed that his touch had affected her.

Angela was shocked to realise that for a moment

she'd felt needy, her breath quickening as a shooting pang of remembered desire curled through her. It was the first time for years that she'd felt anything approaching physical need for a man's touch. Since John's death less than a year before the end of hostilities, she'd been too numb inside to even know that she had a body, let alone want a man to touch her. Yet just for those few seconds she'd wanted to say that the food could wait. What she'd needed was to be held in strong, warm arms and loved, made to forget the world and all its pain, to forget that her heart was a desert.

Realisation and guilt soon swept the aching for physical release aside. John was dead; he couldn't feel love and nor must she. To give herself to another man would be a betrayal of the man she'd adored – still adored.

'I'm sorry,' she whispered to the empty room. 'Forgive me . . .'

It had just been a foolish moment and she was glad Mark hadn't noticed, because if they had given in and begun an affair it would have ended in tears. Angela might need physical comfort but she would never love again and nothing less would do for her. Besides, she was fairly certain that Mark would have been shocked, perhaps even disgusted. He had been John's best friend and he wouldn't see her as a woman he could take to bed just for a fling.

No, it was all in her mind and the sooner she forgot it the better.

CHAPTER 16

'What's the matter?' Mary Ellen asked when she saw Billy sitting on the wooden backstairs, which led up from the back scullery and were used mostly by the staff. He brushed his hand over his eyes and sniffed, and she saw his eyes looked red, as if he'd been crying. She went to sit beside him on the stairs, looking into his face. 'Was it that rotten old witch Sister Beatrice?'

Billy gulped and wiped his nose on his sleeve. 'She's got it in fer me, I reckon. She caught me runnin' again this morning and made me go to her office and then she give me three whacks of the cane on me knuckles . . . that's the second time she's whacked me.' He held out his hands to Mary Ellen so that she could see the red marks. 'I ain't cryin' fer that, though – it 'ud take more than that old witch to make me cry. I reckon as I've got a chill, that's all. It's turned cold all of a sudden and it's only early October.'

'I'll ask Sally to wrap them up for you,' Mary Ellen offered and stroked one hand gently. She'd been here over six weeks now and it was all right, except for rotten old Sister Beatrice. 'She's kind – but that Sister Beatrice is horrid. I should like to kick her ankles . . .'

'I did; she was just goin' to give me a tellin' off but I kicked out at her so she caned me again. Suppose I deserved it. Me pa would have give me a real 'iding. It ain't me 'ands wot made me toot. She said I deserved to be sent away . . . and I don't want ter go, Mary Ellen, not when you're 'ere.'

'She mustn't send you away,' Mary Ellen said, aghast. 'I should hate her forever if she did that – and I'll tell her so right now.' She stood up, prepared to march into battle, but Billy grabbed her ankle above her short grey socks. 'Ouch! What did you do that for?'

'Don't make things worse, Mary Ellen,' Billy warned. 'You'll only get yourself in trouble – and we shall both miss the church treat again this Saturday.'

'Has she said you can't go?'

'I'm on a warning,' he said gloomily. 'If she hears one word out of me I'm banned all treats for the next two months. It will be nearly Christmas by then and I don't want to miss the pantomime. And there's the party for the princess's wedding. There will be street parties, I reckon, and the church is bound ter put on a do next month . . .'

'What pantomime?' Mary Ellen asked, ignoring the possibility of street parties for the moment, because she'd never been to a pantomime. Pa had said he would take her to Olympia one year, but then he'd died and they'd had to move and there had been no money for treats, though they'd had a street party when the war ended. Ma hadn't been ill then and she'd gone out to join her neighbours with Rose and Mary Ellen to celebrate.

'Haven't you heard about it yet? They – Sally and Miss Angela, Nan and Nurse Anna, and Sarah – are going to take all those that are well enough to the theatre up West. We shall go up on the tram and then the underground. It's a special treat for Christmas and supposed to be a secret, but I heard them talking about getting the tickets for the pantomime free. Some big man wot Angela knows is going to pay for them for all of us . . . she was excited and telling Nan all about it the other day.'

'I've never been to a pantomime,' Mary Ellen said, feeling a bubble of excitement inside her. 'What is it like?'

'I ain't never bin neither,' Billy said and grinned at her. 'I've heard other kids say it's fun – actors all dressed up in costumes, singin' and dancin' and silly jokes. We've got to keep on the right side of the old dragon 'til then, Mary Ellen.'

'Ooh yes,' she said and sighed ecstatically. 'I can't wait . . . it is nice here sometimes, Billy. Even if they do have silly rules about running and stuff . . . better than I thought it would be.'

'Yeah.' He rose and took her by the hand. 'I'm all right now. It were just a bit of temper. Let's go and 'ave our tea. I'll get me own back one of these days, but not just yet . . .'

* * *

Nan watched the children file into the dining room and take their places at the tables. Sister Beatrice insisted that there was no running, shouting or pushing in here or anywhere else in the home. It was a good rule in general, but sometimes Nan felt the children ought to be able to let their feelings out a bit more. She didn't quite believe in the dictum that children should be seen and not heard, and she enjoyed hearing their laughter ring out.

She'd seen a gradual improvement in the health of the children over her four years at St Saviour's and that she was quite certain was down to the good food and even better care they received here. Sister Beatrice knew the name of every child and Nan knew she cared deeply for them all, but her manner was more that of a strict Victorian matriarch than a loving mother – and what these children needed was love. Nan tried to give them that and she also tried to soften Sister's attitude whenever she could, knowing full well that Beatrice listened to her where she would reject advice from Angela out of hand. It was all very well to teach them discipline, but what about making them confident, and showing them that love was what made life worth living?

Hearing a sound she loved, Nan looked at the two children as they put their heads together at the table and giggled. They seemed to be settling in at St Saviour's and the pair of them were inseparable. Up to some mischief she would be bound; they were a lively pair, but the little girl was very loveable and usually easy enough to manage, though she could be stubborn when she chose. In Mary Ellen's case, persuasion was much better than making demands she didn't understand. Nan watched the pair carefully; they had each loaded their plates with slices of bread spread with margarine and jam, fairy cakes and two small sausage rolls, which were the treat of the day.

Turning her head, Nan saw that Marion had ventured into the dining room for the first time. Sally was pushing her in a wheelchair and the child looked apprehensively about her, for although her arms were perfectly recovered she could not yet walk. It was her first time out of the sick ward and she would be going back there after tea, but Sister Beatrice thought she needed to start getting used to the other children, because St Saviour's was likely to be her home for the next few years. Marion's mother had died a few years previously and her drunken father was now awaiting trial for nearly killing his daughter, and would certainly go to prison.

'Take her to sit with Mary Ellen and Billy,' Nan said as Sally hesitated, looking for a seat in the crowded room. 'They have a spare seat at their table. Have you got all you want, Marion dear?'

'Yes, thank you, Nan,' Marion said, looking nervously at the table where Billy and Mary Ellen were sitting. 'It's very noisy in here, isn't it?'

'I expect it seems that way after the sick ward,' Nan said, then, glancing at Sally, 'I'll introduce her and ask them to look after her for me. I'm sure you have plenty to do?'

'Yes, I have,' Sally agreed and surrendered the chair to Nan.

'This is Mary Ellen and Billy,' Nan said as she pushed the chair up to the end of the table. 'Children, this is Marion. It is her first time at tea, because she has been poorly, so I want you two to look after her – will you do that, please?'

'Yes, Nan,' the unholy pair chorused; though they looked at each other. 'Hello, Marion. What's wrong with your leg . . .?' This last from Billy.

'I fell down the stairs and broke it,' Marion said timidly. 'My arms were fr . . . actured so the doctor said, but my leg was proper broke in two places.'

'Did it hurt much?' Mary Ellen asked and Marion nodded. 'Poor you. Why haven't you been to tea before?'

'Because I live in the sick ward with Johnny and Jessica, but she's still in bed because her legs are too weak to get up yet, and Johnny's not well enough either.'

'Are you getting better?'

'Yes, I'm much better. Sister Beatrice says it's time I got to know the other children, because this is . . . going to be my home.' A large tear trickled from the corner of one eye. 'I've got nowhere else to go now . . . they're going to put my pa in prison . . .'

Nan smiled as the children talked naturally. She was usually right about the kids and she'd thought that pair were sound enough underneath, even though she knew that Sister Beatrice had her doubts about the boy. They'd discussed him over a cup of tea once or twice. Mary Ellen could be stubborn too, but the two of them were much alike and would look after another misfit, and perhaps take her under their wing. Nan thought there was a lot of good in Billy, but he'd got a bit of a chip on his shoulder, didn't take to authority.

Satisfied that the three children were getting on well, she walked away, leaving them to get to know one another.

'Nan's nice,' Marion said as they watched the motherly figure walk from the room, looking worried. 'I was so frightened when they brought me here to St Saviour's, but she cuddled me and made me feel better. She's like my ma used to be when she was alive.'

'I can't remember mine much, but I know she was warm and nice,' Billy said. 'Me ma and me pa are both dead – but I've got a bruvver.'

'I've got a sister and a mother,' Mary Ellen said. 'My pa was lovely. He used to cuddle me and kiss me, so did Ma once, but she's ill now so she can't. One day she'll come back from the hospital and I'll go home.'

'I ain't got a home to go to now,' Marion said and sniffed, the tears hovering.

'Yes, yer 'ave,' Billy grinned at her. 'You live 'ere wiv us. We're yer family now. Me and Mary Ellen. We'll look after yer.'

'Ta,' Marion said, looking shy. 'It's nice havin' friends ter talk to. Will you come and visit me in the ward sometimes?'

''Course we will,' Billy said. ''Sides, you'll be out soon enough and then you'll sleep in the dorm wiv the other girls.'

'I'm tired. I should like to go back now,' Marion said and looked round. 'Where did Sally go?'

'I think one of the carers came and fetched 'er,' Billy offered. 'If you want ter go back to the sick ward we can take yer. I reckon I can push that chair of yours, and Mary Ellen can help me.'

Mary Ellen agreed that she could and the two children experimented with taking off the brake and testing how hard it was to push. Billy was big for his age and strong, and Marion was light; he was soon wheeling her from the dining room, boasting how easy it was.

'You're as light as a feather,' he said. 'But we've got to go up in the lift 'cos I can't get yer up the stairs.'

''Course you can't,' Marion laughed. 'Sally brought me down in the lift. I know how it works.'

They turned towards the lift and pushed the button to summon it. However, it took a while to manoeuvre the wheelchair into the small cubicle and Billy was looking hot and bothered by the time he managed it. Marion pushed the button inside that took them whizzing up to the first floor, where the sick ward was situated, and after banging the chair against the sides of the door opening a few times, Billy got it out and they set off down the corridor.

'I'm sorry,' Marion apologised, because he was breathing hard. 'We should have waited for Sally. It's too hard for you to push me all the way.'

'Nah, 'course it ain't,' he said. 'I can make you go faster if you like.' He gave the chair an almighty shove and let go and it flew off down the corridor, taking all three children by surprise and making Marion cry out in fright as it hurtled towards a trolley left outside the door of the sick ward.

'I'm going to crash,' she yelled as Billy ran after her, trying vainly to catch up with the chair before it went into the trolley and either overturned that or Marion. 'Help me . . .'

Billy made a desperate bid to stop the crash just as the door opened and someone came out. That someone saw what was happening and rushed forward, putting herself in front of the chair so that it rammed into her and stopped, avoiding what might have been nasty since the trolley was loaded with glasses. She gave a little scream and yelled in pain as the child tipped over onto her and they both crashed down to the floor.

Billy's heart sank as he arrived in time to right Marion's chair and pull her off Sister Beatrice. He saw at once that the chair had caught the older woman's leg and he thought she might be hurt because she rubbed at it beneath the horrible old dress thingy she was wearing.

'I might have known,' Sister Beatrice said, looking

at him balefully as she got to her feet and straightened her habit. 'What did you think you were doing, Billy Baggins? You have no right to be here – and certainly not in charge of a wheelchair. If Marion's leg has been damaged it will be your fault.'

'I'm sorry about your leg . . .' Billy mumbled, eyes down.

'It's all right,' Marion said quickly. 'I didn't hurt my leg, Sister. It wasn't Billy's fault. I asked him to push me faster and he slipped and let go of the chair by accident.'

Sister looked at her through narrowed eyes, then back at Billy. 'It hardly matters who was at fault, you should not have been in another child's care. Where is Sally?'

'She took me down to tea and then got called away,' Marion said. 'Please do not be cross, Sister Beatrice. I wanted to come back. It wasn't Billy's fault – or Sally's. I should have waited until I was fetched.'

'He knew he should not have brought you up, let alone used the lift.' Sister frowned at him. 'Since it appears you are all equally to blame I shall not cane you this time, boy – but you, and you, Mary Ellen, will lose all privileges for the next two weeks. Now leave Marion to me and go back to your dorms or wherever you are supposed to be.'

She glared at them as for a moment they both stared at her defiantly, then turned and walked off, their heads in the air. They could hear her scolding Marion as she took her into the sick ward and closed the door.

'Miserable old witch,' Billy muttered. 'I'll get even with her one of these days. You see if I don't.'

'Don't let her upset you,' Mary Ellen advised. 'Who wants to go to the rotten old church do on Saturday anyway?'

'They're havin' a slideshow,' Billy told her. 'I heard it was Mickey Mouse cartoons but I don't know fer sure.'

'I've never seen Mickey Mouse, excepting in a comic,' Mary Ellen said, feeling and looking a bit regretful. 'She's mean, that's what she is, but at least she didn't cane you.'

'That's 'cos Marion spoke up fer me. I'm goin' ter sneak back later and talk to 'er, see if she's hurt, though I reckon it was Sister wot took the brunt of it, but I'll 'ave ter wait until the coast's clear. Angela might be on duty tonight. She won't split on me. She's a good 'un.'

'Yes, she is,' Mary Ellen agreed. 'Sounds a bit posh when she talks but I like her. She's got laughing eyes. Mind you don't get caught, Billy. If Sister catches you out again, she'll have your guts for garters.'

''Ere you, watch yer language,' Billy mocked and winked at her. 'She'll give you wot for if she hears you say that an' all.'

CHAPTER 17

'I believe Markham's stories have done some good,' Mark Adderbury said to Angela as they left the sick ward together that evening. 'I wasn't sure they would, but I've seen a definite improvement in both Marion and Johnny as far as their attitude is concerned. His health isn't getting any better but at least he seems more cheerful, and Marion is a ray of sunshine. Jessica is perfectly normal apart from a spinal condition that makes her legs weak but she's over her fever now and will be up and back in her wheelchair before long.'

'I think her father is having her transferred to a special home for disabled children in the country now that he is back from the Army. He only put Jessica here on a temporary basis, and obviously cares for her, but he's a busy man and can't look after the child himself so she'll be going into a permanent home, because her mother died recently. That was the reason she was brought here, you know: her aunt couldn't cope with looking after her. Jessica wasn't ill-treated but she felt rejected when her aunt wouldn't have her. We shall be losing her shortly – but the other two have settled in well.'

'Yes, I think they are both happier now. Marion has accepted what happened to her and is no longer puzzled by it. She knows her father was drunk and she understands that his violence is something he is unable to control – but she doesn't burst into tears every time one of us speaks to her. I think Markham's stories have something to do with that . . .'

'The children love him.'

Mark smiled warmly. 'I enjoyed our drink the other evening, Angela.'

'Yes, I did too.'

'Is everything all right now?'

'I don't think Sister truly approves of me but we're treating each other with cool politeness at the moment. I'm afraid we've had words again – but I do not approve of using a cane on a child, Mark. I'm sorry but I made my views clear.'

'I'm not sure I approve of that either.' Mark frowned. 'I didn't know Sister used the cane?'

'She has more than once on Billy Baggins quite recently. I asked her to stop the practice and we disagreed. It is something I feel strongly about, Mark. I hope to persuade her against using the cane – but if she feels she has the right I must ask the Board for their ruling. I do not think I could continue here if they supported the practice.'

'I'm sorry to hear that, because in principle they may well do so, and the Bishop is almost certain to agree with her, because he is all for strong discipline. It would be a pity to fall out over such an incident, Angela. I dare say she thought the boy needed to be taught a lesson. She is an excellent warden and wonderful with the children as a rule. You must try to make friends with her . . . perhaps if you were able to speak to her as a friend, you might try to persuade her to put the cane away in a deep, dark cupboard. I might have a word one day, just casually, suggest that it is not helpful for a child's mental state. She does listen to me sometimes, but only now and then.' Mark laughed, hesitated, and then, 'I'm staying in London over the weekend. I wondered if we might go out to the theatre and supper afterwards . . . perhaps tomorrow evening at about seven.'

'Yes, why not? Will you call for me here – and shall I dress formally?'

'Oh, we'll go somewhere really nice, so yes, do dress up for it – and I'll call for you here if you wish.'

'Yes, that will be perfect,' she agreed and gave him that lovely smile of hers. 'I must leave you now. I have to speak to Nan before she leaves for the evening . . .'

'Yes, of course. It was nice talking to you, Angela. I'm going to pop in on Sister Beatrice before I leave. There are some things we need to discuss. Remember what I said, Angela. No point in making an enemy of Sister?'

'No, of course not,' she said, a flush in her cheeks. 'I shall look forward to tomorrow evening.'

Mark turned to watch as she walked away. He was thoughtful as he approached the Warden's door, wondering if he might have been a little impulsive in tailoring this position for Angela. She was just right for the work she was doing, but it would be unfortunate if the unease between her and Sister Beatrice caused them to lose their excellent Warden: they couldn't do without Sister Beatrice – and yet he knew that they needed Angela's efficiency and her drive if they were to bring the home up to the standard required of them for the future.

He stood outside the Warden's office and knocked just as he heard a loud crack of laughter and realised that Sister Beatrice had company. If he were not mistaken that was Father Joe, the Catholic priest who devoted so much of his time to the children of the East End, not just here but in the mean streets that wound their dirty web about the home and its vulnerable inmates.

'Come in, please!'

Mark entered and saw that he was correct in his assumption that Sister's visitor was Father Joe. There was a bottle of pale sweet sherry on her desk and two glasses still half full. Clearly, they had settled down for one of their long and bantering evenings spent arguing over their various beliefs.

'I hope I do not intrude?' he asked as Father Joe

rose to his feet. 'Please sit down, sir. I'll sit here, if I may?'

'Of course,' Sister Beatrice said and smiled. 'How fortunate I am to have two visitors this evening. Would you like a glass of sherry, Mr Adderbury?'

'Yes, thank you,' he said and then frowned as he saw her move awkwardly to fetch another glass. 'Have you hurt your leg?'

'Oh, it was that Billy Baggins,' Sister said carelessly. 'He pushed Marion's wheelchair too fast, slipped and let go apparently. She would have careered into a trolley loaded with glass had I not stepped out in front of her just in time. She could not stop and came into me, knocking me down and landing on top of me – but at least I broke her fall and her leg was not further damaged, thank goodness.'

'Well, as long as you're not badly hurt. If he is too disruptive I could see about getting him moved somewhere more suitable.'

'I've offered to talk to him,' Father Joe said. 'I know the lad and his family – the father was a drunken brute but he's dead now. Billy isn't a bad boy, but a little wild and cheeky. He needs to be given duties to make him more responsible. If you send him to a house of correction he will get worse, the wrong punishment will make him resentful, whereas with a little patience I think we might rescue him from the devil. There's a lot of good in him, it just needs coaxing out . . .'

'You'll have me believing he's a saint next,' Sister said wryly.

'No, I'll not be doing that.' Father Joe looked serious. 'But I see the good in all God's creatures, Sister, and if I can fetch it out of him so much the better.'

'Well, you can try,' she conceded. 'He makes me want to give him a good birching on his backside sometimes, but so far I've kept it to three strokes on the hands. I was told about the violent father – and the no-good brother, who is being searched for by the police apparently, but we *are* here to do what we can to save these children, not to make their lives a misery. I shall listen to your advice, Father, and try to control him by other methods. By all means do what you can with him, Father Joe, but forgive me if I venture to think he will lead you a merry dance.'

'There's many a tune played on an old fiddle.' The priest tapped the side of his nose. He looked at Mark, raising his brows. 'If it's private speech you're wanting with the good Sister here, I can leave you together?'

'Not at all,' Mark said. 'I thought I would pop in and say hello after visiting some of the children. I was wondering what we'd planned for them this Christmas – and whether we are holding any fund-raising events.'

'As for the fundraising, I've left that entirely to Angela,' Sister Beatrice contributed. 'She said something about a Christmas party at the church

227

hall, and seems to think that she will hold a bring and buy sale a couple of weeks before, with raffle tickets, a tombola and other stalls, in the church hall again. She has already obtained free tickets to a pantomime for the children and staff – and, I think she said her mother was having a small dance one weekend at their home in the country, which will fund future projects. Her parents live in your village, I believe?'

'Yes, they do. I hadn't heard about the charity dance yet, but if Mrs Hendry is organising it, it should raise quite a bit. She has a lot of wealthy friends.'

'I dare say.' Sister Beatrice's lip curled as if in distaste.

Mark hid his smile. It seemed that the antipathy was not all on Angela's side.

'I think we should have a big tree in the house with presents – and Father Christmas to give them out to all the children and staff.'

'That would be a rather large expense.' Sister frowned. 'None of them have been used to such extravagance and I'm not sure it is a good thing.'

'Yes, but I intend to meet that expense myself – and to play Santa Claus,' Mark said. 'I also think we should have carols, nurses and staff going from room to room and singing to the children. Lots of mince pies, sweets and cakes – if we can get hold of what we need. I have a few friends who may be persuaded to chip in with a jar or two of mincemeat and some extra sugar. I shan't ask where they got them of course, though I suspect the black market, but what I don't ask I don't know . . .'

'You will spoil them,' Sister Beatrice said, and Mark thought she sounded disapproving. 'These children do not have much to look forward to when they leave us. If they are lucky perhaps an adoption into a good family, and a reasonable education, but in most cases it will be an apprenticeship or work in one of the factories – and living in lodgings until they can afford a home of their own to rent. If we give them ideas beyond their station they may find the real world hard.'

'All the more reason to give them some good memories. I think we all agree that the children need to have more innocent fun in their lives now that the war is over. We've all been through a terrible time and if we can we should spoil them a little at Christmas. St Saviour's needs to be a home they are happy in, a place they think of fondly even if life is hard once they leave. If we make it too hard they will only run away as soon as they're fourteen or so. It is happening at homes all over the country. Surely we can do better here?' Mark said, and appealed to Father Joe. 'Don't you agree, Father? Shouldn't we try to make this a home rather than just an institution?'

'Spare the rod and spoil the child?' The priest was thoughtful for a moment. 'Providing the true meaning of Christmas is brought home to them, I see no reason why they shouldn't have a bit of pleasure while they can. After all, we've all been under a shadow. I don't think a few treats will endanger their immortal souls – do you, Sister?' He was smiling as he spoke and her stern features relaxed a little.

'I can see I shall be out-voted,' Sister Beatrice said, a reluctant smile in her eyes. 'But if we are to have carols I think those children that can sing should learn their own and perform for the rest of the inmates and the staff, earn their treats by working for it . . . You like music, Father Joe. Perhaps you'd take it on?'

'Why not?' he asked good-naturedly. 'I shall have to discover if young Billy Baggins can sing. Just the thing to keep him out of mischief between now and Christmas – even if he only turns the pages for the music.'

CHAPTER 18

Alice was just preparing to leave for the evening when Nan came up to her in the corridor. She stopped and smiled, asking Alice how she was getting on with her work now. For a moment Alice wondered if she'd done something wrong, but then she saw the kindness in the older woman's eyes and relaxed.

'Was there something you wanted me to do, Nan? I don't mind staying on for a bit if you need help.'

'No, I was just a little concerned for you, Alice my dear. You've seemed a little quiet recently. If there is anything troubling you, I'm always willing to listen. I always have time for the staff as well as the children, you know.'

'Yes, I do know,' Alice said and her throat caught because Nan's kindness made her feel like crying. She was anxious and there was no one she could talk to – but Nan wouldn't understand if she told her what was on her mind. 'It's just a little problem at home.'

'Well, if there is anything at all I can do, just let me know.'

'Thank you, I shall,' Alice promised, though she knew she wouldn't – couldn't – confide in Nan.

How could she tell her that she was frightened of doing something foolish? How could she explain that she was being shadowed and haunted by a man who wouldn't let her go? Nan would say she should go to the police or tell her father – but it wouldn't help if she did either. The police would simply say she should make sure she was always home before dark or have a friend with her – and her father would go after Jack and probably end up with a knife in his belly.

Besides, Alice was more afraid of herself than Jack. She was beginning to like him, and the excited feeling in her stomach whenever he came up to her made her ashamed. How could she feel like this about a man she knew was no good? Yet she'd always known him at school, and she'd liked him even then. Why couldn't she feel as excited at the thought of meeting Bob? He had written her a cheerful letter saying he was coming home that weekend and wanted to take her out. He'd explained that he wasn't much good at dancing, but would take her out to the pictures or a meal at a nice restaurant.

Alice had shown the letter to Michelle, when they'd met briefly between her arriving and her friend leaving.

'You've got a decent bloke there by the sound of it,' she'd said. 'I've only met him a few times when I've been out with Eric, but I like him. If I were you I'd go steady with him for a while – that's if you like him enough?'

'I do like Bob; he's good company and very generous – but he doesn't make me feel like I want to melt into puddles when he touches my hands.'

Michelle looked at her oddly. 'Do you know someone who does?' Alice nodded. 'But you don't want to go out with him – why?'

'Dad says he's rotten; into all sorts,' Alice told her. 'He keeps following me – and he threatened to harm Bob if I keep seeing him. Jack thinks I belong to him, though I've told him I don't want him.'

'Not Jack Shaw?' Michelle looked incredulous. 'I saw him pestering you at the dance a few weeks back, Alice. You would be a fool to get mixed up with his sort. I've heard what his boss is into and it's horrible. A lot of men aren't to be trusted, love, that's why you want to grab a good one when you get the chance.'

Alice stared at her. 'You sound as if you've been let down?' Alice had suspected something of the sort, but it was before they'd got to know each other so well, before Michelle started to work at St Saviour's, and her friend hadn't talked about it before.

'I was . . . before the war. I haven't told you before, because I felt such a fool for being taken in. I really liked him and I thought he liked me, but he was married all the time. I promised myself I wouldn't get taken in again like that. That's why

233

I'm telling you now, Alice. Don't be fooled by Jack Shaw. He'll let you down. I know how much that hurts.'

'Is that why you wouldn't go to the flicks with Eric when he asked you?'

'He told you I'd turned him down?' Michelle looked cross. 'No, I don't think he's married or a womaniser – I just don't want to get serious with anyone and I think your cousin is the sort who would want to get married. He's going to stay in the Army as a career and I would have to give up my job if . . .' She broke off and blushed. 'Not that he was thinking of marrying me, of course – but I'm just saying.'

'And yet you think I should encourage Bob?' Alice felt a bit annoyed with her friend.

'It's different for you, Alice.'

'Why?' she demanded, cross because Michelle was interfering, though in her heart she knew her friend was right. Jack was no good for her, but however many times she told herself that, she still liked him.

'Because I'm a nurse and if I dedicate myself to my job I could become a Sister and in time I might even go higher. I think you want to get married one day, don't you?'

'But don't you want a family ever? You love kids.'

'And I spend my life looking after them,' Michelle said. 'Your job is all right, Alice, but unless you train as a nurse you'll never get any higher.'

'I'm not clever enough to be a nurse,' Alice said

gloomily. 'Sally is bright. She can do it if she tries, but I just want to get married one day and have my own kids.'

'There you are then,' Michelle said and laughed. 'That's the reason you should encourage Bob and give Jack Shaw the elbow. He won't give you a home and a family – though he might give you a child if you're not careful.'

'Michelle! I wouldn't,' Alice said indignantly, but the trouble was, she knew her friend spoke the truth. At first it had been easy to send Jack off with a flea in his ear, but she was finding it harder to resist his charm and his good looks. The last time she'd seen him, Jack had been wearing a smart suit and good leather shoes. He looked so handsome and his smile made her heart race, but her father was right: no one else had clothes like that round here and they certainly didn't have a motor car. He was waiting for her most nights when she left work and he seemed to know which shift she was on.

He'd been pestering her to let him take her somewhere nice and he'd given her a present. Lying on the black velvet inside a jeweller's box was an engraved silver locket on a lovely thick chain; it opened so that she could put either a picture or a lock of hair inside. Jack had grinned at her as she exclaimed, because no one had ever given Alice anything of value before.

'You can put a lock of me hair inside, Alice, then you'll always have me with you wherever you go.'

'I don't want that, Jack – and I can't accept this from you. I'm not your girl and I never will be.'

Jack had moved towards her, a hard, angry expression on his face. His eyes seemed a glacial blue and his mouth was set, the black shine of his slicked-down hair making his skin seem pale in the lamplight. He had the looks of a Hollywood film star and Alice couldn't understand for a moment what he saw in a girl like her. She'd never had a decent dress in her life and coming from work she must look a sight, in her overall and flat lace-up shoes. 'If you're not mine you ain't anyone's,' he growled and pulled her against him, his breath hot on her face as she trembled and waited for the kiss she knew was coming. The intensity of his gaze made her feel funny inside and she swayed towards him without wanting or meaning to. Once his lips met hers, Alice felt herself melting into his body, her heart thumping wildly as the hardness of his need pressed into her, making her very aware of how he felt about her. That look deepened as he muttered, 'You're not still thinking of that Army boy, Alice?'

'No, of course not, Jack. I just don't want to be your girl.'

'Why?' he demanded furiously. 'I've got money. I'll give you a good life – a better life than your ma ever had. I might even marry you if you behave yourself.'

Alice gasped, because he was tempting her even though she knew she would be a fool to trust him.

There was nothing special about Alice, at least in her own mind. She longed to be slender like some of the glamorous women she'd seen only on the posters outside the cinema, to have long hair that waved down her back, but hers was collar-length and, although it had a natural curl and was fine and fluffy, it wasn't special. Knowing she was plumper than she wanted to be, Alice couldn't imagine why she seemed to inspire passion in Jack. Maybe if she had beautiful clothes and wore expensive makeup she would look all right, but she only used them occasionally, when Michelle lent her some nail polish and lipstick. Besides, Ma would knock her to kingdom come if she'd seen her at that dance.

'I can't marry you, Jack. You do things . . . bad things. I won't go out with a man who works for . . .' She couldn't even bring herself to say the name, because everyone in the East End knew of them and feared them.

'Butcher Lee?' Jack scowled at her. 'You shouldn't believe half of what folks say, Alice. He ain't that bad – and all I do is stand around and look fierce. We protect those that are loyal to us, Alice – and no one interferes with anyone the Butcher looks after.'

Alice suspected he was lying to her, making it sound less than it was. She'd heard all sorts of things about the man he worked for and none of them were good. People said Jack's boss ran a shady gambling club called The Glitter Ball and

237

sold the services of fallen women for money. It all sounded sleazy and unpleasant to Alice and she didn't want to believe it, but why would her father lie? And if he was right, Butcher Lee and his gang were responsible for half the robberies in London – and Jack had to be a part of all that, didn't he? She moved away from him with a shake of her head.

'Dad says that club of his is just a front for gambling and prostitution. It's a wonder the police don't close it down.'

'It's a legitimate club,' Jack said. 'Your dad's got it all wrong, love. Butcher's got all sorts in his pocket, including a judge and some real top-notch nobs. They wouldn't come if there was anything illegal goin' on, now would they?'

'Well, you can do what you want, Jack, but I'm never going out with you while you work for that man. Give it up and find a proper job and I'll consider it.'

Jack glowered at her once more. 'No woman dictates to me, Alice.'

'Then stay away from me. I shan't change my mind – and take this with you.' In a fit of temper Alice had thrown the jeweller's box at him. He didn't attempt to catch it and it fell into the gutter.

She had walked away, fearing that he would come after her. She hadn't looked back but she was sure Jack wouldn't pick the box up. Perhaps he would leave her alone now.

Alice had hoped Jack would give up after the

incident over the locket. She'd looked in the gutter on her way to work, but of course the jeweller's box had gone. If Jack hadn't taken it someone else would.

When she returned from work that evening, Jack was leaning against the wall waiting for her in the same place. Again, he was wearing his posh suit and looked so handsome with his black hair and bold eyes that her heart jerked. She tried walking straight past, but he moved like lightning to prevent her, his hand catching her wrist.

'Wait until you hear what I've got to say,' he said urgently and something in his voice caught at Alice's heart. She lifted her head and saw that he was looking wretched, and for the first time it occurred to her that he might be telling the truth when he said he cared about her. 'Please, Alice.'

'I meant what I said, Jack. I don't want to spend my life waiting in fear for a knock at the door and seeing a police constable standing there telling me my husband's dead or locked up in the cells.'

'You don't understand what it means, Alice. Once Butcher gets his claws into you, you're his for life – unless you go right away from London. He's a devil, Alice. He'd as soon slit your throat as look at you. Everyone is afraid of him when he gets into one of his rages, though he could sweet-talk a bird from the trees when he wants. You don't know what you're gettin' into until it's too late. If I broke with him we'd have to leave London fast and we couldn't come back, because he would kill me for certain – but it's what he might do to you . . .' His voice broke and she saw pleading in his eyes. 'I do love you, Alice, I really do.'

'Jack . . .' Her stomach cramped and she knew her will to resist was crumbling. 'I wouldn't mind leaving London if . . .' Her voice died away as his eyes gleamed and she knew she'd betrayed herself. 'All right, I'll admit I like you. If you'd been an ordinary bloke I might . . .'

Before she could finish Jack had her in his arms. His kiss was so tender and sweet that she nearly swooned and just let herself relax into his body, feeling the strength and the life pulsing through him. It was so good there that somehow she couldn't fight him any more.

'I don't understand why you care so much?' she whispered, knowing that her heart was no longer her own. 'I'm just ordinary . . . plain and plump . . .'

He put a finger to her lips, hushing her. 'No, you're not. You're warm and lovely and sexy. And I want you – that's all you need to know. I'm goin' places one day, and if you're my girl I'll look after you.'

'Oh, Jack.' Alice gave a little sob. 'I've told you what I think of you working for . . . him. I can't change me mind, because I know one of these days you'll end up dead in the gutter.'

'And you'd care if I did?'

''Course I would!'

Jack laughed triumphantly. 'I knew I'd get you

in the end, Alice. I'll take you to a dance this Saturday. You love dancing, don't you? We'll go to a club I know up West and we'll have supper and dance for as long as you like.'

'Jack . . .' Alice began, but Jack had hold of her and he wasn't going to let go.

'I'll change for you, Alice,' he told her, his eyes gleaming with a possessive hunger as he gazed down at her. 'I'll take you away, somewhere they won't find us – to America.'

Alice gasped in dismay. 'America? Do you really mean it?'

'The further we go the safer we'll be,' Jack said, his expression unreadable. 'It's goin' to take a bit of time to get free. I can't just say thanks for the memory and walk away from things, Alice – but I promise I'll do it if you'll be my girl and come out with me. Just be a good girl and don't go causing me trouble.'

Alice hesitated, not sure that his promises rang true, but it was too late to say no. He knew she liked him . . . more than was good for her if the truth were known. Jack was like a terrier. Once he had hold of his quarry he never let go.

'Will it be dangerous for you to leave them?'

'It would be if the gang knew what I had in mind. What I know about Butcher and the rest of them would get them in a lot of trouble. I've got a mate, Arthur, and he's terrified of Big Harry; he's Butcher's bodyguard and Arthur says he'd stick a knife in you as soon as look at you. We've got a few ideas, Arthur and me,' Jack went on. 'I need to get my life sorted, sell a few things and put the money somewhere safe until I can get our passage booked. If I'm careful, they won't even know I'm leaving until we're on the ship and out of reach.'

Alice felt a chill at her nape, and she clutched his arm. What was she doing agreeing to any of this? The more she heard about the men he ran with the less she liked it. Her father was right, they were bad, dangerous men and she was a fool to let herself be drawn into his net – and yet she loved him. No one else had ever made her feel like this, as if her insides turned to liquid honey and set her whole body alight with feverish heat. She held on to him, suddenly very afraid.

'Be careful, Jack. Please . . .'

'Don't you worry about me,' Jack said and kissed her again. 'I can do anythin' I set me mind to, you just watch me and see.'

CHAPTER 19

'I ought to get home now,' Sally said. They'd just left the floor after waltzing to the music of the crooner Bing Crosby, and she'd noticed again how good Keith was at old-time dancing. He didn't like the modern American-style jiving that had become a craze during the war and Sally wasn't keen on swing either. At the local Pally they mixed both kinds of dancing but Keith always sat the fast ones out. 'I have to get up early and Mum will worry if I'm late home.'

'All right,' he said and smiled, then, 'Listen, I like this; it's Glenn Miller's "In the Mood". Why don't we just have a drink and listen to the music?'

'You listen while I get my coat, Keith.'

Sally walked away from him, feeling she'd had enough of the evening and regretting she'd agreed to come with him on her own. Keith had used every opportunity to show her that he wanted more than mere friendship and she'd had difficulty in maintaining her normal friendly manner.

Sally wasn't sure why she'd suddenly realised that she didn't want her casual friendship with the young plumber to develop further, but it might have had something to do with the fact that she liked Mr Markham more and more each time they met. So far it was just a few words and a smile as they passed in the corridor, though he often came into her morning classes and watched her, before reading to the children himself.

Of course, she was probably reading too much into the smiles and words of encouragement he offered, but she couldn't help being attracted to him, and it had made up her mind where Keith was concerned. She must not encourage him to think of her as his girlfriend.

The ladies cloakroom smelled of lily of the valley and Evening in Paris scent and two girls Sally knew slightly were primping their tightly waved hair in front of the mirror. They both wore cheap copies of the New Look dresses that Christian Dior had brought in earlier that year, but neither of them was wearing stockings. Like Sally, they had to make do with gravy browning or go without; nylons were fabulous, much better than the silk stockings they'd had before the war, but they disappeared out of the shops so fast it was almost impossible to buy a pair, and if you were daft enough to buy from the spivs who hung about on street corners and sold them out of suitcases, when you opened the packet they had all kinds of faults in them.

Keith was waiting for her when she emerged from the cloakroom. He was frowning, clearly annoyed that she'd insisted on going home before he was ready to leave. It was chilly as they left the over-warm dance hall and Sally shivered. He turned his head to look at her.

'Are you cold?'

'Not really. It was very warm inside there.'

'Come here, and I'll put my arm about you, keep you warm.' The suggestion in his tone and the smile on his lips made Sally frown and take a step away from him.

'I'm not ready for anything more than having fun,' she told him, deciding that she had to get this thing sorted. 'I like going out with you but I want to do my training and it will be at least three years until I'm a fully qualified state registered nurse, and even then I shall want to work for a while . . .'

'Doesn't stop us gettin' married, does it?'

'I'm not ready, Keith . . .'

'I can wait if I have to.'

Sally caught the smell of frying and wanted to change the subject. 'Oh, that smells good. I'm hungry. Shall we get a packet of chips?'

'Good idea.' Keith grabbed her hand and they ran across the road together. He stopped outside the door and looked in through the steamy glass. 'Isn't that your Mr Markham? I saw him leaving St Saviour's when I came round to fix a toilet last week; someone spoke to him. I remembered you sayin' he was a top surgeon or something. What is he doing in a fish and chip shop here?'

Sally looked and laughed. 'He's buying a bag of

chips just like us,' she said. 'Did you think he was one of the gods and lived on nectar and honey?'

'Cheeky monkey!' Keith retorted.

'Hello, sir,' Sally said as Mr Markham emerged from the shop with a packet of chips in his hand. 'What are you doing here?'

'I've just finished an operation that took hours longer than we expected and I was hungry. I like to walk for a while after I've been working intensely and I smelled these . . . so here I am. Try one of my chips, Sally.' He offered the paper. 'I've put plenty of salt and vinegar on.'

'That's kind of you, sir.' Sally took a chip and smiled, as she tasted it. 'Oh, yes, that is nice. I shall want a big bag of these, Keith.'

'I'll go in and get them.'

'You're out late?' Mr Markham said, showing no desire to move on. 'Been somewhere nice?' His eyes went over her, taking in the pretty dress and seeming to approve. 'You look lovely . . .'

'Thank you.' She blushed. 'We went to the Pally, but it was very hot and I fancied some fresh air so we're walking home.'

'You look as if it suits you, Sally; your cheeks are nice and pink, like delicate roses . . .' There was a teasing look in his eyes. 'I don't think I've ever seen you in anything but the overall you use for work.'

'No . . .' She felt a little breathless, and yet she was more alive than she'd ever been, her whole body jinglingly aware of him. She wished that she'd been alone and that she could spend time with him . . . that he was the one walking her home.

'I suppose I'd better go,' he said but she heard the reluctance in his voice and his eyes seemed to speak to hers, making her heart race. 'You'll want to get back to your boyfriend.'

'We're just friends,' she said quickly and then felt embarrassed. 'I'm going to train as a nurse once I've finished my course at night school . . .'

Sally saw the smile in his eyes, but he just nodded and walked away as Keith emerged from the shop with the packets of chips.

She watched as the surgeon headed off down the street eating his fish and chips, only turning as Keith came up to her.

'Has he gone?' Keith asked. 'What did he want, talking to you all that time?' There was a note of jealousy in his voice. 'He's not your sort, Sally. You want to be careful of men like him. They only want one thing from a girl of your class.'

'What do you mean by that? I'm as good as anyone!'

'Yes, of course you are. I didn't mean anything – only be careful of him.'

'Shall we eat these as we walk to the next tram stop?' Sally bit into one of her chips. Keith was right in a way, she had seen the interest in Mr Markham's eyes, but a man like him wouldn't be serious about a girl like her, would he? She suspected Keith might be right, but that didn't give him the right to speak to her like that, did it?

Her family might be hard up at times but they were decent.

'I'm sorry, Sally, don't be angry with me,' Keith said, looking regretful. 'I was wondering if you'd like to go and see *Annie Get Your Gun* at the theatre one night. It's a musical and all the reviews say it's good.'

'Well . . .' Sally hesitated; she wasn't keen on going out with him alone, but the offer was tempting. 'Yes, why not? I don't think I've been to a musical before but it sounds nice. As long as you remember it's just friends, Keith.'

'If you like,' Keith said but looked sulky again. 'What about if I call for you on Monday night?'

'Yes, thanks. I'd like that,' she agreed. It was nice to be asked somewhere special Yet she was already wondering if it was a good idea. Perhaps she ought to have just said no, because in her heart she knew that Keith wasn't the one for her and perhaps letting him take her out wasn't really fair on him . . .

Sally noticed the atmosphere as soon as she entered the kitchen. It felt warm after the chill of the evening air and smelled of wood smoke. A pile of ironing, ready to go up to the airing cupboard, was laid on the shabby old sofa. Mum talked vaguely of getting a new one but so far there wasn't anything in the shops and she didn't want second-hand this time. They'd all had enough of make do and mend these past few years. Her father's working boots had been set by the fire to dry out and they had the radio on. By the sound of it they were listening to Henry Hall's big band dance music, and she knew they would have had 'In Town Tonight' on earlier, because they always did on a Saturday. Her mother and father were sitting at the table over a cup of tea from a large brown pot, slices of fruitcake in front of them, but neither of them had touched it and they both looked worried.

'Is Bren all right?' Sally asked, because it was the first thing that came into her head.

'Yes. She is upstairs in bed,' Mrs Rush sighed. 'It's your father – he's just been told that he's been put onto a two-day week.'

'Only two days now?' Sally stared at her in dismay. 'That's rotten luck, Dad. What reason did they give you?'

'It's just a shortage of work, that's all. They keep telling us that it will only be for a short time, but unless more work comes soon I can see them closing down altogether.'

'And then what shall we do?' Sally's mother asked. 'You can't give me any more and neither can Brenda. I've looked for work. I'll take anything . . . but a few hours scrubbing office toilets is all I can find.'

'And you are not doing that,' her husband said sharply. 'I mean it, Millie. I'm going to start to look for another job tomorrow. If anyone has to scrub toilets it will be me, not you. I'm telling you so listen to me for once. I won't have my wife demeaning herself like that.'

'Listen to Dad,' Sally urged. 'I can give you a little bit more if I don't save for a while . . .'

'That's your money for nursing college,' her mother objected. 'It's your dream, Sally. I can't bear that you should give up everything. You've worked so hard through night school as well as your job. It wouldn't be fair.'

'I agree with your ma,' Mr Rush said. 'Keep your savings, girl. I'll find something to take the place of the wages I've lost. I worked for Bill Saunders through the war, because he applied for and got exemption for his workers. I wouldn't have been much good in the Army anyway, bit too old the second time round, and I did my bit in the first one. Bill will see me right as soon as he's got the work. We're not desperate yet.'

'No, and I want to help,' insisted her mother.

'Not scrubbing toilets for other people. You have enough to do here.'

'Dad is right,' Sally agreed. 'You work hard here, Mum. We'll manage somehow. I don't mind waiting another year to apply for college. Dad is sure to find something before then . . .' Her heart bled for him, because he was a proud man and she knew that it must hurt him because he couldn't keep his family as he always had.

Sally was feeling tired when she went into work on Monday morning. She hadn't slept very much, because her mind kept going round and round in circles, but she couldn't find a solution to her family's problems. If they were to keep paying their rent and live, one of them had to make sacrifices, and Sally had quite a few pounds saved for nursing college. If she had to she would give it to her mother to pay their rent for a few weeks.

However, Sally soon forgot her own problems as she got into the routine of looking after the children. Many of them were perfectly healthy, very resilient despite the traumas they had endured, and acted like normal kids, running in the playground and yelling at the tops of their voices. She gathered them up after breakfast, and first washed hands and faces to get rid of strawberry jam, then took them into their own schoolroom.

This was a large, sunny room at the back of the house and looked out into the small garden and the playground. Bookcases lined the walls and there were two long tables, at which the children sat to draw or do simple sums. In one corner of the room was a rush mat next to a cupboard where the toys were placed. Sally was most often the carer who looked after the children during the day and she had established a routine. First of all they had to do simple lessons, like adding up or forming their letters, and then they had a break for a glass of milk and a plain biscuit. Afterwards, they went out into the garden for half an hour to play games. Only when they returned were they allowed to play with the dolls, building bricks, wooden train set and the wonderful Noah's ark that someone had donated to the home.

Several children tried to make a beeline for the toys as soon as they came in, but Sally was firm with them, making them sit down and do their drawings or, if they had started to write, to form their letters. One little girl was only three so Sally normally sat and showed her picture books, teaching her what the letters spelled by showing her the pictures of a cat and various other animals.

Valerie liked the reading but she also liked scribbling with crayons, and this morning Sally allowed her to have her way, giving her a large sheet of paper and the box of wax crayons. She was walking round, watching over the children's shoulders to see what they were drawing, when the door opened and Mary Ellen walked in, followed by Billy Baggins.

'Sorry I'm late, miss,' Mary Ellen said. 'Nan asked me to help her find Lizzie. She'd locked herself in the toilets and couldn't get out, so I crawled underneath the door and opened it for her. Lizzie was cryin', 'cos she said they were going to stick needles in her, and she wouldn't come out for Nan, but I got her to in the end. And I don't have school because I've still got a bit of a cold.'

Sally nodded, then, 'Why aren't you at school, Billy?'

'I've got the morning off,' he replied innocently. 'It's football practice and I'm no good at football so they told me to stop home today.'

'Billy, you love football,' Sally said. 'Now tell me the truth. Why haven't you gone to school?'

Billy hung his head and kicked the ground. 'It's a spellin' test, miss. I can't do spellin' and Mr Saunders will whack me round the legs if I get them wrong again.' He pulled a dirty-looking piece of paper from his pocket. 'I was supposed to learn them words and I forgot.'

'Let's have a look,' Sally said and took the paper from him. 'You haven't tried to learn them, have you?'

'No, miss.'

'Look, I'll chalk them on the board for you, and you and Mary Ellen can copy them down over and over again. Do it together and speak them aloud and then they will stay in your head.'

'I know what they are,' Mary Ellen said. 'I'll help you learn them, Billy. Why didn't you tell me before?'

'All right then,' he agreed.

Sally went to the board and chalked up the list. She was looking at it as she said, 'Anyone who knows how to form the letters can copy these down if they like and then we'll say them together.'

'I know the first one.' A voice spoke from the back of the room, and Sally spun round, staring in disbelief as she saw who was standing there. 'It's horse, isn't it, miss?'

The children tittered with laughter as Mr Markham sat down on one of their chairs and drew a piece of paper to him on the table. Two of the little ones gravitated to his side, leaning against him as he began to write.

'The first letter is an aitch,' he said. 'And the second is O – round like an orange. Does anyone know what the third is?'

A chorus of voices told him it was an r and then the class started chanting the letters as Sally chalked them on the board, and Mary Ellen and Billy wrote them down studiously.

'Horse, cat, house, donkey . . . that's a big word, miss,' Mr Markham said and the children went into ripples of laughter again.

He continued until everyone was chanting the words, even Billy and Mary Ellen joining in, and then asked if anyone would like to hear a story. All the children shouted out that they did and Sally sat down, listening as he began to tell them one of his stories about monsters and giants who ate children, and of the brave animals who rescued them.

No one wanted to stop for the milk break and they all groaned when Mr Markham announced he had to leave now, begging him to tell them another story.

'Well, I shall have to love you and leave you . . . for now,' he said, winking at Sally. Her heart jumped and she felt the breath catch in her throat as her gaze dropped from those wicked eyes. 'I shall be here on Saturday – and that's a promise.' He kissed the tips of his fingers towards her and then the room in general, producing a few more giggles amongst the children.

Something in his manner at that moment made Sally look at him and she felt that the kiss was just for her, that there was more in his words than he could say in front of the children.

'I shall look forward to it,' Sally said, lifting her eyes to his suddenly. Her mouth felt dry as she saw the look in his and knew that she was right; he did like her a lot! Heart racing, she gave him a shy smile. 'Thank you for helping us. Children, say thank you to Mr Markham.'

'Thank you, Mr Markham,' they chanted as he left the room.

He smiled again at Sally from the doorway, and her pulse raced as she met what seemed to her an intimate look, promising much more than mere liking. She felt tingly all over, butterflies fluttering in her stomach, but then she realised she was being foolish. Mr Markham probably smiled at all the pretty girls like that and she was an idiot.

'Time for milk and then we'll play games outside,' Sally said, making herself think straight. 'Billy, I think you should go to school now, please. Tell your teacher you had to stop to help out here and perhaps he won't cane you.'

'All right. I think I can remember most of them words now, miss.' He touched Mary Ellen on the arm and went out.

'Billy's all right really, miss,' Mary Ellen said after he'd gone. 'I'm starting back at school next week, so I'll make sure he goes in future.'

'Yes, he really should,' Sally said. 'Now do you

want to help me give the milk out? And then we'll go outside for some air . . . and after that you can all play with the toys . . .' Sally was still in a pleasant dream that consisted of Mr Markham taking her in his arms and kissing her, but she was rudely interrupted by one of the children pointing and giggling.

'Miss has gone all soppy over her boyfriend.'

'Don't be silly, David,' Sally said and laughed. What an idiot she was for engaging in daydreams over a man who probably had half the women at his hospital drooling over him!

Sally was thoughtful as she walked home late that afternoon. She had really enjoyed her day. The little incident with Mr Markham had had her floating on air for most of the morning, and the afternoon had been spent taking most of the children on a trip to an exhibition of mechanical toys that had just opened, a kind of toy fair, with exhibits from the past and new ideas for the future. Angela had arranged it and she'd asked Sally and Nan to help her manage the children.

There had been a stall outside selling hot roasted chestnuts and Angela had bought all the children a small bag to eat. Then they'd crowded onto the tram and gone back to St Saviour's for tea. When the older children came back from school some of them had sulked when they learned what they'd missed, so Angela said she would take them on Saturday afternoon and asked Sally if she would come too. It was Sally's half day, but she'd agreed, because she liked Angela a lot and knew she couldn't manage alone, and Nan had other duties that day. There would be just the two of them, but the older children didn't take so much looking after as the young ones.

Sally thought that her job at St Saviour's was all right really. Perhaps it wouldn't matter if she never managed to put herself through nursing school, because one day she would want to get married – wouldn't she?

Sally had never really thought about this, because she hadn't met anyone she would want to spend the rest of her life with – not in that way. Keith was nice as a friend, but she wanted something different when she married – someone good with children. Someone like Mr Markham, whose smile could make her melt inside like warm chocolate. No, that was daft! She was a fool even to imagine it . . .

Lost in her thoughts she didn't realise what was going on ahead of her until she heard the screeching of brakes. Suddenly, a lorry skidded across the road trying to avoid hitting an old lady . . . and crashed into a young lad on a delivery bike. Giving a cry of alarm, Sally rushed to the lad who had been knocked off his bike and was lying in the road. His face had blood on it and his eyes were closed, as if the blow had rendered him uncon-scious. She knelt by his side, bending over him to smooth his hair back from his face and comfort him, wishing that she knew more about nursing.

She was sure he ought not to be moved until a doctor had seen him and said as much to a man who wanted to get him out of the road because of the traffic.

'Let me through there. I'm a doctor . . .'

Sally looked up as she heard a voice she knew. She felt the relief wash over her as she spotted Mr Markham and saw his quick nod of recognition as he knelt beside her and began to examine his patient. She saw how efficient and gentle he was, his calm air of assurance settling the frightened boy. He looked so vital, so handsome and clever and in control that she was filled with admiration; at St Saviour's he was funny and friendly, always teasing the children, but here he was the cool, efficient doctor and she suddenly realised that he was the sort of man she wanted in her life.

'That's it, old chap,' he said as the lad gave a little moan. 'Let's have a look at you – make sure nothing is broken.'

'It hurts . . .' the lad said. 'My leg . . .'

'Ah yes, I can see.' Mr Markham ran his hands over the lad's leg. 'Yes, I can see you have done a bit of damage here. I think we shall have to get you to hospital . . . steady, let's see if you've done any damage anywhere else.' He carefully moved the lad's head and nodded at Sally. 'No real damage to the head or neck, that's good, but we'll give him an X-ray and make certain.' He turned and looked at a police constable who had been speaking to the lorry driver and now came up to them. 'We need an ambulance please, Constable. Can you phone St Andrew's clinic and tell them Mr Markham asked for an emergency ambulance and to prepare theatre for the patient I am bringing in, please?'

'Yes, sir. I'll see to it right away, sir – and I'll get rid of this crowd.'

Mr Markham turned to Sally, who was holding the lad's hand and talking to him. 'What is worrying him?'

'He's bothered about his bike, because it belongs to the shop he works for and he's afraid he'll be in trouble for damaging it.'

'Don't worry about that, lad. Miss Rush will take it back for you and explain – won't you?' Sally agreed and the doctor smiled his approval. 'There you are, nothing to worry about. Now can you tell me your name and where you live so we can inform your family where you are?'

'Jimmy Noakes of Brick Lane, sir. I work for the butcher's shop in . . .' He swooned before he could name the street and Mr Markham looked at Sally. 'Just as well. I wish I had my bag with me, but I didn't bring the car. I hope that damned ambulance isn't long. Do you think you can return the boy's bike for him?'

'It has the name of the shop printed on it,' Sally said. 'I'll go as soon as you've got him in the ambulance.'

'I hope you didn't have anything special planned this evening? Not going out with that boyfriend of yours?' He arched his brows teasingly. 'No hot date planned?'

'Keith is just a good friend. We're not courting. I only see him now and then,' she said and flushed, then remembered that Keith was taking her to the musical that night. Taking the boy's bike to the butcher's shop would make her late, but she couldn't go back on her word now.

'That's all right then. Ah, I think I can hear the siren. We shall be on our way in no time at all.'

Sally nodded, but didn't reply. Knowing that without his help she would have been lost, she realised more than ever how much she wanted to do her nursing course. Sometimes saving life could be a matter of acting quickly and with resolution. Mr Markham hadn't done very much, but he had made sure that the lad had no injuries to his spine or neck, and that could make all the difference because well-meaning people might have moved him and done irreparable damage. At least she'd been able to keep them at bay until he arrived, but how she wished that she had even a half of his skill . . .

Sally tried to gather her thoughts as she hurried through the dark streets to return the delivery boy's bike. She was getting quite a crush on Mr Markham and she really ought to stop now, while she could.

Keith was just about to leave when she arrived home, and she knew at once he wasn't pleased because she was late. The butcher had been so grateful to her for returning the bike and wanted to know all the details, and then his wife came in from the back and insisted on giving Sally a cup of tea. After she'd finally got away, Sally had run all the way but she was nearly an hour late and she could see by Keith's face that he was furious with her for letting him down.

'Where the hell do you think you've been?' he asked as they stood on the pavement outside her home. 'We'll have missed the first half now and we shan't know what's going on. It's hardly worth going at all . . .'

'I'm sorry, but I couldn't help it,' Sally said. 'There was an accident with a boy on a bike. He was knocked off and his leg was injured and . . .'

'What has that to do with you? You're not a bleedin' nurse,' he said and glared at her.

'Not yet,' Sally replied, her face white. 'But I am a caring human being and naturally I stopped to help. Not that I could have done anything much – but Mr Markham stopped too and he was wonderful. The way he took control and calmed the child and then he ordered an ambulance and went to the hospital with him . . .'

'So that's the way of it.' Keith's look of jealous dislike shocked Sally. 'You'd rather be with that bloody toff.'

'I shan't put up with language like that,' Sally said. 'Please go now, Keith. I don't want to go to that show with you – and I think you should be ashamed of . . .'

He moved towards her threateningly, and Sally flinched, thinking he might be going to hit her, but then the front door opened and her brother came out with his girlfriend. Keith looked at them, back at Sally, and then stormed off.

'What's wrong with him?' Madge asked.

'I stood him up because there was an accident to a young lad,' Sally said. 'Well, that shows what kind of a man he is, doesn't it?'

'Stay clear of him, love,' her brother advised and kissed her cheeks. 'Madge and me are on our way to the flicks – want to come?'

'No thanks, I'll find something to do,' Sally said and laughed. 'I don't want to be a gooseberry.'

She went into the kitchen. Her mother was washing the dishes and looked up with a lift of her brows.

'Did you see Keith? He's been here nearly an hour.'

'Yes, I know.' Sally explained why she was late. 'I had to take the bike back, Mum. It might have got stolen – and they were so pleased.'

'Yes, I expect so. It's a pity your evening was spoiled, though.'

'I don't mind. I'm not sure I want to go out with Keith again anyway.'

Sally went to change into a dress, thinking she might pop next door for a while and visit a friend, unless Brenda wanted to go out for a coffee. Just as she finished her hair, she heard a knock at the door and voices. Then her mother called her name and she went into the kitchen to see they had a visitor – one that made her heart race wildly.

Mr Markham's smile made her heart jump for joy and she looked at him uncertainly, waiting for him to speak.

'I thought I would just let you know the boy is comfortable,' he said.

'Oh, good, I am glad. They were so pleased that I took the bike back.'

'Yes . . .' He looked at Sally's mother. 'I'm sorry if your evening was ruined.'

'It doesn't matter. I'll find something to do.'

'Why don't I take you for a drink?' he said. 'If you've nothing better to do?'

'Yes, I'd like that,' she replied quickly, ignoring her mother's frown. 'I'll just get ready . . .'

Sally felt as if she were walking on air as she hurried to get her best jacket. She'd missed going to that musical but now she was going some-where far better with a man she really liked and admired. She couldn't help smiling as she rushed back and found him talking to her mother about the accident.

'Don't be late,' her mother said sharply.

'I shan't,' Sally replied, and looked regretfully at her companion as they went out. 'I'm really looking forward to this . . . you can tell me all about your books and how you started to write them.'

'That will take five minutes,' he said and smiled at her in a way that made her heart race. 'I would rather talk about you, Sally. You can tell me about your ambition to be a nurse . . .'

CHAPTER 20

Alice came off duty that Friday night to find Bob waiting for her outside St Saviour's. He was wearing his Army uniform and smiled at her, then held out a bunch of flowers, looking a bit shy as if he felt daft for bringing them. His smile lifted her spirits, because she was dreading going home. Her parents had been at it hammer and tongs the previous night, yelling and screaming so much that the next-door neighbour had banged on the wall and told them to leave off. It was getting so that she felt desperate enough to run off and find herself somewhere else to live, but she knew she couldn't afford it on her wages. She longed for an escape, somewhere exciting and new where people lived better lives than they did round here.

She took Bob's flowers with a smile, though she had no idea what to do with them, but it was lovely of him to buy them for her. However, she felt awkward because she'd started going with Jack and she hadn't meant to keep Bob on a string.

'They're lovely, Bob,' she said and sniffed at the

chrysanthemums. 'You shouldn't have spent your money on me.' She hesitated. 'You didn't get my last letter, then?'

'Letter? No, I've been away on a course and I've got another coming up soon. I'll be a highly skilled man one day, Alice. I might go into business myself when I leave the Army.'

'What do you do exactly?'

'I don't talk about it much, but I've been learning to protect people.'

'Oh . . .' Alice hadn't expected that answer and wished she hadn't asked. She looked round warily. Jack normally waited for her much closer to her home, but she didn't want to be seen with Bob, because Jack would be angry if he heard she'd been seeing his rival. She handed him back the flowers.

'I'm sorry. I can't take these, Bob. It wouldn't be right. I wrote to tell you I couldn't see you again. I'm with someone else now.'

She was shocked by the look of disappointment she saw in Bob's eyes. He must think a lot more of her than she'd imagined and for a moment she felt a sense of guilt but then it was gone, because Jack would be waiting for her. She would talk with him in the shadows for a while and he would kiss her, and then they would plan their future in America. Jack was full of plans. He was going to open his own club in New York and make their fortune. If only she could believe that, because she was desperate to get away from the home she'd begun to hate. When she was with him it all seemed possible and yet when she was alone the doubts crept in.

Sometimes, Alice wondered if Jack's dreams of getting rich in America would work, because she couldn't see it all going as smoothly as he seemed to imagine, but perhaps he would find himself a job in a club and settle for second best. She knew he looked smart when he dressed in his good suits and wore shoes you could see your face in, and she believed that he could find himself a decent job somewhere – even if it was as a car salesman. He would be good at that, she thought, clutching at straws. Yes, he could find a job in America and they would have a nice house and a car . . . and the future he'd promised was so enticing that she tried to believe it would happen, though the sane, sensible side of her kept telling her it was all a pipe dream.

'It's that flash wide-boy I've seen you with,' Bob said after a moment or two of silence. 'You're making a mistake if it's him, Alice. Perhaps I'm too dull for you – but he's bad news. If you get mixed up with him, you'll be sorry.'

'You don't know him,' Alice said sharply, feeling cross, because what right did he have to criticise Jack? 'Besides, he's going to change . . .' She was about to say they were going away together when she remembered that it had to be a secret until Jack was ready to leave.

'A leopard never loses its spots,' Bob said. 'Keep

your flowers, Alice. I wouldn't know what else to do with them – but I shan't bother you again.'

Alice took the flowers back and stood watching as Bob walked away. She didn't know what to do with them either, because Ma didn't have a vase to put them in and they wouldn't fit into a milk bottle. She hesitated, then went back inside St Saviour's and thrust them at the first person she saw, which happened to be Angela.

'Would you like these?'

Angela looked surprised. 'They are lovely. Why don't you want them?'

'Someone gave them to me, but we don't have anywhere to put them,' Alice said ruefully. She couldn't tell Angela she didn't want Jack to see her carrying them. 'Take them if you like. I shall leave them here otherwise.'

'Yes, I will have them, thank you,' Angela said. 'I've been meaning to ask you if you would like to come to the pictures with Sally and me one night. Make it an all-girl night? I'll ask Michelle too.'

'Thanks. Yes, please,' Alice said. 'I don't know when though. I'm going to a dance tomorrow. My . . . boyfriend is taking me somewhere nice.'

'Oh, well, have a good time. We'll arrange it when you can all come.'

They left St Saviour's together and Angela walked off down the street. Alice resumed her journey home. When she reached the spot where Jack usually waited, she saw that he wasn't there and looked about thinking that he would pop out suddenly. She didn't think she was late and she felt slightly uneasy, because it wasn't like Jack to miss meeting her from work.

After waiting for some minutes, Alice went home. She was only working in the morning tomorrow and she hoped she would see Jack on her return, because otherwise she wouldn't know where to meet him that night.

She was sorry that she'd had to let Bob down, because he'd looked disappointed – and hurt too. Alice felt guilty, which was daft, because she hadn't promised him more than friendship . . . yet she still felt upset. In her heart she knew she was a fool to throw him over for Jack Shaw, because Bob would make a good husband, and she did like him – but he just wasn't Jack.

At Saturday lunchtime Alice left work and walked straight home, rather than going to the market as she often did on her half day. She'd decided to save her money for America. Jack was going to pay for their tickets, but Alice would need whatever she could manage to put by to take with her. She didn't want to feel completely dependent on him . . . although a part of her still didn't quite believe that it was all going to happen. Things like that did not happen to girls like her. Her sister would tell her not to be daft and so would Michelle.

Jack was in his usual spot, leaning against the wall at the top of the lane. As she came up to him, she saw the dark bruise on his cheek and around his left eye.

'Jack, what happened to you?' she cried, her heart thumping. 'Have you been in a fight?'

'It looks worse than it is,' Jack said defensively. 'There was a bit of trouble at the club last night and I had to throw the culprits out – they didn't want to go, but I won in the end. It's usually Big Harry's job, but he's in the hospital . . . got knocked down by a car they say, though I reckon it was more than that . . .' Jack saw her face and laughed, then winced. 'Don't look like that, Alice. I don't normally get involved in fights. I'm Mr Nice Guy, believe me.'

She almost believed him, because she wanted to believe he was better than everyone said.

'Your face must hurt?'

'You should see the other bloke's,' Jack said and grinned.

'It wasn't to do with . . . anything you're planning?'

'Nah, 'course not. They trust me, especially after last night. Someone tried to knife Butcher and I saved his life. I'm their blue-eyed boy at the moment, luv. Don't worry, Alice. I'll be careful. I've got everything to live for now – haven't I?'

'Yes . . .' Alice shivered. 'Are we still going out tonight?'

''Course we are,' Jack said. 'I don't break my promises – not to you, Alice. Have you got something to wear?' He grinned as she hesitated and took some money from his jacket. 'Buy yourself a nice dress – from a shop, not the market.'

She stared at the money, far too much of it and more than she needed for a nice frock for dancing. 'I don't want all that, Jack. You'll need the money for the future.'

'Don't worry about money. I've got plenty put by. You don't think I've worked for the Butcher all this time without making it worth my while?'

Alice shuddered at the use of the thug's name, because although no one could prove it people said he was a murderer. She'd never met him; Jack hadn't taken her to the club and she didn't mix in the world the violent thug belonged in, but she'd heard whispers. People said he looked like a country gent, but there was a scar on his face and she knew that even Jack was afraid of him. 'Just give me two pounds, then,' she said. 'I can get a pretty dress for that – but you don't have to give me stuff, Jack. All I want is for you to keep your word.'

'Trust me,' he said and thrust all the notes into her hand. 'Keep it in case. You never know what may happen in the future, Alice.'

She stuffed the notes into her jacket pocket, trying not to think what he meant, though she knew in her heart. If Jack hadn't been strong and clever, he could have ended with a knife in his guts rather than a black eye.

He was living a dangerous life and Alice felt a sick knot of fear in her stomach, because now that she'd let herself care about him too much, it would hurt her if anything happened to him. She'd begun to love him in a way she'd never dreamed she could and to believe in the life he'd sworn they would have if she went away with him. If anything went wrong, she didn't think she could bear the disappointment. Jack had to keep his promise and take her away with him . . . he had to!

Alice bought herself a calf-length, pretty green voile dress with a satin petticoat underneath, and a sweetheart neckline. She wore it with a pair of black patent shoes she'd bought from the market a few weeks back; they were almost new, because whoever had owned them first hadn't worn them. She'd used up all her clothing coupons, but she wasn't likely to need them for anything else – and she wouldn't need them in future.

'And where do you think you're goin', madam?' her mother's voice asked when she came out of the bedroom she shared with her sister and brothers. 'I haven't seen that dress before.'

'I've been saving up and got it cheap in a sale,' Alice said.

'If you can afford things like that you can start giving me more money.'

'Leave the girl alone,' Alice's father said, surprising her by defending her. He usually cleared off to the pub when his wife started to nag, because he couldn't bear to listen. Alice despised him for turning to drink rather than standing up to his wife, but she pitied him too.

'She gives you what she can afford, why shouldn't she have pretty things sometimes? Where are you goin', luv?' Alice was surprised because her father had never stuck up for her like that before; she hadn't thought he cared about any of them, but it seemed he did a bit.

'To the dance with a friend,' Alice said and felt awful because she'd deceived her father, but if she told the truth both her mother and father would forbid her to go.

Giving him a quick kiss on the cheek, Alice left the house and walked quickly to meet Jack. He was waiting for her in the usual place, wearing the smartest suit she'd ever seen in her life, his car parked at the side of the path. Her heart raced as he grinned and opened the door for her to get in. The seats were leather and smelled lovely as she slid into the passenger seat. Alice had never expected to ride in a posh vehicle like this and she turned to him with a look of awe.

'This must have been expensive?'

'I bought it second-hand.' Jack shrugged and looked pleased with her comments. 'It's a Daimler but it ain't new. I ain't that rich yet, Alice, but I shall be when we get our own club in America.'

Alice nodded but didn't say what was in her mind. It would seem as if she doubted him if she asked what he would do if things didn't work out quite the way he thought. Alice knew very little about these things, but she'd seen American gangster films and she suspected things were much the same there as they were in London; the bullyboys would rule the clubs there and Jack would have to join them or give up all idea of one of his own.

It wasn't the sort of thing she could question him about when he was taking her out for the evening. Besides, she wanted him to break with the gang. It would be time enough to talk about the future when they were on the ship to America.

Although Alice couldn't believe it was ever going to happen, she'd gone too far to draw back now. Much as she loved Jack, she knew he would never let her go. It was best to just go along with what Jack said and hope that he would keep his word and break with the criminal world for good.

Alice woke up to hear Mavis still gently snoring beside her. She was back in her own bed and everything was normal, but no, it could never be normal again. She closed her eyes against the hot sting of tears as the memory of the previous night flooded back into her mind and she felt hot all over. She couldn't have been so stupid! She, Alice Cobb, had fallen for the oldest trick in the book.

The evening had started so well. Alice had been thrilled to find herself in a real nightclub in the West End. The lights were low and had a slightly pinkish glow as they took their seats at a secluded table in the corner. There were tiny lights on each table and everywhere smelled lovely, like perfume, Alice thought.

'This is wonderful,' she breathed as the waiter pulled out her chair and smiled. She'd noticed the way they'd been greeted with respect by the head waiter and he'd snapped his fingers for one of his underlings to show them to *Mr Shaw's* table. 'That man at the door knows you too, doesn't he? You've been here before.'

'Yes, he owes me a few favours. I got him the job here – and I look after them, make sure they don't get trouble from outsiders.'

'Do they pay protection money?'

'Best you don't ask questions like that. Just accept that I'm welcome here. I have connections . . .'

'Do you bring other girls here?'

'In the past,' Jack said, 'but none of them meant anything to me, Alice. You're the only girl I'll take anywhere in future.'

Jack had ordered champagne for a start, and then a white wine to have with their meal. 'I think you would find red too heavy,' he said. 'Besides, we shall be having the lobster bisque and the roast chicken and white is best with them.'

Alice was impressed with his knowledge. She'd never tasted champagne and at the first sip wasn't sure about the taste, but the bubbles went up her nose and made her giggle, and after her second glass she realised she liked it. In fact it was all rather special and exciting and she'd been carried away by the glamour of the evening.

'I could take to this,' she said and Jack chuckled.

'I knew you'd enjoy it,' he said, 'but take it easy,

275

luv. Have a glass of water and then it won't go to your head.'

'I've never had lobster bisque – what does that mean?'

'Soup made from lobsters and it's delicious,' he said. 'They make it well here. Just try it, Alice, I think you'll like it.'

Alice had liked it, even though she hadn't thought she would. In fact she'd loved everything about the evening. Jack had danced so well. Alice couldn't believe the way it made her feel when he took her in his arms and guided her expertly round the floor. It was so lovely to dance with someone who really knew what he was doing and she felt proud to be with a man of his sophistication. No one would know he was Jack Shaw from Thrawl Street, once one of the most disreputable places in London, who had gone to school with his backside hanging out of trousers that were too big for him and holes in his shoes.

Jack had made something of his life and he was going places – and he was taking Alice with him. She felt very grateful and happy as she drifted through the evening, drinking a sip of wine every now and then but not overdoing it.

Jack cared about her. He didn't want her to get drunk and make a fool of herself and so Alice followed his instructions to drink some water. Besides, she didn't need too much wine, because she felt as if she were floating on clouds.

When they went out into a cool evening, Alice

shivered and Jack took off his jacket and put it around her shoulders.

'You'll get cold,' she said and he smiled down at her.

'We'll be in the car in a minute, besides, you're my girl, Alice, and I want to take care of you.'

Alice let him tuck her into the car; he was careful to make sure her dress wouldn't get caught in the door and spoil. She felt like the luckiest girl in the world. Not many girls she knew were taken to posh nightclubs, nor did they go out in cars like this.

Alice was feeling a bit tired when they stopped. She glanced out of the window and realised they were in a place she didn't recognise. Jack leaned across and kissed her on the mouth.

'Feeling sleepy?' he asked softly. She nodded and he laughed. 'Thought so, luv. I've brought you to my place, Alice. I'll take you in and give you some coffee to sober you up before I take you home. Don't want your ma seein' you like this.'

Alice had gone with him, still feeling dreamy, only half-awake and trusting him. What a damned fool she'd been!

A little moan broke from her as she relived the way Jack had drawn her in and lulled her into a feeling of peace, while the coffee was brewing. He'd sat beside her on the large and very comfortable sofa and told her to put her head back and relax. Alice had done so, closing her eyes for a moment. When she woke Jack was lying on the sofa with her, kissing her with such tenderness and passion that she'd been swept away by the feelings this aroused.

'I love you, want you so much,' he'd whispered in her ear as his hand caressed first her cheek, then her throat and then her breasts. 'Let me love you, Alice. You know I'm going to look after you. We'll go to America and we'll be married . . .'

Alice hadn't been able to think clearly. His touch thrilled her, making her tremble with need and desire. When he opened the front of her dress and pulled down her petticoat to caress her breasts with the tip of his tongue she moaned with pleasure. His hand stole beneath her skirt, caressing her with a gentleness that sent thrills through her and she felt herself strain to meet him, her mouth opening beneath the assault of his tongue.

Vaguely, at the back of her mind, Alice knew she should not be letting Jack do this, but she wanted it. Her breath was coming in hot little pants and she found herself quivering, rising to meet him as he suddenly thrust into her. The shock of his entry stilled her and she cried out, begging him to stop. She'd been enjoying his caresses but she'd never dreamed he would go this far and it shocked her.

'Please don't,' she begged. 'I didn't want this to happen, Jack. Not until we're married.'

Jack ignored her protests, and she didn't fight him, because she couldn't. Her body was betraying her and she liked what was happening, even though it was wrong – it was so very wrong!

When it was over and Jack left her, Alice wept silently. She knew what her parents would think of what she'd done and she was ashamed. But it wasn't all Jack's fault, she'd gone into his arms eagerly and she'd liked him touching her.

'Don't cry, luv,' Jack said and wiped her tears away with his fingertips. 'It had to happen sometime and it won't hurt again, I promise.'

'I'm not crying because it hurt. I've shamed meself.'

'Why should you be shamed?' Jack asked a little huffily. 'You know you're me girl, Alice. We're going to get married. I'll get you a ring tomorrow. I shan't let you down, I promise.'

'Supposing something happens – you know.'

'It won't, not the first time,' Jack said confidently and stroked her cheek. 'Stop crying and I'll get you that coffee, Alice. You belong to me, you always will. I'll marry you as soon as I sort things out. I don't want anyone to know how important you are to me, so you'll have to keep your ring hidden. You can hang it on this chain under your dress.' He took the silver locket from his pocket and gave it to her, laughing as he saw her face. 'You didn't think I was goin' to let some down and out find your locket?'

'Oh, Jack,' Alice said, bending forward so that he could fasten it around her neck. She swallowed hard and smiled at him. There was no

279

point in making a fuss now, because she couldn't change things. 'I didn't want you to lose your respect for me.'

Jack shouted with laughter. 'If that's all you're worried about, Alice, you can stop frettin'. I've put me mark on you, luv, and that's an end to it. I've made sure you can't go runnin' off with that Army bloke.'

'Oh, Jack, as if I would when I've given you my word.'

'That's all right then,' Jack said. 'As soon as I've made plans, we'll get married but we can't before I've got the money together. I don't want to leave valuable stuff behind when we make the move. I just need a bit more time and then we'll be off to a new life in the States.'

'Just what are you up to, Jack?'

'The less you know the better,' he said and grinned confidently. 'Now, you're goin' to drink your coffee and then I'll take you home . . .'

Alice had been late getting back, but thankfully her parents were having one of their rows and didn't notice as she slipped into the bedroom. Mavis had been asleep and Alice thought she might have got away with it. She'd been a fool, but she would be careful it didn't happen again . . . until she'd got Jack's wedding ring on her finger.

'Where were you last night?' Mavis now murmured sleepily as she yawned and stretched. 'Ma will kill you if she finds out what time you came in.'

'She won't know if you don't tell her. I went up West with someone, that's all.'

'Not with Jack Shaw?'

Alice was silent and Mavis poked her in the ribs.

'Pa will kill you if he finds out. He says he's scum. You've haven't done anything daft, Alice?'

''Course not,' Alice lied. 'What do you take me for?'

'Just be careful,' Mavis said. 'I don't trust his sort. Whatever he says or promises, you would do well to keep him at bay. If you keep on seeing him, Alice Cobb, you'll land in trouble.'

'Stop nagging,' Alice said. 'I'm going to make a cup of tea. Do you want one?'

'If you like but I'm not gettin' up yet.'

'I'll bring it back,' Alice promised. She knew there was some blood on her underclothes and she wanted a chance to stick them in the copper to soak before her mother or Mavis saw them and guessed the truth.

She just had to cross her fingers and hope that she wasn't already in the kind of trouble her sister was warning her about.

CHAPTER 21

It was the day of Princess Elizabeth's wedding at last and the streets were filled with crowds wanting to get a glimpse of her as she went past in the royal State Coach, escorted by the Household Cavalry and dressed in a beautiful gown. Those close enough to see told their friends that it was made of ivory silk and embroidered with flowers of beads and pearls and her tulle veil hung from a circlet of diamonds. The gown had been designed by Norman Hartnell and must have taken more material than anyone else could dream of, but people said that the princess had refused to have a trousseau to take on honeymoon, because she knew that other people were struggling to buy new clothes. Not that the cheering crowds or the majority of people in England would have grudged it to her. They were happy to enjoy the pomp and ceremony of a royal procession and believe that things were bound to improve for everyone soon. After all, the Food Ministry was hinting that everyone would have more meat, sugar and sweets for Christmas.

The ceremony itself was simple, because of the austere times, but the procession had been lovely and everybody milling around in the Mall after-wards felt happier than for a long while. It was times like these that people were unconditionally proud of the royal family and felt as they had during the war, that the values and traditions of old England were worth making sacrifices for. Only a few envied the royal couple the wedding breakfast, with the huge cake that the newspapers said would be cut with the sword of the bride-groom's grandfather, or the fifty thousand pounds that had been voted for Clarence House to be done up for the young couple.

Sally had managed a few hours off to come and watch with all the thousands of others as the coach passed by. Brenda had been given a day off work and the sisters stood together, waving flags and cheering until they were hoarse.

'Shall we go and have a cup of tea to celebrate?' Brenda asked when the procession had passed. 'My feet are killing me.'

'I have to get back,' Sally said apologetically. 'Angela's filled in for me. They're taking most of the children to the church party this afternoon, because Sister said we were only having the commemorative mugs. She thought it was too close to Christmas for us to have our own party.'

'Mean old thing,' Brenda grumbled. 'Everyone is celebrating, why not you?'

'Because the funds won't stretch to it, I suppose,' Sally said. 'It isn't easy to be the Warden of a children's home, you know.'

'I suppose not.' Brenda linked arms with her. 'I'll walk back with you then. I'm going out tonight with Gerald Jones; he's taking me to the pictures. Are you going out with Keith? Most people will be celebrating down the pub tonight.'

'Keith hasn't asked me out since I was late for that show he got tickets for,' Sally said with a sigh. 'I think he paid a lot of money for them and we had a row over it. Besides, he wanted to get serious and I didn't. I wouldn't have gone out with him tonight, even if he'd asked.'

'You were late because of that accident?' Sally nodded. 'How is that boy by the way?'

'Doing all right, I think,' Sally said. 'I fancy a bar of chocolate. I was saving my coupons for Christmas, but I'm going to treat myself. After all, it isn't often the future Queen gets married.'

Alice listened to the broadcast on the radio in the staff room. She'd volunteered for duty because she didn't want to accompany the girls who were going to watch the procession. Tomorrow's papers would be filled with pictures of the wedding and she wasn't likely to get close enough to see much on a day like this; besides, she wasn't in the mood for celebrating much. The previous night, she'd asked Jack when they were going to leave London, but he'd gone moody and wouldn't talk about it.

'I'll tell you when I'm ready,' he'd flared at her when she'd tried to push him into telling her about

284

his plans. 'It's best you don't know anythin' – then you won't get into trouble.'

'Pa keeps asking me where I'm going nights and Mavis knows I'm seein' you, Jack. I'm worried she'll tell me pa and then he'll give me a right hidin' for goin' out with you behind his back.'

'He'll be sorry if he lays a hand on you,' Jack growled. He'd pulled her closer on the big sofa where they'd first made love, his kisses hungry and insistent as his hands roamed over her breasts and then began to inch up her skirt. 'You're mine now, Alice, and I protect what belongs to me.'

'Don't,' Alice said and tried to push him off as he eased her down on the sofa. 'You know I don't want to do it again until we're married. If I get pregnant me dad will kill me.'

'I told you, we'll be out of here soon,' he murmured huskily against her throat. 'I want you, Alice. It's daft to keep sayin' no when you know you don't mean it. You want me as much as I want you . . .'

The trouble was it was true and Alice had given into him on two or three occasions. She was terrified her period wouldn't come and lived in fear of her father finding out that she was going with Jack, but he was a law unto himself these days and wouldn't take no for an answer.

Switching off the radio, Alice went back to work. If she was another day late for her monthlies she was really going to start worrying – and she would make Jack listen. If he was going to leave the gang he could do so sooner rather than later, couldn't he? Alice wouldn't feel safe until they were on that ship to America.

She looked up and smiled as Michelle entered the staff room.

'You got stuck with duty as well then,' she said. 'I didn't mind but I thought you were a fan of the princess?'

'I am,' Michelle said, 'but someone had to stay so I told Anna to go and I'd hold the fort. I shall see it all on the Pathé news when I go to the flicks tomorrow.'

'Are you goin' with some of the girls?'

'No . . .' Michelle's cheeks reddened. 'Your cousin Eric asked me and I said I would. He walked home with me the other night – actually, he stepped in to stop some louts who were pestering me. It was good of him, because it was late and no one else was about, so I said I'd go, but you needn't grin like that. I'm not going steady with him or anyone.'

'Eric is all right,' Alice said. 'I'm off to get ready for when Angela and Nan bring the kids back from the church party. Have a good time.'

Michelle stared after her friend. Alice had been a bit quiet lately, but she seemed more cheerful today. She'd been on the verge of asking if something was worrying Alice, but decided not to pry. Michelle had reason to think her friend was being foolish with Jack Shaw, but she didn't want to fall out with her and risked it if she nagged her too much about the undoubtedly charming rogue. Yet perhaps she should have spoken out, because she didn't want Alice to be hurt.

Michelle shut out a memory she didn't want to intrude – a memory she'd pushed to a far corner of her mind long ago. She'd been as trusting as Alice once and she had fallen for a handsome face, but she'd paid for it.

Michelle knew that she'd been lucky to get away with a sore heart. Alan had seduced her with promises he never meant to keep – promises he couldn't keep, because he was already married and had a child. Perhaps she should have told Alice how she'd been seduced by a sweet-talking rogue. She would, next time she got a chance, because that might bring her friend to her senses.

Thank God she'd discovered the truth in time, before she got caught in the trap he'd set for her and ended up alone and pregnant. Her experience had made her wary of men, however pleasant and honest they seemed, and the thought of her best friend being mixed up with someone like Jack Shaw made Michelle's stomach turn sour. One of the reasons she'd agreed to go to the cinema with Eric was because she intended to ask him to keep an eye on Alice if he could.

Eric might be stationed away for most of the time, but he had plenty of East End mates and if he asked around he would soon discover what was going on. Michelle knew Alice might be angry if she knew that her cousin was looking out for her, but it was better than letting her get into trouble . . .

Angela kicked her shoes off and put her feet up. She was thoroughly exhausted after spending all afternoon looking after a horde of excited children at the church fete. They had played games and watched a slide show on a large white screen; they'd been entertained by a magician and given a bag of homemade toffee and fudge to take away at the end of the party. And that was not until a wonderful spread of sandwiches, cakes, jellies and *tinned fruit* – all the way from some good people in America, thank God for the Allies! – had been consumed and washed down with glasses of orange squash.

The telephone rang and she reached for it, glad that she didn't have to get up, because she wasn't sure she could. Her father's voice came over the phone, asking if she'd managed to see any of the royal wedding.

'No, I was busy with a party for the children,' she said. 'I might have gone to watch the coach pass, but one of the carers wanted to go with her sister so I volunteered to do her job.'

'Your mother and I saw the princess go into the Abbey. We got a good view because someone let us through to the front, even though we didn't get there until an hour before she arrived.'

'I had no idea you were coming up. If you'd let me know I could have met you . . .'

288

'That is why I'm ringing you now. Your mother misses you, love. We thought you might like to come and have dinner with us – as it is a special occasion?'

'Yes, of course, Daddy,' Angela said. 'I shall enjoy that – but I need to get washed and changed. I shall be more than an hour.'

'All the time in the world, my love,' he said. 'We both miss you, you know.'

'I'll be there as soon as I can,' Angela said and replaced the receiver after being instructed to take a taxi to the Criterion. Her father was doing it in style, and suddenly her tiredness had fled. She would enjoy spending the evening with her parents for a change – even though she'd hoped she might hear from Mark. It was a week or two now since she'd seen him to talk to, though he'd visited St Saviour's. She was conscious of missing him, though that was just foolish . . .

Beatrice opened the account books in front of her and ran her finger down the column of figures. A frown touched her brow as she added them up for the sixth time and came to the same total. She was going to be fifty pounds down this month again, and that wouldn't please the Bishop when she attended the meeting tomorrow.

Perhaps those commemorative mugs had been a mistake. She had wanted to give the children something to mark such a special day, but even at the cheap rate they had stretched her budget. She ought to have been firmer and ignored the idea. After all the children had been to a party and that should have been enough. Goodness knows, she did her best, but there was always another child to take in, another mouth to feed, and another body to clothe. Even with all the gifts and the extra money Angela had raised, it was a stretch each month.

Oh, well, the money was spent and she couldn't change her mind now. She closed the book and got up to pour herself a glass of sherry. She thought regretfully of the small bequest her father had left her, which she had immediately donated to her order. Since her vocation forbade her to own or think of worldly goods, she'd given the money to the Abbey, but she sometimes thought that the order was well-endowed and St Saviour's could have done with that three hundred pounds. Too late to think of that now.

What she really needed was for Angela's fund-raising to do well. Beatrice hadn't asked how much was in the fund, because she didn't want to admit that she'd overspent again this month, but perhaps she would just inquire how the Christmas fund was coming along in the morning.

Frowning, Beatrice poured herself another sherry. Her liking for the drink was undoubtedly a failing. Mother Superior would say she must curb her weakness, but Beatrice pushed the guilt from her conscious mind. She only ever drank in moderation, and if it was a sin it was surely a small one. After all, it was a special day, wasn't it? Princess

Elizabeth had married the man of her choice and all was well with the world. Yet there was a shadow haunting her, hovering at her shoulder.

Perhaps it was that boy . . . Jake who had died of the chicken pox. Something about him reminded her of another child, a child she had been unable to protect. The old memory flickered for a moment before she managed to banish it. She was not to blame, though God knew she still felt the guilt of what had happened after all this time.

A sigh left her lips and then her brooding thoughts fled as someone knocked at the door and she heard a voice she knew well asking if he might come in.

'Of course,' she called and Father Joe walked in. She felt her mood lighten instantly. She knew he'd come to spend an hour or two with her because he was carrying a small bottle of her favourite sherry. Her loneliness fled and she produced another glass, inviting him to sit and tell her all about his day. He'd been organising a children's party at the Catholic church hall and by the look of him he was exhausted. 'Tell me how you've been getting on – and perhaps you might give me your opinion on something that has been bothering me . . .'

'I'm always ready to listen and share your burdens,' he told her with his ready smile. 'Fire away, me darlin'; there's nothing so bad it can't be lightened by sharing the load.'

★   ★   ★

Sally was listening to an account of the royal wedding on the wireless with her mother. She'd brought a few souvenirs home for her and they settled down in the parlour, with a glass of ginger wine and a piece of fatless sponge, when the front doorbell rang.

'Who can that be at this hour?' her mother said, looking a bit cross. 'You go, Sally. I couldn't face all those crowds earlier and I want to listen to this.'

Sally nodded and got to her feet. She hoped Keith hadn't come round expecting her to go out with him and she jerked the door back impatiently, but her annoyance melted as she saw who was standing there.

'Mr Markham . . .' she said, suddenly a little breathless.

'Why don't you call me Andrew?' he asked. 'I did suggest it when we had that drink – in private anyway.'

'All right,' Sally said, feeling oddly shy. 'I wasn't expecting you – will you come in please?'

'Yes, thank you,' he said. 'I wondered if you would like to come out for a little celebration – a meal somewhere quiet and nice if you haven't eaten, or just a drink. I know of a new Italian restaurant that everyone says is good . . .'

'Who is it, Sally?' Her father had come into the hall, dressed in his trousers and braces and a shirt with rolled-up sleeves, and looked startled. 'Mr Markham, is it?' he said and offered his hand. 'Is there a crisis at St Saviour's?'

'Oh no, nothing like that,' Andrew Markham replied, shaking his hand. 'I was hoping to persuade Sally to let me take her out for a celebration as it is a special day.'

'I've eaten, but I wouldn't mind going for a drink. I'll just get my jacket . . .'

Sally hurried through to the kitchen and took her jacket from behind the door. She could hear the two men laughing and, when she returned, her father was smiling and Andrew Markham was looking perfectly at ease.

'I'm ready,' Sally said and her father winked at Andrew.

'These young girls are always in a hurry these days. Off you go, then – but remember you have to get up in the morning.'

'Of course,' Sally said, kissed his cheek and then went out of the door Andrew Markham was holding for her. Her heart fluttered as she saw the way he looked at her. Last time they'd gone for a drink it had been a wonderful evening. Sally hadn't stopped talking and laughing and the time had flown by.

'Your father told me you went up the Mall earlier – did you see much?'

'Yes, we were lucky, we got a good view,' Sally said and when he offered his arm she hugged it and smiled up at him, her heart beating joyously. 'I loved it, Andrew – all the horses and the men in their smart uniforms marching, and the bands, and everyone in a happy mood. It was so lovely. Did you get to see it?'

'Unfortunately, I had to work, but I did manage to listen to a bit of it on the radio, and we heard the crowds cheering all the way.' He smiled down at her. 'I'm glad you got to see it. I thought about you and wondered if you were there.'

'Yes, I thought about you too,' she admitted.

'Good.' He paused. 'You're lovely, Sally, special, and I feel happy whenever I see you.'

Sally giggled and held his arm tighter. She'd loved the procession and the feeling of excitement and joy that had spread through the crowds at their first sight of the princess as she went by in her coach, but this . . . going out with Andrew again was even better.

'I feel the same,' she whispered softly. 'This will make a very special day even more special. Thank you for thinking of it.'

'Thank you for coming with me,' he said and then bent his head towards her, just brushing her lips with his own. 'I want us to do this more often . . .'

Sally's head was spinning and she could hardly breathe because her heart was behaving so foolishly, beating so hard she thought he might hear it.

'I shall never forget this day. I'll remember it always.'

CHAPTER 22

Angela woke feeling unusually tired and reluctant to get up. She'd stayed up late the previous evening celebrating with her parents – but she hadn't drunk much and that wasn't the reason for her unease. She remembered that they'd been seated at their table when a party of men and women entered, and she'd been surprised to see Mark was one of them. They'd been shown to a large table on the other side of the room, and it was obvious they were enjoying themselves, ordering champagne and laughing.

Angela had avoided looking in his direction, but Mark had seen her just as she was ordering her sweet course and he came over to the table. Angela's father had risen to his feet and the two men shook hands.

'How are you, sir? Mrs Hendry?' Mark had paused before he turned to Angela. 'I didn't know you were coming here this evening? You've been busy at the home recently, I know.'

'Yes, there is rather a lot to do,' Angela agreed. 'But they do let me out now and again, you know.'

'She works far too hard,' Mrs Hendry said. 'Why she bothers I have no idea. If I had my way she would come home.'

'I think Angela enjoys her work,' Mark said.

'I love it,' she said. 'There's never any time to be bored. After several delays, the builders have been hard at work for a couple of weeks now, Mark. Have you seen what an improvement they've made already?'

'Yes, and it is going to get better,' he said. 'We must meet for a drink soon and talk about the changes. Excuse me, I must get back to my friends, but I wanted to say hello. Goodnight, Mrs Hendry, Edward . . .'

'I'll give you a ring tomorrow,' Angela's father said. 'Would it be convenient to talk – perhaps in the evening after we get home?

'Of course,' Mark said but looked puzzled. 'I hope nothing is wrong?'

'Oh no, just a small matter I'd like your advice on.'

'Of course. Enjoy yourselves – Angela.'

Mark walked back to his table but Angela refused to watch. It was ridiculous to feel slightly jealous of the beautiful brunette he appeared to be with, because she had no hold on him, none at all. He was a good friend and that was all she wanted him to be, because she could never bring herself to love again, and if she didn't want Mark to be her lover she couldn't be jealous of his happiness with someone else. Of course she couldn't – and she wasn't!

'Is anything the matter, Father?' Angela asked but he shook his head.

'Just something I'd like to speak to Mark about, that's all.'

Sighing now, Angela washed and dressed. If her father wanted her to know he would tell her in his own good time.

A little later that morning, Angela entered the staff room and found Nan there before her, collecting dirty cups and saucers. It was just one of the tasks that the woman often did. Employed as the head carer or supervisor, everyone saw her as a substitute mother and ran to her with their problems. Nan always seemed to have time to listen. Although she was wearing a white apron, she did not have a uniform.

'Your hair looks lovely. Have you had it styled differently?'

'Yes.' Nan looked a little self-conscious and touched her hair, which was cut in a stylish DA. 'I thought it was time for a change so I had a restyle . . .'

'It certainly suits you,' Angela remarked as Nan fetched a cup someone had left on the windowsill. 'Couldn't one of the kitchen staff do that?' she asked and reached for the kettle.

Nan laughed and stopped what she was doing to sit down and look at Angela. 'I'm ready for a cuppa if you're making tea?'

'Yes, of course,' Angela agreed. 'Have you got time for a chat?'

'We are all of us busy most of the time,' Nan said. 'Especially when we're short staffed.'

'Have you got casualties again?'

'Kelly has a cold. She should collect the dirty cups and supply fresh, and do the washing up – but she is a little unreliable.'

'Yes, I've seen Kelly a couple of times. Is she Welsh?'

'Her father is . . .'

'How long have you been here?' Angela asked as she poured boiling water into the pot and gave it a stir.

'I joined the staff when Sister Beatrice came here. We've known each other for some years, before she became a nun. Then we met again, when I took a cleaning job at the hospital she worked for and she was very kind to me when . . . I needed help. My husband and son had both died of typhoid fever and my daughter . . . well, to cut a long story short, when Beatrice was asked to take this on, she approached me to help her out here.'

Angela handed her a cup of tea. 'I hope that's as you like it?'

'Lovely, thank you. Beatrice told me it has made a difference you being here.'

'Has it? I'm glad if she's pleased with my work – though I must admit I would love to do more for the children.'

'You would be wasted simply as a carer,' Nan said earnestly. 'I know you're raising money for us, money that we really need. It's something that neither Beatrice nor I could do half as well. Yes, I appreciate that you help out with the children too, and that's good – but you mustn't think we don't notice what you do, because we do. The children enjoy all the things you arrange for them.'

'Yes, I think they do,' Angela agreed. 'Billy was fascinated by that working steam engine at the toy fair. He hardly moved from the stand, and he told me afterwards that he liked engines. He wants to work with them when he leaves school.'

'He'll have to work a bit harder at school if he's to pass the exams he'll need. I like the boy myself, but there's no doubting that he's been taught the wrong values. He never had the love he needed and it isn't easy to break down the barrier he's built inside. Once people set their minds a certain way, it isn't easy to change them . . .' Nan sounded weary for some reason and Angela thought she saw a flicker of sadness in her face. What was Nan's secret? Angela guessed she had one, but didn't feel she should press for details.

CHAPTER 23

'We need someone to keep cavey when we do the boot factory,' Jack said and Arthur Baggins nodded agreement. 'There's a night watchman and he ain't one of them that goes to sleep on the job, so we need to make sure we aren't disturbed.'

'Yeah, I reckon I know someone we can trust.'

'Who?' Jack's eyes narrowed in suspicion. He and Arthur worked well together but he didn't trust anybody and this job was important. 'I don't want to cut anyone else in on this. Both of us are on borrowed time, Arthur. I need the money to get away, and you'll go too if you've got any sense. Since we did that safe in the lawyer's office I've been sweating about Butcher finding out it was us. All that expensive jewellery was stuff Butcher fenced and he needed to keep it safe until the heat died down and he could sell it. Nearly as bloody priceless as the jewels at the flamin' royal weddin' yesterday.'

'We didn't know it was Butcher's,' Arthur said gruffly. 'I wouldn't have bleedin' touched the stuff if I'd known.'

'Well, we did and we can't sell it in London, any of it. I need money quick, Arthur, and there's bound to be loads of cash at the factory on Thursday night, ready for the wages on Friday. I've been watchin' what goes on and I know the boss fetches it regular three o'clock on Thursday and his secretary makes up the wage packets ready for the next day.'

'I'll get me bruvver,' Arthur said. 'He's a stroppy little devil, but he'll do what I tell him, and we don't 'ave ter give 'im anythin' but a bag of chips sometimes. If he plays up I'll give 'im a slap or two to quieten 'im.'

'Give the lad a couple of bob now and then, keep him sweet,' Jack said. 'Right, we'd better be careful for the next few days. We don't want anyone to know what we're plannin'. If Butcher got wind of it, he'd kill us both . . .'

Arthur's eyes moved restlessly from side to side; he was sweating and obviously scared. Jack cursed inwardly. Arthur was more of a liability than an asset. If Butcher got to work on him, he'd scream like a stuck pig. He was a bully and like all bullies he couldn't take it.

Jack would have blown the safe at the factory on his own if he could manage it, but it was a two-man job. He preferred easier targets, but he needed enough money to take both himself and Alice to America. It wasn't often that Jack bothered about girls after he'd got what he wanted, but there was something about Alice that made him want her; perhaps because when he'd been a ragged-arsed urchin with bare feet, Alice had always had a smile and good word for him.

He was going soft in the head. Jack scowled at his thoughts. He was a fool if he bothered to take her with him; he would travel lighter and faster without her . . . and yet he still wanted her, still thought about the softness of her skin and the way her mouth tasted sweet when he kissed her . . .

'Get your brother to help, then,' he said. 'I've got something to do. Keep yer nose clean, Arthur. Don't go gettin' up Big Harry's nose or the deal's off. I want to keep Butcher and Harry sweet until I'm ready.'

Billy was running home after school the next afternoon, eager to tell Mary Ellen what had happened at football that afternoon, because for the first time he'd been picked for the school's first eleven and was going to play for the team that Saturday. He was excited, because if there was one thing he enjoyed at school it was football practice.

'Where do yer fink yer goin', young'un?'

Finding himself grabbed from behind by a strong arm, Billy kicked out and had the satisfaction of hearing his attacker yell. He looked round and then his grin faded as he saw his brother seconds before Arthur's fist struck out and caught him on the ear, nearly knocking him off his feet.

'What did yer do that fer?' Billy demanded, rubbing at his ear.

'You kicked me,' Arthur growled. 'I'll have respect from yer, Billy lad, or you'll feel me fists more than yer want.'

'You're just like Pa,' Billy was resentful. 'Why did you grab me like that? You startled me. There's some rum coves round 'ere and I thought you was after . . . well, you know what.'

'I ain't one of them,' his brother growled, pushing his face close to Billy's. 'I've bin lookin' fer yer, Billy. Where yer bin hidin' yerself?'

'I'm livin' at St Saviour's,' Billy said reluctantly. Once he would have been glad to see his brother but now he was suspicious, apprehensive. 'What do you want? I ain't seen nuthin' of yer for months, why now?'

'I've bin keepin' me 'ead down,' Arthur said. 'The coppers were after me so I hopped it up North for a while, see, but now I'm back – and you can leave that place and come with me. I've got a use for yer. You behave yerself and I'll give yer a few bob; you'll like that, I reckon.'

'Nah, I'm all right where I am.'

Arthur cuffed him round the ear. 'You'll do what I tell yer or I'll make yer sorry yer were born,' he grunted, and there was a vicious gleam in his eyes that made Billy shiver. 'I ain't found a place to stay yet. I went to Nanna's old house thinkin' you would be there, but they told me she's in a home and won't come out. Someone else has her house now – and no one seemed to know for sure where you were so I came lookin' fer yer.'

'I want to stay at St Saviour's. I've got friends there now and I like it.' Billy looked at him defiantly and dodged the next blow. 'I'm no use to you.'

'Hoity-toity, speakin' posh now, ain't we? There's lots of times when a young'un like you could be useful,' Arthur said tersely. 'You can get in windows where we can't – and you can keep watch. I'll treat yer right and give yer a share of the money we get from robbin' houses – and shops too, if we get the chance. Come on, Billy, me and you – for old times' sake?'

Billy eyed him uncertainly. If Arthur had come for him when his father died, he would have gone with him without a murmur, but he was beginning to like his life. He'd managed to get seven out of ten of his spellings right and he was going to be in the school football team. Living rough with Arthur in a derelict house with no heat and only rags to lie on wouldn't be much fun, and he was used to having enough to eat at St Saviour's. Besides, there was Mary Ellen . . .

'I've got a football match at school this week on Saturday afternoon. I ain't coming with you before that,' he said, backing out of reach.

'I shall come for yer to the home on Saturday evening,' Arthur told him, lifting his fist. 'You'd better come out to me or I'll have to come in and get yer – and if some of your friends get hurt that will be your fault.'

'All right, Saturday night after dark.'

'I'll be there at ten,' Arthur said. 'We can't start work until then anyway, too many people about. Jack is working on a good crib for us – but we got to find somewhere to hide the stash first, see. We shan't be ready to start until Saturday. But remember, if yer ain't there when I come, I shall make you sorry – and them people at the home. I might set fire to it when they're all in their beds.'

'You wouldn't,' Billy cried in horror and then knew he'd made a mistake as his brother's eyes lit up. Now that Arthur knew he cared about St Saviour's, he would hold that threat over him even if he had no intention of doing any such thing. Knowing him, he was just mean enough to do it if Billy defied him.

'Clear orf, then,' Arthur muttered. 'Go to your football match if yer want – won't have no time fer school once I put yer to work . . .'

Arthur turned and strode off through the market, which was packing up for the day, the debris of rotten fruit and vegetables lying in stinking piles in the gutters until the man came to sweep it all up before the morning. Billy looked about for a policeman, wild thoughts of informing on his brother flitting through his head, but even as he sought and didn't find one, he realised it was useless. As far as he knew Arthur hadn't done anything they could arrest him for yet, and threats meant nothing unless they were carried out. Besides, where he came from the worst sin of all was to be a copper's nark. He didn't want to go with his brother, but he couldn't shop him to the police.

Wiping his dripping nose with the sleeve of his coat, Billy walked slowly back to the home. He'd got a blooming cold again, but he wasn't going to report sick, because he would lose the chance of playing football if he stopped off school too much.

The shadow of his brother's threats hung over him, because he knew his days of living in safety at St Saviour's were almost over – and there was no one he could tell. No one who could stop his brother forcing him into a life of crime. Even if he went against his upbringing and told the police they probably wouldn't believe him; they all thought he was a troublemaker and none of them knew what he'd suffered at the hands of both his father and brother. He dreaded the thought of being hungry all the time, in fear of his brother's temper and reduced to living on the streets again. At St Saviour's he'd begun to think there might be more to life than he'd ever dreamed, even for a boy like Billy Baggins. He'd even tried to correct his speech, wanting to sound like Mary Ellen, and he meant to learn all he could at school, to do something with his life – but now it wouldn't happen. He'd probably end up like one of them shifty spivs, hanging about street corners selling rubbish nylons to girls daft enough to buy them, and running for his life every time a copper turned up.

He sniffed, holding back the silly tears that stung

his eyes. Boys didn't cry. That was only for girls –
and Mary Ellen wouldn't cry whatever anyone did
to her. He wanted to tell her he would be leaving
St Saviour's on Saturday, but if he did she would
be sure to tell someone. And if the police went after
Arthur he would get away and then they would all
be burned in their beds . . .

'What's wrong, Billy?' Mary Ellen asked when she
saw her friend moodily kicking a ball at the wall
in the schoolroom after tea, because if Sister had
caught him he would be in trouble again. 'Are you
worried about something?'

He shook his head, but Mary Ellen guessed he
was lying. She knew by the way he avoided looking
at her.

'Is it Sister Beatrice? Has she been at you again?'

'Nah, I ain't scared of her . . .'

'But you are scared of something.' Mary Ellen
saw the answer in his eyes even though he didn't
speak. She knew that not much scared her friend
and stared at him hard. 'What's wrong?

'It's Arthur. He wants me to go with him . . . to
leave St Saviour's and help him.'

'Billy, you mustn't go,' Mary Ellen said, aghast.
'He's rotten through and through. He'll get you
in trouble and you'll end up just like him.'

Billy seemed on the edge of telling her something
but then he shook his head. 'You don't understand,
Mary Ellen. You don't know what he'll do if I
don't go with him.'

'Tell someone,' Mary Ellen urged. 'The police are after him. If they knew they would arrest him and put him in prison.'

'I can't do that.' Billy looked miserable. 'Leave it alone, Mary Ellen. You can't do anything to help me.'

Mary Ellen watched as he ran off. It was obvious he didn't want to talk to her so she decided not to follow him. She was frightened for her friend, but she didn't know what to do. If she told one of the carers they would speak to the police – or Sister Beatrice would. Yet she couldn't just stand by and see him ruin his life. She would just have to wait and see what she could do to stop Billy getting into the worst trouble of his life.

Billy had sought desperately for an answer to his problem, but he could find none. If he told on his brother Arthur would know and he was a mean, spiteful man. He would disappear until the police stopped hunting for him and then he would come back and set fire to St Saviour's. No one could stop him, because he was sly and clever and Billy was afraid of him, though he would never have admitted it to anyone else.

The weather was bright and crisp, just right for playing football that afternoon. The excitement had been mounting in Billy all the previous day, because despite his fear of Arthur, he was looking forward to playing for his school; it was an honour and one he hadn't expected.

He ate his lunch in the dining room with Mary

Ellen, though he couldn't bring himself to munch more than a cheese and pickle sandwich and an apple. Mary Ellen looked at him in surprise.

'Why didn't you want one of Nan's jam tarts?' she asked. 'She's doing the cooking today because it is Cook's day off.'

'I mustn't eat too much,' Billy said and drank a big gulp of his orange juice. 'I've got a lot of runnin' to do this afternoon, because I'm the centre half.'

'You're playing football?' Mary Ellen looked puzzled. 'But didn't Sister Beatrice stop all your privileges for another week?'

Billy stared at her, stunned as he realised it was true. He was grounded for all pleasure outings and it would be just like the old witch to class playing football for his school as pleasure.

'I've got to go, it's for the school and it's an honour,' Billy said. 'She won't know if I sneak out the back way. I'm going whatever she thinks – you won't tell her if she asks, will you?'

'Of course I shan't,' Mary Ellen promised. 'I wish I could come with you, but I'd have to get special permission, and if I asked they would know where you'd gone.'

'Never mind,' he comforted her. 'I'll tell you all about it this evening – and perhaps if I do well . . .' He broke off as he remembered there would be no next time. It felt as if he'd been stabbed in the chest and he nearly choked as he realised that after today there would be no more St Saviour's

– no more sitting with Mary Ellen and sharing his problems, no more football. He would be on the streets with Arthur and forced into a life of crime.

It wasn't fair and it wasn't right, but what else could he do? If Arthur had threatened to break his bones, he would have defied him, but he couldn't risk his spiteful brother carrying out his threat against St Saviour's, and all the friends Billy had made.

'I'm going to slip away now,' he whispered to Mary Ellen. 'You're me best mate, don't ever forget that.'

She gave him a puzzled look and Billy's heart felt as if it would break but he got up and left. Just as he was exiting the dining hall to go out the back way, he caught a glimpse of Sister Beatrice coming down the hall. She called out to him by name but he ignored her and slipped out of the side door and into the garden, stopping to pick up his football boots, which he'd hidden under a bush earlier.

Sister Beatrice would be on the warpath when she discovered he'd missed the detention she'd set him, but what could she do to him? Billy had always been more afraid of his brother than the stern nurse, whom he suspected of having a softer heart than she let on. He would face what came when he returned from his game, but after that evening it wouldn't matter what she thought, because he was going to have to do as Arthur told him.

CHAPTER 24

Mary Ellen left the dining hall and made her way to the schoolroom. She was supposed to be in detention this afternoon, too, which was why she'd remembered about Billy. Finding the room empty, she sat down at the table and began to write out the lines: I must not run in school. I must obey the rules. She wrote them over and over again. Sister had told them they must do one hundred lines each, which was quite a task for Mary Ellen as she carefully inscribed each letter, but after some perseverance she had finished her lines.

About to leave the schoolroom, she realised that a little extra effort on her part would accomplish another one hundred lines, which she could print Billy's name on at the top. If Sister found both sets of lines here she would not know that he had played truant for the afternoon, and he might escape further punishment. It was so unfair that he should be punished just for running in the corridor Billy thought Sister had it in for him, and Mary Ellen believed him.

She put Billy's name at the top of a second sheet,

printing it carefully so that it looked different to her own, then she began to write the lines he had been given, slowly and painstakingly printing every letter so that no one could be sure who had done it. It took twice as long as her own lines, and by the time she'd finished her hand hurt and her shoulders ached from crouching over the table, but she was able to place both lists neatly on the desk. She was just about to leave when the door opened and Sister Beatrice entered, looking stern.

'Have you finished your lines, Mary Ellen?'

'Yes, Sister,' she answered in a scared whisper. 'I left them on the desk.'

'And where is Billy Baggins?'

Mary Ellen swallowed hard. 'I don't know, Sister.'

'Well, you may not, but I do. A little bird told me that he is playing football for his school team this afternoon – it is considered an honour, I understand.'

Mary Ellen stared hard at the floor, wishing it might open and swallow her up. She wished she hadn't written those lines and put Billy's name on them now, because Sister would know what she had done and be angry with her. There was a sick feeling in her stomach as Sister walked past her to the desk and she bolted quickly out of the door and fled along the hall, heading upstairs to the dorm.

It was empty at this time in the afternoon, but Mary Ellen didn't want the company of other girls. Billy was her best friend and she was very much afraid that she might have made things worse for him. Sister would think Billy had asked her to do it, and it was all Mary Ellen's fault.

She felt apprehensive but knew that if Sister demanded an explanation, she must tell her the truth, because otherwise Billy would be in worse trouble. Sister Beatrice had threatened to cane him next time he did anything wrong and a little voice in her head told her that cheating would be considered much worse than running in the corridor.

Mary Ellen was in the dining room having tea with Marion when Billy came in. He looked flushed and triumphant, and she knew immediately that he must have done well in the football match. He loaded his plate with shrimp paste sandwiches, two sausage rolls and a slice of sponge cake, and brought them to the table where they sat.

'We won,' he announced as he set his plate down. 'And I scored the winning goal.'

'Oh, that's wonderful,' Mary Ellen said, her heart lurching. He looked so pleased with himself and she was carrying a guilty secret she just knew was going to get him into a lot of trouble. 'I'm so glad, Billy. Tell us all about it. We want to hear it all, don't we, Marion?'

'Oh yes,' Marion agreed and looked wistful. 'I used to like playing football in the lane with my friends, but I wasn't very good – not like you, Billy.'

'I don't know if I'm very good,' Billy said, 'but

the sports master said he would make me a regular member of the team and . . .' His face clouded and Mary Ellen thought he might burst into tears, he looked so miserable.

'What is it?' she asked. 'Is it because of Arthur? Or is it Sister Beatrice? Has she got on to you about the lines . . .?'

'What lines?'

'You were supposed to be in detention and write one hundred lines so I did them for you and put your name on the top, but she came in just as I was leaving and she said she knew you'd gone to a football match at school . . .'

'No, did she?' Billy stared in surprise. 'How could she know that? I never told anyone but you – and you didn't tell?'

'No, you know I wouldn't. But she'll know you didn't do the lines and be angry with you. She might think you asked me to cheat for you . . . but I shall tell her the truth if she blames you. It was all my idea.'

'It was a good idea,' Billy said. 'If she hadn't found out I was playing for the school she wouldn't have guessed.'

'No, because I printed the letters like you do, Billy. It was ever so hard and took ages, but I thought it would save you getting into more trouble – and now you may be in worse.'

'Oh. Look.' Marion ducked her head down. 'Sister Beatrice has just come in and she's looking for someone – I think she's coming over, Billy.'

'I don't care,' Billy said on a note of bravado. 'There's nothing she can do to me now.'

'Billy Baggins, so you've returned to us, have you?' Sister boomed in a tone that brooked no good for errant boys. 'Well, I'm sure I hope you enjoyed your afternoon, because it is the last time you will have any privileges until Christmas – and now I should like you to come to my office if you will. Playing truant is one thing, but getting another person to write out your lines is quite another.'

'It wasn't Billy's fault,' Mary Ellen said quickly. 'I'm the one that did it – and I thought of it myself. Billy didn't ask me . . .'

'Indeed?' Sister's gaze narrowed intently. 'Why should I believe you?'

'Because I'm telling the truth,' Mary Ellen replied, meeting her angry stare. 'On my life, Sister. It was all my idea . . .'

'Then you should be ashamed of yourself, Mary Ellen. Cheating is something I just will not accept here at St Saviour's. If you were not asked to do this . . .'

'It isn't her fault,' Billy put in quickly. 'Don't lie for me, Mary Ellen. I made you do it. You should punish me, Sister, not her.'

Marion started to cry. 'It isn't Mary Ellen's fault,' she wept. 'Don't punish her – and Billy won his football match and now you've gone and spoiled it . . .'

'Stop that snivelling at once,' Sister Beatrice

commanded. 'Is this a mutiny? I shall have something to say to you, Billy. Finish your tea and report to me in half an hour. Marion, you must learn not to take sides when it doesn't concern you – and as for you, Mary Ellen, your privileges will be cancelled for the next two weeks.'

Mary Ellen stared at the Warden but she didn't reply, nor did she cry, even though her eyes stung with tears. She wished she hadn't cheated, because now she saw how shameful it was, but she'd done it to save her friend. Instead of that, Billy was in even more trouble and she might miss the Christmas party at the church hall unless Sister relented before then.

She turned to Billy as Sister walked away, feeling sick with misery. 'I'm sorry; I've just made things worse for you. I meant to help – but she's really angry with us now.'

'She'll probably give me the cane,' Billy said. 'It don't matter. It only hurts for a minute and me pa used to hit me far worse.'

Mary Ellen knew that he was putting on a brave show, because he was bound to suffer, but there was a look in his eyes that bothered her because it was caused by something worse than a punishment from Sister Beatrice.

'Is there anything you haven't told me?' she asked and saw him look hesitant. For a moment she thought he was going to speak, but then he checked and grinned in his old way, almost reassuring her.

'Nah, there ain't nuffin' wrong,' he lied, and she

knew he was lying. 'I don't care about the old witch – she can't hurt me no more.'

'What do you mean?'

Mary Ellen didn't understand, because she knew Billy had been trying to keep Sister Beatrice sweet so that she didn't send him away from St Saviour's, but now he seemed resigned – as if he'd given up trying. She reached out and touched his hand, but he drew it away as if he'd been stung, jumped up from the table and ran from the room, leaving most of his tea untouched on the table.

'What's wrong with Billy?' Marion asked. 'He loves sausage rolls and fruitcake, but he's hardly eaten a thing.'

'I'll wrap them in a paper serviette and take them for him,' Mary Ellen decided aloud. 'I can smuggle them up to him after lights out.'

'If you get caught you will be in trouble,' Marion objected. 'Why not take them to his dorm when you go and put them by his locker? He will find them when he goes up and you won't get into trouble for being out of bed later on.'

'Yes, I shall, thanks for the idea,' Mary Ellen said. 'And thanks for sticking up for us to Sister Beatrice. I've never seen her cross with you before.'

'She never has been, though she's always firm, but she was very angry. I haven't seen her like that before.'

'She seems to pick on Billy all the time,' Mary Ellen said. 'I don't know why she's unkind to him, it only makes him do silly things – he goes and

317

defies her but she doesn't seem to understand that it's just him proving he isn't afraid.'

'I don't think Billy is afraid of anything.'

Mary Ellen didn't answer. She had sensed fear in Billy just now but she didn't think it was to do with Sister Beatrice threatening to cane him. No, it was his fear of his bully of a brother, fear that went much deeper than his dislike of Sister.

As she took the remains of his tea upstairs and put it by his bed in the empty dorm, Mary Ellen sensed a shadow hanging over her friend. She couldn't guess exactly what was troubling him, but she knew it was bad. If he would only tell her they might find a way of solving it. Angela and Sally were both approachable and Mary Ellen felt that if she confided in them they would find a way to help – but if Billy wouldn't tell her what was wrong, she couldn't do anything for him.

There was no sign of Billy when the children gathered for prayers and a glass of milk before bedtime, and Mary Ellen was truly worried. She couldn't shake off the feeling that something bad was about to happen, but she didn't know what to do. Even if she went to the boys' dorm to look for him, there was no guarantee that she would find him.

She had to try because her instinct told her something was wrong. Billy had looked so miserable and he'd won his match so he ought to have been happy.

Jumping out of bed, Mary Ellen dragged on her clothes and left the dormitory. She would go down in the garden and throw stones at Billy's window. If he woke up he would come out to see what was wrong.

She crept along the hall, finding her way to the back door. One small light was always left burning at night in case anyone came down, and the carers were about all the time. The back door was unbolted, which was unusual, and the back of Mary Ellen's neck prickled, because it should not have been opened. Someone had got here first.

'Billy . . .' she called softly as she went out into the darkness of the garden. 'Are you here?'

For a moment there was silence and then a small shadow came towards her. 'Mary Ellen, what are you doin' here?' Billy's voice hissed at her. 'I'm waitin' fer Arthur. I've got to go with him.'

'No, you mustn't,' she cried and grabbed at his arm. 'I shan't let you. Billy, he's trouble. Please don't be foolish . . .'

'You don't understand,' Billy said and his face was pale in the light of a moon suddenly revealed by shifting clouds. 'If I don't go he'll hurt you all – he's threatened to set the place on fire . . .'

'Billy!' She was shocked and anxious. 'Don't you see, he's bad? You mustn't go with him.'

'I've got to,' he said, and his voice broke. 'He could hurt all of you.'

'I told you to come alone, you little bugger. We need yer to help us do a job tonight.' Arthur's harsh voice broke into their speech. 'Get rid of her or I'll break her neck.'

'You just leave her alone or I'll kill you!' Billy said and stood forward. 'Why do you want to come back 'ere? I don't want anythin' to do with . . .'

'It won't be just her I'll hurt if yer don't behave,' Arthur muttered and moved threateningly towards them. 'I'll give the pair of yer a good hidin'.'

'Run for it, Mary Ellen, he means it,' Billy warned.

Mary Ellen gave a screech of fright, but instead of running off, she lunged at Arthur, kicking and screaming at the top of her voice. He gave a grunt of pain as she kicked his ankles and then swore furiously, making a grab for her hair and tugging it until she yelled in pain. Mary Ellen turned her head and sank her sharp little white teeth into Arthur's hand and he cried out in anger. He hit out at her and caught her in the face, knocking her to the ground where she lay gasping for breath. Her head was swimming and the last thing she heard was Billy's cry of horror before the outside light was switched on and a woman came out into the garden.

'What's going on out here?' Angela's voice called. 'Who is it? Whoever you are I've got a poker here and I've already sent for the police.'

'You'll pay for this, you runt,' Arthur's voice hissed. 'I'll be back and when I do you'd better be ready to come or I'll kill your little friend here.'

Billy was on his knees helping Mary Ellen to her

feet when Angela came out to them. 'What's going on here? Did I see a man running away?'

'It was just a tramp,' Billy said. 'Me and Mary Ellen came down to get a drink of water and saw him trying to get in the window so we tried to stop him . . .'

Mary Ellen looked at Billy. She wanted to blurt out the truth but was too scared. Angela was looking hard at Billy.

'This door was unbolted,' she said. 'I don't think a tramp could have done that. Are you going to tell me the truth, Billy?'

'It is the truth,' Billy said defiantly. 'I ain't got nuffin' else to say – and nor ain't Mary Ellen.'

'You should tell Angela the truth,' Mary Ellen said quietly. Her cheek felt sore and she was close to bursting into tears, but her pride wouldn't let her.

'Well, I shall have to tell the police and Sister,' Angela said. 'Because if there was someone trying to break in we shall need to call the police . . .'

Billy looked at Mary Ellen. 'I'm sorry he hurt you, but he'll do worse if I don't go,' he said. 'It's not her fault, miss. She was just tryin' to help me.'

He turned and ran off through the garden. Mary Ellen watched him go but she couldn't stop him and she was hurting too much to try.

'Can you tell me the truth?' Angela asked, but Mary Ellen shook her head. 'This is serious, you know. If Billy has run off with someone we need to know, Mary Ellen.'

'I can't tell you, miss. I want to but I can't . . .'

'Well, by the look of you, you've been taught a hard lesson. Come on, I'll take you in and clean you up and you can have a drink of hot milk before you go to bed – but I shall have to lock up and I must report this to Sister Beatrice in the morning. And I'll have to let the police know what happened here.'

'Please, miss,' Mary Ellen begged. 'Billy didn't want to go. He might come back in the morning – and if you tell the police he will be in trouble . . .'

Angela hesitated, because an intruder was serious, but she wasn't sure anyone had actually been trying to get in and she didn't want to stir up trouble for Billy if she could help it. 'Well, I shan't disturb Sister just now. I'll make sure everything is safe and I'll talk to her in the morning – it will be for her to decide whether we need to inform the authorities. I suppose Billy might come back and it might be best to see what he has to say before we go to the police.'

When Mary Ellen woke on Sunday morning Alice was opening the curtains and calling to the girls to get up and wash. 'You shouldn't be yawning when it's morning,' Alice said, coming to her bed. 'Didn't you sleep well?'

Mary Ellen shook her head and stretched. Her cheek felt sore and she thought she must have a bruise. Sally would have asked her why she hadn't slept, but Alice seemed preoccupied and just walked on to the next bed, as if her mind was elsewhere. Mary Ellen wished that Sally was there, because perhaps she might have told her how worried she was about Billy and the threats his brother had made the previous night. The horror of what had happened flooded over her and she jumped out of bed, in a hurry to get washed and go down to breakfast to see if Billy had come back. Surely, he wouldn't have gone to join Arthur? His brother would make him do bad things and Billy would get into trouble. She was scared, because Sister was going to be cross when Angela told her about what had happened in the garden.

Mary Ellen's clothes were muddy from where she'd fallen when Arthur hit her and she had to get clean ones out, and put the others in the washing basket. That would earn her a black mark, because they'd been clean on the day before – but that was nothing compared to the danger Billy was in if he hadn't returned.

She ran down to the dining room on fire with the need to find her friend. Please let him have come back; please don't let him be in trouble . . .

Billy wasn't in his usual seat, and that sent a chill through Mary Ellen, because he was always the first down. If he'd really run away anything could happen to him and she felt anxious just thinking about it.

Selecting two slices of toast with a spoon of marmalade, Mary Ellen carefully carried her tray to their table. She sat sipping her orange squash waiting for Billy to come in and join her, but he still hadn't arrived by the time she'd finished eating. She was just thinking of going to look for him when she saw Angela coming towards her and her heart began to pound madly.

'Sister Beatrice wants you to come to her office. Don't look so frightened, Mary Ellen. She just wants to ask you a few questions about last night.'

'She'll give me the cane . . .'

'No, I am sure she won't. I'll stay with you, if you like?'

'Yes, please, miss.'

Mary Ellen pushed away her used plate and stood up, following Angela from the dining room through the hall and up the stairs to Sister Beatrice's office. Her mouth was dry and her heart beating so fast that she thought her chest would burst. She was in trouble, she was sure of it!

Angela knocked at the door and then pushed it open and went in, Mary Ellen following behind like a scalded mouse. Sister was looking out of the window, her hands crossed behind her back and she looked stiff and straight. She must be very angry!

'What do you know of what happened last night, child?'

'We heard a noise in the garden and went out.' Mary Ellen fidgeted as she lied. 'A man was trying to get in . . .'

'You heard a noise and went out – what were

you doing out of your dorms and why were you together?'

'Billy was upset,' Mary Ellen fabricated desperately. 'I went down for a drink of water and he was there and . . .'

'Billy did not come to my office as I asked last evening. I believe he intended to run away – and perhaps you tried to stop him. Is that what really happened?'

'Billy thought you were going to whack him.'

Sister frowned, looking concerned rather than angry.

'Had he come to my office, I merely intended to inquire whether he wished to remain here. We have certain rules at St Saviour's, which I consider necessary for the safety and comfort of my children and staff. However, apart from sensible rules I do not believe the life here is hard or unhappy for most of our children – and I have to consider all my children. One unruly boy cannot be allowed to upset the smooth running of the home for all the others. I meant to ask Billy to think carefully whether he could accept these rules and continue to live here – or whether he would prefer to live elsewhere. It seems I have my answer. He has run off without a word, making more trouble for all of us.'

'Sister Beatrice,' Angela intervened. 'We do not know what the reason behind Billy's disappearance may be. It is possible that he will turn up later with a perfectly good explanation. Doesn't

Billy have an older brother? Mary Ellen, is that who it was?'

Mary Ellen hung her head and wouldn't answer.

'I hope that you are right, but I take leave to doubt it.' Sister Beatrice seemed annoyed with Angela for speaking up for Billy. She stared coldly at Mary Ellen. 'I hope that you are speaking the truth when you tell me you knew nothing of Billy's plans to run away. I am disappointed in you, Mary Ellen. You cheated by writing out those lines and putting Billy's name to them. I want you to promise me you will not do anything so underhanded again.'

'Yes, Sister.' Mary Ellen's bottom lip trembled. 'I just wanted to save Billy from getting the cane . . .'

'I very seldom cane anyone, child. Just a rap over the knuckles occasionally. But some children need discipline. I am not a cruel person, please do not start to think of me as an ogre, for it was not my intention to cane Billy this time, whatever he may have thought, because it clearly does not work for him – and if you know where he is hiding, tell him to come to me and we shall discuss his position here.' She paused, then, 'Very well, you may go. I have decided that I shall not withhold your privileges since you confessed your crime – but any further transgressions will be severely punished. Do you understand me?'

'Yes, Sister.'

'Very well, run along.'

Mary Ellen looked at Angela, who smiled and

nodded. Making good her escape, she went out of the door but did not close it and heard Angela speak to Sister Beatrice.

'Shall you inform the police?'

'Not immediately. I hope the foolish boy is simply hiding somewhere. If that is the case he will come out sooner or later, when he gets hungry.'

'We must hope you are right,' Angela said, sounding anxious. 'I'm not sure it wouldn't be a good idea to let the police know he's gone missing. He is out there on the streets somewhere and I don't like the idea that a man may be hanging about in the garden.'

'I cannot imagine what he hopes to find here. We have nothing of value for him to steal. Besides, you were not certain there was an intruder, were you?' Angela shook her head. 'I believe that we shall discover my version was the truth and the boy has run away – but, because I think I may have frightened him into it, we shall give him a few hours to return. If he does not then I shall have to report this incident to the police.'

'If they knew he was missing the police might find him and bring him back . . .'

'If I report Billy missing the matter could be taken out of my hands. It might then be a decision for the magistrates as to whether Billy could remain here. I am as worried about his welfare as you, Angela, but I believe he is just as likely to be hiding here in the house and will give in when he's hungry.'

Mary Ellen felt a shiver down her spine. She didn't think Billy was hiding. He had run away like Sister said – and she was afraid that he'd gone to his brother to stop him setting fire to the home. Arthur would make him do bad things. Perhaps she ought to have told Sister about Arthur, but Billy would never forgive her for being a snitch. All Mary Ellen could do was to pray that he was safe and would come back when he was ready.

CHAPTER 25

Sally was listening to the radio as she helped her mother clear the table and wash the supper dishes with hot water and soap powder. It was a music programme and they were playing all the popular tunes of the last few years. She hummed one of the latest hits and then started to sing the words: 'Maybe it's because I'm a Londoner . . .'

'Sally, can I borrow your blue dress tomorrow?' Brenda asked, entering the kitchen, her hair in wire curlers and wearing only her pink rayon pyjamas. 'I've got to see the office manager first thing Monday and I think I may be in line for promotion. If he makes me a secretary rather than just one of the typing pool I'll get a rise and I'll take you to the flicks.'

'You don't have to bribe me,' Sally said. 'Of course you can wear my best dress, Bren – but don't get ink all over it.'

'You're a love,' Brenda laughed and grabbed her about the waist as a dance tune came on the radio, waltzing her round the kitchen. 'The office manager is absolutely dishy. I should love to work for him.'

'I thought you were going out with that chap from the accountant's office?'

'I am sort of, but it isn't serious,' Brenda said. 'It's a bit like you and that apprentice plumber. Why don't you go around with him any more?'

'Keith doesn't come round any longer, because we quarrelled. Besides, I don't think of him as anything but a friend.'

'You don't mind that he doesn't come, do you?'

'No, not a bit. It was fun going out with him for a while, but I'm not in love with him.'

'Good, because I saw him out with another girl. He was in the queue at the Rex last week and they seemed to be very lovey-dovey.'

'Oh, well, good luck to him and her,' Sally said. 'I really don't mind what he does, Bren.'

'Is it Mr Markham?' Brenda whispered confidentially as their mother hung the tea towel over the kitchen range to dry.

'You know I think a lot of him, but he hasn't said anything definite yet. We're still getting to know one another, Bren.' Sally turned her head so that her sister couldn't see her face. She was falling deeper and deeper in love with Andrew every time they met, but although he'd told her he liked her an awful lot, and he'd kissed her a few times, she wasn't sure if it was more than a flirtation on his part. Sally sometimes felt that he was the one and longed for him to tell her he loved her as much as she loved him, but she knew he was way above her and it seemed unlikely that he could really be serious about her.

'I hope you're not falling for him,' Brenda said. 'You know it would never work, don't you? He isn't our sort. The folks wouldn't like it – they wouldn't feel comfortable asking a man like that to tea, let alone seeing him married to their daughter.'

'Stop being daft,' Sally said, although she knew her sister was right. Dad had seemed to get on all right with Andrew when he'd called round to take her out, but her mum had made it plain she didn't approve. 'I'm tired and I'm going to bed.'

She snapped off the radio, feeling out of sorts with her sister. Brenda was just being priggish. What did it matter if they did come from a different class to Andrew? Besides, there was never going to be anything between them so it was all nonsense. As she'd told her sister, she admired Andrew for his work with the children and as a surgeon. The fact that his smile turned her insides to mush was neither here nor there.

She pushed the silly ideas Brenda's words had aroused to the back of her mind and went up to bed. They were busy at St Saviour's and she had another long day ahead of her in the morning.

'Hi, Michelle,' Sally said when she went up to the sick room with a parcel containing sterilised dressings and various medications that had been delivered the following morning. 'Sister said you needed these so I brought them up. How are you? I haven't seen you for a chat for ages. I wondered if you'd like to go to the flicks one night.'

'Yes, why not? I should like to see *The Ghost and Mrs Muir* – it's the new Cary Grant film and I like him. I think that might be fun.'

'Yes, I'd like to see that,' Sally agreed. 'When shall we go?'

'What about tomorrow?'

'That suits me. I don't have a class that night. I'll bring a change of clothes and we'll go straight after work. Have a cup of coffee somewhere first, perhaps?' She hesitated, then, 'Are you worried about anything? Only you've seemed a bit quiet lately.'

'My father isn't well,' Michelle said. 'He has a bad cough, that's all.'

'Oh, I'm sorry about that,' Sally said, accepting her word, though she had a feeling there was more. 'I'll see you on Tuesday, then?'

'Lovely,' Michelle agreed. 'I shall have to get on. I need to check these supplies and then I have a dressing to do. Jilly Watkins has a nasty sore on her leg and I'm afraid it might turn septic.'

'Poor little thing; I'll leave you to it. I'm glad we had a chat,' Sally said and left her to get on with her work. Michelle was friendly enough, but she obviously had something on her mind, but whatever it was she didn't intend to share it.

Sally wondered if it concerned Alice, because she'd noticed that the other carer hadn't been paying as much attention to her work recently as she ought, and perhaps Michelle had noticed too. Sally would have liked to ask Alice what was wrong, but didn't like to intrude.

Oh, well, it wasn't her problem. She'd better get on with her own work or she'd be the one in trouble! And the last thing she needed was to lose her job.

Sally was reading to the children when the door of the schoolroom opened and Mr Markham entered quietly so as not to interrupt her, but the children had seen him and started to whisper, giggling and looking at each other excitedly. Sally finished her story and closed her book.

'Children, say hello to Mr Markham.' Her heart jerked as she saw the little expression of expectation on his lips, and she felt the happiness dancing inside her. How handsome he looked with his soft, slightly overlong hair and that teasing smile, but she had to behave as if he were just another staff member and stop herself wanting to laugh for the pleasure of seeing him.

'Hello, Mr Markham,' they chorused and looked expectant. Then one little boy piped up, 'Have you come to tell us a story?'

'Well, I do happen to have a copy of my latest book about the Big Hairy Spider . . .'

Cries of delight greeted his announcement and then absolute hush as he took a seat next to Sally and opened the large picture book. His story finished, he left them to peruse the latest book and puzzle, and he joined Sally as she stood by the window, her face half-turned from him. His nearness sent her senses spinning but she forced herself to act naturally.

'Perhaps we could go somewhere this evening?'

Sally felt a crushing disappointment as she said, 'I have evening class tonight. I'm sorry . . .'

'What time does it end?'

'Eight thirty.'

'I'll meet you and we'll go for a snack somewhere. Perhaps some of those excellent fish and chips we once shared?'

'Yes, lovely, thank you,' Sally said and blushed as she became aware that the children were watching.

'Say thank you to Mr Markham, children.'

'This evening, then,' he said and walked to the door.

The children chorused their thanks and he left them, sending Sally what she thought of as his special smile. He really was a lovely man and he did seem to like her, which made her happy. It was the odd the way his smile made her heart beat faster and her tummy tumble with excitement, because no one had ever made her feel like that before.

Her thoughts turned for a moment to her future, because she wasn't sure if her hopes of becoming a nurse would ever come true. With the present state of her father's finances she simply could not afford all the books she would need.

She sighed deeply as the bell rang and she ushered the children into the dining room to drink their milk. She was an idiot to feel this way about Andrew Markham, because, as Brenda had told her, nothing could ever come of it – their worlds were too far apart.

CHAPTER 26

Alice looked for Jack in vain as she reached the corner where he normally stood in the shadows to wait for her. He was nowhere in sight and her breath caught in her throat. This was the third evening in a row that he hadn't been waiting for her – and she was sure now that she'd missed her period. It was the twenty-fifth of November now and she was due the previous week. She'd always been as regular as clockwork until now. The trickle of fear went down her spine as she thought about what would happen if Jack didn't come any more. How long would she be able to keep her condition a secret – and what happened when her parents found out?

Choking back the tears that threatened, Alice looked about her one last time before moving on. It was too chilly to stand about long and she already had a bit of a cold. She wished she'd told Jack of her suspicions the last time they'd met but she hadn't wanted to say until she was sure. He got angry if she went on about things, especially when she asked about his plans to leave Butcher's employ.

'Are you tryin' to get me killed, Alice?' he'd demanded the last time she said anything. 'If I go too quickly they'll get suspicious and then I'm for the chop.'

'Sorry. It's just that I'm scared. I couldn't bear it if anything happened to you. I just want us to be together.'

'It's what I want too,' he told her and kissed her, smiling down at her. 'I'm not goin' to break my promise, Alice luv. We'll go away together and we'll be married. I shan't change my mind.'

'Shall I see you tomorrow?'

'I'll be here and we'll go for a meal and then back to my place,' he'd promised, but he hadn't come and Alice had been on thorns for days.

She had started to walk home when a car drew up beside her; the door opened and Jack's voice told her to get in quick. She obeyed and he glanced over his shoulder and then set off down the lane, driving as if all the bats in hell were after him.

'Is something wrong, Jack?'

'Butcher has had someone following me for the past couple of days. He thinks I've done somethin', but he doesn't know what – and if he discovered the truth I'd be dead. I couldn't meet you as usual, because I was scared he would cotton on to us goin' steady. If he knew, he would use you against me – threaten to harm you if I didn't do what he wants.'

'Does he want you to do something bad?' Alice turned her head to look at him fearfully as he shot down one lane and up another, doubling back on himself several times until he finally parked in the seclusion of a pub yard. It was dark in the shadows away from the lights of the building and Alice couldn't see his face. 'Why is he having you followed?'

'Because Butcher wants me to kill someone and I've told him I won't do it. I've done some things I'm not proud of, Alice, beaten up a few men who wouldn't pay up – but I stop short of murder. He knows that and they've never asked before, but now they say it's a test to prove my loyalty. I reckon they know I want out, girl. And some stuff of theirs has been pinched . . . some stolen stuff they had stashed away in an office safe. Butcher reckons Arthur Baggins had a hand in it and they want me to kill him – but I've refused, told him I won't do it.'

'Jack! You haven't taken that stuff, have you?'

'Nah, I ain't a thief,' he protested, but she thought he was lying. 'He wants me to kill the bloke he suspects of stealing the stuff. Butcher says that if I'm not in with Arthur, I'll do as he asks, but I ain't goin' to do it, Alice. I ain't goin' ter swing for him – even if it means we have to go sooner than I intended. I've got to get hold of some more money. I know you won't like this, Alice – but me and Arthur are goin' ter do a job together. And then we'll clear orf and I promise I'll go straight. I'm only doin' it fer you, so we can have a decent life in America.'

'Oh, Jack, please don't do whatever it is you've planned . . .' Her breath caught in her throat. 'We'll manage with whatever you have. I don't need much if I have you. I just want to get away from here and I couldn't bear it if you were killed. How soon can we leave? What do you want me to do?'

'Just carry on workin' same as usual, Alice. You can't tell anyone or I'm a dead man. If they got wind of what I've been up to they would kill me without a thought.'

'I thought you said they were suspicious?'

'They are but they don't know what I'm really doin', Alice. I just need to get a bit of extra money, and then we'll go. I promise, Alice. I really care about you, love – and I'll look after yer. Just trust me and it will all be all right.'

'Don't do anything silly!' Alice cried. 'I want you, not money. I need to tell you something, Jack – I'm pretty sure I'm pregnant . . .' Her voice died away as she saw the shock in his eyes and his quick frown. 'I knew you wouldn't like it . . . I'm sorry.'

'It takes two,' Jack said gruffly. 'I'd say I'm pleased, Alice, but it just complicates things – makes it all the more important that you don't get dragged into this.' He was silent for a moment, and then nodded as if his mind was made up. 'I can't take you with me when I go, Alice. I'll have to make a quick break for it – and you would just slow me down.'

'But you promised . . .'

He leaned forward, touching his mouth to hers. 'I'm not abandoning you, Alice. You must stay here and carry on as if nothing was different. As soon as I get settled and I'm sure I haven't been followed I shall send for you. I'll send you a letter with some money and you can come and join me wherever I am.'

'Oh, Jack.' Alice's eyes filled with tears but she struggled to hold them back. Jack would be angry if she made a fuss but she was frightened – frightened that once he'd left London he would simply forget her. Why should he bother with a pregnant girlfriend who was plump and plain? He swore she was lovely and that he loved her, but Alice didn't feel glamorous or pretty and she knew Jack would always be able to sweet-talk a girl into bed with him. She'd fallen for the charm and the kisses that drew her heart from her body.

Alice was about to say she would risk anything to be with him when car headlights swept into the car park. A man got out and started to walk towards them. Jack swore loudly, grabbed the steering wheel and took the brake off, revving his engine as he attempted to swivel about and leave the car park by another exit.

'Get down,' he hissed at her. 'I don't want him to see you.' He put his foot down, deliberately crashing his car into the other as he swept past. His car was bigger and sent the other swerving off at a tangent. Jack reversed into a dark lane, and then took off down another at terrific speed, leaving Alice trembling and shaken. 'Damn them to hell! That was Big Harry and I'd bet my last shilling that he was going to kill me. I can't go back to my place. I'm going to leave you near St Saviour's and keep goin', Alice. You'll have to get home yourself – and remember to carry on as normal. I'll get back to you when I can . . .'

Alice held her breath as he drove through the darkened streets, narrowly missing a bus pulling out from a stop and an oncoming lorry. She was trembling when he screeched to a halt and told her to jump out.

'Jack, I love you,' she cried despairingly but he didn't answer her, simply speeding off into the night.

Alice ran into the alley at the side of St Saviour's and stood there trembling. She was afraid to move in case she'd been seen getting out of Jack's car and she felt like bursting into tears.

'Alice, are you all right?' Nan's voice brought her head up and she shook it, unable to speak. 'You're trembling. Come on, I'm going back into St Saviour's for a while before I go home. I'll make you a cup of tea and you can tell me what happened.'

Alice didn't want to go with her, but Nan had her by the arm and was pushing her gently but firmly towards the back entrance of the home. Alice felt too weak to resist. Her mind was in a whirl, fear and shock at what had happened, fear for Jack – and what was going to happen if Jack didn't write to her again.

Nan took her into the warmth of her sitting room and put the kettle on a small gas ring to make tea. 'What happened to upset you like this, Alice?'

'Someone came after Jack. He thinks they were going to kill him and he drove fast to get away from them . . .'

'Who is Jack?' Nan asked, frowning.

'My boyfriend. He wants to marry me. We were going away but they won't let him go because he knows too much about them. He went off and left me here . . .'

'Oh, Alice.' Nan looked at her sadly. 'What have you got yourself into?'

'I didn't want to at first.' Tears were slipping down her cheeks. 'Pa would half-kill me if he knew . . . but Jack wouldn't leave me alone and I fell in love with him.'

'Oh, you poor girl,' Nan said. 'Dry your eyes. Nothing happened to you, did it? It's Jack they're after and not you, so stop worrying.'

'But if Jack doesn't come back . . .' Alice choked back the words that would shame her. She couldn't tell Nan what a fool she'd been. She couldn't tell anyone, even her friend Michelle or her sister. 'I don't know what to do . . .'

'Here, drink this; it's brandy and it will help with the shock. You ought to have something or you'll be no good to anyone. After you've calmed down we should go to the police.'

'I couldn't do that.' Alice was horrified. 'You don't understand about these men, Nan. If I went to the police they would have me killed – even if they were inside a prison cell. Jack warned me to carry on as usual and tell no one. I shouldn't even have told you.'

Nan studied her in silence for a while and then nodded. 'Don't think I do not understand, Alice. I probably understand more than you think. Things happened to my daughter that I couldn't stop . . . I can't talk about it, but I do know something of what you've been through. I thought there was something wrong recently.'

'I've been such a fool . . .'

'Is there something more you want to tell me?'

Alice shook her head. She sipped her tea and began to feel better. The brandy had stopped her shaking and the tea was comforting.

'I'm all right now. I'm sorry I was foolish . . .'

'You're not foolish at all. Would you like me to walk home with you?'

'No, I'll be all right.'

'Take the bus . . . here, let me give you the fare.' Nan took her purse from her coat pocket. 'Go on, take it. You can't walk in the state you were in. Remember I'm always here to help if you need me.'

Alice thanked her and went back outside. It was cold and there was a bus just coming that would take her most of the way home. She ran to catch it because she couldn't bring herself to walk home in the dark.

CHAPTER 27

It was nice being home for a short break, Angela thought as she finished arranging the flowers in the church hall. She'd come down late on Friday so that she could help her mother on the day of the dance and this was the first she'd seen of the arrangements. The people from a local and very popular inn had just arrived to set up the bar and the tables for the buffet. Mrs Hendry never did things by half. The buffet would be high quality and everyone would be given a glass of white wine on his or her arrival. After that the bar would be charged for and a percentage of the profits would be donated to the charity. Mrs Hendry had used the caterers before and said they were always reliable.

Angela had invited several of the nurses and carers from St Saviour's, offering them the tickets for free as a reward for all their hard work, but only Michelle and Sally had taken her up on her offer and they were coming down that day and would stay at her home overnight.

Angela wandered over and introduced herself to the caterers, studying the menu with awe: tiny pastry tarts filled with smoked salmon or cream cheese with chives; game pâté on squares of toast, and cold asparagus wrapped in thin brown bread – wherever did they get that at this time of year? Out of a jar perhaps, or was it imported? Harrods often had out-of-season imported foods that no one else would think of selling. Also prawns in a rose sauce in flaky pastry cups, special game pies, venison and herb tartlets, and local cheeses with fresh bread and butter and pickles.

Just looking at the smart menu made her mouth water. It was an age since she'd tasted anything as good, not since she'd gone to London – except for the times Mark had taken her out, of course. Even then, she hadn't had half the choice there was on her mother's enticing menu. No wonder people with money thought it worth the price of the tickets! Yet even though the food made her feel hungry, a part of her was revolted at the thought of all the money squandered on luxuries like this. Remembering the shortages they'd all endured for several long years, and the homes the St Saviour's children came from, where they were fortunate to have a bit of bread and dripping, she felt angry. Where was the justice when some people had so much and others had nothing? It made her feel ashamed of the things she'd taken for granted all her life, and determined to do more to help those in need.

Yet she was a sane, sensible woman and she knew that she couldn't expect everyone to have her own sense of social justice and fair play. Reading the menu again, she was amazed. How on earth did the caterers make a profit out of what her mother was charging for the tickets? Angela realised that her mother had pulled out all the stops to make this a special affair and had gone to so much trouble with all these tasty morsels that made her feel hungry just at the thought of them.

Angela thanked the caterers, and then went to put on her warm red coat. She was just leaving the hall when a car drew up and Mark Adderbury waved to her. He was casually dressed in slacks and an open-necked shirt under a tweed jacket, very different from the smart suits he wore in London.

'Are you on your way home? Mrs Hendry told me you were here – may I give you a lift?' He got out to open the door for her, and Angela paused to glance round at the quiet country scene, so very different from the grime of Spitalfields, before she slid into the passenger seat, appreciating the smell of leather.

A wry smile touched her mouth as she realised that she had conflicting emotions: Mark was one of the well-off people she'd been angry about earlier, but he used his money and his time to help others less fortunate. Yet that didn't stop him enjoying a nice car or a pleasant home, and good food too. Perhaps this need inside her to help the people who were in desperate straits sometimes led her to be too harsh. Her mother was undoubtedly a middle-class snob, who admired people with money – but she'd worked very hard to make this event a success and Angela would be sure to thank her properly for that.

'It should be a good do this evening?'

'Oh yes, I think so,' she said, glancing at him as he started the car. 'You are coming, I hope?'

'I wouldn't miss it for the world. Mrs Hendry's charity affairs are always worth attending. Your mother has the knack for this sort of thing, Angela.'

'Yes, she really does,' Angela acknowledged. 'You should see the menu for the buffet. I'm used to piles of sandwiches and fruitcake without much fruit in it, and mostly pastry sausage rolls, if we're lucky. It made me feel ravenous just to see what they have planned for tonight.'

'Your mother's dinner dances are famous,' he said. 'I'll take you out for lunch if you like – treat you to something special?'

'Sorry, I can't. I've got masses more to do at home and I can't leave it to my mother; she's done enough as it is . . . and she's looking a bit tired, I thought. Mother has invited you to her drinks party before the dance, hasn't she?'

'Yes. I imagine you will be busy helping with that,' Mark said, a little sigh escaping him. 'I was hoping I might get you to myself for a while.'

'Lunch tomorrow?' she said on a teasing note. 'I can catch the later train back to London.'

'Why don't I drive you back? We can stop for

lunch at one of my favourite restaurants on the way.'

'Lovely,' Angela said. 'Yes, I shall enjoy that far more than trying to squeeze a hasty lunch in today.'

'That is a date,' Mark said, drawing to a halt in front of her father's modern red brick house. It had large gardens all round, though at the moment they looked a little forlorn. 'I shall see you this evening – don't work too hard.'

'Oh, I enjoy it,' Angela said as he opened the door for her to get out. 'I shall enjoy this evening all the more because you will be there, Mark. I have you to thank for my job at St Saviour's and I'm so grateful.'

'Getting on better with Sister Beatrice now?'

'I think I understand her a little better. We had a long discussion after I apologised for speaking out of turn and Sister has been thinking about some ideas of her own, which she will no doubt tell you when she's ready . . .'

'Well, keep trying. We need both of you at St Saviour's, Angela.'

Angela turned to wave as he drove off. She was trying very hard to keep the truce with Sister Beatrice but there was a slight feeling of tension between them and one of these days it was going to boil over.

Michelle and Sally had arrived and were unpacking in their room. Angela smiled as she saw the tasteful flowers her mother had arranged, the clean towels, fresh individual soaps and flannels that had been put out for them. Everything was as perfect as Mrs Hendry could make it, and most of it she'd done herself, because she only had a daily for the rough work and a cook when she was entertaining.

Sally turned as she came in. 'Your parents have a lovely home, Angela. I'm not sure I'd want to work in London if I lived here.'

'It is nice but I was bored. I hope you will be comfortable here.'

'It is very nice,' Michelle said and smiled. 'We're both looking forward to this evening.'

'I'm sorry I couldn't manage tickets for your boyfriends but they were all gone. I only managed to wangle two in the end.'

'I don't really have a boyfriend,' Sally said and laughed, though her cheeks were flushed and her eyes did not meet Angela's.

'I haven't got anyone special either,' Michelle said.

'Is there anything we can do to help Mrs Hendry?' Sally offered and Michelle nodded agreement.

'I'll ask her after lunch, but I expect she will say you're here to enjoy yourselves and tell you to walk down to the river and explore for a couple of hours – and you are here to relax. You both work extremely hard at St Saviour's and that's why I offered free tickets, because all this is as much for you as the children.'

Angela walked away, leaving the girls to hang up

their dresses for the evening. She herself intended to help prepare canapés and polish glasses ready for their guests that evening, but her mother would never allow guests to help.

'Well, your mother has done herself and you proud, my love,' Mr Hendry said, coming up to Angela as she stood by an open window, surveying the crowded room. It was filled with prosperous men and their wives and daughters, all of them wearing expensive gowns and diamond rings on their fingers, the scent of French perfume heavy on the air. 'I think everyone is enjoying themselves – including the friends you invited down.'

'Yes, they've both been dancing most of the time.' Angela had noticed that Sally had drunk lemonade all night, though Michelle seemed to enjoy the wine and punch cups on offer and might have been just a little merry.

'What about you? Too tired to dance with your old man?'

'Oh, Daddy, of course I'm not,' Angela said and put down her lemonade. She too had steered clear of both the wine and the heady punch cups. 'I should love to dance with you.'

He took her hand and led her onto the floor just as the band struck up for another waltz. Smiling, Angela followed his lead. Her father was a good dancer and he'd taught her when she was fourteen at one of her mother's charity events.

'I've missed you, my love,' he said, smiling down

at her. 'Are you happy up there? If not you can come home and help me in the office again.'

'Thank you for asking but I love my work. It's the children, Daddy. Some of them tug at your heartstrings and you want to scoop them up and protect them from all harm.'

'Yes, children have a way of doing that to you,' he murmured. 'It's the way I feel about you, even though you're grown up and you've been married. You see, you will always be my little girl. When we lost your brother you became all the more precious to me.'

'Oh, Dad. I'm glad I'm precious to you, but I wish you hadn't lost Steven.'

'At least he was spared the horror of war. Besides, you are enough for me – my special person in all the world.' He squeezed her hand and smiled down at her. 'That's why I want to look after you.'

He was still a very attractive man with silvered hair at the temples and a distinguished air, but there were slight signs of strain in his face that she hadn't noticed before. She wondered but then he smiled at a friend and the look had vanished.

'I love you too, but I don't need protecting now. I have to go out into the world and fight dragons for myself.'

'And for some of those children?'

'Yes, particularly one little girl and boy at the moment. I'm worried about him, Daddy. He's gone missing and I'm not sure why. Sister Beatrice thinks he ran away because he'd been naughty, but Mary Ellen is sure it's something different; but won't tell me why, though I think it may be something to do with his bully of a brother.'

'If you're worried you should go to the police.'

'We have but Sister is anxious not to cause too much fuss in case they think Billy ought to be sent elsewhere –'

'I could put you in touch with a lawyer who would help if it comes to that.'

'Yes, thank you.' She looked up at him. 'Are you all right? Nothing wrong?'

'Of course not, why do you ask?'

She shook her head. 'No reason, just asking . . .' she murmured as their dance ended.

Angela was about to seek out her mother and ask her if she needed any help when Mark Adderbury came up to her.

'That is a wonderful dress, Angela. Red always suits you.'

'I bought it before the war,' she said and laughed. 'But thank you for the compliment.'

'You haven't danced with me yet this evening,' he said. 'Do you have a spare dance for an old friend?'

'Of course I have,' Angela said. 'I had to dance with all those businessmen Mother had invited to meet me. I'm after donations for my fund for the children and so far it looks promising. I might get even more than the dance itself will raise if they all keep their word.'

Mark led her into the quickstep and there was

little time for small talk, because it took all her concentration and breath to keep up with the pace of the intricate steps. By the time they'd finished she was laughing, out of breath and warm. She smiled up at him, wondering at the look in his eyes. Just for a moment there was something that made her catch her breath . . . but then it had gone and he was his normal caring and calm self; the man who had helped pull her through the months of sorrow and despair.

'I must go and dance with those St Saviour's girls,' Mark said. 'I shall see you in the morning, Angela.'

She smiled, watching as he walked away to speak to Michelle, who was standing with a glass in her hand. Sally was dancing with someone. Angela looked again and realised it was Mr Markham. She hadn't known he would be there that evening; Mark must have sold him the ticket. He and Sally seemed to be getting on well. Sally was laughing and gazing up at him, her eyes bright with excitement – and was that something more? Angela was surprised and then pleased, because they looked so right together. Her mother might say the two were worlds apart, but Angela didn't agree. If they loved each other – and from what she could see she was guessing they did – then let the world say what it liked. Angela was just glad the girl she liked so much was enjoying herself.

'Well, are you satisfied, Angela?' her mother's voice said from behind her. 'I really don't know what you expected from this evening – but I've done my best for you. Just do not ask me to do it again. I'm really not sure I could raise the enthusiasm for such an event twice.'

'Don't spoil it, Mum, please.' Angela turned to look at her mother, who had come up to her unnoticed, and frowned. 'It's a lovely evening, Mum. You've done us proud. I know you don't approve of me working at St Saviour's but it is something I wanted to do and I am grateful for this evening.' Angela noticed that her mother looked a little flushed, which was unusual for her.

'Well, I wanted it to be special.' Her mother stared at her. 'You're looking thin. Why don't you come home and settle down? There are several perfectly eligible men here this evening. I'm sure you could find someone if you tried – and stop all this charity nonsense. You're letting yourself down, Angela, and us. If you want to help others, I could give you some work writing letters and raising money for the vicar's latest project overseas.'

'Mum, why can't you see what's under your nose? There are children in London close to starving . . .'

'Well, I'm sure they needn't be if their parents stopped drinking and went to work. You've changed since you married, Angela, and I don't like it. Why can't you be as you were before the war?'

'Because it changed everything . . . including me, Mum.'

'I suppose you're still grieving over John. Surely, it's time to move on, my dear? I'm only thinking of your happiness.'

'I know but I'm happy doing what I'm doing, and I have no intention of remarrying for a while.'

'You can't still be grieving after all this time?'

'I loved him very much, Mum. I shall never forget but, yes, I can think of John without breaking down now. However, I'm not ready to move on – and I certainly don't want to get married.'

'Well, I don't understand you, and I think you're a fool. Anyone can see that Mark . . . but you won't listen to me. I may not approve of what you do, Angela, but I hope you know I would help if you needed me.'

'You've been wonderful.' Angela kissed her cheek and caught the smell of strong alcohol, a smell she'd never associated with her mother. She must have taken a stiff whiskey to keep up her strength for the evening. 'A real brick . . . but you're looking tired. I hope all this wasn't too much – it hasn't knackered you?'

'Really, Angela. Language, my dear! I hope you are not learning bad ways at that orphanage of yours.'

Angela stared at her and then started to giggle. Her mother looked bewildered but she just shook her head, unable to find the words. She'd spent all this time working to make this evening a success for the children of St Saviour's but that didn't mean she approved of them.

'Why are you laughing? For heaven's sake, Angela, I cannot understand you.'

'Nothing,' Angela told her, seeing the flicker of annoyance in her eyes. Her mother would never accept why she did what she did and that made her sad, but she would try to ignore her barbs and keep the peace between them, for her father's sake if not her own. 'I'm just happy, that's all. And I do appreciate you, Mum, even if we don't understand each other all the time.'

'I have enjoyed this weekend,' Mark said as they left the splendid but very ancient inn where they had enjoyed a wonderful lunch of fresh salmon in a delicious sauce, salads and tiny sautéed potatoes. 'I can't recall when I've felt so relaxed and free of care.'

'It has been fun,' Angela agreed. 'Mother outdid herself last evening, and this was a lovely idea, Mark. Much nicer and easier for me than dragging that heavy suitcase on the train.'

'Is all that stuff for the church jumble sale?'

'It's a "bring and buy" sale, I'll have you know,' she said, her eyes sparkling with mischief. 'An upmarket jumble sale I'll grant you, but I scrounged some good things from my mother's friends as well as my own bits and pieces. Some of it is old-fashioned but the cloth is good and can be remodelled – and there was so much stuff in Mother's wardrobe that she will never wear. I don't know where it came from, because most of it isn't her style at all and I'm not even sure it would fit her. I asked if she could spare anything and she said take what I want so I did – but nothing she really likes, of course.'

'Well, you certainly deserve success,' Mark said approvingly. 'You've worked very hard, Angela, and justified my faith in you.'

'I'm so grateful to you,' she said as she slid into the front passenger seat. 'I am finding this work very rewarding.'

He stood looking down at her before closing the door. 'And how do you feel in yourself? Not just putting on a brave face, I hope?'

'No, I'm getting there little by little,' she replied, the smile leaving her eyes. 'I still think of John most days but it is becoming easier. Now I can remember the lovely times – the happiness we shared for such a short time.'

'It would never have been long enough, Angela. When you love someone you carry that with you for the rest of your life.'

'Is that how you felt when your wife died?'

'I felt and still feel mostly guilt.' There was a sombre look in his eyes. 'I didn't love her as I should and I neglected her when she needed me most – and so I blame myself for her death.'

'I'm sure it wasn't your fault, Mark. You're a busy man and . . .'

'Don't make excuses for me. I should have known how she felt about the death of our child – but I chose to throw myself into my work.'

'We can all find reasons to blame ourselves.'

'Not you, Angela. You adored John and he knew it.'

'Yes, that is true – but we quarrelled on his last leave. I told him he was too controlling, because he objected to me wanting to join the Wrens. I told him I wanted to carry on working for the hospital after the war and he didn't agree. We made it up before he went back, but it has stayed with me and I've regretted it so bitterly . . . for a long time I wondered if he felt I'd regretted our marriage; if he was careless because of it . . .' She choked back a sob. 'So stupid of me. It was just a little quarrel and he forgave me but . . . I cannot forgive myself. I spoiled a day of our time together by insisting on my own way when I should have been making the most of every second.'

'Yes, I do see how that would feel,' Mark said. 'Believe me, John wouldn't have harboured a grudge; he wouldn't have thought badly of you. He probably blamed himself, because it *was* old-fashioned of him to expect you to give up the work you enjoyed, and there could have been no harm in your carrying on – at least until you started a family. Personally, I think it does married women no harm to work outside the home if they wish, but I know that not many men agree with me. When the children come it is different, of course.'

'Unfortunately, that never happened. Besides, why should that stop women having a career? As long as there is love and the children are cared for properly – why should a woman not go on with her career? Why shouldn't the man help with childcare – or is that too outrageous even for you, Mark?' Angela looked at him provocatively and he gave a shout of laughter.

'Well, that is something I'd never thought about, Angela. It's a bold idea and I'm not saying it's wrong, but I should like time to consider before making my plea, your honour.'

She looked at him in amusement. 'Did I get on my soapbox? I do that sometimes when I feel something strongly, I'm afraid.'

Mark was silent for a moment, then, 'Would you like children of your own?'

'Perhaps but I'm not ready to think of marriage yet, Mark.'

'I know, but one day you may want a family – and I'm sure your father would enjoy grandchildren.'

'Yes, perhaps.' Angela acknowledged in her heart that he was right. Yet how could she think of a domestic life without John? To contemplate having children with another man was a terrible betrayal of their love. 'We must hope that both of us find love again, Mark.'

'Yes,' he said, but there was an odd look in his eyes as he turned away and inserted the key, starting the engine without looking at her. 'I hope we shall both be fortunate one day . . .'

CHAPTER 28

Angela was thoughtful as she locked away the takings from the sale of second-hand clothes that morning. She'd raised more than seventy pounds, and sold every last thing she'd collected, because it was all good quality and people were so fed up with finding nothing worth having in the shops. The Utility fashions that had been imposed during the war had been universally hated and all Angela's things had been stylish, even if most of them were pre-war. Some women had suggested that she have sales on a regular basis and someone else had proposed a shop where women could bring the things they were tired of and swap them. Angela wasn't sure what the Board would think of that, but because there had been so much interest she'd raised a decent sum for the home.

It would take a lot of thinking about, Angela decided as she left her office that evening. She wasn't sure that it would be worthwhile to devote so much time to such a venture – but she wouldn't dismiss it out of hand just yet. There were all sorts of possibilities for raising funds in the future.

'Oh, Angela, I'm glad I've caught you,' Nan said as she was heading towards the stairs. 'I'm sure you're longing to get back and have a nice bath and a cup of tea. It's just that a couple of the children have gone down with nasty coughs and colds today, and I'm rather shorthanded. The sick children are feeling very poorly and I wondered if you would make them some hot cocoa and take up to the ward? I know you've been on your feet all day, but the kitchen staff have left for the night and Sister Beatrice has gone to the convent to speak to her superior about something this afternoon and may not be back until late . . .'

'Yes, of course. I shall be only too pleased.' Angela smiled at her, happy that she'd been asked to stay on and help. She was so busy with other things that she didn't get as much time as she would like to spend with the children. She thought about what Mark had said, about having a family of her own, and realised that it was probably something she wanted one day – if she hadn't left it too late.

Tears stung the back of her throat, because she would have liked to have John's children, but that could never happen now . . . and she wasn't sure that she would ever be able to give her heart again.

Sometimes she thought that perhaps she could love Mark; he understood her more than anyone else did – perhaps more than John had. A smile touched her mouth as she thought of the look in his eyes when she'd thrown that outrageous idea at him. She wasn't sure where it had come from; she wouldn't have said it once upon a time – but what was wrong with a man sharing the care of his children?

Poor Mark had looked shell-shocked, but he'd soon rallied. She thought that of all the men she'd ever met, she probably had more chance of a decent life with him than any of the others. He might not always agree, but at least he would give her views a fair hearing.

Still smiling at the thought, Angela went off to carry out Nan's request. She'd almost forgotten about Sister Beatrice, though it had struck her as odd that the nun had gone back to her convent. Surely she wasn't thinking of giving up her position here?

Beatrice had been kneeling on the cold stone floor for more than an hour and she felt the stiffness strike through her as she stood and genuflected before the large cross on the altar. For a moment her fingers touched the large silver crucifix on its heavy chain at her breast; it had belonged to her mother, and the Abbess had granted her permission to keep the symbol of her faith when it had been willed to her. The feel of the raised figure beneath her fingers gave her comfort and for a moment she permitted herself a smile. She'd asked the saints to intercede for her and gradually the peace of the old convent had come back to her, easing the anxiety that had been building inside for some weeks.

She had never considered herself as being either cruel or unkind, but Angela's reaction to her caning that young lad Billy Baggins had made her question herself. Billy had run away rather than come to her with whatever was troubling him and perhaps that was because she'd been too much the stern guardian and not enough the kind protector she was meant to be.

Perhaps Angela was right about corporal punishment, even the mild form that she had applied in the case of young Billy. Her own life had been hard, perhaps because of her pride and the same kind of defiance she'd seen in that boy's eyes. Had she learned to control her pride sooner maybe so much pain would have been saved . . . but that memory belonged to the distant past and she refused to let it torment her.

She worried about Billy being on the streets for several days and nights, perhaps alone, perhaps with that rogue of a brother of his, as Angela had suggested. In either case he would be in danger and she would feel responsible if anything happened to him.

As she left the chapel the Abbess approached her with a comforting smile.

'I trust that your time in prayer has helped you, Sister Beatrice?'

'Thank you, Reverend Mother,' Beatrice replied.

'I fear that I am still guilty of that sin of which you warned me so many times as a young woman.'

'Yes, you were always proud and independent, Sister Beatrice. I remember that you found the vow of humility the most difficult to take.' A gentle smile touched her lip and then she sighed. 'With myself I fear it was gluttony that caused me trouble. I did like my food, but I have curbed the need for sweet things – and in time you too will find peace of mind. We all carry a little sin with us,' the kind elderly nun said and made the sign of the cross over her. 'Go in peace, my sister. I shall pray for your soul – and you are always welcome to return to your home whenever you wish.'

'As always, I find strength in coming here and speaking with you as well as in prayer,' Beatrice said. 'When you first took me in I was consumed with bitterness and hate, Reverend Mother. Through your gentleness and love, I found a way to forgive those that had hurt me so grievously. I have never regretted my decision to give myself to the service of God – but I do fear that I fail to achieve the humility expected of my calling. I sometimes think I am simply not worthy . . .'

'The Lord gives us strength, my dear. I am but His servant, but I am happy if He chose me as His vessel to reach you. I pray that you have found peace here today.'

Beatrice thanked her and left. She'd needed a short time to reflect and pray, to ask for forgiveness and the strength to do God's work – but she knew that her life was not here amongst these quiet cloisters. She belonged at St Saviour's, where the children needed her.

As she walked away to catch her bus back to Spitalfields, her thoughts were still with Billy Baggins. Where was he – and was he safe? She had prayed for him to return to them and she could only trust that her prayers had been heard.

CHAPTER 29

Mary Ellen couldn't sleep. It had happened as she was walking home from school that afternoon. Billy had darted out at her as she passed a narrow alley, tugging her into it so that no one else would see them.

'Billy!' she'd cried. 'Oh, Billy, are you all right?'

'No, I bloody ain't,' he said and looked over his shoulder. 'Arfur is a bully and I hate him, but I have to do what he says or he'll kill me.'

'Oh, Billy, you mustn't swear!' she exclaimed. 'I've been so worried about you.'

'I have to do what Arthur says. If I don't, he'll come after you – and he's threatened to set fire to St Saviour's. I don't want that to happen, Mary Ellen.'

'I miss you something awful . . .'

'I miss you as well. I wish I could be back with you at St Saviour's, but I'm frightened of him. Me only chance is if the police catch him when he's doing a job.'

'Does he break into all sorts of places?'

Billy nodded. 'Him and his mate did the tool factory and got away with some money. They thought it would be all the wages for the week, but they got it wrong. Thing is, Arthur and Jack need to get away 'cos they broke into a lawyer's office the other week and stole a lot of stuff from a safe. Now they're in big trouble, because the stuff belonged to some dangerous men, and now they're scared.'

'What do you mean?'

'Have you heard of Butcher Lee and his gang?'

'No, I don't know who they are.'

'They're gangsters, see, and they're mean. Arfur wanted to make a break for it as soon as he realised what they'd done but Jack Shaw said they can't sell the stuff in London so they need cash before they can clear off up North . . .'

'Will your brother make you go with them?'

'I'm going to sneak off as soon as I can,' Billy said. 'I reckon Butcher will put the word out on them, and they won't dare to come back for years.'

'Come home with me now, Billy. Sister will be all right if you tell her the truth, and Miss Angela is on our side.'

'He needs me to keep watch when they do the boot factory office tonight,' Billy said. 'If I run off he will come after me and then he'll set you all on fire in your beds – that's what he says.'

'But you could be in danger . . .'

'I ain't goin' to let him hurt you again,' Billy had said. 'Don't you worry, Mary Ellen. I'll get away somehow and then I'll come back to the home.'

Billy had assured her that he would be all right,

but now Mary Ellen kept thinking about him all the time. She was frightened of what was going to happen and it all kept going round and round in her mind.

If only Billy had come with her for tea, but he was terrified of his brother and what he might do to them all. Mary Ellen didn't know what she'd do if Billy didn't come back. Rose hadn't been to see her for ages and she'd had nothing from her mother other than a joint card for her birthday soon after she arrived at the home. Tears slipped down her cheeks, because she felt so alone at times, and she needed her best friend here, because Billy loved her like family and she loved him.

Billy stood shivering in the dark, hugging his arms about him and constantly moving his feet to keep them from losing all feeling. It was a bitterly cold night and he could hardly stop his teeth chattering; he hadn't eaten all day and his stomach rumbled with hunger. His left eye ached where Arthur had hit him the previous day for defying him and he wished with all his heart that he were back at St Saviour's in his bed with a good big breakfast of bread and jam to look forward to in the morning. The most Arthur ever gave him was a pie and chips and that was only when he was pleased about something.

Billy hated being forced to help him by keeping watch while Arthur and his mate Jack were inside the houses or small grocery shops. In the houses they took gold, old coins, medals and money but nothing bigger, because it was too much trouble to sell. Jack's father was a pawnbroker and he bought any gold, medals or bits of silver and jewellery they took for him, fencing them through his shop or through other men who sold them away from the area. The money was split between Arthur and Jack; Billy was given nothing except his food, and he didn't want anything else, because it was dirty money. So far he hadn't been forced to go into a house through a small window and let them in, because Jack didn't trust him, and they'd simply smashed their way through windows or doors.

They were rotten to the core and Billy hated them both. He heard them laughing together after they'd done a break-in, boasting of what they'd stolen and the way they'd smashed up people's homes. Why couldn't they see that although the glass and china they smashed was worthless to them, those things probably meant a lot to the owners of the damaged property? He'd tried to tell them it wasn't fair and got a smack round the ear and a fat lip for his pains. Arthur told him to keep his gob shut and if he did anything that either of them didn't like he didn't get anything to eat that day.

It was worse than living at home with his drunken father. At least Pa had been all right on the days when he didn't drink. Arthur was a mean pig all the time and Billy would've run away, but he knew that his brother would come after him – and then he would set fire to St Saviour's and Mary Ellen would burn in her bed and so would Marion and all the others. Even the carers and the nurses would be hurt . . . and Sister Beatrice. Billy didn't want any of them to die in a fire. He knew now that it had been the best time of his life, even when he was in trouble, and he swore that if he could just go back he would keep Sister Beatrice's rules. Of course, she wouldn't have him back now.

Billy racked his brains to try and find a way out of the trap he was caught in. If he could find a way to stop Arthur . . . but the police would never catch him because he was too sly. Billy was keeping watch now as they broke into the office at the boot factory; it was the reason Arthur had come looking for him, because if Billy warned them when anyone approached, they could get away before the coppers realised they were inside.

If only Billy could be sure of what he suspected, but he'd never been one hundred per cent certain that Arthur had been behind the attack on Pa that had ended his life. It had happened down the Docks the night after Arthur walked out of their house in the middle of a blazing row with their father. Pa had accused him of being a dirty little thief, because whatever else their father had been, he'd been honest and worked for his living. It was only the drink that let Pa down, and that was only after Billy's mother had died.

Billy had been sitting on the bottom of the stairs

listening to their row and he'd heard his brother say he'd get even with Pa for going to the police and laying evidence against his own son.

'I'll do fer you,' he'd yelled at the top of his voice. 'You're an old bastard and I'll see yer in hell – see if I don't. You'd best watch your back 'cos there's a knife headin' there soon enough . . .'

Arthur had stormed out and Billy had rushed upstairs and locked himself in his room, because there was no telling what Pa would do when he was in one of his moods. Billy didn't think his father had really informed on Arthur, because they didn't do that in the narrow, mean little streets where they lived. People were poor, often hungry and sick, but they stuck together, though some of the men were capable of handing out punishment if they thought it necessary. Should they consider a man had gone too far, a few of them might get together and give him a good hiding, but they didn't tell tales to the police. If he'd been able, Pa would have taken his belt to Arthur, but he wasn't strong enough to best him in a fight now. He'd lied about informing the police about Arthur's thieving because it was the only way he hoped to stop him, but instead Pa had got a knife between his shoulder blades the next evening when he left work.

He hadn't come in all night and in the morning the police had called to tell Billy his father was dead. They'd asked for Arthur, said they wanted to speak to him, and told Billy that he must go and stay with his grandmother or live in a children's home.

Billy had wanted to tell them he thought it was his brother that had murdered his pa, but he was too afraid to say it – and felt it would be snitching. Around here, the folk sent any coward known as a police informer to Coventry, which meant they wouldn't speak to them and if they went in the pub, everyone turned their backs on them. Billy knew murder was different from simple stealing, but he couldn't tell the police anything more than the threats Arthur had made – and that wasn't enough to convict him of murder. If Billy had dared to tell, Arthur would've found out and given him a good thrashing; he might even have killed him the way he had Pa . . . if it had been him.

Billy wished there were some way he could get away from Arthur without putting his friends at risk. It was soon going to be Christmas and he would miss the parties and the trip to the pantomime . . . and he missed seeing Mary Ellen every day; that was the worst thing of all.

Billy stiffened as from his hiding place behind a load of wooden crates he saw a dark shadow moving stealthily towards the office of the boot factory. His brother and Jack Shaw were inside so what was going on? Was someone else intent on robbing the factory of its wages?

He was about to give the warning whistle when the dark shadow suddenly threw something directly at the door of the office. Even as he saw a flash of light, he realised that the missile was a petrol bomb. He whistled as loud as he could, but the flash of fire as the bomb hit and a roaring sound nearly knocked him backwards as the door seemed to explode and flames were shooting up the wooden door.

Billy hated his brother and Jack Shaw; it would serve them right if they got burned in the fire, but he couldn't just stand by and watch and knew he had to warn them somehow. The fire was too fierce for him to get in through the doorway. He darted at the caretaker's office, going round to the side window, though which his brother had entered earlier. Already the flames were shooting into the narrow passage that led up some steep stairs to the main office containing the big old-fashioned safe Jack had said would be easy to break. The strong smell of dyes and leather made the air stuffy in the dark passages leading to the workrooms and Billy gulped before placing a hand over his nose and mouth, because smoke was billowing through the darkness towards him. Scrambling through the window, Billy ran towards the bottom of the stairs. He saw the body of a man lying face down on the floor, and it looked as if someone had hit him hard, because there was blood on the back of his head. Billy felt sick to his stomach. It must be the night watchman and either Arthur or Jack had hit him so hard they'd killed him.

He almost turned and ran out without warning

them but then he knew he couldn't because that would make him as bad as they were, and he yelled at the top of his voice, but the noise of the fire was surely loud enough to warn them of the danger.

Arthur appeared from the office at the top of the stairs. 'What the hell do you . . .' he began and then saw the fire licking at the door and already eating its way through piles of leather stacked in the hall, smoke curling through the darkness and making Billy cough and cover his nose with his hand. 'Bloody hell! Jack, we've got to get out – there's a fire . . .'

Jack appeared at the top of the stairs and swore. In the eerie light of the flames, his handsome features reflected his fury. 'I ain't goin' without what we came for . . .'

'Don't be a bloody fool!' Arthur said. 'Money ain't worth dyin' for.'

As he spoke the external door seemed to erupt as it fell in and the sparks went everywhere. The flames from the petrol-soaked door were licking at the piles of leather and the fumes were choking Billy as he stood indecisively. Arthur came charging down the stairs, nearly knocking him over as he rushed for the open doorway, his jacket over his head.

'Get out while you can, Billy.'

Billy turned back towards the window by which he'd entered and had almost reached it when another missile came smashing through it and seemed to explode in a wall of flame. He halted, terrified, uncertain whether to turn back or go through the flames. Seeing a door at the end of the passage, he tugged at the handle and it opened. He went into what he thought was a store room and shut the door quickly to hold back the flames and the smoke. At first he couldn't make anything out. He was choking, the fumes he'd already inhaled making him feel dizzy and ill. He couldn't see another way out and it looked like he was trapped.

He would die here, because the smoke was already seeping under the door and soon the flames would get to it. Billy's mind was fuzzy as he tried to think what to do. If he went back out into the fire he would get burned and yet if he stayed here . . . his eyes stung with tears as he thought of Mary Ellen and his friends. What was he going to do? There had to be some way out of here, he just had to find it, but the fumes were drifting into the store room and he was beginning to feel faint . . .

It was then that he sensed a slight breeze on his face. His eyes were adjusting to the darkness and he noticed a faint chink of light coming from the floor. He felt his way along the wall towards it and bent down to investigate. It was a grating and he knew that it must lead to the airey, a cellar that had been used for coal and storage, perhaps still was for all Billy knew. A lot of old properties had them in London so that the coal didn't have to be carried through the building. If he could wrench open the grating, he might be able to get out into the back yard and escape that way.

He dropped to his knees and tried pulling the metal grate; it was stuck and he couldn't move it. Billy could smell the stench of the smoke and hear flames roaring outside the door. Before long the fire would envelop this room and he'd be trapped. He was beginning to feel the sting of the smoke in his eyes and throat. He had to find something to help him prise the grate open. Moving around the room, feeling his way in the darkness, he bumped into a pile of wooden crates and yelled as he grazed his hands, but then his fingers touched something metal. He grasped what he guessed was a crowbar and then felt his way back to the airey, inserting the long metal bar into the grating and pushing it downward to lever it up. He pressed with all his strength but it wouldn't budge and he felt the fear rise in his throat as the roaring of the flames came closer and he knew he couldn't get out of the door. Almost in despair he jammed the bar into the grate again as hard as he could and suddenly felt it give. Bending down, he grabbed it and pulled it back. The opening was big enough for him to enter it easily and he found he was standing on steps that led down into the blackness.

Billy's heart was pounding as he sat on his bottom and worked his way down, wary of slipping and knocking himself out in the darkness. He could smell the sharp, acrid stink of coal and a musty unpleasant odour that told him the cellar hadn't been used for a long time. When his feet touched the bottom, he scrabbled on loose coal scattered on the floor; it caused him to stumble a couple of times and he scraped his hand and his knees. Now he could see where the faint shaft of light was coming from; it had an eerie redness about it and he guessed that it was the glow of the fierce fire reflected in the sky. It must have spread swiftly because of all the chemicals the factory used for its leathers, and even down here Billy could smell the smoke.

He felt his way round the wall until he came to some steps at the other end, which led up to a second grating. There was more air now and he gulped it gratefully, because down here the atmosphere was foul and he guessed the stink came from rat droppings and probably their corpses too.

When he reached the grating, Billy pushed against it, but, as he'd feared it was stuck fast just like the one he'd somehow managed to prise open. From above he'd been able to get some leverage and that gave him extra strength, but here there was no way he could shift the grating. It was stuck fast and would not budge one inch, even though he strained with every ounce of will he had.

Tears pricked at Billy's eyes. He wasn't a coward but he didn't want to die down here like a rat in a trap. Sitting on the steps with his head on his knees, he tried to think of a plan. Perhaps the fire wouldn't get down here. Perhaps if he just stayed here and didn't panic, he could get out through the ruined factory when the fire had burned itself out.

It was then that he heard the loud clanging of the fire engine's bell and he realised that help was at hand. There were people shouting up there, running about as they prepared to try and put out the flames. Clawing up, he rushed to the top step and started to yell.

'Help! I'm stuck down the airey. Please help me!'

Billy yelled and yelled until he was hoarse but no one answered his pleas and he realised there was too much noise and chaos up there for them to hear his voice. It was useless to call out; he would just have to sit and wait until it quietened down up there and then he would try again.

He sat down on the steps, pulling his knees up and laying his head on his arms. So far the smoke hadn't penetrated the cellar; he could only hope that the firemen would put out the flames before they got to him. His left hand hurt where he'd scraped it on something and so did his head, and he was worn out with his efforts to attract attention; hungry, tired, cold and miserable, incredibly Billy fell asleep.

Mary Ellen was feeling tired when it was time to get up that Friday morning. Sally asked her what was wrong when she dragged herself out of bed and went through the motions of washing and dressing, but Mary Ellen couldn't tell her. She kept thinking about Billy and where he was, what he was doing, but she didn't know what to do. Surely it would all be over by now, and perhaps Billy would turn up later that day. If Arthur was intent on leaving London in a hurry he might be careless enough to let his brother slip away – or perhaps he just wouldn't care.

She went down to breakfast and sat with Marion and a girl called Sarah Morgan. Sarah was a few months older than Mary Ellen, and she'd been ill for a long time before she came here, though she was well enough to share their dormitory now. She was nice enough, but not a special friend. Mary Ellen couldn't confide in Marion that she was worried for Billy while the other girl was with them.

It was as she was getting ready to leave in order to help Sally in the playroom that she saw Nan enter the dining room and speak to the carer. They looked worried and after Nan left Sally came over to their table.

'We've just heard that there's been a dreadful fire at the boot factory,' Sally said, sounding concerned. 'Julia's father works there as a caretaker and he didn't come home this morning, which may be why she didn't come into work. Nan has asked me to go round to Julia's house and find out what's happening.'

'Has someone been hurt at the factory, Sally?' Mary Ellen asked urgently, her heart pounding. She was frightened because she knew that Billy's brother and his mate had gone there to rob the safe. Had they set the fire and what had happened to Billy? 'Please tell me . . .'

'I don't know the details,' Sally said, 'but they say a man's body was found at the factory.'

Mary Ellen gasped. She felt sick and started to shake, because if Arthur or his mate had been killed, perhaps Billy had too.

'It may not be Julia's father,' Sally said in a reassuring tone. 'I'm sorry, I shouldn't have told you. Look, Angela is coming to take the little ones into the playroom. You should go with her. Nan wants me to see if Julia is all right.'

She watched as the carer went off hurriedly, stopping for a quick word with Angela before leaving. Angela spoke to one of the kitchen girls for a moment and then approached Mary Ellen.

'Will you help me with the little ones, please?'

'Yes, miss,' Mary Ellen said but her bottom lip trembled.

If anything had happened to Billy she would never forgive herself. She ought to have stopped him going on that robbery with his brother. It would have been better to tell Angela about it and let her tell the police than have this happen. Yet how could she have known there would be a fire?

'Is something wrong, Mary Ellen?' Angela asked, looking at her intently. 'You're upset about something, aren't you?'

'No, miss,' Mary Ellen lied and swallowed hard. 'Have they put the fire out at the factory yet?'

'I don't know much,' Angela admitted. 'Constable Sallis told us there was a fire when he called in earlier to speak to us about some children he wants us to admit, but I imagine the fire service will have it under control. Why? Do you know someone who works there?'

Mary Ellen shook her head. She wanted to blurt it all out, to tell Angela that she was afraid Billy might have been trapped in the fire, but she was afraid that he would be in trouble. The police wouldn't care that he'd been forced to work with his brother; they would simply say he was a bad boy and send him away to a place of correction. No, she couldn't say anything yet, but as soon as she could slip away she would go to the factory herself and see what was happening.

Billy woke with a start. He was feeling stiff and his neck ached, and his eyes were bleary, as if he had a cold, or perhaps it was the effects of the smoke. The firemen must have got it under control quickly, because it hadn't penetrated this far after all, though the air in the cellar stank of it. He'd shivered through the night, sleeping intermittently. Each time he'd woken, he'd gone to the top of the steps and shouted but no one had answered, and now his throat felt sore and his eyes had started to sting. He had to get out of here!

He heard some noises in the yard above his head and climbed to the top of the cellar stairs, calling out for help, but his voice was only a croak and he knew no one could hear him. He was never going to get out this way, but he could hear men talking close by. One of them said it had been a close thing.

'I thought the whole damned place would go up.'

'The fire was concentrated in the office and store area. There's something suspicious here, if I'm not mistaken. I don't think this was an accident.'

'No, it was definitely deliberate. Do you think the caretaker had something to do with it?'

'He says he went out into the yard to investigate a noise and was hit over the head. It was him that raised the alarm so quick – said he came to himself when the door to the office went up with a whoosh. In my opinion it has to be an arson attack. Someone had it in for the folk at the boot factory.'

'He can thank God he was knocked cold outside in the yard,' the first voice said and then someone else chimed in, 'He thought he saw a face at the office window just before the whole thing went up. Thieves, do you reckon?'

'We shan't know that until we can make a thorough search of the place. It should be cool enough soon. Whatever happened, the poor devil caught upstairs didn't stand a chance. If the explosion didn't kill him the fire would have.'

'He couldn't have known much about it after that blast . . .'

The voices moved away and Billy shuddered. If the caretaker was still alive, who had been lying dead at the bottom of the stairs? Had there been someone else in the building when Arthur and Jack broke in – and why had they killed him?

Billy reckoned it must have been Jack who was caught in the blast, though whether it was from the fire or the explosive he'd set Billy couldn't guess. He was pretty sure Arthur had escaped, though he might have suffered a few burns.

He listened for a while longer, straining to hear voices, but it seemed to be quiet up top. Billy had come to a decision. He wasn't going to get out this way, so the only alternative was back up to the store room and out through what had been the office doorway. The men had said the fire was out so he thought it was time he took a risk and tried to make a move.

It was lighter in the cellar now and as he climbed the stairs the stink of the smoke grew worse and he felt it choking him. He took off his jacket and put it over his face and nose, leaving just enough space to see where he was going. His heart sank as he saw the grating had fallen back across the opening and for a second he panicked; he was going to die in here!

Taking a deep choking breath to steady his nerves, Billy grabbed the grating and pushed hard. To his relief it swung back but the metal was hot and he felt it burn his hands. He yelped with pain but it added to his determination to get out of here and he scrambled out of the opening into the store room. It was lighter in here now and he saw the fire had been kept back as the door had not collapsed, although the paint had blistered and the smoke that penetrated underneath had covered everything in a fine dust and made the air almost too thick to breathe.

Billy made a run for the door, but stopped as he noticed the metal handle. Doubling his jacket over, he took hold of the handle and pressed. It yielded and he yanked the door back, half-stumbling into what had been the passageway. For a moment the stink of burning was almost too much for him and he choked, spluttering as it grabbed at his throat. Everywhere was black and as he steadied himself, he became aware that piles of debris were still smouldering between puddles of water, and he had to watch where he stepped. Avoiding the smouldering rubbish, he squelched through the water, which soaked into his boots. Looking up, he saw that at the end of the hall there was a gaping void; the stairs had gone and there was a huge hole in the roof. Billy ran, feeling the heat through the soles of his boots as he stepped on ashes that were still hot and in some cases still glowed red where he kicked them. A part of the roof had been clinging precariously to burned-through struts and a large section came crashing down just ahead of him.

Billy yelled and ran for it, just making it to the hole in the wall where the door had once been, and staggered out into the yard before everything inside collapsed and everywhere was showered with sparks and debris; he gasped for air as a load of smouldering wood fell where he'd been standing moments ago. His lungs felt as if they would burst and he stood gasping for air as he tried to think what to do next.

'Here, you, nipper!' a man's voice yelled and Billy saw one of the firemen waving his fist at him. 'Get away from there, you idiot. It's still dangerous; the fire isn't out completely yet.'

Billy saw that a policeman had turned to look at him. 'What are you doing here, lad?' he called. 'How did you get in here?'

Billy didn't wait to answer. They knew the factory had been set on fire deliberately and he could guess who would get the blame. Billy thought he knew the real culprit, but even if he told the police they wouldn't believe him – and if they did and they went to arrest the Butcher, Billy would be dead meat. If the gang discovered he'd snitched on them, he would be murdered.

Billy started to run. His only chance was to get away before they recognised him and took him down the station.

'Come back, lad. I want to talk to you!'

Billy ignored the policeman's voice and kept running. He knew what he had to do now. For the moment he was going to lie low and hope that the coppers wouldn't know who he was. Arthur must surely be running scared. His brother was caught between a rock and a hard place. If he stayed in London, either the coppers or Butcher

385

Lee would find him and in both cases he was in trouble.

Billy had to find somewhere to hide until tonight and then he was going to creep into St Saviour's and somehow get hold of Mary Ellen. He knew where he could hide for a while, just until it was safe to come out . . .

CHAPTER 30

On Saturday morning Mary Ellen ate her breakfast with Marion. She'd been on thorns all the previous day and had found it difficult to sleep again. Her guilty conscience was torturing her, because although she'd managed to run down to the damaged boot factory she hadn't been able to get near; the police had it cordoned off and they were ordering anyone who tried to get close enough for a good look to keep clear. Its walls were blackened and there were great holes in the roof where the fire had destroyed it. If Billy had been caught in there, it didn't bear thinking about and she shuddered in fear for him.

On her return, she'd asked Sally and Alice for news but all the carers told her was that Julia's father was all right and the police thought the dead man was a burglar who had been committing a series of robberies in the area.

If Billy didn't come today Mary Ellen was going to have to tell someone that she was afraid he'd been caught in that fire, but if she did that he would be in such trouble and then even if he was all right, Sister Beatrice would send him away.

387

'Are you all right?' Marion asked. 'You look as if you want to cry.'

'I'm worried about Billy,' Mary Ellen admitted. 'I keep thinking he may be hurt.'

'He's going to miss all the Christmas treats if he doesn't come back,' Marion said. 'And I've got him a present – have you?'

'Not yet . . .'

Mary Ellen received three pennies in pocket money each week, which Rose had left with Sister Beatrice for her. Rose had been to see her once at the beginning and she'd given her a shilling for herself. Mary Ellen hadn't spent any of that shilling and she'd saved most of her pocket money, because living at St Saviour's she never needed to buy anything. The children were given cakes and nice things to eat, and on Saturdays each of them was allowed two boiled sweets from a jar. Mary Ellen had never had much money to spend on sweets and the two she was given were enough for her so she'd saved her money, and she'd been planning to buy Billy a school scarf so that he would keep warm on his way to classes, but now he wouldn't be here for Christmas.

She'd already purchased a box with some coloured crayons for Marion, six sugar mice to give to the other girls in her dormitory and a bar of fancy soap that smelled of roses for her sister. Rose had told her she would come to visit before Christmas but Mary Ellen wasn't sure when that would be; she just hoped it wasn't on the day they were going to the pantomime, because she didn't want to miss that – whatever else she missed. She'd hoped Billy would be taken too, but now he wasn't here. She had other friends at St Saviour's but none as close as Billy.

'I bought him a magazine about football,' Marion said and rubbed at her eyes to brush away her tears. 'I'm worried about him too.'

'It's so cold out now – and I'm sure he has nowhere to sleep. I should think he's hungry and miserable.'

Marion looked sympathetic. 'We could look for him tomorrow, 'cos it's Saturday. Perhaps you could push my chair . . . I can't manage my crutches outside yet, but I shall soon.'

'Sister wouldn't let me push your chair. Remember what happened last time? Besides, Billy wouldn't be anywhere near here . . . would he?'

'He might come back if he was cold and hungry.'

'Yes.' Mary Ellen looked at her hopefully. 'I wish he would.'

'Sally is coming to take me back upstairs. You'd better get ready to help her with the little ones when she comes down.'

'Yes, I suppose so,' Mary Ellen said and sighed. 'I'd better go and get my books. I left them in the schoolroom last night, because I wanted to do my homework there . . . it reminds me of being there with Billy.'

Sally had arrived to take Marion's chair and Mary Ellen got to her feet. She heard Sally telling the other girl that Mr Markham was coming that morning to tell them some stories and was glad it was a Saturday. She liked Mr Markham and it had been fun that morning she'd helped Billy with his spelling.

She ran upstairs to the empty schoolroom. Collecting the books she'd used the previous evening, Mary Ellen slipped them into a little cloth bag that she'd made in needlework class for the purpose. It had a drawstring and she could loop it over her shoulder.

'Psst . . .' Mary Ellen heard the odd sound and looked round, wondering what it was, and then she heard it again and recognised the voice. 'Mary Ellen . . .'

'Billy – is it you?' Her heart was racing as she spun round. The door to the big cupboard where Sally stored toys and books was slightly ajar. She ran towards it and pulled it open, to find him crouching in the bottom. 'Where did you come from? Where have you been? I was so worried because I thought you might be hurt in the fire. I almost told Angela but I knew you wouldn't want me to . . .'

'I got in last night through the back scullery window. I'm going to hide up in that attic store room we found – remember?' Billy was always exploring the cellar and the attics once he'd found the key, and he'd taken Mary Ellen with him a couple of times.

'Why do you have to hide? I think Sister would be all right if you told her why you ran away.'

'I daren't. I was at the factory when it was fire-bombed and I saw it happen,' Billy told her. 'I got trapped inside when I warned Arthur and couldn't get out so I crawled in the airey and tried to get out that way but the grating into the yard was rusted in the ground.'

'You might have died.' Mary Ellen's breath caught on a sob.

'I thought I was going to for a while. I shouted but no one heard me and then I couldn't shout no more, because me throat hurt. So I waited until the fire was out and then I went back up. It was all black and the air was enough to choke yer; there was a hole in the roof and the stairs to the office where the safe was had gone . . .'

'A man was found dead at the factory . . .'

'That could be Jack Shaw.' Billy nodded, but he didn't tell her about the body he'd seen lying at the foot of the stairs, because it was murder and might give her nightmares. 'I went in to warn them of the fire and Arthur ran out through the flames, but his mate wanted the money and wouldn't leave so he might have been killed. I reckon Arthur must have got some burns . . . I burned me hand getting out the morning after 'cos it was still hot.'

'You should tell the police what happened.'

'I ain't sure what happened to Jack, see. If I told they would go after me brother – and if they believed me about who started the fire and why, they'd arrest the Butcher Lee gang and then they'd have me killed. Even in prison they could do it . . .'

391

'Oh, Billy, don't say it.' Mary Ellen felt scared. 'We should tell someone.'

'No, not yet; I've got ter lay low fer a bit, just until it's safe. If I say what I know Sister Beatrice will tell the police – and then I'm done for.'

'What are you going to do?' Mary Ellen looked at him anxiously. He was in such terrible trouble and she didn't know how to help him.

'Stay hidden in the attics fer a bit – if you'll bring me food and somethin' to drink, Mary Ellen?'

'Of course I will,' she said loyally. 'Go up there now before Sally comes. Be careful because if anyone sees you they will tell Sister Beatrice.'

'No one saw us before. I can sneak up the back way like we did last time. Them old stairs ain't ever used these days – but I'm 'ungry. Me belly's rumblin'. I went lookin' fer somethin' last night but I couldn't get in the pantry 'cos it was locked, but I did have a glass of water.'

'That's 'cos Cook has been making cakes and special sweets and stuff ready for Christmas and she thinks someone got in and stole some the other day so she keeps it locked at night.'

'Can you get me somethin' now?'

'I'll go back to the dining room and see if I can find anything,' Mary Ellen said. 'I'll bring it up to the attic as quick as I can.'

'I knew you wouldn't let me down,' he said. 'You're a true friend, Mary Ellen. See if you can find a bit of grease and a hanky to bandage me hand; I burned it on the grating, but it ain't too bad 'cos it weren't scorching.'

'I'll find food for you,' she promised. 'And I'll smuggle something out every time we have a meal. We'll manage, Billy – but I think you should tell someone what a wicked man Arthur is. And what you saw at the fire.'

'I will but not just yet,' Billy promised. 'Sister Beatrice won't believe me. She'll think I've made it up just to get out of a caning.'

'She might listen,' Mary Ellen said. 'Angela or Sally would know what to do. I must hurry or I'll be late – but I'll come to you as soon as I can, I promise.'

Picking up her bag she walked quickly back to the dining room. Most of the food had been cleared away, but there was one hard-boiled egg left in a dish and two slices of bread and marge. Snatching them up, she wrapped them in her handkerchief and shoved them in her cloth bag just as one of the kitchen staff came back into the room to finish clearing.

'Did you want something, Mary Ellen?'

'No, miss. I just came back for my book,' Mary Ellen lied, feeling hot all over because she didn't like to tell fibs. 'I'm going now.'

There was no way she could find anything for Billy to drink yet, but she would go out later and buy him a big bottle of lemonade and then when it was empty she could fill it with orange squash or water. For now all she could do was take him

393

the food she'd found, and then she would have to run because Sally was expecting her to help with the little ones.

Mary Ellen stopped to purchase a bottle of orange squash on her way home the following Monday. She left it in the cloakroom and went into tea, but just as she had loaded her plate with enough for two hungry children, Angela came up to her.

'Ah, here you are, Mary Ellen. Sister Beatrice asked me to find you and take you to her office immediately.'

'But I've just got my tea, miss.'

'Leave the plate with Marion,' Angela suggested. 'She will look after it for you and see that no one eats it, won't you, Marion?'

'Yes, miss. I'll wait until you get back, Mary Ellen.'

'All right, thanks.' Mary Ellen thought of Billy waiting. She hadn't been able to get anything much for him at lunch, because there was nothing she could wrap in her handkerchief, other than an apple and that was already in her bag with the squash. He must be so hungry!

Worrying about her friend took the fear out of the visit to Sister's office. She sensed from Angela's manner that it was important, but she just hoped it wasn't that Billy's presence in the house had been discovered.

When Angela knocked and then led the way into Sister's office, Mary Ellen's stomach curled in fright as she saw the burly policeman standing by the window. He looked serious and so did Sister Beatrice and Mary Ellen's mouth was suddenly very dry. If the police were here, Billy must be in trouble.

'Ah, there you are, Mary Ellen,' Sister said, looking at her in a way that made her tremble inside, though she lifted her head defiantly, determined not to show her fear. 'I am glad Angela was able to find you, because this police constable wants to ask you some questions.'

'Yes, Sister.' Mary Ellen waited, nerves tingling, because she must be careful not to betray Billy.

'Sister Beatrice tells me that you are Billy Baggins' friend – is that so, miss?'

'Yes, sir,' she replied in a small voice. 'He's always been my friend.'

'Did he say anything to you about why he was going away before he left?'

'No, sir.' Mary Ellen crossed her fingers behind her back as she lied. 'He was upset about something but he wouldn't tell me what was wrong.'

'Did he seem nervous or bothered at all?'

She hesitated, then inclined her head, 'Yes, sir. I thought he was frightened – but not of getting a caning from Sister.'

The police constable glanced at Sister Beatrice, a grim smile on his lips. 'It's as I thought; the brother came for him and forced him to go with him. He was their lookout while they burgled people's houses. The boy was seen running away from the boot factory some hours after they put the fire out. He may know what happened, especially if was watching out for his brother.'

Mary Ellen wanted to shout out about Billy being forced to help his brother and seeing the man who had deliberately set fire to the factory, but if she betrayed her knowledge of that night, they would make her tell them where he was. She set her mouth, her stomach churning as the policeman turned to her again.

'Now, Mary Ellen, I want you to tell me the truth – have you seen Billy today?'

'No, sir,' Mary Ellen lied, crossing her fingers behind her back. She could feel the heat rushing through her because she hated having to lie, but she must for Billy's sake. 'What makes you ask, sir?'

'Well, it may be best to tell you. Billy will not be in trouble if he comes forward and tells us what we wish to know. We're looking for his brother and when we find him we're going to arrest him for several crimes. If Billy helps us in our investigations he will be doing a service to the community.'

Mary Ellen was so tempted, but she held her silence. She couldn't tell on Billy, because the police might take him away – he might be arrested for his part in the crimes. She was torn between wanting to confess why Billy had done what his brother ordered him to do and keeping his secret. She believed that Angela and perhaps Sister Beatrice might stand up for him . . . but he would think she was a snitch and a traitor, and Mary Ellen knew what happened to people who told tales. She didn't want that to happen to her, because it would break her heart if Billy turned against her. Besides, she wasn't sure you could trust the police. Her pa had always thought they were sly and stupid so perhaps she couldn't believe this one when he said Billy wouldn't be in trouble if he told his story. She could pass the message on but she wasn't going to tell.

'I haven't seen Billy for a long time, sir.' *Well, she hadn't seen him since breakfast so that was a long time, wasn't it?*

'Well, if you do, I want you to tell Sister Beatrice. Billy need not be afraid; we shall protect him. His brother won't be going anywhere for several years once we get him.'

'Yes, sir; if I see Billy I shall tell him he should come to Sister Beatrice.'

'Very well, I'll be on my way, Sister – Mrs Morton. This is very important, Mary Ellen. Arthur Baggins is a bad lot. We suspect him of a lot worse than theft and we should like to send him down the line for a long time.'

Mary Ellen was so uncomfortable that she couldn't look at him, let alone answer.

'Just a moment, Mary Ellen,' Sister said as she turned to follow him out. 'I want a word with you myself.'

Mary Ellen looked up at her, quaking inside as she saw Sister's stern look.

'Well, now you can just tell me the truth,' Sister said as the door closed. 'I know you lied to the police constable – so why? I think you have seen Billy recently so why won't you tell us?'

'I haven't seen him,' Mary Ellen said in a voice not much above a whisper but she couldn't look at Sister, because she felt so awful. She didn't like Sister Beatrice much, because she was mean to Billy, but she did know she was right. The police needed to know everything, because it was the only way they could do their job and put a bad man in prison.

'Please do not lie to me, Mary Ellen. I ask you again, have you seen Billy since he left St Saviour's?'

'No, Sister . . .' Mary Ellen was close to tears and the words hardly discernible.

'I shall not ask again, but I warn you: if you do not give me the truth, I shall punish you in a way that you will find unpleasant.'

Mary Ellen hung her head, refusing stubbornly to answer, her insides tying themselves in knots as she waited for Sister to fetch her cane, but all she did was to stare at her in silence. Mary Ellen felt that she couldn't breathe, but as each second ticked by so her determination not to betray Billy grew.

'Very well, you leave me no choice. You will not go with the other children to the pantomime on Saturday. That is your punishment. You may go now.'

Mary Ellen looked at her, the tears burning behind her eyes but she refused to let them fall.

She dreaded the cane but would have accepted it rather than seeing the treat she'd looked forward to for weeks being withdrawn.

How could Sister be so cruel? She wanted to fly at her, to tell her she was mean and nasty, but instead she just raised her head and looked at her in silent misery, and then she turned and walked from the room.

The injustice of her punishment burned inside her as she went back to the dining hall. Most of the children had gone but Marion was still sitting there guarding the plate of food.

'What's wrong?' she asked but Mary Ellen just shook her head, because it hurt too much to talk about it. She'd been counting the hours until the pantomime, hardly able to contain her excitement as the weeks passed, and now it was only a few days and she couldn't go. Sister Beatrice was just horrid, and it wasn't fair.

Mary Ellen couldn't have eaten a thing. The food would have choked her so she took two large clean handkerchiefs from her pocket and tipped all the cake, sausage rolls, and sandwiches into them, folding them neatly to slip into her bag when she reached the cloakroom.

'Why don't you want your tea?' Marion asked, staring at her.

'I'm in trouble with Sister,' Mary Ellen said, blinking back her tears. 'I can't go to the panto-mime on Saturday – you mustn't worry, Marion. I'll eat this later.'

'That's not fair,' Marion said indignantly. 'I don't want to go if you can't.'

'You must,' Mary Ellen urged her. 'You can't give it up just for me – and you can tell me all about it when you come back.'

Marion also had tears in her eyes. 'Sister is wrong. You haven't done anything wicked, Mary Ellen. I know it. She is being mean to you and it isn't fair.'

'Sister Beatrice is doing what she thinks right,' Mary Ellen said, desperately trying to hold back the tears of disappointment. She wished she could share the secret with Marion, but if she did that, her friend might give her away – or even worse, she might be blamed too when it all came out, as it might one day. 'You must go and bring back a programme to show me at tea.'

Marion promised she would, but when Sally came to fetch her she was resentful on Mary Ellen's behalf and refused to smile as she was wheeled away.

Mary Ellen hurried to the cloakroom and added the food to the other things she'd acquired for Billy, which included a packet of toffees from the shop where she'd bought his orange squash. It was a good thing she hadn't wanted her tea, because he was bound to be starving, and knowing she was under suspicion with Sister Beatrice might make it difficult to take food to Billy every mealtime. She was going to have to watch her opportunity and slip away. Most of the children would have gone into the games room to play before supper and she couldn't keep Billy waiting any longer. He would be thinking she had deserted him.

Angela looked at Sister Beatrice as the door closed behind Mary Ellen. She'd kept her silence during the interview with the police constable and what happened afterwards, but now she felt compelled to speak.

'Was that truly necessary?'

'What do you mean?'

Sister looked angry and Angela knew she was treading on thin ice, but she had to speak out. The look on that child's face had struck her to the heart and she knew how much Mary Ellen had been looking forward to going to the pantomime.

'Could you not just have given her a few lines or something? To take away the best of the Christmas treats – it is very unkind to say the least.'

'It is not for you to question my judgement, Angela. This is not the first time Mary Ellen has lied to me. I do not approve of liars, even if you do.'

'If Mary Ellen held back something she did it for a friend,' Angela said. 'I think she was hiding something, as you do, and Mary Ellen is certainly tense and upset over Billy. I do agree that she isn't telling us everything – but punishing her in such a manner is not likely to gain her trust. She isn't to blame for whatever Billy has done. Why should she bear the punishment?'

'Because I will not have the children lie to me. Had she chosen to tell me the truth I should have sorted it out. Billy need not be in trouble with the police if he will come forward and do the right thing – but does he even know what that is? Some of these children learn to lie at their mothers' knees and it is not acceptable here. This place is run on trust. Yes, I do see that she is upset for her friend, and had she chosen to confide in us, we could have helped them both.' Beatrice looked anxious, uncertain. 'Believe me, it gives me no pleasure to punish her but I cannot condone this kind of behaviour. Sometimes I make mistakes, but in this instance I believe I am right. What I do is for the good of all, Angela. Discipline must be maintained or we shall have chaos. I wouldn't expect you to understand. You've never known what it is like to have your trust utterly betrayed – to learn firsthand what lying and cheating can do.'

'No, perhaps I haven't,' Angela said. 'But I've known grief and I saw real grief in that child's eyes. She hasn't much to look forward to in life. How can you take away something so precious?'

'You make too much of it,' Sister Beatrice said coldly. 'Have you no work of your own? Did you not say that it is better to take away a privilege than smack a child? Now, if you will excuse me, I have a great deal to do personally so I would appreciate it if I could be left in peace.'

Angela bowed her head and left without another word. She was so angry that she might have said something that would make it impossible for her to work with the other woman. Having made her protest against the injustice of the punishment there was no more she could do if she wanted to stay here. She had begun to think more kindly of Sister Beatrice and to make allowances for her harshness at times. The older woman had hinted at a hard life, of suffering that she could know nothing of – but Angela had known the depths of despair herself and yet was still able to care for the children, to understand their point of view. It was arrogant of Sister to dismiss her as having no notion of suffering.

Angry and frustrated that there was nothing she could do to help the child, Angela went in search of Mary Ellen. Perhaps she could talk to her, ease her disappointment a little by telling her of other treats planned – though she feared nothing would equal the pantomime.

Entering the dining room, Angela saw that all the tables had been cleared and the children had gone. She would try the large room that the younger ones gathered into to play games and do puzzles or read books before going to prayers and then bed. It wouldn't be easy to find the words to comfort Mary Ellen, but she must try.

Sally, who looked worried, stopped her on her way from the dining hall.

'I wanted a word,' the carer said. 'Marion tells me that Sister Beatrice has cancelled Mary Ellen's trip to the pantomime?'

'Yes, that is true. The police came asking after Billy Baggins. Mary Ellen said she hadn't seen him, but Sister thought she was lying – and that was her punishment.'

'That's a bit unfair, isn't it?' Sally said. 'Mary Ellen is always good with the small children. If Billy is in trouble, it is his fault, not Mary Ellen's.'

'I'm not sure that he would be in trouble if he came forward, but we do not know where he is. Sister is sure that Mary Ellen knows – and she hates lies. In general I agree with her, but in this case . . .' Angela shook her head. 'Have you seen Mary Ellen? I wanted to talk to her – to discover why she won't tell.'

'Mary Ellen is very loyal. She would never tell on her friends.'

'Yes, I think that is what the problem is – but in this case it might be better all round . . .'

'Well, if I see her before I leave I'll come and tell you. Shall you be in your office?'

'Yes, for a while – but I'm going to look for her first.'

'Let's hope you find her. We don't want her running off as well.'

Angela nodded her agreement. Mary Ellen was just the independent sort of child who might decide to run off if she felt she'd been unfairly treated.

CHAPTER 31

Sally looked up from the book she'd been reading to the little ones as the door of the schoolroom opened and Andrew entered. She smiled, her heart giving a little hop, skip and jump as she saw the answering smile in his eyes. She was almost sure she was in love with him now, and when he smiled like that she believed he loved her, really loved her. Her mother and sister had both warned her not to take his attentions seriously, but surely her own heart was a better judge?

'I hope I do not disturb you? I wanted a word with you if you have time?'

'Yes, of course. Children, you may play with the toys for now and we'll continue the story tomorrow.'

The children got up, running to be the first to the toy cupboard, pushing and quarrelling in an effort to get their favourite before someone else snatched it. Sally walked towards the other end of the long room where it was quieter, before turning to her visitor, keeping her voice light because the children were listening, and asked, 'What can I do for you?'

'I thought you might like to know how Jimmy

Noakes was getting on. The young boy who was injured in that nasty accident.'

'Yes, I remember. His father came to see me at home yesterday evening. He told me his son was coming out of hospital soon and thanked me for helping the boy before you arrived – and for taking the bike back to his employer.'

'Ah, that was well done of him, because it was kind of you to go out of your way to help the lad.'

'It was the least I could do. Mr Noakes seemed to think that his son was recovering well, is that correct?'

'Yes. We managed to patch up his leg, and apart from a few bruises elsewhere he was lucky. Had he suffered a head injury he might have lost his life or been brain-damaged. As it is, he will be back to normal in no time.'

'I'm so pleased. It was fortunate that you came along when you did, Andrew.'

'I was wondering whether you would have dinner with me soon. Please, Sally. I know we've been on a casual footing, just drinks or a coffee until now – but I want us to start going out properly. I suppose I'm asking you if I can court you – isn't that the right term?' His eyes teased her, the laughter in them making her pulses race with excitement. She wished they were somewhere else, because she wanted to feel his arms around her and his lips on hers.

Sally swallowed hard, her heart beating so fast that she felt short of breath and did not know how to answer him. Common sense told her that she was out of her depth and it would be best not to start something that could only end in disappointment for them both. Yet her heart was telling her this feeling was right and special and she wanted it so much . . . so very much.

'I have my nursing classes tomorrow evening and I can't afford to miss one because there are exams coming up. I'm sorry . . .'

'And I am busy for most of next week,' he said and looked disappointed. 'Christmas is looming and I'm not sure . . . but we'll fix something soon, because I'm quite serious in wanting to court you, Sally.'

'Yes, it's what I want too,' she said softly. 'I shall look forward to seeing you again soon. I shall see you at the children's Christmas party shan't I?'

'Yes, of course. I couldn't miss that. I may be able to pop in sooner and perhaps I'll know by then what my arrangements are and we can fix up something.'

'Yes . . .' Her breath caught in her throat when his eyes lit with pleasure and she felt that she had suddenly taken a leap into space. She had no idea where this was going, but she wanted to know him better. 'Yes, I should like that . . .' She smiled dreamily as she watched him leave.

Glancing at the clock on the wall, Sally realised it was almost time to take the children to wash their hands before lunch. It was the pantomime the next afternoon and they were all anticipating it eagerly. Recalling that Mary Ellen had been denied the privilege, Sally felt saddened. The girl had been looking forward to it so much and it didn't seem fair to punish her like that, even if she had lied to protect her friend.

Angela said Sister thought Billy was hiding and Mary Ellen was helping him, but Sally couldn't think of anywhere the lad could successfully hide. All the rooms were in constant use, because there were more than fifty children in residence at the moment. It was too cold for him to hide in a garden shed; he would be frozen if he did that, because the frost was deep each night even though it hadn't snowed yet. Sally knew he wasn't hiding in the cellar, because Angela had been down there twice to look. If Billy was hiding at St Saviour's he must have found a very good place that neither she nor Angela could discover.

Billy was frozen all over. He kept moving his hands and feet to instil some warmth into them, but he was still very cold despite the thin blanket Mary Ellen had somehow managed to smuggle up to him under her coat. The old house was heated by a boiler in the cellars and the heavy cast-iron radiators kept the rest of the rooms at a comfortable temperature, but because the attics had been sealed off, not much heat found its way up to him.

He was hungry too, because he'd been up here for days now and Mary Ellen couldn't always get enough food for him. She did her best and brought him bread and butter, cake, a hard-boiled egg and now and then some cold meat or a sausage roll, but she couldn't bring hot food and his drinks were water, lemonade or orange squash. He thought constantly of steak and kidney pie, mashed potatoes and sponge pudding with lashings of hot custard, and longed for a cup of creamy cocoa.

Billy had managed to wash off the coal dust that had covered his hands and face after his adventures in the cellar, but his clothes still stank of the smoke from the fire. Mary Ellen hadn't been able to sneak into the boys' dorm to bring him clean, and though she'd brought one of her own woollens to help keep him warm, she couldn't get his shirt or trousers.

In the early hours of the morning, he crept downstairs to the kitchen and emptied the chamber pot he'd found in the attics down one of the toilets. Every time he was sure he would be caught. Once, a carer had come through the back kitchen to the toilet and tried the door, but Billy had locked it. He'd heard her mutter something and go off again, his heart beating as he escaped back up the narrow stairs to his hiding place. It was beginning to seem more like a prison than a sanctuary.

There were mattresses but they were damp and smelled fusty and he'd caught a chill the first night he was up here. He kept wiping his running nose, conscious that he was dirty as well as cold and miserable. Mary Ellen had tried to persuade him that he should come down and confess everything to Sister Beatrice, but he was frightened of being sent away.

'The policeman told me,' Mary Ellen said over and over. 'You won't be in trouble if you tell what you know, Billy. None of it was your fault. You can't stay up here much longer. You might be ill and then what would I do?'

'You won't tell on me?'

'You know I shan't,' she promised him, although there was a look in her eyes that made Billy wonder. 'Are you in trouble 'cos of me?'

She'd shaken her head, but he sensed that something was upsetting her. He almost made up his mind to give himself up then, but decided to wait a few more days. If he confessed to Sister she would know that Mary Ellen had been helping him and she might withdraw his friend's privileges. He could hold out a bit longer and he would . . . just until the Christmas party was over . . .

Mary Ellen was worried about Billy, who had been sneezing and his nose looked red, as did his eyes. She had taken him some paper napkins to blow his nose on but she knew he didn't feel well and she was torn between her loyalty to him and her fear that he might become really ill. She knew that the food she was managing to get to him wasn't enough, but she couldn't find a way to take more than she was already doing, because the serving girl kept giving her a peculiar look when she loaded her plate with enough for two.

They'd had plum tart with thick yellow custard for tea that afternoon. It was a favourite with Billy and Mary Ellen racked her brains for a way to take a bowl of the delicious treat to him. She dared not go for second helpings and even though she was willing to give up the pudding for his sake, it wasn't going to be easy smuggling out a bowl of tart and custard. She wrapped it round with the paper napkins and looked over her shoulder to see if she was being watched before hurriedly sliding the dish into her bag. Her own stomach was rumbling, because she'd been giving more than half of the food she took to Billy, but his need was greater than hers.

'What did you do that for?' Marion asked, and Mary Ellen realised her friend had seen her hide the plum tart. 'You should eat it now while it's hot.'

'It isn't for me . . . Oh, I shouldn't have told you . . .'

Marion stared at her, eyes opening wide. 'I've seen you hide food before. You're taking it to Billy, aren't you?'

'You won't tell anyone?'

'Sister will be so cross if she finds out . . .'

'I know but I've got to. Billy can only come down at night and there's no food about then.'

'Can you get enough for both of you?'

'No, because they watch me; I know they think I'm greedy, and Cook complained that someone had pinched some food and I don't want them thinking it's me.'

'Here, take this,' Marion said and pushed her plate across the table. 'Give Billy my cake. I've had enough anyway.'

'Thanks, Marion. If you can bring a bit extra in future it will help.'

'But surely . . . he isn't going to stay hidden forever?'

'Of course he isn't. I can't explain, because I promised I wouldn't say anything – but he's not hiding from Sister, not really.'

Marion nodded. 'Does Billy know you can't come to the pantomime tomorrow because you wouldn't tell on him?'

'No, and I'm not going to say. He would do the same for us.'

'Yes, he would.' Marion looked solemn. 'But if he stays up there any longer he'll miss Christmas dinner and we're havin' a special one.'

'I know.' Mary Ellen sighed. 'I keep telling him but he's . . .' She stopped, because she couldn't reveal that Billy was frightened he might be in trouble with the police. 'I'm going to slip away now, because this tart is better while it's warm.'

'All right.' Marion's gaze followed her anxiously as she left the dining room.

It was Marion's anxious gaze that alerted Sally. She'd seen the hasty way Mary Ellen had left the table and, coupled with the fact that she'd noticed the girl slip a bowl of tart and custard into her cloth bag, her suspicions were fully aroused. She'd noticed the girl hiding food in her bag before, but children did sometimes take a piece of cake up to the dorm, even though they were not supposed to because crumbs could attract mice. A bowl of tart and custard was different, because it could spill all over and was better eaten warm. Most of the children devoured their share before eating their bread and butter and Mary Ellen was usually the same. Sally knew that both she and Billy Baggins loved plum tart and custard . . .

Of course! It was obvious that the child was helping him to hide somewhere in the home. The police had looked for him without success but if he was here at St Saviour's they wouldn't have a hope of finding him on the streets – but where? Neither Sally nor Angela could find the lad. But Mary Ellen knew where he was.

Leaving the dining room hurriedly, Sally was in time to catch sight of the girl disappearing up the stairs at the far end of the hall. Those back stairs had once led to the warders' rooms when it had been a fever hospital in the bad old days, and were still used as a shortcut to the sick wards, but Sally had thought the attic rooms were boarded up. The children must have found a way in that no one else knew of.

Walking swiftly after Mary Ellen, she wondered what she ought to do if she discovered their secret. Could she persuade them to give up this masquerade or was it her duty to go to Sister Beatrice? She was torn between catching the guilty pair and forcing them to confess their secret and waiting to see whether they would decide to come clean themselves. It would be a betrayal of the children's trust if she told Sister Beatrice and yet it was her duty to let someone know where Billy was hiding.

As she reached the landing, there was no sign of Mary Ellen. She had simply disappeared, but Sally had followed her too quickly for her to go far. Where had she disappeared to?

There were three doors along this landing. One led to the dormitories and was used by the carers in the mornings, the other to a short flight of stairs leading down to Sister's office, the sick ward and the isolation ward. The third door had always been kept locked. Sally tried the handle and discovered that it turned easily. Opening it cautiously, she saw there was another set of stairs, narrow and dark, the walls hung with cobwebs, as if they hadn't been used in years – but there were quite clearly footprints in the dust: a child's footprints.

Sally had known there was a staircase up to the old attic rooms, but she believed it had been boarded over at the top. Obviously, Billy had somehow gained access to the staircase – but how could he get into the attics themselves if they were boarded up?

Should Sally go up and investigate? She hesitated, then started up the stairs, taking care to tread softly. It was very dark but with the door at the bottom left open, there was just enough light to see that the stairs ended abruptly with what looked like a solid panel of wood. How could the children get past that? She wondered about it and then touched it experimentally, jumping as it swung back at the bottom, revealing a dark space. So the panel had not been secured properly – or had Billy somehow managed to force it? She imagined it was he that had discovered the way in, for Mary Ellen would not come exploring here alone.

Sally got down on her knees and peered through, unable to see much at first until her eyes became accustomed to the dark, but then she heard voices and turned her head towards the sound; as she did so, she realised that there was just a flicker of light under a door. Billy or Mary Ellen must have a small torch – or worse, a candle. A candle up here could be dangerous, because the wood was so old and dry that a fire could start in an instant.

To burst in on them now might startle them and in the dark an accident could happen. Sally decided that it would be better to go back downstairs, find Angela and come back with a torch. There might even be an electric light, but she didn't want to go stumbling about up here in the dark in case she or the children were injured.

Creeping back down the stairs, her pulse was racing because she was anxious to sort this out without Sister Beatrice discovering what they were doing. Once she had the children safely back in the house, she and Angela together would sort out what was the best thing to do.

Sally just hoped that Angela would be in her office and alone.

Knocking at the door, she found Angela working at her desk on what looked like some accounts. She looked up and smiled a welcome.

'Sally, it's lovely to see you. Is something wrong?'

'I've found Billy,' Sally said and put a finger to her lips as Angela rose quickly to her feet. 'Do you have a torch? He is in the attic and it is very dark. Only, I don't want Sister to know yet . . .'

Angela nodded. She opened the drawer at the top of her desk and took out a good-sized torch. 'I use it for crossing the garden late at night, because it can be dark outside the Nurses' Home.'

'We need to go quickly,' Sally urged. 'If Mary Ellen locks the door we shall have to make her give the key up.' Angela looked puzzled and Sally explained about the old attics and how everyone believed they were securely boarded up.

'I didn't even know they were there. I never use the back stairs, only the main staircase or the lift.'

'We carers sometimes use the back stairs as a shortcut in the mornings, but when I first came here that door was always locked. I think Billy must have found the key somewhere. I have no idea where it was kept. At the top of the stairs there's a solid panel but it moves to one side. Whether the work was never finished off or whether Billy managed to work it loose I don't know . . .'

'How long has he been there? Not since he first disappeared?'

'No, I don't think so, probably only a few days. I noticed Mary Ellen piling her plate rather high a couple of days back, and today at tea I saw her putting food in her schoolbag.'

'She has been taking him food?'

'Yes, of course. Billy wouldn't be able to get any otherwise. Cook is keeping the pantry locked at night so that the Christmas food doesn't get stolen. She thinks one of the new carers might have taken some food she was saving for Christmas Day.'

'Surely it would more likely be one of the children?'

'Some of the girls come from poor homes and have families to feed. I can understand the temptation to take a few tarts or something. I've been tempted myself since Dad went on short time, but he'd be furious if I did anything like that.'

'Oh, Sally,' Angela said. 'Why didn't you tell me? If you need money I might be able to help . . .'

Sally shook her head, putting a finger to her lips. She tried the door to the attic stairs and found it open. 'Shine your light on the stairs until we get up there. It was too dark inside without a torch and I didn't want to fall over something and frighten them – they will think they're in trouble as it is and may panic.'

She showed Angela how the seemingly solid panel swung back at the bottom. The narrow gap would be easy for children to squeeze past but Sally needed Angela to hold it while she wiggled through, and once inside the aperture, she held it up for her colleague to follow.

The torch showed that they could stand upright and look about them. At some time, the attics had been used as sleeping quarters and were divided by wooden partitions. Old mattresses still lay on the floors and there was a Victorian chest of drawers and some broken wooden chairs lying on their sides, abandoned, also commodes and wash-stands with their china basins still intact.

At the sound of some scuffling, they guessed the children had heard them coming. The faint light showing under a door had gone out as Billy and Mary Ellen tried to hide their presence, but this was the only way out and they were caught. Pushing open the dividing door, Sally shone her light and saw the guilty pair huddling together and looking scared in the yellow beam.

'Thank goodness you're safe,' Angela said. 'Do you think there's a light switch up here? Have you got a torch, Billy?'

'No, miss, I just brought an oil lamp. I found it in the cellar and it still works.'

'That is very dangerous,' Sally said. 'You might have set the house on fire, Billy.'

'No, miss. I was very careful, I promise. I wouldn't set you alight in your beds.'

'His brother threatened to,' Mary Ellen burst out. 'That's why he had to go with him. Tell them, Billy. Tell Sally why you ran off. Arthur made you do it. And tell them how you saw the fire start at the factory and went in to warn them and got trapped yourself for hours.'

'Is that all true?' Angela asked.

'Yes, miss. He made me help him, because he hit me – and I was scared he would kill all of you in a fire.'

'Well, you can't stay up here,' Sally said. 'You've got to come down and let us help you, Billy. Angela will talk to Sister. You won't be in trouble if you explain why you went off – and tell the police what you know.'

'If I come she'll know Mary Ellen 'elped me and she'll be in trouble. Sister will stop her goin' to the pantomime and the party . . .'

'I've already been stopped going to the pantomime,' Mary Ellen said. 'You've got to come down now, Billy. He's got a cold, miss, and he's hungry.'

'Yes, I expect it has been very uncomfortable up here for you,' Sally said. 'Come with me, Billy. I'm going to put you in the isolation ward for tonight – and I'll bring you some hot cocoa and a ham sandwich in bed.'

'You didn't tell me you was in trouble wiv Sister over me.' Billy stared at Mary Ellen.

'It was 'cos the policeman asked if I'd seen you and I said no – and Sister knew I was lying. She wanted me to tell and I wouldn't so I can't go tomorrow . . .'

'Rotten old witch,' he muttered.

'Now, Billy, that is enough,' Sally said. 'I'm going to take care of you – and Angela will talk to Sister

419

about you. She'll ask her if Mary Ellen can go to the pantomime after all, seeing as you had a good reason to run off.'

Angela added her mite. 'We must go down. You cannot stay up here, Billy. It's freezing cold. You could die of pneumonia, and we don't want that – think of Mary Ellen and Marion. They are your friends and it would upset them. You owe it to them to come down and let us look after you.'

Billy muttered something rude, but gave in. Angela looked round for the oil lamp and picked it up.

'It's out, honest, miss.'

'Yes, but I think we'll make sure and put it back in the cellar where it belongs. You wouldn't want to cause a fire, now would you?'

'No, miss. It upset me when Arthur said he'd burn you all in your beds.'

'The police are looking for your brother. They are bound to find him sooner or later – and you could probably help them if you wished.'

'I ain't a snitch, miss. He's a bully and I hate him, but I ain't never been a snitch.'

'If you tell the police what happened, they will see he goes to prison for a long time. You'd like that, wouldn't you?'

'He's me brother, miss. Sometimes I 'ate him for what he does, but he were all right when we were little . . . it were only after Ma died that he went bad . . .'

'Yes, I understand that, Billy – but you don't want him to hurt your friends, do you?'

He shook his head, but she sensed that he had conflicting emotions about the prospect of telling the police about his brother. It could never be easy to inform on family, but in this case she hoped he would realise it was necessary.

Angela shone the torch for them all to squeeze through the hole. It was even darker now for there was no light even from the passage below.

When they were all safely down the dark stairs, Angela switched the hall light on. Sally looked at Billy and exclaimed in dismay as she saw his condition. He had a blanket over his shoulders, but his face was streaked with dirt, as were his hands and legs.

'You look as if you haven't washed in weeks.'

'I ain't, miss. Me brother lived in bombed-out houses and there weren't no water to wash – and me hand hurts where I burned it. I've been in the attic for five days I reckon and I daren't wash in case I got caught.'

'Right, it's in the bath with you and then I'll bind your hand for you,' Sally said and, taking hold of his arm, marched him off through the end door towards the isolation ward.

Mary Ellen looked at Angela fearfully. 'Do you think Sister will be angry with Billy?'

'I expect she'll be cross, don't you? He should have gone to her instead of running off and then hiding in the attics. Don't worry, I'll do what I

421

can to explain – and I'll see if she will change her mind and let you go to the pantomime. Run off to your dormitory now and do whatever you're supposed to do at this hour.'

Mary Ellen cast her a woebegone look and then ran off through the door that led up to the dorms. Angela sighed and followed in Sally's footsteps. She wasn't looking forward to the interview with Sister Beatrice, because she suspected that the Warden was going to be very angry indeed.

CHAPTER 32

'Where are they now?' Sister Beatrice asked when Angela had finished her lengthy explanation. 'I trust you removed the oil lamp?'

'Yes, of course, but it was out. Billy is quite responsible and I truly believe he would never harm anyone here at St Saviour's.'

'That is beside the point. He was reckless and thoughtless and I am not sure we can keep him here after this.'

'Surely his behaviour is understandable? His brother is a bully and a rogue. Billy was afraid of him. He still has bruises on his face where Arthur hit him, and a couple of small burns from being trapped in that fire. He is lucky to be alive, and I'm inclined to think him a bit of a hero. Sally is giving him a bath and putting him to bed in the isolation ward for the night. I expect he is hungry – and he has a nasty cold.'

Sister Beatrice gave her a disbelieving stare.

'Please do not let him bamboozle you, Angela. Boys like that know how to make themselves appear in the right when they are in a tight corner.

It is a wonder he hasn't got pneumonia,' she said. 'Those attics must be freezing at this time of year. I cannot understand how he gained access to them. The key to that door was lost years ago, after they were boarded up.'

'I think Billy found it in the cellar, where the lamp was,' Angela said. 'The caretaker uses the cellar to store all kinds of things and he has to go down there to look after the boiler so that is why Billy chose the attics instead.'

'Had he been honest he would have come to me and confessed.'

'I think he was frightened in case his brother came looking for him – and then he wanted to protect Mary Ellen. He said he was going to come out after Christmas when all the treats were over and she wouldn't lose privileges.'

'Indeed?' Sister Beatrice frowned. 'So now I am an ogre?'

'No, of course you're not. It's just that he and you . . .' Angela's words trailed away. 'In the circumstances, could you not allow Mary Ellen to go to the pantomime?'

Sister Beatrice glared at her. 'You would have me condone lies?'

'No, not in the general way – but she was only protecting a friend. It's not as if she did anything for her own gain; in fact she'd been going without food to feed him. I think it was noble of her.'

'Well, your notions do not accord with mine!'

'He really did no harm hiding in the attics . . .'

'And that could have led to goodness knows what. If that lamp had fallen over and set fire to the attics, it could have been a disaster.'

'I told Billy it wasn't safe. He will not be as foolish again.'

'You have more faith in his common sense than I,' Sister Beatrice said. 'You will please leave the running of this home to me, Angela. I am the warden here and what I say stands.'

'Yes, of course. I didn't mean to suggest . . .'

'Yet you do not hesitate to tell me I am wrong? I have good reasons for what I do, let me assure you. The punishment stands. Neither of them will attend the pantomime.'

'If that is your final word, then I must accept it. I'm sorry, Sister. I didn't mean to usurp your position; I couldn't. Forgive me – but think again about the child going to that pantomime.'

Angela turned and walked from Sister's office, feeling angry. She'd been forced to apologise because she knew that Sister Beatrice was far more important to St Saviour's than she was, but she wasn't sorry for standing up for the children. It was a pity that she had only made things worse, because a small boy and girl would suffer. Yet there was little she could do about it other appeal to the Board, which would mean a showdown and might lead to the Warden leaving her position.

Angela had been sent here to help Sister Beatrice to bring St Saviour's into a more modern world, not to cause such a breach that one of them was forced to leave. It certainly ought not to be the nun, because her expertise was essential for the children's welfare.

At the moment Angela wasn't sure whether she wanted to carry on working here. Sister Beatrice could be very sharp and Angela didn't like being treated as though she were irresponsible or a foolish child. Sister might be a good nurse and she worked hard for the children, but it wouldn't hurt her to listen once in a while. Angela might not have her experience of running a children's home, but she knew instinctively that some children needed encouragement and love, not punishment – and Mary Ellen was surely one of those. Her small, pale face had touched Angela's heart the first time she saw her, and she wanted to protect her as much as she could.

There were so many children in need of love and care and Angela knew that Sister Beatrice was very necessary to the running of St Saviour's – but surely there was room for other opinions?

Beatrice glared at the door as it closed behind the younger woman. She was not sure what had made her more angry, to discover that Billy Baggins had been hiding here all the time, or being told that she was in the wrong by a middle-class woman who had no idea what it was like to suffer the conditions prevalent in many East End homes. How dare she presume to tell Beatrice her job?

She snatched up a small silver vase from her

desk and went through the motions of hurling it at the door, but it never left her hand because such actions were childish and against her vocation; she would not allow herself to lose her temper. Goodness knows she'd been driven to the verge enough times of late. Angela was so obviously disapproving of her actions and even though she'd apologised she clearly felt herself in the right.

The trouble was that in her heart Beatrice knew some of what Angela had suggested would be good for the children. At first she'd rejected the list of points the younger woman had given her simply because she was not ready for changes. Surely the time-tested ways were the best; children needed to be disciplined for their own good – and yet she'd never enjoyed caning a child and had to steel herself to deliver the punishment. At the convent she'd learned the power of self-discipline, learned that a strong will could overcome personal pain and grief.

It was the right way for her, because she could never let herself remember the past that had shaped and scarred her – but that did not make it right for everyone. Perhaps Angela was correct when she said that sometimes the children had suffered so much that even if they were naughty they deserved love and understanding rather than discipline.

Even so, could she stay here and work side by side with a woman who so clearly disapproved of her and her methods? Angela was determined to sweep away the established disciplines of years and bring in the modern thinking she considered beneficial. Yet Beatrice knew that Angela was not alone in thinking as she did; there was a new mood abroad in the country. You read it in the way the newspapers wrote scathing reports on some children's homes and the way the Government was still being condemned for having sent children away from their homes without proper planning during the war. Some of the evacuees had been treated appallingly and some were even lost to their parents.

Was she perhaps letting the sin of pride cloud her judgement? Her hand closed over the silver crucifix she wore at her breast and she murmured a silent prayer asking for the strength to know what was right – and to accept it, even if perhaps it meant she had to adjust her own thinking.

Remembering that she'd been so very worried about Billy, Beatrice wondered at her own intransigence and honesty forced her to admit that if Angela hadn't gone straight into battle over the children she might have been more lenient; it was a sad thing that she'd allowed the younger woman to get under her skin in this way.

Could she adjust sufficiently to work with her? Beatrice wasn't sure but the alternative was perhaps even worse. St Saviour's was her home and the children were her children, the reason that made her go on with her life. To give it up now because of that upstart . . . no, it wasn't to be borne!

CHAPTER 33

Angela was sitting in her office on Saturday morning when the phone rang. Answering, she heard her father's voice. 'Hello, Daddy, how are you?'

There was a slight hesitation, then, 'I'm all right. I was just ringing to ask if you were still coming home for Christmas.' Something in the way he spoke sounded like a plea to Angela and her heart caught. He'd sounded unlike himself . . . vulnerable.

'Yes, I'm coming down Christmas Eve after the carol service – and I'll stay until the afternoon of Boxing Day.'

'Good . . .' Was that relief in his voice? 'We shall both be pleased to see you, my love. Your mother has been planning a special lunch. I mustn't tell you, because it is a surprise – but I didn't want her to go to all that trouble and then be disappointed.'

'No, I shan't disappoint her. I'm looking forward to it.'

'So am I,' he said. 'Bye for now, love.'

'Are you all right?' She was anxious, because

instinct was telling her he was keeping something back. 'Is anything wrong, Dad?'

'No, not at all, never better,' he affirmed and yet she sensed that it was an effort, his hearty voice put on to reassure her.

Angela replaced her receiver, slightly uneasy. Even if something was wrong, her father wouldn't tell her on the phone. It made her frown, because he was usually so cheerful. She was about to ring him back when her phone rang once more.

She picked it up and relaxed as she heard Mark's voice. He hadn't rung her since they went to the theatre, for which he apologised now.

'I've had such a lot on, a rush of private patients on top of my hospital work. I think this time of year always brings on bouts of depression,' he said and laughed deprecatingly at himself. 'Do you have time for dinner one evening soon – next Monday?'

'I'd love to, Mark – that's the 15th isn't it? After that things will start to get pretty hectic here with all the preparations for Christmas. I have a lot to tell you. We've found Billy – you remember the lad who went missing? He was forced to work for his rogue of a brother and got mixed up in that fire at the boot factory. But I'll tell you on Monday.'

'Yes, you do that,' he said. 'By the way, are you going home for Christmas?'

'Yes. I thought I'd go down on Christmas Eve, after the party here.'

'Good. I'm going then so I'll drive you – if you'd like?'

'Lovely. I shall look forward to it – and I'll see you on Monday.'

Angela smiled as she replaced the receiver. Mark was such a good friend and she missed him when they didn't meet for a while.

She sat staring into space for a few minutes, thinking about the past year or so during which she'd gradually been learning to live with her grief. John's death had left a gaping hole in her life and an ache in her heart she sometimes thought would never leave her – and yet since she'd come here Angela had begun to feel things more sharply. She thought about the children she saw every day, the new arrivals looking frightened and pale when she and Nan admitted them, and the gradual blooming of roses in their cheeks as good food and security helped them recover from terrible experiences. Most of them had been half-starving; they had never been as well fed in their lives as they were here – and Angela was determined they would grow up in a place that would make them smile when they were older and looked back.

The new building was still a shambles. Sometimes the noise of hammering penetrated Angela's office and she felt like asking them to stop for a while, but the sooner the new dorms were ready the better. Mark had taken her ideas to the Board and they had agreed to keep the size of the rooms down to six pupils, making two for the boys and three for the girls rather than two huge ones. Mark had told her some of the Board had grumbled about the extra running costs it might incur, but Angela had got her way. That was one big tick on her list but she had a long way to go. The next step was to discuss the idea of team leaders with Sister Beatrice . . .

It was a pity they'd had words over Billy Baggins and Mary Ellen again. Particularly the girl. Angela sighed and tried not to think about the child's woebegone face. She pulled on her thick coat and picked up her bag, preparing to leave.

Saturdays were actually her time off, and she usually spent the morning shopping and then helped out at St Saviour's in the afternoons. This morning she intended to spend her time buying Christmas gifts for her parents, the staff at the home and small things to put on the tree for the children.

Mark Adderbury would be putting up the tree one day the following week and she knew he intended to give out gifts on Christmas Eve at the party. The children had heard whispers and were growing very excited, but Angela could not forget the look of misery in one child's eyes because she was to be denied something that meant more to her than anything else.

It was so cruel of Sister Beatrice to deny Mary Ellen this chance, which might never come again, during her childhood anyway. Angela had wangled the tickets from a friend this year, but she might not be able to do it again next year – and if she wasn't here . . . her thoughts came to an abrupt end, because she had to be sensible. She couldn't overrule Sister Beatrice. Mary Ellen could not go to the pantomime and that was the end of it, but . . . supposing another treat was substituted?

The idea came to Angela as she was passing a cinema showing a Walt Disney cartoon. The pictures of Mickey Mouse and Bambi posted in glass cases outside made her linger, and temptation raised its ugly head. Sister hadn't said the child could not have any treats, just that she could not go to the pantomime with the others. Supposing Angela took her to the Disney film instead and then to tea at Lyons' Corner House?

She ought not to do it. Angela knew that, because it would be flinging Sister's authority in her face, not an actual flaunting of her wishes but a defiant action that would make her furious . . . but with Angela rather than Mary Ellen.

Angela knew she was taking a great risk but for some reason Mary Ellen had touched her heart, making her want to protect and care for the vulnerable child. Many of the children at the home were sad cases, but none of the others seemed to be in trouble all the time.

On the bus back to St Saviour's, Angela still hadn't made up her mind to do it, because she knew that it would be wrong to flout Sister's wishes. She was punishing Mary Ellen for lying to her and the child *had* been wrong, but her reasons were unselfish and loyal and Angela felt that Sister could have relented this time.

She went up to her room and placed the parcels

on the bed ready for wrapping later. Angela seldom went anywhere in the evenings, preferring to stay at home and listen to a concert or a play on the wireless or read a book. If she had her own flat she could have her gramophone and her baby grand piano sent up from the country, which would provide her with endless entertainment, also more of her clothes, books and other treasures, which she missed. She might feel as if she had a home again then, but so far she hadn't found a flat she liked well enough to take on a lease, perhaps because she was so uncertain about staying at St Saviour's. Had she got on better with Sister Beatrice the job would have suited her – better than any other she could think of. She would be sorry if she had to leave, but there were other charities, other places she might find work with children if she tried. Yet she liked it here, was making friends . . .

And then there was Mark Adderbury. Angela suspected that Mark thought of her as more than a friend, but she wasn't ready to contemplate a relationship with a man yet: far from it. Much as she enjoyed their time together, Angela was still too raw inside, too much in love with John to think of . . . no, she couldn't imagine being another man's lover or wife.

'John, my love . . .' A wave of longing overtook her as she remembered the first time they'd met at that Young Farmers' ball. He'd looked so handsome in his dark suit and white shirt, his silvery blond hair waving back from his forehead, and his disconcertingly blue eyes. 'I loved you so very much. So much . . .'

John had swept her off her feet, claiming every dance with her, refusing to give her up to anyone and then taking her off to walk by the river. She remembered removing her shoes, sitting on the edge of a grassy bank and dangling her feet in the cool water. He'd kissed her and the feeling was so heady and sweet that Angela had known instantly this was different. He was the one she'd waited for all her life.

She'd been a virgin when he married her and carried her off to the sea for a brief honeymoon. John's lovemaking had been all that she'd dreamed of, making her come to life, as if she'd been a sleeping princess in her dark tower until that moment – but her happiness had lasted such a short time. John had only weeks of training before he was sent abroad; twice he'd returned to her on a brief leave and then . . . the telegram that told her he wouldn't come home again.

No, she couldn't think about that or she would let in all the grief and pain that she'd conquered. She treasured her short marriage and she could not think of giving herself or her heart to another man. Mark was a good friend, a wonderful listener, and she was eternally grateful to him for all he'd done for her – but she didn't want more than friendship from him or anyone else.

Dismissing Mark from her thoughts, she returned

to the problem of Mary Ellen. Billy wasn't going to the pantomime either, but he couldn't have gone anyway, because his cold had turned worse and he'd been running a fever. Sister Beatrice would no doubt have banned him if he'd been well, because she would have had no choice in the circumstances. Billy was confined to the isolation ward until he got better, but Mary Ellen would be alone while all the others went off to the theatre.

Angela left her room and went in search of Sally, to make sure she had the tickets and money necessary for the children's treat. She and Nurse Anna, Nan and Jean, one of the newer carers, were getting ready to assemble the children ready for the pantomime.

'Are you coming with us?' Sally asked, but Angela shook her head.

'I'm sorry. I can't manage it,' she said. 'You can cope without me, can't you?'

'Cook asked if there was a spare ticket. If you're not going, could she have yours?'

'Of course.' Angela hunted in her jacket pocket. 'Yes, here it is. You've got all the others?'

'Yes. And the five pounds you gave us for ice creams and sweets.'

'Good.' Angela smiled at her. 'It is so kind of you all to give up your time off to take the children.'

'We're all looking forward to it,' Anna said. 'Come along, Michael . . . Ruth, put your coat on, all of you must wear a coat. Hats for the girls and caps for the boys, please.' She mustered the crowd of excited children into some sort of order, checking that everyone had gloves, hats and scarves to combat the bitter weather.

Angela left the girls to it. She need not worry that they would find so many children difficult to manage, because they all adored Nan and did whatever she told them. With Cook there would be five of them to make sure the children didn't get lost or run across the road in their excitement.

It was in Angela's mind to look for Mary Ellen. She tried the isolation ward first, thinking the girl might be with Billy, but he was sound asleep, having been dosed with medicine for his sore throat and aching limbs, and Nurse Michelle said she hadn't seen the girl since first thing that morning when she'd come to ask if her friend was any better.

'I told her not to come in, because we don't want her catching it and being ill for Christmas.'

'No,' Angela agreed and walked away, feeling anxious.

Mary Ellen wasn't in the schoolroom, which was quiet and abandoned. She went up to the dorms but Mary Ellen wasn't there either and the fear built inside her. Could she have gone up to the attics to hide? Surely she couldn't get in now, because Sister Beatrice had the key safe in her desk, but she ought to look.

Mary Ellen was sitting on the back stairs, her shoulders hunched and her head bent. Angela knew she was crying and in that moment her anger became a fiery flame that roared in her head. She knew she was going to burn her boats and defy Sister Beatrice when the child raised her head and she saw the tears trickling on her cheeks, and the utter grief in her eyes. It must seem to Mary Ellen that they were all against her and that she had nothing to look forward to. All the letters for the children came first to Angela's office and she passed them on to Nan, who gave them to the children after first making sure there was nothing upsetting in them. She knew that Mary Ellen had not received so much as a postcard from her sister for some weeks. Either Rose must be exceptionally busy or there was another reason for the lack of communication of any kind. Angela couldn't understand her, because surely she could have walked here once every week or so, after she left the London hospital in the evenings.

The child had so little to look forward to anyway: her mother in a sanatorium, her sister too busy to visit often, her best friend lying sick in his bed – and all the other children off to the pantomime. It just wasn't fair or right and Angela wouldn't put up with it.

'Here, wipe your face,' she said and handed Mary Ellen a clean handkerchief. 'And then you can put your coat on. I'm taking you out.'

'To the pantomime?' Mary Ellen's face lit up like a candle.

'No, I cannot disobey Sister's instructions; she forbade us to take you there – but I can take you somewhere else.' She held out her hand, holding the child's gently in her own. 'Tell me, Mary Ellen, have you ever been to the cinema?'

'No, miss. That's where they have the pictures, isn't it?'

'Yes, and there's a Walt Disney cartoon programme today. If we hurry, we shall just be there in time for the start . . .'

For Angela her abiding memory of that Christmas period would always be Mary Ellen's face as they took their seats in the darkened cinema and the screen suddenly lit up. For a start there was a short cartoon of Mickey Mouse followed by Donald Duck, and then an interval, during which Angela bought them both an ice cream in a little tub with a wooden spoon, from the girl who came round with her tray. Then the lights dimmed again and the big feature began.

Disney's film about the young fawn losing its mother had come out in the war years and was so popular that it did the rounds of the cinema every few months, especially on school holidays and Christmas. Of course Mary Ellen had never seen it. She'd once seen cartoons reflected on a white screen at her local church hall, but that was nothing compared to this, and her face throughout was a picture of wonder and delight. She shed a few tears at Bambi's plight but in the end she was smiling and happy, sitting absolutely still and staring at the screen until the last credits had finished.

'Did you enjoy that?' Angela asked, even though she knew the answer.

Mary Ellen nodded, too bewitched by all she'd seen to speak, and it was not until they were eating their tea at Lyons that the excitement came bubbling out of her and she kept asking Angela if she seen Thumper show Bambi how to do this or that . . . and then, all of a sudden, she went silent.

'Thank you for bringing me, miss,' she said. 'It was wonderful. I wish Billy had seen it too, but I shall tell him all about it when he feels better.'

'I'm sorry you didn't get to the pantomime.'

'I liked this even better,' Mary Ellen assured her. 'Nothing could be as lovely as Bambi, miss. I shall never ever forget it.'

Angela had to agree with her. Seeing it through the eyes of a child had made her realise what a lovely film it was, and she knew she would never forget this afternoon – even if it meant she had to leave St Saviour's.

'I'm glad you enjoyed yourself. Perhaps we might go another day to see something else, not yet . . . but one day.'

She couldn't promise anything definite, because her time at the home might be over soon enough. If Sister Beatrice was as angry as she had every right to be, Angela might be forced to resign.

Angela told Mary Ellen to join the other children in the schoolroom before supper. Seeing her run off happily, she felt content and well rewarded for what she'd done, even though she knew that her next interview with Sister Beatrice might be very unpleasant. She went up to her office and removed her outer coat, sitting down at her desk and taking a list from her desk drawer.

She was running her finger down the items when the door opened abruptly and Sister Beatrice walked in. The look on her face was grim and Angela knew at once that the Warden had discovered what she'd done – and she was furious. Rising to her feet, Angela prepared to meet the onslaught she knew must be coming.

'You're angry,' she said.

'I believe I have every right to be angry.'

'Yes, perhaps,' Angela agreed. 'I didn't override your instructions – but I didn't see why I shouldn't take the child out myself.'

'No one is permitted to take the children out unless I am aware of it. Surely you know the rules? I have been looking for her. I was afraid she had run away.'

'No, Mary Ellen wouldn't do that. She was sitting on the back stairs crying when I found her. I took her to a Disney film and then to Lyons for tea. Please do not punish Mary Ellen. I am the one who broke the rules, not her.'

'I am well aware of that. I dare say you think I am cruel and stubborn, making stupid rules and expecting them to be obeyed? This is a home for disturbed children, Mrs Morton, and it has to have rules. If one child is allowed to get away with flouting them, they will all think they can do the same. I had to make an example of her whether I liked it or not. Had you any sense of loyalty to me, you would have understood that and, had you asked, I would have allowed you to take her to the cinema another day. To take her out on the very day I had punished her was to show everyone that you think I am a crass fool who gives out punishments for the pleasure of it . . .'

'I didn't mean it like that. I just couldn't bear to see her in such distress.'

'Do you imagine I enjoy punishing her? She is a taking little thing – and that friend of hers is a cheeky devil but I mean him no harm. I am not an ogre, and I do understand how children suffer. Good grief, I've seen enough of it. Being denied a trip to the pantomime is nothing compared to the beatings many children receive . . . but you are so certain you know best, aren't you?'

Sister Beatrice was almost shouting, but she broke off and turned away, her back towards Angela, shoulders heaving and clearly in distress.

Angela blinked, stunned by Sister's sudden outburst. For a moment she was silent, then, 'I'm sorry. I didn't realise how it would seem. I thought only of the child's disappointment. I knew I was wrong, and if you want me to resign, I shall do so when it is convenient to the Board.'

'I think one of us may have to go. I leave it to your conscience to decide which of us it should be.'

'Obviously it has to be me. I'd like to see the setting up of the new wing finished . . .'

'We shall carry on as usual until after Christmas. You must send your resignation letter to the Board; they asked you to take up the position against my better judgement . . .'

Angela stared at the door as Sister went out and closed it. A swathe of bitter regret went through her. Perhaps if she'd tried a little harder to understand the older woman . . . but it might not have made a difference. Sister Beatrice hadn't wanted her here.

It was going to wrench the heart out of her to leave. She'd been feeling so empty when she came here, the space in her heart where John had been open and ready for invasion. Mary Ellen and, to a lesser extent, Billy, had crept in and she had wanted to make the girl happy, to fill her own life with the things that might have been hers had John lived. Because she would have welcomed children; a career was nothing beside the joy that a child could bring.

Now she would have to make a new life for herself, start over again. Angela didn't think she wanted to go home to her parents' house. The first thing was probably to find herself an apartment and then, when she was settled, she could look for a new job; something working with children who needed her.

CHAPTER 34

Michelle was thoughtful as she joined the others in the canteen that day. She'd started her monthlies that morning and was feeling a bit under the weather, but she'd taken an Aspro and she thought the ache was easing a bit. Munching her share of fish pie, she worried at the problem that had been nagging at her for a while. Something was wrong with Alice, and she was afraid she might know what it was, because Alice's cousin Eric had met her after work the previous evening and suggested going for a drink.

'I've heard a rumour about Alice and I want to talk it over with you.'

'Did Alice tell you why Jack Shaw left London in a hurry?' Eric had asked over their first drink and Michelle shook her head, 'It was because Butcher Lee put a contract out on him.'

'Why would he do that?' Michelle had asked.

'Because Butcher reckoned he must be betraying them. The word is that Jack was selling up stuff and they thought he was getting ready to leave – and he knows too much about them. They can't afford to let him get away, because his evidence would hang them.'

'Alice hasn't looked very happy lately. I've tried asking her out, but she's always busy. I think she's avoiding me.' Michelle had hesitated, because she'd noticed little things, like how pasty she looked in the mornings, and a certain look that pregnant women had in their eyes. 'I'm not sure so don't get angry but I think she might be in trouble . . .'

'If that bugger's done the dirty on her . . .' Eric had scowled. 'Butcher Lee won't be the only one after his blood.'

'Some people think he was the man found dead at that factory fire.'

'Nah, not him,' Eric said. 'There's another way out of that office and I reckon he went down the fire escape at the back while everyone was watching the front. Jack Shaw is too cunning to get trapped like that; he would have cased the building before he decided to rob it . . . that's if he was even there and, despite the speculation in the papers, no one knows that for certain yet.' He scowled. 'He won't get away so easily if I catch up with him.'

Michelle had looked at him intently. 'You're very fond of Alice, aren't you?'

'Yeah, suppose I am. Alice has a rotten home life, but she's always been a good friend. She was the only one who understood when me Da died . . .'

Michelle hadn't asked him what he meant,

because she didn't want to become involved with him. Eric was all right for the occasional drink or a trip to the local dance hall, but she didn't want to get too close – to him or any other man.

Oh, well, this wasn't going to get her anywhere. Alice would confide in her if she wanted to and in the meantime Michelle had a job to do.

When she returned to the sick ward after she'd eaten it was to find that Marion had left to join the other children who were going to the pantomime.

Checking on Johnny, Michelle could see little change. He was still pale and quiet, but he wasn't running a temperature and there was no reason to think he was any worse. Perhaps she'd imagined that look in his eyes, a look she'd seen in other patients who were close to the end. She bent over him and touched his face gently.

'How do you feel, love?'

'I feel tired, miss, that's all,' he said wanly.

'I'll get you a nice warm drink,' she said, because she knew there was little else she could do for him.

After she'd made Johnny as comfortable as possible, Michelle felt her stomach ache returning and took another Aspro with a cup of tea.

Michelle popped next door into the isolation ward to look at Billy Baggins. One of the new carers was with him and had just given him a warm milky drink and some biscuits. He grinned at Michelle as she entered, obviously on the mend and no worse for his adventure. She reflected that he had his interview with Sister Beatrice to come and wondered what would happen. Would he be sent somewhere else? He had caused a lot of trouble by running off like that, but if he'd been frightened of what his brother might do . . . well, surely that was a consideration, wasn't it?

Michelle felt it would be a shame if he were sent away from his friends, and was glad that she didn't have to decide things like that, but she wouldn't have dreamed of questioning Sister Beatrice's right to make those decisions.

With nothing much else to do, she wrote up her report and then made herself a cup of tea and some more drinks for the children. One of the kitchen girls brought up a tray of sandwiches and cake a little later, and Michelle helped the children decide what they wanted. Billy asked for a sausage roll. Johnny didn't want anything, though she persuaded him to have a ham sandwich, because ham was such a treat, but he took one bite and kept chewing it round for ages before swallowing it.

'Couldn't you eat any more, love?' she asked, looking at the lovely food he'd left. Ham had been one of his favourites, and it worried her that he hadn't eaten it.

'I can't chew it enough, miss. I'm sorry . . .'

'It's all right, Johnny. It doesn't matter.'

She thought she might ask for some jelly and ice cream or a blancmange for him for his supper.

Perhaps that would slip down easily and tempt him to eat something.

Marion arrived about half an hour later, having had her tea downstairs, and Johnny bombarded her with questions. Michelle turned as Mary returned from her afternoon off.

'Johnny is no worse,' she told her in a low voice, 'but I'm going to see Sister before I leave just in case. Keep an eye on him but don't fuss. He does not have a temperature so he may be fine; it was just a feeling I had, that's all.'

Leaving the ward for the day, Michelle walked towards the Sister's office. If she still wasn't here, she would put a note on her desk.

However, she was invited to enter as soon as she knocked. Sister was frowning but her face lightened as she saw Michelle and she listened attentively while the nurse told her what was on her mind.

'I know what you mean about that look in the eyes. I've seen it for a while now,' Sister Beatrice said. 'Do not worry, Staff Nurse Michelle. I shall be here all night and I will keep an eye on him. Go home now and enjoy your night off. I think you are free until Monday morning?'

'Yes, that's right, Sister. I just wanted to be sure you were aware of a change in him.'

'That was very conscientious of you. Thank you.'

Michelle left her office, feeling as if a weight had been removed from her shoulders. Some of the staff – Angela in particular – thought Sister harsh, but Michelle admired her. Sister had a lot of responsibility and knew what she was doing. Now Michelle could stop fretting over Johnny for the time being, rather than worrying that Nurse Mary might not be able to cope if the child needed help during the night . . .

CHAPTER 35

Alice was more than three weeks late now and Mavis had been giving her suspicious looks recently. Sharing a bed, as they did, it was impossible to keep secrets from one another; Mavis knew if she had a headache and she certainly knew when Alice was suffering from the dreadful stomach cramps that the *curse* caused her each month.

'You're not on duty this Sunday, are you?' Mavis asked when she crawled into bed beside her sister that Saturday evening.

'No. Why do you ask?'

'I want to buy a new outfit. I've been invited to a wedding; Ted's elder sister is getting married and he's asked me to go with him . . .' Mavis hesitated, then, 'Besides, we need to talk, Alice, and we can't do it here – too many ears listening.'

Alice felt her stomach catch, because Mavis had guessed something was wrong. She'd probably noticed that Alice had been sick in the mornings and she was bound to have spotted that she hadn't had her period for a while. Her sister could be stubborn and when she got hold of something she would worry at it like a terrier at a rat. She was going to get Alice's secret out of her one way or the other – but perhaps it was what she needed, someone to tell her story to before it was too late. Mavis might tell her she was a fool, but she would be on her side, and she might be able to think of something to help her – which was more than her parents would do once the truth came out.

'All right, thanks,' she whispered. 'We'll go down the lane tomorrow, Mave. I need some new shoes for work and I got some decent ones there last time.'

'Go to sleep then – the brats are all ears.' Mavis nudged her sister and then said loudly, 'Anyone telling tales to Ma will be boiled in oil and skinned alive.'

'You'd be dead if you was boiled in oil,' Saul called out cheekily.

'And if I tell Ma that you've been skipping off school to go down the Docks and hang about with Bertie and his mates, she'll whack you until you bleed.'

A chuckle issued from the other side of the curtain as the brothers whispered beneath the bed covers. 'We ain't snitches, Mave.'

'Go to sleep then, 'cos I ain't either.'

Some time later Alice turned on her side, burrowing down into the lumpy feather mattress. It needed a really good shake because the feathers were old and stuck together, but it was best done out in the yard or the dust would fly everywhere.

Conscious of her sister already snoring and her brothers giggling beneath the covers of the bed they shared, Alice allowed a few tears of self-pity to slide down her cheeks. She was almost out of her mind with worry over Jack, because she hadn't heard from him since she'd seen the car speeding away into the night. Everyone had been talking about that fire at the boot factory, and Alice had heard that a man's body had been found. At first they'd thought it might be Julia's father, because he was the night watchman, but he was all right. So who could it have been?

Alice wasn't sure Jack had been one of the thieves attempting to rob the factory, but she'd heard Billy Baggins' brother had been one of them and Alice suspected that Jack would have been the other. The police were looking for Arthur – so was it Jack whose remains lay in a police mortuary, too burned and mutilated to be recognised? Her imagination ran riot because all the paper had said was that the body was unrecognisable.

No, please no, don't let it be Jack. Yet who else could it have been? Alice didn't know and nor did anyone else, because the papers called him a mystery man.

Alice felt sick at the thought, because she really loved Jack, even though he'd gone off and left her; she knew he was a rogue, but his smile made her insides go weak and she couldn't bear to think of him dead.

No. He couldn't be dead, because Alice would

know. Something inside her kept telling her that Jack was alive. It was the only reason she hadn't given way to grief, because she just knew Jack was still alive. She clung to the promise that he would come back for her, but as each week passed she knew it was more unlikely.

Why was she worrying about Jack rather than herself? Alice buried her face in the pillow and gulped back a sob. Men like Jack could look after themselves; it was Alice who was going to be in all kinds of trouble. For a start she would lose her job as soon as her condition became noticeable, and then she would probably be out on the street, because her mother would yell at her for being a filthy little slut and her father would disown her.

She was going to be on her own, Alice realised, because there was no one she could turn to for help. Nan was lovely but she would think Alice a fool and probably advise her to go to one of those Church-run places where they gave you a home until the baby was born and then took it away from you, giving it to a deserving but childless couple.

Instinctively, Alice curved her arms protectively over her stomach. She wouldn't have chosen to have this child until she was married, but the idea of being compelled to give it away made her feel sick. It wasn't as if she'd been raped by someone she hated.

It was too late now. She wouldn't show much for ages yet; time to make her plans and decide what to do. No one but the sister she shared so much of her life with would have guessed, Alice comforted herself. She still had some of the money Jack had given her so when the time came . . .

Alice fell asleep with that thought still unresolved in her mind.

'I love comin' here,' Mavis said, her arm firmly tucked through Alice's as they wandered through the flower market, its busy vendors crying their wares to catch the first of the eager shoppers on their way to spend their wages in the network of narrow lanes and alleys. There was an air of Christmas festivity, because this was the 14th December and people were getting in the mood for the coming holidays, despite the frost that nipped at their noses.

Columbia Road market had started out in the nineteenth century selling all kinds of bits and pieces, but now most of the stalls were offering flowers and plants, sprigs of holly and mistletoe. Even in winter the smell was lovely, Alice thought as she looked at the buckets of huge chrysanthemums, tall lilies and asters. Some enterprising traders were offering twigs and sprays of dried flowers with a kind of snow or glittery stuff on them.

The chill of an east wind reminded Alice that it would soon be time to think about Christmas and she decided that she would volunteer for duty. It wasn't much fun being at home all day, because Ma would grumble and Dad would probably take the port off to his shed and get drunk by evening.

Leaving the flower market, they walked through a street made up of shops and stalls selling mostly second-hand clothing; there were a lot of Jewish people here and the smell of spicy foods being sold in tiny alleys nearby drifted on the air. Some of the traders spread sheets on the ground and the things they offered were laid out to be picked over by anyone who passed by. People were pulling them about and trying on jackets or anything they fancied.

Mavis walked past this clothing, because a lot of it looked as if it were hardly fit to wear. Some of the shirts and underclothing being tossed about even had yellowed stains on them and Mavis wrinkled her nose at the sour smell that came from the bundles.

'Ugh,' she said as a man with green teeth and greasy hair thrust a pair of silk drawers under her nose. 'They stink. Please take them away.'

'Nuffin' a good wash wouldn't cure,' he chortled. 'Looking for yer winter furs are yer, me lady?'

'Ignore him, Mave,' Alice said as they sidestepped a pile of horse dung that was still steaming and smelled even worse than the stained silk drawers. 'You won't find anything much here. It's much better in Petticoat Lane.'

Mavis had stopped to look at one of the more expensive stalls. She was attracted to a pink tweed two-piece with a large fur collar and inquired about the price from the woman behind the stall.

'Luverly bit of cloth, that,' the woman said. 'I got it off a toff only recent. She said it didn't fit her 'cos she was expanding . . .' She cackled with mirth and held her hands suggestively over her stomach. 'Wiv her money she'll be after the latest fashion once she gets shot of the brat. I want two quid fer it if yer interested.'

'Don't buy it,' Alice whispered in her ear. 'You'll see better things in the lane.'

'I'll give you a pound,' Mavis offered, ignoring her sister's advice.

'Clear orf out of 'ere,' the woman said, her smiles disappearing. 'That's less than I give fer it.'

'Suit yourself,' Mavis said and grinned at her sister as they mingled with the ever-growing crowds swelling the lanes and through to Club Row – or, as the locals called it, the Dog Market. Cats and dogs were on sale here and the street attracted many children, who stood watching and admiring the fluffy creatures. Just ahead was the bird market, the noise of which could be heard above people calling out and the rumble of wheels.

From the flower market, they made their way through the commercial dinginess of Brick Lane, where it sometimes seemed that every other building was a sweat shop producing clothes made by downtrodden seamstresses. Here there were stalls selling fruit and vegetables, the gutters filling up with rotten waste as the day progressed, a stall selling bagels and the jellied eel stall: the sight of the eel flesh in jelly, which eager buyers would sprinkle with vinegar and pepper, turned Alice's stomach.

In Petticoat Lane there was barely room to move, and Alice reminded her sister to keep her hand tightly on her purse, because there was always a danger of a hand slipping into your pocket to relieve you of your hard-earned wages. The traders were vying with each other, offering what they promised were fantastic bargains. On the crockery stall the man had boxes of blue and white willow-pattern china resting in white straw.

He held up a pile of plates, saucers and cups for his audience to see and tossed them in the air, catching them expertly and with ease which brought a gasp of delight from the crowd.

'I ain't offerin' these fer twenty pound fer a whole dinner, tea, and coffee set, which them fancy shops up West would charge yer. You'd be lucky to get wares like mine for a score I'm tellin' yer. I ain't offerin' 'em fer eight pound or seven or even five . . .'

'I should think yer bleedin' givin' 'em away,' one man jeered.

'Too right, mate,' the trader came back at him. 'I'm givin' them to yer for four quid – the whole bleedin' lot of 'em. Now who wants me first set?'

'I'll give yer thirty bob,' the same heckler cried. 'I bet half of 'em are cracked or chipped.

'Honest Bob never cheats a customer,' the trader

quipped back. 'If me wares are rubbish I'll be 'ere next week and yer can bring 'em back. You're breakin' me 'eart, ladies and gents. I tell yer what – I'll give 'em to yer for three quid, now I can't say fairer than that . . .'

'I'll take one,' a woman near the front cried out. 'Me daughter's getting wed and she'll like bein' posh wiv a set like that – not the one you've been throwin' ahbat . . .'

'They look good,' Mavis said. 'I'm tempted to buy one, but if I do I can't afford to get a new costume for the weddin'.'

'If you took that home Ma would go on somethin' awful,' Alice said. 'She would probably pinch bits out of it for herself. Leave it for now, there's plenty of time to buy things for your home.'

'Plenty of time for me,' Mavis agreed and her gaze narrowed. 'But what of you, Alice? How much time before you have to get wed?'

'I don't know,' Alice admitted and her cheeks flushed. 'I'm late but that doesn't mean . . .'

'Alice, you fool,' her sister said, taking hold of her arm to steer her away from the stall where the buyers were now scrabbling to buy the trader's bargains. 'Let's go and find something to drink and sit down and talk.'

'What about your new costume? If you leave it all the bargains will be gone.'

'I might go back and get that costume with the fur collar. It was nice, Alice, but too expensive. If she comes down to thirty bob I'll buy it –

if not, I'll wait until next week and see what I can find.'

Alice nodded, feeling glad to get away from the crush around the china stall. Two women were fighting over the last set now, punching and kicking each other as they squabbled.

They found a stall in Cheshire Street selling brightly coloured glasses of fruit cordials, strawberry, orange, pineapple and all kinds of exotic mixtures, but the two sisters went for the hot blackcurrant, and then bought a bag of hot roasted chestnuts. They found a bench at the side of the pavement and sat down, watching the flow of life as it passed by: a mongrel dog hunting in the gutters for abandoned food; children playing with hoops and one small boy on roller skates wobbling all over as his sister followed him, crying and telling him it was her turn now. There were all kinds of people here: Jewish people; people with dark skins; others with Asian clothes and black eyes, and the good old Londoners in all shapes and sizes. A Pearly King was gathering a small crowd about him as he played a squeeze box and collected money for charity; some people had begun to hurry home clutching heavy bags of shopping.

Mavis looked at Alice. 'It was that Jack Shaw did you down, wasn't it?'

'Yes,' Alice admitted, glancing away from the accusation in her sister's eyes. 'I kept saying no, Mave, but he wore me resistance down. I fell for

459

him, like the fool I am, and in the end I couldn't resist him. He promised to marry me. We were goin' away . . .'

'You didn't tell me any of this?'

'Jack made me promise not to. The people he works for . . . he knows too much about them. They wouldn't let him walk away so he had to get his money together on the quiet – but somehow they found out and they tried to kill him. I was in the car when they did it . . .'

'Alice!' Mavis was shocked. 'You weren't hurt?'

'Jack told me to get down and he drove off like a madman. He dropped me outside St Saviour's and went speeding into the night. I haven't heard from him since.'

'And you won't,' Mavis said. 'His sort are all charm and no substance. They promise you everything and then let you down – leaving you in trouble.'

'You don't know that, Mave.'

'He hasn't let you know he's all right. Do you really think he is going to risk his neck by coming back for you?'

'He said he would tell me where to meet him. Jack loves me, he wouldn't let me down. If I hadn't told him I was havin' the kid he wouldn't have been in such a hurry to sell up. It was my fault they nearly got to him . . .'

'Don't blame yourself, love. Jack was a bad 'un. Dad warned you enough times. He'll go nuts when he finds out the truth.'

'Maybe he won't have to . . . if Jack sends word or . . .' Alice's mouth went dry. 'I don't know what to do, Mave. What can I do?'

'You could get rid of it,' her sister said. 'They say if you sit in a hot bath and drink gin . . .'

'Old wives' tales,' Alice said. 'I know one of the girls who used to work with me tried it but it didn't do the trick. She went to one of them places to get rid of it in the end . . .'

'You mean back-street abortionists?' Mavis looked at her in horror. 'They're butchers, Alice. You mustn't do that whatever happens. Promise me you won't. Me and Ted will help you. I'm not sure what we can do, but we'll help if Ma chucks you out.'

'Thanks.' Alice finished her hot blackcurrant drink. 'Come on, Mave. Let's go and see if that old witch will let you have the costume you want for thirty bob.'

CHAPTER 36

The next morning, Mark Adderbury delivered the tree to be dressed, though the presents would be hung just before Father Christmas arrived on Christmas Eve, to prevent prying fingers. It was a lovely big fir and caused a lot of excitement when it was carried in and set up in the hall, from the staff as much as the children, most of whom had never seen such a beautiful one.

Sally and some of the other girls had just finished decorating the tree when Andrew Markham walked in. They had been debating whether to put a star on top, as Father Joe thought proper, or a fairy as some of the girls wanted.

'Oh, a star is much nicer,' a voice said from behind her and Sally swung round, a feeling of delight sweeping through her as she saw who it was. 'I think we should all remember the story of Christ's birth, even though we like to have fun and indulge ourselves with presents, special food and lots of good things.'

'Yes, I think the star is best,' Sally agreed and handed it to him, standing back to watch as he went up the steps and placed it on the tallest point. 'Lovely. We are so lucky to have such a wonderful tree. Mr Adderbury bought it for us. We all contributed to the decorations and found bits and pieces we could bring – and there are going to be lots of sweets and small gifts for the children.'

'It's all very exciting. I understand the carol service and party here is to be held on Christmas Eve? And the big party at the church hall is on Tuesday 23rd?'

'I do hope you will pop in to see us on Christmas Eve?'

'Yes, I can promise that,' he said, and as their eyes met Sally's heart leaped in excitement, because the look in them seemed to promise so much. 'My last appointment is for the afternoon and then I have nothing until after the Christmas holidays.'

'Are you going anywhere exciting?'

'To my aunt's house, for dinner and tea on Christmas Day; it's very quiet but she looks forward to it. I dare say she will try to keep me there over Boxing Day but I have lots of people to visit, people I hardly ever manage to meet because they live in the country. I'll be away three days and then it is back to work for me.'

'You're very busy,' Sally said, a note of envy creeping into her voice as she added, 'It must be wonderful to have your skills. Not only the surgery and the medical stuff – but the books and puzzles too.'

'The books I do for pleasure and the hope they

may help a child. I'm fond of children, Sally. I should like at least three or four of my own . . .'

'Yes, I love them too and one day I want a family.' Her cheeks were warm as she met his teasing look.

'We must go out soon and talk about things,' Andrew said and Sally wondered what that look in his eyes meant. It was almost as if . . . but she mustn't read too much into it, because although he'd taken her out a few times that didn't mean he was thinking of marriage . . . and yet something told her that it was exactly what he was thinking of and her heart began to race wildly.

'Yes, I should like that,' she said softly, hoping that he would suggest a time soon when they could meet, but to her disappointment he just smiled.

'Well, I must not keep you from your duties,' he said. 'I have people to see and things to do – but if we do not meet again I shall see you on Christmas Eve.'

Sally nodded, feeling uncertain as she watched him leave the room. For a moment there she'd thought he really meant something important, that his talk of having children was a message just for her, and yet he hadn't arranged to see her again. Why? She gathered up the tissue and newspaper that had been used to wrap the glass balls and bits of tinsel for the tree. The box would go to the cellar out of the way until it was time to take the decorations down, but that wouldn't be for several days yet.

As she passed the schoolroom she heard the

sound of children's voices raised in song. Father Joe was getting his little choir in good shape and the carol service was something to be looked forward to, along with the present giving and the food. Christmas at St Saviour's was going to be rather special this year, and much of that was because of Angela's hard work.

Angela had been a little subdued when she looked in on them earlier and Sally wondered why. Angela had worked tirelessly to make things nice for them all. It was strange that she'd seemed almost uninterested when she saw they were decorating the tree; it just wasn't like her and Sally wished she'd dared to ask what was wrong.

Beatrice sat at her desk looking through the most recent list Angela had given her some days ago. Some of the ideas here were good despite her own reluctance to change things at St Saviour's. One she thought particularly interesting was about the team leaders Angela wanted to select. Each group of children would have a leader and that leader monitor behaviour and activities.

They would receive stars for good behaviour or for merit. Each month the teams with the most stars would receive certain privileges which could be used for some kind of activity chosen by the children themselves – a trip to the zoo or the pictures was suggested.

Sister Beatrice had rejected the suggestion at first glance because it might cause envy or bad feeling, but then she began to realise that Angela's idea was to give the children pride in themselves, to give them something to strive for and to teach them that hard work and responsibility to each other could earn its own rewards.

Remembering their quarrel, Beatrice frowned. Did she really want Angela to resign? Now that her anger had cooled, she had begun to realise that she might have made too much of the whole thing. It was that old sin of pride again.

Beatrice took the heavy silver cross she always wore in her hand and prayed for guidance. She could not put her sense of humiliation above what was right for the children . . .

The telephone rang and Beatrice reached for it, Michelle's anxious voice jerking her thoughts firmly back to the present.

'Sister, could you please come to the sick ward? Johnny seems very restless and I'm worried about him.'

Beatrice shelved her problems immediately. The children came before anything else and she'd been worried about Johnny when she'd looked in earlier that morning.

'I'm coming now,' she said. The problem of her relationship with Angela could wait.

Angela came back late from a shopping expedition to buy some gifts for the staff. She wanted to give them all a small gift, but one or two of them deserved something really nice. Sally and Michelle

466

in particular had become friends and she was going to miss them when she left. The shops were not yet stocked to pre-war levels, but she'd found some beautiful Swiss lace hankies for Michelle and a pretty silk scarf for Sally, as well as the nylons she'd managed to accumulate for each of the girls, and she was going to enjoy wrapping them in gold paper and ribbon.

She deposited the parcels in her office and then went along to the sick bay, intending to see who was on duty; if it was Michelle, she might ask if she'd like to go to a film together one night the following week.

As she entered the ward, she saw that the curtains had been drawn about Johnny's bed. Wondering whether she ought to leave, she was hesitating as Michelle came out of the curtains and walked up to her.

She put a finger to her lips. 'Johnny isn't very well. We want to keep him quiet today, because his head aches.'

'I'm so sorry,' Angela said in a soft voice. 'Is there anything I can do for him?'

'Sister Beatrice has been to see him. She sat with him for a while and it seemed to ease his spirit. She really is wonderful with the children. I don't know if it is because she is a nun, but when they are very ill she seems to know just what to say to them. I don't know what we would do without her.' Michelle hesitated, then, 'I prom- ised him we would take him to see the Christmas tree. He's too unwell to go in a wheelchair; do you think Mr Adderbury would come in and carry him down?'

'I'll telephone his office and ask,' Angela said but at that moment she saw Andrew Markham enter the room and her eyes met Michelle's. The girl nodded and they both looked at him expectantly as she explained what was needed.

'Yes, I think that would be the best way of taking him down,' Andrew said, looking grave. 'A wheelchair would shake him too much, and he doesn't weigh more than a feather. Sally has just finished dressing the tree. I'll take him now.'

Angela stood to one side as he went behind the curtains, followed by Michelle. She heard his gentle voice ask if the sick boy wanted to see the tree and his voice saying yes, please with more enthusiasm than she'd heard in days.

A moment or two later, Andrew emerged from behind the curtain carrying Johnny wrapped up in a blanket, Michelle following behind as they left and went straight to the lift.

Angela went down the stairs, and then stood in the hall watching as Andrew Markham carried the boy right up to the tree so that he could reach out and touch the glass balls and smell the fresh, sharp scent of the pine. She saw Johnny's face light up with pleasure and her heart caught, tears stinging her eyes as she realised how much the brief visit meant to the fragile child.

After a few minutes, Andrew took the boy back

to the lift, once again accompanied by Michelle. Angela knew that she was crying, because despite all the care and love the child had been given they all feared that this was Johnny's last Christmas. Sister hadn't given up hope but the doctors had told her that he was failing and all the staff knew that his heart was too weak to go on for much longer.

Her own heart aching for Johnny and all the sick children that Christmas, Angela wished that she hadn't fallen out with Sister Beatrice. It was a pity to be at odds with her – and perhaps she was at fault in this instance. She would have to apologise, because it felt wrong to have an atmosphere between them at Christmas, when everyone should be happy and preparing for such a special time. There was enough sadness without her adding to it unnecessarily.

'Sally, I wanted to speak to you . . .'

About to leave for the night, Sally was surprised to see Keith waiting for her outside. She hesitated, because she was tired and would rather just have caught her bus, but he'd been a good friend to her and she didn't think she could ignore him.

'I want to get straight home,' she said. 'But you can walk to the bus stop with me if you like.'

'All right.' He looked at her unhappily as he turned to walk beside her. 'I've been miserable since we stopped seeing each other, Sally. I'd like to be friends again – more than friends . . .'

He caught hold of her arm, swinging her to meet him. 'Please, Sally. You know I love you . . .'

'No, Keith,' Sally said, more sharply than she intended as she pulled away from him. 'I don't love you. I like you as a friend but . . . I can't go out with you again.'

'It's that bloody Markham, isn't it?' Keith flashed at her, his face white with temper. 'I never took you for a fool, Sally Rush. He's just leading you on. A man like that doesn't marry girls like you. He'll get you into bed and then when he's had enough . . .'

Sally's temper surfaced. 'Girls like me? So that's what you think of me, is it? You talk of love and then speak as if I'm some cheap little tart who would fall into bed with someone just because he has money and . . .' She gasped as he grabbed her, pulling her hard against him and she felt the burn of his kiss, his lips grinding against hers. The kiss was more a punishment than a caress and she tasted blood on her lips. Giving a cry of rage, she struck out and hit him with the palm of her hand.

Keith held her fast by the arm, his eyes narrowed with fury. He lifted his right hand as if to strike her, but before he could do so his arm was grabbed from behind and he was prevented from moving by the iron force that held his arms pressed against his sides.

'If you ever try that again I'll make you sorry you ever lived.' Andrew's voice was throbbing with anger. 'I'm telling you and I shall not warn you again. Next time, I'll carry out my promise.' Keith wrenched away, turning on him in hatred. Sally flinched, expecting him to try and hit the doctor, but something in Andrew's face must have stopped him, because he took a step away.

'You can have the cold bitch,' he muttered resentfully. 'She's a bloody fool if she doesn't know what you're after – but why should I care. She deserves what's coming to her.'

He spat in their direction, then turned and strode off, clearly simmering with anger.

'Are you all right?' Andrew looked at Sally in silence for a moment, then reached out to take her into his arms. He held her as she stood there trembling, upset by Keith's spite as much as the threat of violence. 'I'm sorry you had to suffer that, darling Sally.'

'I'm sorry,' she said. 'That was horrible . . .'

'He deserves a good hiding but this wasn't the place to do it,' Andrew said. 'If you know where he lives I'll go round and make sure he never tries anything like that again.'

'Please, don't do anything silly,' she said, pulling herself together. 'I'm all right, Andrew. Keith wouldn't hurt me, not really. He's just angry because I . . . I don't love him and I don't want to go out with him . . .'

'He means nothing to you?' Andrew looked down at her, his eyes questioning. 'Is there someone else you do quite like, Sally?'

'You know I do,' she whispered, her cheeks warm. 'You must know how I feel . . .'

'Darling Sally.' Andrew smiled. 'I should've spoken more openly before, but I've been holding back, thinking I'm too old for you . . .'

'No, I like it . . . I like that you're older and a respected surgeon, because it makes me feel proud to know you and know you like me too . . .' Sally blushed and couldn't look at him. 'Oh, I shouldn't . . .'

'Yes, you should,' he said and touched her cheek. 'I wish I could just sweep you up and take you off somewhere so that we can talk, my dearest girl – but I have meetings this evening and I can't miss them . . . but soon. He touched her mouth with his forefinger. 'Let me put you in a taxi home, Sally . . .'

'No, it's all right. Keith won't come back. I'm not frightened of him, Andrew. You mustn't worry. Just get off to those meetings.'

'Christmas Eve,' he promised, smiled and then hailed a taxi for himself, leaving Sally looking after him. His special smile was just for her. He did care for her a lot, just as she'd hoped.

Angela was about to leave her office to change for the evening when the telephone rang. She picked it up and heard Mark's voice.

'Thank goodness I caught you before you left,' he said in an apologetic tone. 'I'm sorry but I shan't be able to make it this evening. I have an urgent case and this is the only time I can see my patient.'

'Oh, I'm sorry,' she said, feeling disappointed. 'Of course work comes first and I shall see you another time.'

'As soon as I get a free moment I'll ring and we'll go somewhere. I hate to do this at such a late date but there's nothing else I can do.'

'Please don't apologise,' Angela said. 'I understand Mark – and I'll be seeing you at Christmas.'

'I'll be in touch soon,' he promised and the phone went down.

Angela took off her coat. The thought of a lonely evening in her room did not appeal; she would be better off staying here and making herself useful. If Nan was still around she would ask what she could do to help.

Angela had been too busy to bother much about her flat, but it was time she started to look round, because if she had somewhere of her own she could cook a meal for herself in the evenings. She made up her mind to start looking in the London evening papers and perhaps she could move in after Christmas . . .

CHAPTER 37

Alice had been on the early evening shift and the streets were cold and dark, a slight frosting on the pavement as she stepped outside. She shivered and drew her coat tighter about her. It was too cold to walk all the way home but she thought the last bus might have gone, because it was Wednesday, and they didn't run mid-week. Sighing, she set off at a good pace and wanting to get back to the bed she shared with Mavis; at least under the cosiness of the eiderdown she would eventually get warm.

Alice jumped as the shadow moved out of the darkness, blocking her way. She looked up, half-hoping that it would be Jack, but found herself staring into the face of a man she didn't know. He had a scar over his left eye and his eyes were dark, menacing. She shivered but not from the cold this time.

'Someone wants ter speak ter yer, Alice Cobb. He wants ter ask yer a question about a mutual friend.'

The man reached out and took hold of Alice's arm. She gave a little cry of fright and shrank away. 'I don't know you or your friend. Leave me alone.'

'You know our friend though, Alice. Mr Lee wants you to tell him where we can find Jack. Now that's not too much to ask, is it?'

'Who are you? I don't know what you're talking about,' Alice said and struggled, but the man had hold of her arm and was dragging her towards a large car parked at the side of the road. 'Let me go or I'll scream.'

'I think you know me all right,' he leered at her, his face so close now that she could smell the strong drink on his breath. 'Jack told you about his friend Harry, didn't he? I'm just payin' a friendly call, no 'arm in that, is there?'

'Let me go!' Alice screamed and kicked out at him, and as she did so, a man on the other side of the road came sprinting across. He grabbed hold of her attacker's arm and gave him a hard shove. 'Bob . . .'

'Get away from her, Harry,' Bob snarled, not looking at Alice. 'I know who you and your boss are – and I'm not frightened of you. Alice is my girl so just leave her be.'

'Your girl?' the man sneered. 'I was told somethin' different . . .'

'Well, you were told wrong. I'm warning you, leave Alice alone – or you might get a visit from the military cops. I've seen your face before, Harry Miller, and I know you were a deserter from the Army in the war. You're wanted on a hanging charge. I only have to drop a word in a certain person's ear and you're done for.'

A flicker of fear showed in the bully's face, but then he glared at Bob. 'Keep yer mouth shut or you'll get a knife in the ribs,' Harry snarled but a voice from the car called to him and he backed away, getting into the vehicle seconds before it drove off at speed.

'Bob . . .' Alice gasped as she looked at him. 'Thank you . . . but he'll come after you now.'

'I'll be waiting for him,' Bob said. 'But I reckon he'll give me a wide berth from now on. I know too much about him.'

'Is it true that he was a deserter?'

'Yes. I know him from the boxing club Eric and me go to sometimes, but I knew of him before that. He's a murderer. He killed a military cop. They never forget, Alice. They're still looking for him – and I wouldn't want to be in his shoes if they get him, and I'll be putting in a report that I've seen him in London. He'll be glad of the hangman's noose when our lot have finished with him.'

Bob was walking by her side. Alice was glad of his company, because the man with the scar had frightened her. 'How come you happened to be around when I needed you? Eric didn't tell me you were on leave.'

'I just got back. I'm based in London now for a while . . .' Bob looked a bit bashful as he said, 'I've been made a military cop, Alice. It's a career change and means promotion for me. I'm on special detachment at the moment, looking after someone important. I've been training in all the special skills, boxing, martial arts, firearms, so I can qualify as a military bodyguard, and a lot more – and I was on my way to the boxing club when I saw you leave St Saviour's. I followed you, because I wanted to talk to you, but I wasn't sure you'd want to talk to me . . .'

'Oh, that sounds an important job.' Alice wasn't sure what to say next. 'It was good of you to rescue me, Bob. You don't have to walk all the way home with me. He won't come back tonight.'

'Eric will talk to a few friends of his and they'll think twice about coming after you again, Alice – unless they want a turf war.'

'What do you mean?'

'Don't ask, but Butcher Lee and his bullyboys aren't the only ones with influence round here. Your cousin knows most of what goes on, even though he's away a lot. And I've got some good pals at the boxing club, most of them special services Army like me. Big Harry throws his weight around, but he's like all bullies, stand up to him and he's not so clever. If he's got any sense he'll clear off before the Army gets wind of what he's up to.'

'Eric has influence? Did he tell you Jack has gone? Butcher sent Big Harry after him. Jack thought they meant to kill him so he went off and I've heard nothing since. There are rumours that he died in the fire but I'm not sure . . .

'Yes, Eric told me what had been going on,' Bob said grimly. 'I'm not asking you for anything, Alice, but I shall be around for a while – and if you need help, come to me. Eric will always know where to find me.'

They had reached the end of her street. Bob stopped walking and smiled at her. 'I think a lot of you, Alice. I'm just saying if you're in any bother tell Eric to let me know.' He reached out and touched her cold cheek. 'Go on and get in the warm. I'll watch until you're inside.'

'Thanks, Bob.' Impulsively, she reached up and kissed his cheek and then turned and ran, not stopping until she was in the house.

Alice's mother was in the kitchen and she could hear her angry voice as yet another row between her parents erupted. Alice's father sat in his shirt sleeves at the scrubbed pine table, a glass of beer in front of him, while her mother had grabbed a heavy-bottomed saucepan and was brandishing it at him. On the table were spread a few shillings and it was obvious that the row was about money, or the lack of it.

'How am I supposed to pay the rent and pay for our food with that?' Mrs Cobb demanded bitterly. 'I had two pounds in that jar and now there's bloody sixteen shillings and sixpence. You took it for drink, don't deny it, you great fool of a man. Why I ever married you I don't know.'

On the stove a pot was boiling over and the smell of burning potatoes was heavy on the air. Alice moved the pot from the heat, avoiding her mother as she stomped about the kitchen.

'I drink because that's the only pleasure I get in life,' her father said, rising to his feet in anger. He snatched the saucepan from his wife and threw it across the room. 'That's the last time you threaten me, bitch. I wish I'd never seen you, let alone wed you. If you're not satisfied, get off your lazy arse and find a job. A man needs a drink when all he gets is the dirty jobs and all he has to come home to is a scold like you.'

With that he flung out of the room, slamming the door behind him. Alice's mother gave a scream of frustration and started banging pots on the old-fashioned stove.

'There's no tea for you at this time of night, nor anyone else if that pig doesn't start givin' me more money,' she muttered. 'I'll swing fer that man one of these days . . .'

'I've eaten,' Alice said and escaped before she was on the receiving end of more of her mother's vitriol. Going into the room she shared with her siblings, Alice stripped down to her petticoat and climbed into bed beside her sister, huddling up to her warm body.

'What started it this time?'

'It's our Saul again. He pinched some fags from the tobacconists in the High Street and was smoking them with Bertie in the back yard. Ma caught them at it and gave him a good hidin' but Dad came home in the middle of it and told her to leave the boy alone. She turned on him again then and they haven't stopped since.'

'Poor old Dad,' Alice said. 'He'll never do right for her, Mave.' She couldn't help but feel sorry for her father, even though he undoubtedly deserved some of what he got. Instead of clearing off down the pub, he should have stood up to his wife and perhaps then she would respect him more. 'I know he drinks but she would drive anyone potty.'

'He should clear off and leave her,' her sister said sleepily. 'Talk about it in the morning. I'm bushed . . .'

Alice nodded in the darkness. She was safe here in bed with her family around her, but she'd been very frightened when that man tried to snatch her off the street. Somehow they must have found out she'd been seeing Jack before he went off in a hurry. She couldn't have told them anything even if Bob hadn't turned up, but they might not have believed her and she would have been given a beating.

Bob had promised she would be safe, but she wasn't sure he was right. Yet there was nothing she could do, because she had to go on working at night and she had to walk home alone.

Sighing, she closed her eyes. Another busy day was waiting for her tomorrow and there was little she could do to protect herself from bullies like that so she might as well forget it about it as best she could . . . because a black eye from Big Harry was no worse than her father would do once he found out she was having Jack's baby, and her mother would kill her. Yet what choice did she have? She wasn't going to kill her baby at a back-street abortionist, and she didn't think any of the old-fashioned remedies really worked. Besides, if Jack was dead, then the child was all she would ever have of him. Her heart seemed to contract with pain, because she couldn't bear that thought. She didn't want to believe he was dead . . .

Alice suddenly tingled all over, because she'd just realised that Butcher Lee didn't believe Jack had been killed in that fire. He must be pretty certain Jack had got out alive or why was he bothering with her? If he thought Jack dead, he wouldn't have sent Big Harry after her. So who had been burned that night? And why hadn't he got out – unless he was dead before the fire?

Whispers must have circulated through the criminal fraternity. Perhaps someone had seen Jack after the fire or someone knew that he wasn't the body the police had found. The underworld would know details that neither the papers nor the police knew . . . and that meant the dead body could have belonged to anyone.

It wasn't the caretaker because he'd been outside the factory when he was knocked over the head – so if it wasn't Jack, someone else had been inside when they broke in. One of the other workers or . . . but no one else had been reported missing . . . unless it was a tramp! Alice felt a shock run through her as she realised that she might just have stumbled on the truth. London had hundreds of homeless men who would not be missed. A shudder ran through Alice, because if the man had been dead before the fire then someone had killed him . . . but that was too horrible to think about.

Sally had just finished putting up the last of the greenery in the large dining room. It was Friday morning and the preparations were nearly finished. She'd wanted it to look special for the Christmas period and it did. She'd hung a bunch of mistletoe over the doorway for fun, though she had no idea why. They didn't get many male visitors at St Saviour's, except for Andrew Markham and Mr Adderbury, and of course the caretaker who also did a little gardening, and an occasional visiting doctor.

She was just looking up at her handiwork when she heard a noise behind her and turned to see Andrew smiling at her.

'Just caught you,' he said and suddenly took hold of her by the waist, pulled her in close, and kissed her under the mistletoe. Sally was surprised but went into his arms willingly, and a lovely warm feeling curled through her. 'I couldn't resist. You looked so charming . . .'

Sally's heart was thudding and she felt short of breath, her body tingling with the desire Andrew's kiss had aroused, but she managed to say, 'It's what mistletoe is for, isn't it?' Yet the look in his eyes made her want to melt into his arms, because there was such need and longing that it shocked her; she hadn't known he felt like that about her.

'I've been longing to see you, thinking of you all the time, Sally,' he said and his expression made her heart catch and then jump about like giddy lambs in spring. 'I shall see you at the party, of course – but I wanted to make a firm date for dinner, as soon as I return to London after Christmas?'

'Yes, I should like that very much, Andrew,' Sally said. 'I shall look forward to it . . .'

'Good, because I can't wait. I wish it could be before – but my aunt would be disappointed if I didn't go and she was good to me when my mother died. I would rather be with you, Sally, but we'll make up for it next year, I promise.'

'Of course you mustn't disappoint your aunt,' Sally replied and smiled up at him. 'My parents expect me to be with them too – but perhaps things will be different another year.'

'If I have my way they certainly will,' he said. 'I shall have to go, but I couldn't resist popping in on my way to the hospital . . .'

'I ought to get off too. Mum will be wondering where I've got to. I stopped late to finish the decorations in here, because this is where the party food will be set. I've made some pretty paper tablemats and there are homemade crackers for the children to pull on Christmas Eve. All the carers got together to buy some small trinkets to fill them. It's going to be so exciting for the kids. The tables will look so special on the day, and for Christmas Eve – though the carols will be in the hall where the tree is . . .' She stopped, realising that she was babbling, because she was just so happy.

'And up in the wards I think?' His smile was a caress. Sally's heart seemed to turn over and she was aware of a new sensation low in her abdomen . . . a feeling of aching need, a burning desire that she'd never experienced before. For a moment all she could think about was his arms about her and lying in sheets that smelled of lavender . . . Sally recalled her thoughts quickly as she became aware of his quizzical smile as he waited for her answer.

'Yes, the singers will go there first,' she said, a flush in her cheeks. 'Father Christmas is going to pop in there to say hello. Have you been visiting the children in the sick wards?'

'I called in to see them yesterday and thought I would come back this evening. I wanted to see little Johnny as well. He doesn't seem to get any better whatever we do. I'm not sure he will see Christmas.'

'I know. It's so sad – we all love him.' Sally smiled at him tenderly. 'Michelle told me how much it meant to him that you carried him down to see the tree.'

'It was all I could do, but I was glad I could at least make him smile.'

'It's so sad, because he was always such a happy little boy despite his illness . . .'

'Yes, very sad, because he is a loveable child. He managed a smile for me, but he is very poorly. Sister is praying for him and perhaps her prayers will be answered, who knows.' He looked anxious, upset, but then the smile returned to his eyes. 'Well, we must do what we can for all of them – and if Sister's prayers prevail he may rally. I must go, I'm sorry.'

'I must go too. My mother will be expecting me . . .'

They parted and Sally hurried to get her coat, because she would be late for her evening meal and her mother worried unless she knew why. She was thoughtful as she ran to catch her bus. It seemed as if Andrew really cared for her, wanted them to be together, but that didn't mean it would happen. The gap between them was so wide. Andrew didn't realise how bad things were at home now that her father wasn't in regular work. He tried, taking any dirty job that was offered, but they could hardly pay the rent and put food on the table some days.

Her parents would never understand; they would think she was getting too big for her boots, trying to be something she never could . . . betraying her class. Yet Sally knew it would break her heart to walk away from what Andrew was offering.

CHAPTER 38

Michelle looked down at Johnny's face. He was flushed and she had noticed a change in him the moment she came on duty that Monday morning. He had been fretful all day and now he was sweating. She was worried and she knew it was time to ask for Sister's opinion again.

Reaching for the in-house phone, she dialled a number and sighed with relief when it was answered, 'Sister, could you come please? I think Johnny seems worse. He's fretful and he has a temperature.'

'I shall come immediately.'

'Thank you. I wouldn't ask but I'm worried.'

Michelle replaced the receiver and went back to Johnny's bed. She wrung a cloth in cool water and bathed his forehead, because he was complaining of being hot and kept throwing back his blankets. It was not like Johnny to complain, which meant that he had to be feeling very unwell.

The door opening made her turn as Sister entered and came to look down at their patient. She took Johnny's limp hand and checked his pulse, shaking her head as she glanced at the little watch pinned high on her chest.

'He isn't at all well. Keep him as cool as possible. I'll make a soothing drink that may help him sleep for a while, but otherwise there isn't much . . .' Sister's eyes met Michelle's. 'We're doing all we can, Nurse. Just trust in your instincts. Who is on duty this evening?'

'Nurse Anna . . .' Michelle hesitated, then, 'I could stay if you thought . . .'

'Anna is a competent nurse,' Sister said and frowned. 'You cannot get too involved, Staff Nurse Michelle. Do what you can for him, but you must take your time off. Otherwise you will become too tired and then you may make a mistake.'

Michelle nodded as Sister went off to arrange the drink, and continued bathing the child's forehead. Sister returned just as Michelle had finished. Johnny cried when she took his temperature and blood pressure, but then he calmed down after he'd managed the drink Sister prepared for him.

'You may call me if you need me again,' Sister said and went out.

Michelle glanced down at the little boy, who had closed his eyes now. He would sleep for a while, and Sister was right; she must not become too attached to sick patients. Yet Johnny was special and Michelle knew that everyone at St Saviour's would be thinking about him, because they would all know that he was terribly ill. No one ever told the children these things, but they always knew somehow.

Billy had been pronounced better and allowed back to his dorm. He was waiting for Mary Ellen when she came in for breakfast, with Sally and Marion just behind, and waved to her to join him.

'I'm glad you're better,' Mary Ellen said, and brought her loaded plate to the table. 'Have you heard about Johnny? He's poorly, so Sally says, and they've sent for the doctor.'

'That's rotten luck just at Christmas,' Billy said. 'They wouldn't let me visit him in case my cold was still catchin' but you could perhaps get in to see how he is after tea.'

'I've got something to do for Sally this evening. She's . . . well, I can't tell you 'cos it is a surprise, but I'll pop in before I go to the dorms. Here's Marion. She says they've got the curtains round Johnny's bed and they've moved her into my dorm.'

Marion came to join them. She couldn't carry her plate and use her crutches so Sally carried it for her. All the children looked at their favourite carer anxiously as they begged for news of Johnny.

'He is very poorly today,' Sally said sadly. 'You all know that Johnny's illness has left him with a weak heart?' They nodded in unison and she smiled. 'Everyone is doing what they can for him and there is always hope. You must all pray for Johnny to get better.'

They solemnly promised they would and Sally went away, leaving the three together. Her words had made them subdued, because they were all looking forward to Christmas and it seemed entirely wrong for Johnny to be ill at such a time.

Mary Ellen wiped a tear from her cheek, and Billy's hand reached for her other hand beneath the table, giving it a squeeze. None of them was a stranger to death or tragedy, all having experienced it at least once in their young lives, but that didn't make it any easier to accept – and they all liked Johnny.

Billy cleared his throat and sniffed hard, because boys didn't cry. 'I suppose the old dragon will 'ave it in fer me 'cos o' what I did,' he said, trying to change the subject.

Marion giggled uncomfortably. 'You ought not to say things like that about Sister Beatrice,' she said. 'She ain't that bad, honest.'

'I don't mind if she canes me,' Billy said. 'I just 'ope she won't send me packing. I like it 'ere.'

'I'm sure she won't,' Marion said but Mary Ellen wasn't so confident.

'I expect it depends on what the police have to say. Give them details so that when they catch Arthur he goes down the line for a long time. You can say you saw someone throw them petrol bombs but you needn't tell them what else you know about Arthur pinchin' Butcher's stuff unless you like.'

'I ain't a snitch . . .'

'Of course you're not – but he's bad, your Arthur is. Look what he threatened to do to us. And it was wrong to set the factory on fire like that . . . even if Arthur did pinch their stuff; those people should be in trouble too.'

Billy studied her thoughtfully. 'You think I should tell them everythin'?' If he did that he would have to say about the man at the bottom of the stairs – the man who was dead before the fire . . . the man that either Arthur or Jack Shaw had killed . . .

'Yes – and Marion does too, don't you?'

'Yes, I do, Billy. If you do as they want, Sister will be pleased and then she'll let you stay here with us.'

'A'right, I will then,' he said, realising that the police ought to know. People thought Jack was dead, but if Billy told what he knew they would cotton on as he had and guess that Jack Shaw had escaped somehow, perhaps an upstairs window at the back or maybe a fire escape. Billy didn't know if there was one, but he did know that dead man wasn't Jack Shaw. If Arthur had killed that man he should be punished for it, and if it was Jack, why should he just get off scot-free? 'Long as you both think I should.'

That agreed, the atmosphere lightened a little but there was still a feeling of things not being right, a shadow at the back of all their minds, and when they parted after tea to go their various ways, Mary Ellen's thoughts were of little Johnny in the sick ward. It wasn't fair that he would miss all the fun and excitement of Christmas and it made her eyes sting with tears.

She'd made a card for him and decided that she would sneak into the ward and give it to him before she went to bed, even if she got into trouble for it . . .

It was eight o'clock when Mary Ellen reached the door of the sick ward. It was slightly open so she was able to go in without making a sound, her heart beating as she walked softly towards Johnny's bed, which had curtains pulled round it. Mary Ellen couldn't see a nurse, though she could hear the murmur of voices from the rest room next door, which was between the two wards. There was a smell of disinfectant and carbolic that made her wrinkle her nose.

Tip-toeing, she pulled the curtain back just enough to squeeze through and went to the bed, her hand reaching for Johnny's, which lay on the sheet. She touched it and discovered it was ice cold and then she looked at his face. His eyes were closed and his skin was as white as the sheets. His eyelids didn't stir as she touched his cold cheek and then she knew that he was dead. She was too late to say goodbye to him and that made the tears start to trickle down her own cheeks.

Poor, poor Johnny, she thought. Mary Ellen bent over him and kissed his face, and then she stroked his head and laid her cheek next to his.

'I'm so sorry,' she whispered. 'I wish I had come earlier. I wish I could make you better . . .'

Hearing a rustling sound behind her, Mary Ellen glanced round and saw Sister Beatrice looking at her oddly. She drew away from the bed, her heart racing. She was in for it now, because she was not supposed to be in here without permission from a nurse.

Sister came to the bed, looked down at Johnny and nodded gravely. She placed a hand on his brow and said something that sounded like a prayer to Mary Ellen. Then she looked at her and seemed to hesitate for a moment.

'Nurse Anna and Nan were with him when he died,' she said. 'Nan is making some arrangements, but she will return in a moment to sit with him for a while, and Anna came to fetch me. You mustn't think that he died alone, Mary Ellen. I'd seen him just a few minutes before, and he was very peaceful at the end.'

'I'm glad but I wanted . . .' She stopped tearfully.

'Did you come to say goodbye to your friend?'

'Yes, Sister.' Mary Ellen's voice was breathy and scared. 'I wasn't doing any harm. I'd got a Christmas card for him and I just wanted him to know he wasn't forgotten, up here all on his own, but he's . . . why did he have to die, Sister?

It isn't fair. Johnny never hurt anyone; he never did a bad thing in his life.' A sob burst from her and she swiped her face with the back of her hand, trying to wipe away the tears. 'I know I shouldn't be here . . .'

'Do you know why we ask the children not to come here at times like these?'

Mary Ellen shook her head, surprised by the gentle tone of Sister's voice. 'No, Sister. I suppose it's the rules . . .'

'It's because it's hard to witness death, child,' Sister said softly. 'We try to spare you pain if we can. Johnny has gone from us. There was nothing anyone could do, because God decided to take him. His heart was weak, because of the illness he'd had, and it was only a matter of time. We knew this would happen one day. We just hoped it would not be yet. It is a shame for the rest of you that it should happen now, before Christmas, because his death must cast a shadow – but you must try to remember Johnny as he was. He would want you to be happy.'

'It isn't fair,' Mary Ellen said, her bottom lip trembling. 'He was only seven . . . he never had a chance to grow up. There's lots of bad folk in the world. Why doesn't God take them instead of lovely people? Johnny was good . . .'

'Perhaps that is why God wanted him. I like to think that God cares for all our departed children. We can never know the answers to these questions, Mary Ellen. Life is often unfair, as you will already

493

know, and I'm afraid there's little we can do about it – though if we do good things wherever we can perhaps we might make a little difference. Johnny was happy here at St Saviour's, I think.'

'Yes, he was always smiling . . . until the last few days.'

'I expect he felt unwell. Perhaps it is selfish of us to want him to go on living because he did suffer a lot, you know. He wanted to be up and about, running and playing games with the rest of you, but he couldn't, and I expect that made him sad. Johnny didn't make a fuss but I think he was sad sometimes when he couldn't do what the rest of you take for granted. He is at peace now, child, and we must just remember him with love. When you're older you will come to accept that there is sadness in life but also much to be happy about.'

'Like all the fun of Christmas?'

'Yes. You must all enjoy it, because so many people are trying to make it good for you – and Johnny will be looking down and watching you.'

'Is he with the angels? My father always told me that when children die they go to live with the angels in heaven.'

'Then your father was right,' Sister said and took her by the hand. 'No more tears now, Mary Ellen. Remember to pray for Johnny and think of him with the angels. You ought to be in your dorm now, child. Otherwise your carer will be frantic looking for you.'

Mary Ellen shuffled her feet. 'You're not angry with me for coming?'

'I'm not an ogre, child. I know I punished you for lying, and it was wrong of you to lie, do you not agree?'

'Yes, Sister, it was wrong. I did it for Billy, but I won't do it again. I promise.'

'Good. I hope in future you will tell me if you are anxious for your friend, because if I know what is wrong I may be able to help. That is what I'm here for; you must understand that, because it is the only way I can help you.'

'You won't send him away?'

'I shall not do so, but I am not sure the magistrates will take the same view. He did help his brother break into people's houses. I think we all understand why – but it was still wrong, and his fate no longer lies in my hands, I fear. I shall, however, do what I can to keep him here. Now go to your dorm, child. It's the Church party tomorrow and you don't want to be tired for that . . .'

'Yes, Sister.'

Mary Ellen left her sitting on Johnny's bed. She felt heart-sore and distressed by her friend's death, and also by what Sister had told her. The police might say Billy was a bad boy and then the magistrates would send him to a house of correction and she might never see him again . . . but Sister had promised to do what she could. Mary Ellen did not know why, but somehow she trusted Sister Beatrice far more than she had in the past.

Something had changed tonight, and she knew that she was very lucky to be here at St Saviour's. She just hoped that Billy would be able to stay here too.

CHAPTER 39

Sister had gathered everyone together in the dining room the next morning. Looking very solemn, she told them that Johnny had passed away peacefully in his sleep and was now in the arms of the angels.

'Johnny loved being here with all the friends he made at St Saviour's,' she said. 'I know that he would not want you to be too sad, because it is nearly Christmas and that is why the Church party this afternoon, and the carol service tomorrow will go ahead. Father Christmas will come on Christmas Eve as promised, and as we enjoy ourselves we shall remember the child we loved. We shall say a prayer for Johnny and he will be remembered in chapel next Sunday by all of you who attend. However, I should like you all to say the Lord's Prayer with me now.'

'Our Father who art in heaven . . . Hallowed be Thy Name . . .'

Sister Beatrice intoned the popular prayer and the children chanted it after her. Mary Ellen noticed that Sally and Michelle were crying, and so were Nan and Angela. She'd cried all her tears and could only hold Billy's hand tightly and pray that their friend was in heaven, where he deserved to be.

After Sister finished the prayer, she paused and then smiled. 'I am very glad to be able to tell you one piece of good news. Maisie Chapman's aunt has asked if she can go and stay with her after Christmas. I've been told that Maisie will be taken on holidays with her aunt and if she is happy there, eventually she will go to live with her.'

A few of the children cheered. It was always good when someone came for a child, though it didn't happen often enough. Some were silent, because they knew that no one was ever going to come for them.

Mary Ellen was thoughtful as she left the dining room, following the others towards the school-room. Her school had broken up for the Christmas holidays now and Sally had asked her to come and help with some of the little ones; they were making some paper packets, which would be filled with sugared almonds and placed with a cracker by every child's plate on Christmas Day.

Mary Ellen didn't often think of Rose, because she knew her sister was at her hospital and doing well, but now she couldn't help thinking about her, wondering when she would visit – and what news she would bring of their mother. Mary Ellen had written letters to her mother several times and Sally had posted them for her but Ma had only replied once, right at the start. Her sister sent brief postcards now and then but seldom mentioned her mother, just what she was doing herself. Rose's last postcard two weeks previously had said she was going down to visit Ma and would come and see her afterwards, but so far she hadn't.

'What are you doing today?' asked Billy, as he walked along beside her.

'Helping Sally to look after the little ones. We're making Christmas cards. Why don't you come too?'

'Billy . . .' Angela's voice stopped them in their tracks. 'Billy, Sister would like to see you in her office now, please.'

The colour left Billy's face for a moment, but in an instant a look of defiance replaced the fear and he stuck his chin up. 'I'd better do as the old dragon asks,' he said in a low voice and Mary Ellen giggled.

'Good luck. She won't send you away, but the police might if you don't tell them all you know. Be brave and honest, Billy, and I'm sure it will turn out right.'

'Come along, Billy,' Angela said and smiled. 'I'll come with you.'

'All right, miss.'

He turned and followed her, leaving Mary Ellen to stare after him. Tears pricked her eyes but she didn't cry. She would hate it here if they sent Billy away, but there was nothing else she could do.

She just wished that Rose would come and visit

her. If her ma got better she could go home and perhaps Ma would let Billy come too . . .

Angela knew that Billy was scared, even though he was putting a brave face on it, but she couldn't say anything to comfort him because he would hate to be patronised or pitied. She could only hope that Sister Beatrice would be fair and not punish him too harshly.

When they entered Sister's office, she saw the tall, burly policeman standing by the window and felt Billy stiffen at her side. Not knowing what else she could do, Angela put her hand briefly on his shoulder, giving it a little squeeze in the hope that it would comfort him.

'Ah, Billy,' Sister said in what was for her a surprisingly gentle voice. 'I'm glad you've come to see us – and I hope you are ready to answer the constable's questions? I know this will be hard for you, because Arthur is all the family you have – but I think you know right from wrong, don't you?'

'Yes, Sister. It ain't easy but I've made up me mind to do it.'

'I have every confidence in you, Billy – and you know you can trust us. You are safe here at St Saviour's.'

Billy cleared his throat, stood up straight and looked her in the eyes. 'I done wrong to go off, Sister,' he said. 'Me bruvver told me if I didn't do what he said he would give me a good hidin' – but more than that, he threatened to burn you all in your beds. I went 'cos he's mean enough to do it.'

'Is that the truth, lad?' Constable Sallis stepped forward. 'Don't be afraid. We've no quarrel with you. We're searching for him and when we find him, we're going to put him away for a long time.'

'If he gets out he'll kill me – like he did me pa.' He drew a sobbing breath and looked about him wildly. 'I know he's a wrong 'un; he's always been bad and I'm scared of him but that ain't it . . .'

'We understand, Billy,' Sister said. 'You don't want to betray your brother, but it's what you must do to protect others – isn't it?'

Billy hesitated, then nodded. 'Yes, Sister.'

'If you tell us what you know, we can put him away for a long time, perhaps for good if he's a murderer.' The constable frowned. 'What makes you say he killed your pa?'

'Pa said he were goin' ter shop Arfur to the coppers and he said he would do fer him. The next night he were stabbed to death on the Docks. I know it was Arfur, but I ain't got no proof.'

'He hasn't said anything to you to confirm that?'

'He said if I didn't behave I might end up like me pa – but he never said for definite that he done it, though I know it was him.'

'We need something more positive than that, I'm afraid, though we'll look into it. We've suspected him of being a nasty sort for a while. Is there anything more you can tell us, lad?'

'I know every house he robbed and every item

they took and sold. I know who bought the goods and how much Arfur got for them . . . medals, gold coins, and silver watches. I've got a good memory and I remember all of it.'

'Can you write it all down for me?'

'It will take me a while, sir, but I can do it.'

'If you want to tell me, Billy, I will write it all down quicker than you can and then I'll type it up and deliver it to the police station,' Angela offered.

'Yes, miss.' Billy nodded vigorously, and then looked at the policeman. 'Will Arfur know it was me that told on him?'

'Not if we can help it, lad. Once we have the details we can bring pressure to bear – and we may be able to make one of the rogues confess. We shall make some more arrests, because fencing stolen goods is an offence too. So it is unlikely that anyone need ever know where the information came from. If your account of the stolen items matches those from the victims, we shall be sending your brother away for at least twenty years.'

'Good,' Billy said. He raised his head, his eyes bright with unshed tears. 'I ain't a snitch, but he threatened me friends and he deserves all he gets.'

'Yes, he does,' Constable Sallis agreed. He glanced at Angela. 'If you could get that list done as soon as possible, please?'

'Yes, of course. Come with me, Billy. We'll go in my office and do it now.'

'There's somethin' else.' Billy swallowed hard,

then, 'I saw someone throw them petrol bombs at the boot factory . . .'

Constable Sallis stared at him hard. 'Did you see who it was?'

Billy shook his head. 'He had his face and head covered and it was dark . . . but I know somethin' else, only I don't know if I should say . . .'

'Tell the constable everything, Billy,' Sister Beatrice said. 'He needs to know whatever it is.'

'It's like this.' Angela thought Billy looked even more scared. 'Arfur and Jack Shaw done a job on an office safe but the stuff they stole belonged to some dangerous men. They were going to clear off up North, but Jack said they needed the wages from the boot factory before they could go . . .'

'What are you saying, lad?'

'Jack said Butcher Lee would kill them if he found out it was him and Arfur who pinched his stuff. They was both terrified.'

Constable Sallis gave a start. 'Are you sure he said Butcher?'

'Yes, they was messin' their pants over it . . .'

'Billy! Language, please.'

'Sorry, Sister.'

'This makes it all the more important we catch your brother before they do,' Constable Sallis said. 'Don't worry, lad. What you've told us is hearsay and can't be used in evidence so you won't have to go to court – but your brother could help us put some murderers behind bars.' He nodded to

Sister Beatrice. 'I'm relying on you to keep the boy safe until we can sort this business out.'

'Of course, Constable. Is what he told you so important?'

'You have no idea how vital it could be,' the constable told her. He looked at Billy. 'You can go now, lad – and don't tell anyone else what you told me. I don't have to warn you how dangerous it could be.'

'No, sir.' Billy hesitated, then, 'There's more . . . when I went in to warn them about the fire I saw a dead man at the bottom of the stairs. Someone must have hit him on the head and he'd bled but he wasn't bleeding no more . . . and it weren't me brother or Jack . . .'

'Good grief! You are certain of this, Billy? It changes everything. We thought it was Jack Shaw, but they must have been disturbed and killed whoever it was . . . and that means Jack Shaw must have got away, because we only found the one body.' The constable looked at him. 'You don't know which one of them killed him?'

'No, sir. I just saw him lyin' there, dead . . .'

'You've done very well,' Sister said, her face white with shock. 'This has been very hard for you, Billy, but I think you can go now – and give the information concerning stolen goods to Angela.'

'Yes, go along, son. You've done us a good turn and we shan't forget it.'

'Come with me, Billy,' Angela said.

'Yes, miss.' He followed her to the door and then

looked back at Sister Beatrice. 'I'm sorry I caused you so much trouble, Sister.'

'I am willing to forgive and forget,' she said. 'Please come to me in future, Billy. You will find that I am usually willing to listen.'

'Are you going to let me stay here?'

'For the time being, yes. However, it will be up to the police and the magistrates, Billy. Because you ran away they may decide you should live elsewhere . . . that I am not capable of taking care of you properly. You see, your bad behaviour reflects on me.'

'It weren't your fault – and if you let me stay, I promise I won't do it again.'

'Well, we shall do what we can,' Sister Beatrice said, looking regretful. 'I will let you know as soon as we hear – but I can promise you that you will be here for Christmas, whatever else happens.'

'Thank you,' he said and followed Angela from the room.

'I'd better be on my way,' Constable Sallis said. 'I'll put in a good word for him, Sister Beatrice, but I can't promise. The report will go to the magistrates' office. They sent him here on probation because he has a reputation for playing truant and running away.' He shrugged his shoulders. 'You never know what they will say.'

'No, but I shall do my best to keep the child here. Once we have his brother inside, I think he will be no more trouble.'

CHAPTER 40

Angela had just finished typing up what Billy had remembered later that morning, when the door of her office opened and Sister Beatrice hovered on the threshold. She took the last page from the typewriter and placed it on top of the pile.

'Finished?'

'Yes. Billy has a remarkable memory. I should think he could do very well in class if he set his mind to it. In fact I've noticed a small improvement in his speech now and then – haven't you?'

'Yes, I believe he is a remarkable child in his way,' Sister said. 'I wanted to thank you for your help – really for everything you've done since you've been here.'

Angela was surprised, even shocked. 'It was my job – and my pleasure. I've enjoyed every moment of my time here. I shall be sorry to leave.'

Sister nodded, hesitated and then turned and left. She'd looked as if she wanted to say more but couldn't bring herself to do so. Perhaps she believed that it was Angela who should apologise? In her heart, Angela knew it would be correct. She might have the right in principle, but she had been wrong to act so thoughtlessly. Her heart had ruled her head, and Sister had cause to be angry.

Angela stood up and turned to look out at the back gardens. A slight mist hung over everything, moisture dripping from bushes and withered flowers, making it dank and dull. She was restless, unsure of herself or what she wanted to do. Sister had gone a part of the way to apologising in her own fashion. Angela *had* questioned, she *had* challenged the older woman's authority, and, no matter her own views, Sister Beatrice was in charge of the children and the staff.

Wondering what to do for the best, Angela was about to leave the office when the telephone rang. She answered it and smiled as she heard Mark Adderbury's voice.

'Mark, how lovely to hear from you.'

'I've finished my appointments early today and I'm going to treat myself to a decent lunch. I don't suppose you have time to come with me?'

'Yes, of course I have. I would like that very much. Where shall we meet?'

Angela wrote down the name of the exclusive restaurant. She would have to take a taxi to get across town, but as it was a special treat it wouldn't matter for once.

'I'll see you there at a quarter to one,' she said, glancing at her watch.

If she hurried, she just had time to change her clothes. She would deliver her list to the police station later that evening, after the church hall party for the children.

Angela sipped her wine and smiled at her companion across the table. The restaurant had spotless white cloths and flowers on every table, though the swags of imitation grapes falling from oak beams and the piles of exotic-looking fruit and cheeses in glass counters gave it a distinctly un-English look. It was one of the Italian restaurants that had suddenly sprung up again in this part of London, popular with the smart people, who enjoyed a different sensation when dining out, despite the dubious part Italy had played in the last war. The food had been quite delicious, and if they were using margarine instead of butter, Angela hadn't tasted it.

Rationing was still a curse in a Britain only slowly recovering from the devastating war. At St Saviour's they often had to mix what butter they were allowed with the less popular but more available margarine. She'd noticed it at first, because in the country there was always an obliging farmer willing to supply some delicious bits and pieces that had never seen a Government stamp. In London it was much harder to avoid the strict rationing.

Sometimes a grateful relative would bring a few supplies into the home; the butcher down the road slipped them an extra pound of sausages whenever he could. Since they had their own chickens in a wire run in a corner of the garden, they were seldom short of fresh eggs. A butcher in Brick Lane had sent them half a pig for Christmas, because he'd said he was grateful to one of their carers for looking after his delivery boy when he was knocked off his bike.

Angela had no idea how he'd wangled it, but the kitchen staff had put it to good use, mostly for the minced sausage-meat that the children so enjoyed at teatime since that made the meat go further, mixed with breadcrumbs. However, Angela had been told there would be a huge joint of cold pork for Christmas tea, which, with pickles, would be a real treat for everyone. Ham was a favourite with the children, but the only sort they'd had lately was out of a tin from Canada.

'A penny for your thoughts?' Mark said, lifting his eyebrows. 'You seem very thoughtful. Are you bothered about something?'

'Oh, I had another argument with Sister Beatrice a few days ago. I think she wants me to leave, though today she thanked me for my help.'

He frowned. 'Do you want to leave?'

Angela shook her head. 'No, I don't. I like what I do very much . . . but she did more or less ask me to leave and I said I would after Christmas. I shan't go home though. Perhaps I could still help with raising funds?'

'Unless you wish to leave, I should apologise if I were you.'

'Even if she was the one in the wrong?'

'Was she – truly?'

'It was half and half,' Angela admitted ruefully. 'I did rather speak out of turn. She *is* in charge of running things as far as the children are concerned; even though changes are needed, I know we need her approval, because you would not want to lose her.'

'No, we don't want her to leave or you, Angela,' Mark said. 'Could you not apologise, even if it goes against the grain? St Saviour's needs both of you.'

'Yes, I suppose I could – I shall,' Angela agreed and felt very much better. 'I thought she was too harsh with certain children, but I've since realised that she has to carry the can if things go wrong. Billy ran away and the authorities may say that she was not sufficiently in control, that it was indirectly her fault. I hadn't considered that eventuality.'

Mark's approving look warmed her. 'Exactly. If she seems harsh at times it may be just her manner. She has to think of so many things and in the end it is all down to her. We're lucky to have her.'

'Yes, I know.'

'We need you too, Angela. That is why you should stay,' Mark urged. 'I know how much money you've raised for the Christmas fund – and you can continue to do it, if you stay.'

'Yes, perhaps I shall . . . if Sister Beatrice will accept my apology. I have several new ideas I'd like to discuss with you one day, but I should consult Sister Beatrice first.'

'Talk to her. I'm sure you will find her willing to listen and then we'll have a chat.' He glanced at his watch. 'I'll run you back in my car – and then I have a meeting.'

'Thank you.' Angela rose to her feet as he signalled the waiter and placed some notes on the table. 'This was a lovely surprise, Mark. You do me so much good, make me think things through instead of flying into a passion. I really do rely on your sound judgement, and I know Sister does too.'

'Keep the change,' he said, waving the waiter away. 'It was a very nice meal.'

'Thank you, sir. May we wish you a Happy Christmas?'

'Thank you – and the same to you.' Mark took Angela's arm. 'I shall see you on Christmas Eve for the carols and Father Christmas' arrival but now I have to get back.'

'Yes, this has been lovely, Mark, but I have the church hall party to oversee at four and then I really must take that list of Billy's to the police, though I don't suppose they will bother much with it until after Christmas . . .'

CHAPTER 41

Arthur Baggins watched as the taxi drove away at nine that evening and cursed his luck. He was pretty sure that rich bitch in the back was the one from St Saviour's. She was working there as a secretary and Arthur thought she must be good for a few bob. Already he was hungry and cold and he dared not seek out any of his usual haunts, because the bloody coppers were hunting for him everywhere – and he knew Butcher Lee had put the word out on him. He was on borrowed time here in London and he had to get out quick.

The police were making inquiries about him and Jack, and the only way they could have known Arthur was involved in the attempted robbery at the boot factory was if Billy had split on him. Jack would never tell even if he'd managed to get out the back way so it must have been Billy.

Arthur had had one thought in his mind: he was going to get even with that snitch of a brother of his and then clear off up North. However, he would need money for food and it was better to travel by train if he could raise the fare, because if he tried to hitch a lift people would get suspicious and his picture would probably be in the papers before long.

If the coppers got him, it would only be a matter of time before they discovered what had happened at the factory. It wasn't his fault that Jack had hit that fool too hard, but he'd been there and that made him guilty in the eyes of the law. Neither of them had expected to find anyone inside the factory; how could they have known the night watchman allowed a down and out to sleep in the store room during the cold weather? He'd have lost his job if his employers found out, but the poor bugger he'd taken pity on had lost more than that. He'd been going to raise the alarm, but Jack had coshed him, too damned hard.

Arthur wasn't squeamish, far from it. He couldn't care less what had happened to that tramp, but he did value his own skin. He'd killed his own father because he was going to turn him in. The memory of the way that knife had slid into Pa's back made Arthur smile. The old devil had given him a good few beatings when he was young, but he'd got even and that felt good. He'd cleared off for a while but there had been no extensive searches made for him, no hint of a murder charge in the papers, so he'd come back to the East End, but now he was getting out for good. If the cops once got wind that a man had been murdered, even if he was a down and out, they would hang the culprits. If Jack had bought it, which he must have unless he got out of a back window, it was Arthur that would carry the can and that meant he had to get out fast. He would work in the Docks up North for a while, and look for a ship that might take him on. Arthur had always thought he might like to go to America. There were rich pickings there from what he'd seen at the cinema, vice gangs and gambling casinos where a man could get rich if he didn't mind what he did – and Arthur wasn't fussy. He would commit murder for the right bribe and would have been content to work with one of the London mobs, but he'd upset a few of them when he was younger and knew he had no real future here. Robbing folk would never bring him the kind of money he was after. He wanted to be in with one of the big gangs of New York or Chicago and believed he would make his fortune there.

First he needed to get himself some money and then he would burn that little runt and his mates in their beds. Arthur had already found the way into the cellar beneath St Saviour's and he knew that the caretaker kept paraffin in cans down there. Sprinkled liberally, it wouldn't take long to get a good fire going.

That rich bitch had escaped him for now, but she would be back. He'd knock her senseless and snatch that fancy leather bag of hers; she was bound to have a few quid in there. Then he'd set his fire going – and that would be the end of bloody St Saviour's and his brother and all. He just had to wait until everything went quiet. In the meantime, he'd see what he could find to eat in the kitchens at the kids' home. It amused him to think of robbing them before he roasted the lot of 'em in their beds.

Mary Ellen couldn't sleep. She kept tossing and turning in her bed, but something just wouldn't let her go off, though she wasn't thinking about anything in particular. It was just that Billy had told her about the police stepping up their hunt for Arthur, because they reckoned they'd got all the evidence they needed to arrest him for several burglaries, including the factory.

Supposing Arthur discovered that Billy had told on him? Billy hadn't wanted to, but Mary Ellen had persuaded him and now she was anxious in case Arthur came here looking for Billy. If anything happened to him it would be her fault.

Unable to rest, she slipped out of bed and put her shoes and dress on, then tip-toed out of the dormitory. Walking along the landing to the window that looked out into the garden, Mary Ellen stared into the darkness. She couldn't see much other than shadows, but she kept thinking Arthur might be out there plotting to harm them when they slept.

She was creeping downstairs when a whisper behind her nearly made her stumble. Swinging round, she looked at Marion.

'What are you doing?' she asked. Marion had

one crutch and was using it to balance herself as she followed her down to the hall. 'Be careful or you will fall.'

'I saw you get up so I decided to follow,' Marion said. 'What's wrong?'

'I've just got a funny feeling,' Mary Ellen said quietly. 'I think Arthur might be here.'

'What makes you think that?'

'I don't know. It's silly but I can't get it out of my head. I'm going to the kitchen to get a glass of water and have a look round.'

'What will you do if you see him?'

'Yell as loudly as I can.' Mary Ellen grinned at her. 'I expect I'm daft; he won't be there, but I can't sleep until I look. You should go back to bed, Marion.'

'I'm not lettin' you go alone.'

'But if he knocked you down he could hurt you.'

'I'll yell as loudly as you: two are better than one.'

Mary Ellen nodded, turning the door handle into the kitchen. She switched the light on and saw Billy staring out of the back door.

'Put that out,' he hissed. 'I'm sure Arfur's about. I couldn't sleep for worryin'. I've been thinkin' ever since I spoke to that copper and I got up to look out of the window half an hour ago. I saw Arfur across the street. He was tryin' to hide in the shadows but I saw him in the headlamps of a car.'

Mary Ellen's heart caught with fright. She wasn't

pleased that her feeling had been proved right; she would rather be wrong, because if Arthur was here he was up to no good.

'What are we goin' to do?' she asked as Marion switched the light off and the three children stood shivering in the darkness.

Billy shut the door and went into the kitchen. Here there was enough light from an outside light for them to see. 'I'm going to hide round the corner of the dresser and wait,' Billy said. 'If I hear a noise in the cellar or if Arfur tries to get in I shall raise the alarm.'

Mary Ellen was just about to answer him when they heard a cracking sound in the scullery. Billy put a finger to his lips and motioned to them to get under the tables, which were covered with gingham oilcloths. They hurried to obey him, hiding together under the nearest one and holding their breath as they waited to see what would happen. The sound of breaking glass and then something falling over made them clutch each other. For a moment there was silence and then they heard a muffled curse as someone knocked into a chair; seconds later the light flicked on.

Mary Ellen cautiously lifted the edge of the oilcloth and they looked to see what was happening. She could only make out someone's feet moving towards the pantry door and guessed it must be Arthur. Marion grabbed at her arm and Mary Ellen knew she was frightened; she too was feeling nervous and hardly dared to breathe.

They heard a loud curse as the intruder discovered the pantry door was locked, and then the sound of splintering wood. He was breaking the lock to steal their Christmas food. Mary Ellen was incensed at the wickedness of it and without truly thinking of what she was doing, she scrabbled out of her hiding place, followed shortly by Marion. Arthur was returning from the pantry, carrying a plate filled with mince pies and sausage rolls.

'You rotten thief!' Mary Ellen cried. 'That's our Christmas food and you're not having it!'

Arthur had stuffed a sausage roll in his mouth and spat crumbs at her as he made a snarling noise and tried to speak. He pushed the plate onto the kitchen table and made a grab at her hair. She darted out of his way and stared at him defiantly as he spluttered and choked on the stolen food.

'I hope it chokes you, you nasty man,' she cried as he lunged at her again.

'I'll teach you to spy on me, you little brat,' Arthur growled and flung himself at her. This time she wasn't quite quick enough to escape and he took hold of her hair, tugging at it as he attempted to catch her round the waist. Mary Ellen yelled and Billy darted out; he was carrying a rolling pin, which he used to beat at the middle of his brother's back. 'I'll kill the lot of you,' the incensed Arthur roared. 'I'll knock you senseless and then I'll set fire to the lot of . . .'

Mary Ellen had managed to wrench her hair out of his hold and she kicked his shin as Billy went in for another attack with the rolling pin and then Marion launched herself into the fray. Lifting her crutch high, she brought it down on the side of Arthur's temple and the force of the blow sent him staggering. For a moment he leaned against a table, breathing hard and glaring at them. Marion was balancing on one leg and holding onto the back of a chair, her face white with the effort it had cost her. 'What do we do now?'

'I don't know,' Mary Ellen said. The children looked warily at one another as they waited for him to attack again. Then Arthur grunted furiously and shook his head to clear it.

'I'll kill the whole bloody lot of you,' he muttered and made a grab at Billy, catching hold of his arm and twisting it round behind his back until he screamed in pain.

'What are you doing?' Angela entered the kitchen at that moment, taking in that something was going on but not understanding it. 'Let go of that child at once. At once, do you hear me?' She moved in on him menacingly, picking up the rolling pin that Billy had abandoned on the table.

Arthur gave a yell of outrage. 'I'm glad you're back, rich bitch. You can help me get what I want.' He gave Billy a shove and he cannoned into Marion, both of them ending on the floor.

'You wicked man,' Angela said, looking just as angry as he was. 'I shall not give you a penny and the only thing I'm going to help you with is a trip to prison.'

She brandished the rolling pin at him and Arthur moved in, lunging at her and grabbing her arm as they grappled for the weapon, which Angela was unable to use because he had her arm in a tight grip. She dropped it on the floor and Billy, back on his feet now, picked it up and began the attack on his brother's back once more. Angela, left with only her wits for a weapon, went for Arthur's eyes with her fingers, jabbing at him viciously. He screamed in pain and staggered back, tripping over Marion's crutch and crashing against the table again. This time he hit his head and went down, lying still.

'Is he dead?' Marion asked in a scared breath.

'It doesn't matter about him,' Angela said. 'Are you all right – and Billy? Did he hurt you?'

'I've had worse off him and me pa,' Billy said. 'I fell on Marion, though. Is her leg all right?'

Angela looked at her anxiously. 'Did it hurt your leg again, Marion?'

'No, miss. I think it's all right. I'm just shaken,' Marion said, but tears started in her eyes, because she'd been frightened. 'He won't hurt us again, will he?'

'I'm going to send for the police,' Angela began and then a voice spoke from the doorway, startling them all.

'And what is going on in here, may I ask?' The icy tones of Sister Beatrice struck terror into the three children. Sister was staring at the mince pies on the table and then the pantry door. 'And who is responsible for this disgraceful act of theft?' She looked accusingly at Billy.

'It was him,' Marion said and pointed to Arthur as he lay motionless on the floor. 'We caught him breaking into the pantry and tried to stop him stealing the Christmas food.'

'He was going to burn us all in our beds,' Mary Ellen put in quickly. 'We all fought him but Marion hit him with her crutch when he was hurting me, but he was only winded and he got hold of Billy and tried to break his arm and then Miss Angela arrived and fought him.'

'I stuck my fingers in his eyes and he staggered back and tripped over Marion's crutch and hit his head. He appears to have passed out, I'm not sure how badly hurt he is – but I hope severely,' Angela said grimly. 'He deserves no less after what he did to Billy.'

'And Mary Ellen,' Billy piped up. 'He hurt her first because she stopped him stealing the Christmas food.'

'Yes, indeed. I merely came in halfway through,' Angela said. 'These children were fighting bravely and by the sound of it they saved more than the Christmas food.'

'Good grief, whatever next?' Sister said. She held out her hand to Billy. 'Give me the rolling pin, please.' He did so and, grasping it firmly in one hand, she bent down on one knee.

Mary Ellen giggled nervously, because the sight of the stern sister bending over Billy's brother to feel for a pulse with a rolling pin determinedly clasped in one hand was funny. She tried to contain her mirth as Sister struggled heavily to her feet and nodded.

'Is that your brother, Billy?'

'Yes, Sister. He's a bad 'un – is he dead?'

'No, just unconscious.' She broke off as Nan entered the kitchen. 'Ah, Nan,' she said pleasantly. 'Would you mind phoning the police station for us, please? Tell them we have Arthur Baggins here for them and ask them to collect him as soon as possible.'

Nan stared at her, then at the man lying on the floor. 'Did you knock him out, Sister?'

'No, but if he wakes before the police arrive, I shall endeavour to do so. It was these brave children who saved both the Christmas food – and St Saviour's, if his intention was truly to burn us down.'

'Good grief,' Nan said, looking astonished. 'Well done, children. I'll telephone the police immediately.'

Sister Beatrice nodded and then looked at the children. 'Perhaps you should go to bed now?'

'Please, Sister,' Billy said hesitantly. 'We'd rather wait until the police get here in case he wakes up. It took three of us to tackle him and we were lucky he hit his head when he fell, because he's vicious.'

'Well, if you insist,' she said and looked up as

Alice walked into the kitchen. 'Ah, you've come to make a cup of tea before you go home, Alice. Perhaps you would make one for all of us?'

Alice stared at her open-mouthed and Mary Ellen explained it all to her.

'You give me that rolling pin, Sister,' Alice said fiercely. 'If he so much as lifts his head, I'll send him back to sleep for the next year.'

'Yes, well, perhaps it might be more appropriate if I make the tea,' Sister said and Mary Ellen couldn't believe it, because her eyes were laughing even though she managed to keep a straight face as Alice took up guard, her expression so grim that Marion started giggling. Mary Ellen pushed her in the back because she was fit to burst and didn't know how to stop laughing out loud.

Nan came back and took in the scene, her mouth twitching as she saw Alice standing guard over her victim like an avenging warrior.

'Constable Sallis says they're sending a Black Maria and half a dozen police constables to fetch him.' Suddenly, Nan laughed. 'Do you know, I almost feel sorry for the poor man . . .'

The children all started to giggle, and Angela saw the funny side of it too, but Alice didn't see anything to laugh about. She was obviously taking her duty seriously and even when Sister Beatrice gave them all a cup of tea each, she refused to leave her position. If Arthur was unfortunate enough to raise his head, he would soon feel very sorry for himself . . . very sorry indeed.

Fortunately, the police were swiftly on the scene and Arthur was carted off in the back of their van. He was just beginning to come round as they took him out and he started to swear and yell vengeance as the police locked him inside.

'Off to bed with you now,' Sister said, then, 'You can each take a mince pie or a sausage roll for being so brave.'

'No, thank you, Sister,' Mary Ellen said. 'We'll wait until everyone has them, because it isn't fair on the others. That's why I wasn't going to let him steal them.'

'I see.' Sister stared at her for a moment, a strange look in her eyes. 'I think I may have misjudged you, child – and your friends. Very well, we shall put them back in the pantry until we all share them for tea.'

Billy looked at Mary Ellen as the three of them left the kitchen. 'I was so hungry,' he confessed, 'but you did right, Mary Ellen. Marion, you ain't hurt yourself, have you?'

'No, I'm all right,' she said and smiled, clearly proud of herself. 'I thought I might fall but I had to stop him hurting Mary Ellen and my crutch is heavy. It frightened me when he fell over my crutch and I thought I'd killed him, though . . .'

'That wasn't your fault,' Mary Ellen asserted. 'The police should give you a medal, not tell you off.'

'I'm glad they've got your brother in custody,

Billy,' Marion said. 'I hope he stays in prison for a long, long time.'

'So do I,' Billy said. 'I'd better get back to the dorm – you two all right together?'

'Yes, we're all right,' Mary Ellen said. 'See you in the morning . . .'

'Well,' Sister said when the children had left. 'I suppose we ought to be thankful you arrived when you did. Those children were very brave but he might have overpowered them and then . . . it hardly bears thinking about. St Saviour's might have been burned down and many lives lost.'

'It was pure chance, because I'd just been to the police station with that list of Billy's and I kept my taxi waiting. Had I walked back I might have been too late . . .' Angela said with a little shudder. 'If I did my bit I'm pleased, but in my opinion it was all down to those children. I'm very proud of them.'

'Yes, indeed. I certainly misjudged them – especially Billy.'

'Well, we all make mistakes,' Angela said. 'I certainly do.'

Sister sat down heavily, her face white as if it had suddenly hit her what might have happened. 'How could it have been so easy for him to get in? Billy tells me there are several cans of paraffin in the cellar.' Her hands were shaking. 'To think the paraffin was there waiting . . .'

'It would never be hard for a man like that to break in, but I think the caretaker should store his paraffin somewhere else. I suppose he keeps it and the oil lamps in case of electric cuts.'

Sister nodded. 'I totally agree that he should keep it elsewhere, under better security. We'll have something done to make it harder to get in, too. Secure locks on all the downstairs windows, I think, first thing in the morning.'

'If Arthur is in custody, the danger is over. No one else has a grudge against us, why should they? Everyone speaks so highly of you and the work you do. Whenever I ask for money people give what they can – food or goods if they can't spare money. Look at all the gifts we've had this Christmas. Most of the shopkeepers have given us something. I couldn't believe how kind they were when I asked for funds. Arthur was a spiteful evil man, but the police will put him away for a long time.'

'You may be right, but you can't be too careful. I shall have more locks fitted just in case.'

'I'm sure Arthur will not escape.'

'Fire . . . it's such a terrible way to die.' Sister Beatrice's hand was shaking, tears coursing down her cheeks as her words came out of their own volition. 'I've always dreaded it since . . . such a terrible way to die in a fire . . .'

Angela thought she'd never seen Sister Beatrice so disturbed. For a moment she seemed as if she were on the verge of saying more, but she breathed deeply, seemed to take a hold on herself and shook her head, dashing the tears away.

'Such a long time ago . . .'

Angela was certain something terrible had once happened to Sister Beatrice or someone she knew, but the woman obviously wasn't prepared to confide in her and she would not push for her confidences.

'Yes, I know fire is awful, Sister. But the danger is over, truly it is.'

'How foolish of me.' Sister Beatrice blew her nose, her head going up as the barriers came down. 'But we shall take those extra precautions just in case. Well, I shall let you get to bed, Angela.'

'Yes, but I'll make a cup of tea first . . .' Angela hesitated, then, 'I am very sorry that I flouted your wishes that day, Sister. If you felt humiliated, I ask you to forgive me. I did not do it for that reason – but I could not bear to see Mary Ellen so miserable.'

Sister Beatrice hesitated in her turn, then, 'Would you consider forgetting your intention to leave after Christmas?'

Angela smiled. 'I already have,' she said. 'I think we shall do better together from now on – don't you?'

CHAPTER 42

Mary Ellen and Billy were in the schoolroom, because they both wanted to finish making their Christmas cards for friends and the staff who looked after them. Billy had only just started his when Father Joe came looking for him.

'I'm organising a football match for some East End lads, Billy,' he said. 'We're having a practice this morning and I wondered whether you would like to come and see how you get on as part of the team.'

'Yes please,' Billy said, springing up eagerly. 'You don't mind if I go, do you, Mary Ellen?'

'No, of course not – as long as it won't get you in trouble with Sister again?'

Father Joe assured them it would not and took Billy off to join the other boys who were playing that morning. Mary Ellen watched them go a little enviously. She tried to concentrate on colouring her cards, but her thoughts kept drifting away to a previous Christmas when Ma had taken her down Petticoat Lane to buy some bargains as a treat for Rose and her.

Nan came to the schoolroom soon after Billy left. She spoke to the carer on duty in a low voice and they looked at one another anxiously, before Nan called out Mary Ellen's name.

'Yes, Nan,' Mary Ellen said, jumping up from the mat where she'd been playing with the little ones. 'Did you want me?'

'Your sister Rose is here to see you, my dear,' Nan said in a gentle voice. 'I think you had better come down to the hall now, and fetch your coat. I believe your sister wants to take you out for a while.'

'Rose?' Mary Ellen smiled in excitement. Her postcard two weeks ago promised to come before Christmas, but I thought she'd forgotten.' She glanced up and felt a tiny prickle at the nape of her neck, because Nan was looking very serious. Surely there was nothing to look serious about just because Rose had come to take her out?

Nan led the way downstairs. Rose was standing in the hall waiting, and as soon as she looked at her sister's face, Mary Ellen guessed the truth. Rose's eyes were all red and so was her nose. A lump came to Mary Ellen's throat and she wanted to scream, to protest that it couldn't be true, but she knew in her heart it was. Ma had known she was going to die even before she'd gone to that place.

Why hadn't she stayed with Mary Ellen? She would have rather looked after Ma until the end . . . but of course they would never let her do that in case she picked up her terrible illness. Besides, they wouldn't have thought her capable of caring for her mother, but at least she would have had those last few precious weeks with her – and now she would never see her again and that hurt so much. Mary Ellen felt as if she were suffocating, her throat tight and her chest hurting as if it were being squeezed.

Numbed and cold, she walked to Rose and took her hand.

'I'll bring her back after tea,' Rose said to Nan, and then they walked out of St Saviour's together.

'It's Ma, isn't it?'

'Yes, she's gone, love. She was too ill. They couldn't save her.'

'I wish she hadn't gone away. I wished she'd stayed with us.'

'They said she had to, love. She didn't have a choice. She could have passed her illness on to others – especially us.'

She would never again feel her mother's loving touch or see her smile. Mary Ellen couldn't bear it. Pain welled up and spilled over as she gave a wail of grief.

'What will happen to me now?'

Rose stopped walking and turned to face her. 'You're all right here, aren't you? I thought you liked it?'

'I do . . . it's all right, but I wanted Ma to get better so I could come home soon.'

'I had to let the house go, and I sold the furniture

to pay the expenses, but there's a box of Ma's things and you can have your share when you're older. Anyway, it was a horrid place, damp and smelly. We'll find somewhere better when I've finished my training.'

'Where will you live when you have?'

'I'll find another house when I've saved some money – and then I'll come and fetch you.'

'You said Ma would come home and I'd live with her. You lied to me. Why did you lie?' The accusation was there in her voice and her eyes.

'It was what she wanted – what we both hoped. It isn't my fault, Mary Ellen. I didn't want her to die.' Rose looked as if she would cry but blinked hard.

'When did she die?'

'A week ago. We had the funeral yesterday. I couldn't come and tell you until now, because there was too much to do. Besides, I know it will spoil Christmas for you. I almost waited until after but I couldn't let Christmas go without seeing you.'

Rose had known all that time and she hadn't told her. She'd hardly bothered to visit her and Mary Ellen didn't trust her. Tears welled up and she scrubbed them away, angry with her sister.

'It doesn't matter about Christmas. I wanted Ma to come home,' she yelled and pushed Rose, wanting to hurt her because she'd done this – she'd made her leave her ma and now she was gone and she would never see her again. 'I hate you. It's all your fault.'

'For goodness' sake stop going on about it!' Rose gave her a shake. 'We shall both miss her. I wish things were different but they aren't and there's nothing we can do about it – it's just sod's law, that's what it is.'

'That's swearing. Ma would bat your ear if she heard you,' Mary Ellen said, but she was calmer now the first tantrum was over. 'I want her . . . you're so mean to me and you swear awful.'

'Yes, I know, but sometimes you would try the patience of a saint, Mary Ellen.' Rose stopped as she saw the tears in her little sister's eyes begin to flow down her cheeks. 'No, I didn't mean that, love. I'm sorry. I know it's horrid for you having to live in that place – but I have to work hard and take my exams to be a sister so I can make a decent life for us both. I've been too busy to visit much, because it's all more difficult than I thought, and I had to visit Ma sometimes and see to things . . . but I will come more in future; once a month, I promise. Please try to understand. You're all I've got now . . . don't make it worse for me.'

'You won't just forget me and leave me there?'

Rose got down on her knee in the street, her hands on Mary Ellen's shoulders and looking into her face. 'I promise I shall never abandon you, love. You are my sister and I care about you. As soon as I can afford it I'll get a place we can be together. In the meantime you have to promise me to work hard at your schooling so you can get

532

a good job one day. Ma would want you to get on, you know she would.'

'I want to be a teacher and look after little ones,' Mary Ellen said shyly. 'I thought I wanted to be a nurse like you, but I'm good at reading and teaching others to read and learn things – so I'm going to go to college and be a teacher.'

'Ma would be proud of you for wanting to do that,' Rose said and stood up again. 'I haven't bought you a present, Mary Ellen. I thought I would take you out somewhere instead – the pictures and tea at Lyons if you like?'

'I don't want to miss the carols and Father Christmas.'

'We won't bother with tea then,' Rose smiled. 'Don't worry, I've been invited to join in the fun so we'll be back before six when it all starts.'

Mary Ellen looked up at her. 'Can we look at the Christmas windows up West and then . . . could we go to a pantomime?'

'A pantomime?' Rose nodded. 'Yes, if we can get into the early show. A bit of nonsense might cheer us both up. We'll go up West and look at the displays in the toyshops . . . like we did when Pa was alive, remember? He couldn't buy us much but he stood with us for ages while we watched the automatons in the windows.' Mary Ellen nodded. 'And then we'll see if we can get in the cheap seats at one of the pantomimes. I think Mother Goose is on this year . . .'

CHAPTER 43

Angela glanced around her office and gave a sigh of satisfaction. She'd finished all the work she'd set herself to do before she went home for Christmas and would have a fresh start when she got back. Her case was packed and her gifts for her family were inside it. She'd given gifts to the staff and small things for every child in the home were on the Christmas tree. Her heart had urged her to buy something special for Mary Ellen, but she'd remembered Sister's words of warning about having favourites and stuck to little presents for all of them.

Now all she had to do was go down and join the others for the Christmas carols and the party, and then Mark would take her home. A frown creased her brow as she felt faintly uneasy about what she would find. The feeling that something was wrong had been growing steadily since her father's telephone call. He was anxious about something and she had a horrid suspicion it might be to do with her mother; there was nothing she could put her finger on, and the charity dance had been splendid, but little things . . . all that new stuff in the wardrobe and most of it the kind of thing that her mother would never wear . . .

Oh, well, whatever it was she would face it when it came, just as her father was having to. A sigh left her lips but then her frown lifted. At least she would see something of Mark this holiday, because she'd invited him to lunch on Christmas Day. She smiled because she was looking forward to just being with him, listening to carols on the radio and enjoying a glass of wine in the peace of the afternoon.

Her thoughts were interrupted as the telephone rang and she answered it.

'Is that Mrs Morton?'

'Yes, it is. How may I help you?'

'This is Michael Browne, from the department for children's welfare. I wanted to pass on the good news. Your Sister Beatrice has been badgering us for an answer on our decision about Billy Baggins. In view of the news about his brother being in custody and her opinion that he has turned a corner and will now benefit from remaining where he is, we have decided to give him the benefit of the doubt. If you could pass that message on please, Mrs Morton? I've tried to phone her twice this morning, and of course you will receive the official letter but not until the New Year. These things take time and I knew she was anxious . . .'

'Yes, she will be delighted with the news. We are very busy at the moment and Sister has been overseeing the admittance of a young boy who has been in hospital for a long time. He was the victim of a terrible illness and she wanted to receive him herself, because he is going to need special care for some while.'

'Yes, of course. Your Sister Beatrice is a wonderful woman, as I'm sure you know – very persuasive when she sets her mind to it.'

'Yes, I do know. Thank you – and Happy Christmas, Mr Browne.'

'Is anything wrong, Alice?' Michelle asked as they joined the rest of the staff gathering in the hall for the Christmas carols that evening. 'You've been quiet recently – and I haven't seen much of you. I've been meaning to ask, would you like to come to us for Christmas Day? Mum said I could have a friend and you're my best mate – or you were. You haven't fallen out with me, have you?'

''Course not,' Alice said and summoned a smile. It wasn't easy and she knew she'd been avoiding Michelle recently, because of the mess she was in. Her period still hadn't come and she was sure she was having Jack's child. She couldn't deny it even to herself now, but she didn't know how to tell her friend she'd been such a fool.

'I've been busy,' she said, 'but I'd love to come to yours on Boxing Day, if your mum will have me. I'm working over Christmas Day.'

'Poor you,' Michelle sympathised. 'I'll ask Mum about Boxing Day – it will probably be cold meat and bubble and squeak, but she'll save you a few mince pies and a bit of cake.'

'Lovely – and we'll go to the flicks soon,' Alice said.

'And perhaps we can have a cup of tea somewhere later?'

'Why not tonight, after we finish here? Mum will expect me when she sees me and I should like to spend some time with you. I've got a little present for you.'

'I've got something for you,' Alice said. 'Not much – but you are me best mate. That's why I want you to know that I'm havin' Jack's baby – and no, he won't marry me, although he promised to, but he won't because he's gone and I haven't heard from him for ages.'

'Oh, Alice love, I thought it might be the case, but I kept hoping I was wrong. I shan't scold you, because it's too late – but what will you do now?'

'I've decided to keep the baby. I'm going to work for as long as I can, but then . . . I don't know what I shall do when it's born. I just know I can't murder it. I loved Jack even if he is a rogue . . .'

'What do you mean, is? Everyone thinks he is dead, Alice. They hinted as much in the paper. Surely you're not hoping he got out of that fire?' Michelle looked at her sadly. 'Oh, love, you've got to let him go – you have to.'

'I think he did get out, Michelle. How, I don't know and I can't explain why, I think he did, but I'm not the only one that thinks it. I'm not sayin' he'll come back for me. He's gone and I'm on my own, I know that . . . but somehow I'll manage, and I'm goin' to keep the baby whatever happens.'

'Good for you. You know I'll help you all I can,' Michelle said and hugged her arm. 'We'll talk about it later, love. I think they're going to start the carols now.'

'Yes, Mr Adderbury has lowered the lights.' She was suddenly silent as children and staff bearing lighted candles in little holders entered the room. The effect of the steady flames with the sound of their voices joined in praise of God brought the magic of Christmas and its true meaning to them all.

'I have to leave now,' Andrew Markham said, looking at Sally with regret as the carols ended. 'I wish I could stay longer but I have an evening engagement with colleagues – and I'm going home tomorrow. I shall see you when I come back after Christmas, Sally. I should like to meet your parents one day quite soon.' He reached out to stroke a finger down her cheek, then bent his head and kissed her softly on the lips. 'You are a lovely person, Sally Rush. I had thought I should never find a woman I felt I could spend my life with – but I've changed my mind.'

'Andrew . . .' Her protest was mild, Sally's cheeks glowing with a delicate rose blush. 'You don't really know me yet. I like you so much . . . perhaps more

than that but . . . it's much too soon to think of
. . . well, marriage.'

'Yes, of course it is,' he said and smiled. 'I just
wanted you to know that you mean a lot to me.
It's too soon, of course, but I'm hoping you feel
the same way?'

'You mean a lot to me too,' she assured him,
looking shy. 'I know there is a wide gap between
us, Andrew. Yes, there is, you mustn't deny it,
because it is true. My father works on the Docks
and I'm just a carer – though I want to train as
a nurse when I can afford it. Dad has been on
short time recently so I've had to help at home,
but he's trying to find more work and he will,
because he's a hard worker. Someone will give him
a regular job soon. I want it to be right for us but
you have to be sure . . . we both do.'

'Yes, I understand that,' Andrew said and touched
her cheek with his fingers. 'But you mustn't let
class stand between us. I shan't, my love.'

'My mother may and my father will be conscious
of the fact that he is just a dock worker.'

'What does he do actually?'

'He is a carpenter. His real trade is fitting ships'
interiors but he'll turn his hand to anything – why?'

'Oh, just wondering,' he said and sighed. 'We'll
find a way through this, Sally. I promise you that
I shan't let prejudice stand between us.'

'It isn't you . . . it's my family.'

Andrew smiled and nodded. 'I know they have
their pride and we shan't trample on it, I promise

you – but I'm determined never to let you go. After Christmas I'm going to take you to lovely places, the theatre and dancing – and to meet my friends, who I know will welcome you. I don't have that many but those I do are good people I can rely on. And now, my love, I really have to leave. Go back to the party and enjoy yourself. You've worked hard to make it happen, all of you.'

'Thank you.' Sally reached out and hugged him impulsively. 'Happy Christmas, Andrew.'

He reached into his jacket pocket and took out a small parcel. 'Happy Christmas, Sally. I shall come to see you as soon as I get back.'

'Thank you . . . thank you so much.' She took the parcel, a little shyly because of course she hadn't dared to buy him anything. 'I'll open it tomorrow and think of you.'

'I shall be thinking of you too.' He leaned forward and kissed her cheek, then walked away.

Sally stood where she was for a few moments, then turned and went back to join the children and staff, who were just trooping into the dining room to have their special tea. She had slipped the parcel into her uniform pocket to open later when she was alone.

Sally was glowing all over and she wondered if people would notice the difference in her. She was, she thought, truly in love for the first time in her life. Yet she still had a few reservations. Andrew might not think the divide between them too great, but Sally was aware it was there. He was a clever, highly educated man holding down a responsible job, but there was far more to it than that: his family background was so different. The world he moved in was far above her and that frightened her a little.

He'd spoken of taking her to the theatre and out to dinner – but Sally knew her clothes were hardly good enough to wear to the kind of places he was used to. Even if she did love him, and she believed he was serious about her, there was a gulf to overcome.

Then there was the question of her training. She had planned on applying next summer if she could save enough money by then, but . . . no, she wouldn't raise obstacles. Andrew was taking her out after Christmas. She would take things slowly and not worry about silly things like clothes. Michelle would probably lend her a dress if she asked – and Angela certainly would, because she was always giving her things to the 'bring and buy' sale.

Sally took a small glass of wine from the tray and began to follow the others into the dining room.

She was going to enjoy Christmas and think about the future when it happened next year . . .

'Sally, do you know where Sister Beatrice is, please?'

She turned as Angela came down the stairs towards her. She was wearing her coat as if about to leave, but looked excited, and Sally sensed that something had happened.

'I think she is still in the dining room. I believe she was having a sit down and a cup of tea with Cook.'

'I've got some good news for her. I really ought to tell Sister first.' Angela hesitated, then, 'Keep it to yourself for now, but I know you're fond of those two . . .'

'Billy and Mary Ellen?' Sally guessed, sensing Angela's excitement. 'They're going to let him stay here?'

'Yes. I had the phone call just now. I should have missed it had I not stopped to sort a few papers. Mr Browne from the children's department rang me because they've decided Sister Beatrice is the best person to have charge of him now.'

'Is it really settled?' Sally guessed that Angela was bubbling over with excitement but trying to keep it inside.

'Yes; they say if Sister is prepared to vouch for him, and of course, she is, he can stay here permanently. You mustn't tell them yet, because it isn't official until Sister gets her letter, which will not come until after Christmas, but Mr Browne says it's certain.'

'They will be so pleased,' Sally said and smiled at her. 'I think that's the best present you could have given me – though the nylons and scarf were wonderful. I never have enough nylons.'

'Does anyone? I thought all the girls would enjoy a couple of pairs,' Angela said. 'I started buying all I could find weeks ago. I'm glad you liked them.'

'I loved them.'

'You are very welcome, Sally. Happy Christmas! I'll see you after the holidays . . .'

'Happy Christmas!'

Sally watched as Angela set off in search of Sister Beatrice. It was wonderful news about Billy Baggins and made Christmas all the more special, even if they couldn't tell the children until it was official.

Wishing her friends and colleagues a Happy Christmas over and over again as she went to fetch her things from the staff room, Sally reflected on how lucky she was to be here and to have a job where she was respected and liked. She didn't know what the future would bring, whether her father would find better paid work or if she would ever manage to train as a nurse, but she did know she was happy and content at this moment.

Christmas was going to be good for her family, because between them they'd scraped together enough money to buy food, a bottle of sherry and a few small presents. As far as Sally was concerned, the coming year was the start of something new and exciting and she had a nice warm glow inside as she nursed her secret.

She was loved and she loved, and what would be would be.

CHAPTER 44

'Do you think they will let you stay here now?' Mary Ellen said as they sat on the back stairs with their arms about each other, heads together. She'd been telling Billy about Ma and shedding a few tears, but somehow with his arm about her the first sharpness had eased.

Going out with Rose had been all right, but the shadow of her sister's news had hovered at her shoulder even as she laughed at the antics of the pantomime characters on stage, and she'd felt tears on her cheeks when the choir had sung Ma's favourite carol – 'Away in a Manger'.

After the present giving and tea, Billy and Mary Ellen had crept away to sit on the stairs and talk.

'It's rotten her tellin' you today,' Billy said. 'She's spoiled everythin' for you, Mary Ellen.'

'No, because I've got you and Marion and my friends,' she said and offered a chocolate biscuit. 'I always knew, Billy, even though they told me Ma would get better. I knew she wasn't ever coming home. I wish Rose had told me what was going on sooner but she thinks I'm just a kid and wouldn't understand.'

'Bloody grownups . . .'

Mary Ellen nodded and shifted closer to her friend. He was her rock and she couldn't imagine what she would do if they sent him away.

All the excitement of the carol service and the present giving was over, and tomorrow things would be back to normal. On Christmas Day Sister said it would be prayers and a good dinner, but she believed it was a Holy day and should be spent quietly. 'They won't blame you because Arthur came here?'

'It were my fault in a way,' Billy said. 'Arthur wanted to get his own back on me and he knew I care about people here, Mary Ellen. I couldn't bear it if you and Marion and the others were hurt.' There was a faint shimmer of tears in his eyes and she hugged him. 'You're all I've got – me whole family now.'

'It's all right, we're safe now. I keep thinking about when I was little; Ma was always lovely to me, a good mother, and I miss her lots. You and Marion are my family too. We all have to look out for one another.'

'I know.' He gazed at her solemnly. 'I'll always be your friend and look after you and Marion too, if she needs me. I'm just glad they've put Arthur away. I hope he goes down for the rest of his life.'

Mary Ellen nodded, her face grave. She offered him the Cadbury's chocolate fingers Rose had bought with her sweet coupons and he took one, biting into it with a look of ecstasy on his face.

'These are me favourites.'

'Yes, I know – that's why I chose them.'

'You're a good friend, Mary Ellen. When we grow up I'll be a train driver and marry you.'

She smiled at him. 'You'll have to study hard at school to be a train driver, Billy. You have to be clever to do that, Pa told me so. He worked on the Docks and said if he'd got a proper education he could have been a crane driver and earned twice as much as he did for labouring. He told me to study if I wanted to be better than him and me ma were.'

'You won't have to work. You'll have me to look after you.'

'I'm not going to marry for years and years. I want to be a teacher and look after the little ones.'

'But you'll marry me one day, won't you?'

'You'll always be my best friend, Billy. If you ask me when I'm old enough I'll give you my answer then – but not until I'm a teacher. I want to make something of my life, not be like me ma, forced to live in a slum when Pa died.'

Billy frowned over that, because Mary Ellen was the most important person in his world and he wanted to mean the same to her. She offered him another biscuit and he hesitated, wanting it but knowing there weren't many left.

'Rose gave you those for Christmas. You keep them.'

'Have another one. Rose took me to a pantomime instead of giving me a present, and the biscuits were instead of pocket money, because she doesn't bother with sweet rations and saves them for me. I wanted to share them with you – you're my best friend, Billy.'

He grinned at her, his confidence returning as he took another of the delicious chocolate biscuits and bit into it. 'I've got you a Christmas present, Mary Ellen.'

'How did you manage that? You don't get much pocket money, do you?'

'No, only the threpence everyone gets on Saturday, but Constable Sallis gave me a couple of bob for helping him, and I nipped down the shop while you were out and bought something – but I shan't give it to you until tomorrow.'

Mary Ellen had spent most of her pocket money on buying him drink and sweets when he was in hiding so she hadn't been able to get him a scarf as she'd planned. Instead she'd bought him a set of coloured pencils. They hadn't cost her much but it was all she'd had left from the allowance Rose had left for her with Sister Beatrice.

'You shouldn't have spent your money on me, Billy.'

'It's what I wanted. I ain't interested in anything else – and we all got a present from Father Christmas, but I shan't open mine until Christmas Day.'

'Nor shall I – I like the suspense,' Mary Ellen smiled in the darkness. Most of the other kids had torn their parcels open the minute they got them, but she'd kept her little hoard of three brightly wrapped parcels: one from Father Christmas, one from Sally and the other carers, and one from Miss Angela. 'Do you believe in Father Christmas?'

'Nah, 'course not, but we have to pretend to 'cos some of the little kids think he's real. I know it's Mr Adderbury 'cos I 'eard Sally and Angela talkin' about it.'

'I don't care who it is,' Mary Ellen said and smiled. She hugged his arm. 'It's nice being together here, Billy. I just hope they won't send you away after Christmas.'

'If they do I'll run away and come back here. If I keep doing it they'll get fed up and let me stay.'

Mary Ellen laughed. She hoped he was right, because she had to stay here until Rose had finished her training. St Saviour's was warm and comfortable and there was always enough to eat, and more importantly she felt safe here. Outside the ancient walls of the old fever hospital the streets were dark and dangerous and the vulnerable could die of hunger, cold and neglect . . . and in the shadows evil lurked. The kind of evil that she had never known, but sensed was there waiting for the unwary.

Rose had warned her of what their lives might have been like if she hadn't been taken in here and Rose had been left to manage alone. She'd told her to be careful of men she didn't know, even if they seemed nice at first.

'If I had to work all day you would be on your

own, at the mercy of strangers – men who might try to harm you. I couldn't have looked after you properly, Mary Ellen, because sometimes I have to work nights. In a few years you will be older and I shall be earning good money. I can pay someone to look after you at night if I can't – but until then you have to stay at St Saviour's. You don't know how lucky you are to have a place there . . . some of these homes . . . well, you hear bad things whispered about what happens to the children in them.'

Rose was wrong to think that Mary Ellen didn't know how lucky she was. She'd rebelled against Sister Beatrice and her rules, but now she knew they were there for a purpose, and she'd made up her mind to obey them – and if Billy were allowed to stay she would make sure he did too. St Saviour's wasn't a bad place to grow up if she couldn't go home to her mother. Her throat tightened with grief, but she didn't cry. Ma was in heaven with Pa and the angels, and not suffering any more. Rose said she had suffered and they had to be glad for Ma's sake that she was at peace now so Mary Ellen would try to be, even though it hurt so bad.

'Come on,' she said to Billy, offering him the last two biscuits. 'One each, and then we'd better go up to the dorms or Sister will have our guts for garters.'

'She will if she 'ears you say that,' Billy retorted and grinned. 'She ain't all bad, you know, Mary

Ellen. I reckon it's time I pulled me socks up. I want to get somewhere when I'm older and if that means doin' as I'm told for a bit and learnin' things – well, I don't mind, as long as they let me stay here.'

'Well, that is good news,' Father Joe said and lifted his glass, which contained not the usual sherry but a drop of the good Irish whiskey Mark Adderbury had provided with his compliments of the season. 'Sure the lad is a tearaway, but he'll calm down. After what he's been through in his short life 'twas only to be expected he would kick a bit.'

'Yes, I think I agree with you,' Beatrice said and sipped her sherry. She didn't care for the taste of whiskey despite Father Joe's claims that she would change her mind, if she once tasted the Irish variety. 'He was inclined to rebel when he first came here, but I think that business with his brother sorted him out. I do not think we shall have any real trouble with him now.'

'Mary Ellen is a good girl. She'll keep him on the right track now that she's settled in herself. It was a sad thing that she lost her mother – and so close to the Lord's birth.'

'Yes, I'm afraid she is going to have to stay here for several years. Her sister is set on becoming a nurse and that takes years of training. Even when she has her certificates she may find it isn't easy to find work that allows her to live independently.

Many of the hospitals still require their nurses to live at the home provided.'

'Unless she came here?' he suggested with a provocative lift of his brow. 'You might be more flexible, I think?'

'Perhaps.' Beatrice was feeling mellow. She couldn't remember having a better Christmas, not even when she was a girl at home. Her parents had never been short of money, but there was no warmth in their home for they loved neither each other nor their daughter. Had they cared for her she might never have suffered so much grief and her life might have been very different. 'Yes, I should welcome her here if I had a place for her.'

'We none of us know what's round the corner – except for the dear Lord and He's not telling. Look at the troubles we've been after having this year, and haven't they all resolved themselves?'

'Yes, most of them have. Angela has done a wonderful job of raising money. I understand we're to have some of it towards the extras the children need and the rest may be used for improvements. I'm relieved she has decided to stay on, because we should miss her now. I can't do everything myself.'

'Of course you can't and that's why Adderbury asked her to come, because he didn't want to lose you. You are everything this home and the children need and Adderbury knows it.'

Beatrice looked at him, feeling surprised and touched by the compliment but then she knew he was right. Adderbury did appreciate her values. Sentimental tears pricked behind her eyes. She'd been a fool to feel threatened. Her work here was valued and appreciated. She might not always agree with Angela but they could manage to get along well enough if they both tried a bit harder.

'Yes, we've come through pretty well when you think about it,' she said and lifted her glass to salute him.

Beatrice realised that she'd learned to bend a little in the past few weeks, to see things in a different light. Her old-fashioned notions about children being kept in their place seemed to have become less important. Billy and Mary Ellen had shown her that they were strong characters and both honest and fearless. Had it not been for their courage and the combined efforts of the three friends, St Saviour's might have been burned to the ground.

Because she did not believe in making too much of things, she'd thanked them and sent them to bed, but in her own mind they were heroes. Perhaps it was time that the individual was encouraged, and she would tell Angela on her return that she backed her all the way with the idea of team leaders and monitors. It was time to give the children more responsibility and to trust them to behave rather than threatening them with strict rules.

'Here's to 1948 and let's hope it is the start of better things for all of us: the people, the country and most of all St Saviour's and our children,' she said and sipped her sherry.

'I'll drink to that,' Father Joe said with his lazy smile – and he did.